Opening her eyes, Ch............... her bed with her foot. The early morning sun streaming in through the leaded-light window warmed the gentle mounds and crevices of her naked body as she brushed the veil of long black hair from her pretty face. Sighing, she stretched her limbs lazily, basking in the comfort of her bed as sleep left her. The room coming into focus, she gazed bleary-eyed at her school blazer hanging over the back of a chair.

Also by Ray Gordon in paperback from New English Library

Lust Quest
Sinful Deceit
Depravicus

Schoolgirl Lust

Ray Gordon

nel

NEW ENGLISH LIBRARY
Hodder & Stoughton

Copyright © 2001 by Ray Gordon

The right of Ray Gordon to be identified as the Author
of the Work has been asserted by him in accordance
with the Copyright, Designs and Patents Act 1988.

A NEL Paperback

10 9 8 7 6 5 4

All rights reserved. No part of this publication may
be reproduced, stored in a retrieval system, or transmitted,
in any form or by any means without the prior written
permission of the publisher, nor be otherwise circulated
in any form of binding or cover other than that in which
it is published and without a similar condition being
imposed on the subsequent purchaser.

All characters in this publication are fictitious
and any resemblance to real persons, living or dead,
is purely coincidental.

A CIP catalogue record for this title
is available from the British Library

ISBN 0 340 73330 6

Typeset by Hewer Text Ltd, Edinburgh
Printed and bound in Great Britain by
Mackays of Chatham plc, Chatham, Kent

Hodder and Stoughton
A division of Hodder Headline
338 Euston Road
London NW1 3BH

SCHOOLGIRL LUST

Chapter One

Opening her eyes, Charlotte pushed the eiderdown off her bed with her foot. The early morning sun streaming in through the leaded-light window warmed the gentle mounds and crevices of her naked body as she brushed the veil of long black hair from her pretty face. Sighing, she stretched her limbs lazily, basking in the comfort of her bed as sleep left her. The room coming into focus, she gazed bleary-eyed at her school blazer hanging over the back of a chair.

She thought about her English project. She should have finished it by now. Miss Chambers would question her, rebuke her. Propping herself up on her elbows, Charlotte looked at the bedside clock. Eight-fifteen. She was going to be late. Why hadn't her mother called her? Something must be wrong – perhaps it was the clock. Her head flopping onto her pillow as she realized that it was Saturday, she grinned. No school. There was no need to get up, no rush to do anything.

Looking around the room, she scrutinized a picture hanging on the far wall. A vase of flowers, daffodils. Another picture caught her eye: her grandparents dressed in Victorian clothes. Grandfather was leaning on a walking stick, his wife sat on a chair by his side. No smiles: they were posing stony-faced and rigid for the camera. Below the black-and-white photograph stood an antique ottoman. Charlotte used it to sit on when she tied her shoelaces.

Charlotte's bedroom might have been decorated and furnished at the turn of the century. There were no posters of teenage idols like The Backstreet Boys or Robbie Williams. No mini hi-fi system or CDs, as would be found in most seventeen-year-old girls' bedrooms. No make-up adorned the old oak dressing table, no vivid colour embellished the bland room. Although the third millennium had arrived, Charlotte might have been living in the late eighteen-hundreds.

Running her hands over the violin curves of her naked body, the firm mounds of her young breasts, the smooth skin of her inner thighs, Charlotte frowned. Sitting bolt upright, she parted her thighs and focused on the sparse black fleece veiling her girl crack. Her pubic curls matted, sticky, her inner thighs starched with a cream-like substance, she tentatively peeled open the fleshy lips of her vagina. Her virginal sex valley was hot and wet, the intricate folds of her inner petals dripping with opaque liquid. She parted the soft hillocks of her intimacy a little further and examined the pinken flesh forming a funnel around the entrance to her unsullied sex sheath. Milky liquid oozed from the mouth of her vagina, trickling down between the firm orbs of her pert buttocks. Sure that something was wrong with her, she leaped out of bed.

Biting her lip as she gazed at the wet patch on the sheet, Charlotte ran her fingers up her drenched sex valley. As the lubricious cream-like liquid flowed in torrents from her young body, streaming down her inner thighs in rivers of warm milk, she grabbed her dressing gown and crossed the landing to the bathroom. She could hear her mother calling as she filled the bath. Breakfast would be ready. Tea made in a china pot, wholemeal bread with home-made marmalade, fresh grapefruit . . . No waffles or croissants or white sliced bread.

Her gown slipped off her shoulders onto the cold lino beneath her feet and she stepped into the bath. Her naked body sinking into the hot water, gentle waves lapping at the fleshy lips of her vagina, she lay back, immersing her head to her temples. Closing her eyes, her long dark hair floating about her pretty face like a huge black lily, she massaged the soft folds nestling within the divide between her swollen sex cushions.

Charlotte had never discovered her clitoris, the delights of masturbation. Her strait-laced upbringing by her strict mother in a homely cottage had shielded her from all forms of carnal knowledge. The village school had barely changed since it was built in the late nineteenth century. Classrooms with long wooden benches and antique desks, disused gas lamps hanging from the oak beams – Miss Jean Brodie would have felt at home there. Charlotte knew little of the real world, having only left the village occasionally to visit an ageing aunt in the neighbouring county of Hampshire. A television wasn't something her mother deemed necessary, neither was a telephone. Their only contact with the outside world was an ageing valve radio permanently tuned to BBC Radio Four. Or, as her mother still insisted on calling it, the BBC Home Service.

But Charlotte was happy within the confines of her small world. What she hadn't had, she didn't miss. As she lay in the bath, her mind drifted back to her childhood days. She'd been taught that her young body was to be veiled at all times, shrouded as if it was something ugly to be hidden from the eyes of others. On the rare occasions when she was taken to the beach, she wore a full swimming costume and rubber bathing cap. Playing in the garden during the hot summer months, she'd been fully dressed in a frock and thick knickers. Not only had she been taught to veil her young body, she'd been told that certain parts 'down there' were dirty.

Running her fingers up her inner thighs to the swell of her girl lips, Charlotte listened to the music of the lapping bathwater. Guilt engulfed her as she massaged her sex valley with soap. Washing 'down there' was to be done quickly. No rubbing or caressing. Brainwashed by her mother, she'd come to deny her femininity, never exploring between her legs, never scrutinizing the intricate folds of her inner sex lips. When her breast buds had inflated into firm rounded melons, she had been ordered to wear a thick bodice. Although her body had developed fully, her feminine curves and mounds were shrouded by heavy clothing.

'Charlotte!' As her mother's voice bellowed up the stairs, Charlotte placed the bar of coal-tar soap in the china dish and rinsed her young body. Climbing out of the bath, she dried herself with a towel and slipped her pink dressing gown on. 'Charlotte!' her mother called again. Charlotte opened the door and trotted down the narrow staircase to the kitchen. The familiar smell of tea and toast filled her nostrils as she smiled at the middle-aged woman.

'You're always having baths,' her mother sighed, her beady eyes scowling at the girl. 'When I was your age, Sunday night was bath— Where are your slippers? You'll catch your death of cold standing on the stone floor with bare feet. And you shouldn't walk around like that, Charlotte. It's slovenly to parade around in your dressing gown. You haven't even brushed your hair, girl.'

Charlotte looked down at the red quarry tiles. Her feet weren't cold, but she wished she'd put her slippers on.

Mother knew best. Watching the woman dump a pile of washing in the stone sink and wipe her hands on her apron, she smiled. She loved her mother despite the older woman's Victorian attitudes, her grouchiness. She had no one else to love. Her father had passed away when she was a baby. Pneumonia had taken him, her mother had told Charlotte when she was twelve. Never having had a father figure or a brother, Charlotte had known nothing of the male species. An only child, the only people of her own age she mixed with were a few school friends.

'Emily's coming round this morning,' Charlotte said, sitting at the well-scrubbed pine table.

'I don't like that girl,' her mother returned irritably, pouring the tea. 'She has no values, no morals.'

'She's all right, mother,' Charlotte countered.

'She's far from all right. Look at her father, for goodness, sake. He's nothing but a—'

'He's nice,' Charlotte murmured, taking the lid off the stone marmalade pot.

'Nice? He's a drunkard.'

'Mother!' Charlotte laughed.

'I've seen him going into the public house.'

'Lots of people go into the pub.'

'Well, they shouldn't,' the woman returned, brushing her lank dark hair away from her ashen face. 'And don't call it a pub, it's common. If I ever hear that *you*'ve been into that place, I'll disown you. Now, hurry up and eat your breakfast. I want you to go down to the shop.'

'Emily will be here soon.'

'She can wait, can't she?'

'I suppose so.'

After breakfast, Charlotte dressed in a long skirt and white blouse. Tying her shoelaces, she brushed her dark hair, twisting it at the back and slipping an elastic band around the ponytail. Walking to the local shop, she smiled politely at people she passed. The vicar, the milkman, the postman. Village life was confining in its familiarity. Everyone knew everyone else. People talked and gossiped. Not least, Charlotte's mother. She referred to the couple at Mill Cottage as outsiders. They'd only lived in the village for twenty years. Their eighteen-year-old son was vulgar. Why her mother thought that, Charlotte had no idea. Perhaps there was something she didn't know about the lad. Perhaps there were many things that Charlotte didn't know. The small bell tinkled as she opened the shop door and stepped inside.

'Good morning, Charlotte.' The middle-aged man behind the counter smiled.

'Good morning, Mr Goodhugh,' Charlotte replied in a monotone as she had done since she was four years old. 'May I have—'

'Soap suds?' he interrupted her with a triumphant grin.

'Yes. However did you know?'

'Your mother was in yesterday. She was saying that there was something she'd forgotten. When she'd gone, I thought, seeing as she does her washing on a Saturday, she'd be needing soap suds.'

'That's very astute of you, Mr Goodhugh,' Charlotte smiled.

'I should have been Sherlock Holmes,' he chuckled, placing a box of suds in a brown-paper carrier bag.

Mr Goodhugh gazed at her white blouse clinging alluringly to the firm mounds of her young breasts as she passed him a five-pound note. Charlotte noticed his gaze, wondering why he'd always looked at her like that. She recalled the days when she'd call in for sweets on her way home from

SCHOOLGIRL LUST

school. He'd had that same glazed look in his eyes as he'd stared at her young legs, her white ankle socks. As she'd grown, he'd put his arm around her and felt her chest, the small bumps there. She'd never understood why he'd used to do that, and she still didn't understand.

'You're growing into a fine young woman, Charlotte,' he said, mopping his brow with a handkerchief. 'A very fine young woman.'

'Thank you,' she smiled, wondering what he was toying with beneath the counter.

'How old are you now?'

'Seventeen,' she replied.

'Charlotte, I've been thinking.' He hesitated, looking around the shop as he leaned on the counter. 'I've been wanting to talk to you for some time but the shop's either full of customers or you come in with a school friend. I've never been able to catch you alone.'

'Oh?' The girl frowned.

'Would you like to help me out on Saturday mornings? I could do with some assistance in the shop.'

'Well, I . . .' she murmured hesitantly. 'I'd have to check with my mother.'

'Yes, of course. I'll have a word with her the next time she's in. It would only be light duties. Nothing strenuous.' His face reddened as he again eyed her clinging blouse. 'Er . . . tidying the stock room and other small jobs. No doubt the money would come in useful.'

'Yes, it would. Thank you, Mr Goodhugh.'

'Right, I'll speak to your mother about it.'

Taking her change, Charlotte grabbed the bag and left the shop. Making her way home, she became aware of a stickiness between her thighs. Her knickers felt wet, and she again pondered on what she was beginning to look upon as a medical problem. She would have gone to the doctor but he knew her mother well. He knew everyone well. He wouldn't be discreet, Charlotte was sure as she walked up the path and opened the front door. Everyone knew everything in the village.

Charlotte's mother announced disapprovingly that Emily was in a state of near-undress and waiting upstairs. Dumping the bag on the kitchen table along with the change, Charlotte stared at the sheet from her bed crumpled in the wicker basket by the sink. She should have washed it herself, she knew as her face flushed. Praying that her mother hadn't noticed the wet patch, she bounded up the stairs and walked into her room.

Emily was standing by the window, the sun accentuating the golden hue of her long hair. Wearing a red miniskirt that did nothing to conceal her naked thighs and a tight T-shirt clearly outlining her elongated nipples, the young girl radiated an air of sexuality. Charlotte gazed at the band of flesh between her T-shirt and her skirt. Focusing on the small indent of her navel, she felt an unfamiliar sensation within the crack of her vagina as she lowered her eyes to her friend's red leather boots.

'You are lucky,' she smiled, lifting her head and gazing admiringly at Emily's red glossed lips.

'Why's that?' Emily asked, sitting on the bed and crossing her long legs. Her blue eyes sparkling, her fresh face beaming, she tossed her long blonde hair over her shoulder. 'Why am I lucky?'

'Because . . . Never mind. So, what shall we do today?'

'I thought we might go to Ravensbrook,' the other girl replied, a grin on her pretty face.

Charlotte didn't like Ravensbrook. The town was only a ten-minute bus ride away, but it was always bustling with people. The warm scent of diesel fumes hung heavy in the air and the noise of the traffic was disconcerting. She'd have preferred to go to the woods behind the village hall. There were birds there, wild flowers and peace and tranquillity. Pine trees reached up to the sky and the smell of the undergrowth was invigorating. When she listened to the music of the small stream running beneath the wooden footbridge, Charlotte felt at one with the woods.

'There's a new wine bar opened up in the high street,' Emily said enthusiastically.

'A wine bar?' Charlotte frowned. 'I really don't think—'

'They also sell coffee, Charlotte. You don't have to drink alcohol. And your mother won't know where we've been.'

'I don't know,' Charlotte sighed despondently as she thought of the woods, the sound of the running water. 'What if someone sees us and my mother finds out?'

'For God's sake, you *are* seventeen,' the other girl sighed, reclining and lying full-length on the bed.

'Yes, but you know what she's like.'

'Too right, I do,' the girl said mockingly. 'I don't know how you put up with it. If my mother was like—'

'But your mother's *not* like mine, is she?'

Perching on the end of the bed, Charlotte gazed at the smooth unblemished skin of Emily's slender thighs. Following the milk-white flesh up past the hem of her friend's short skirt, she focused on the swelling triangular patch of red material concealing the other girl's feminine intimacy. There were times when she'd wanted to be like Emily, times when she'd wished she was *allowed* to be like Emily. Charlotte wore thick woollen knickers and heavy long skirts. Emily wore flimsy tops and . . . There was no point in thinking about it.

As Emily talked about the wine bar, Charlotte couldn't

take her eyes off the bulge of the girl's tight panties. The thin, tight material faithfully following the contours of Emily's fleshy sex lips, the crack of her vagina clearly defined by the tight red silk, Charlotte felt her stomach somersault. Again aware of a stickiness between her thighs, she wasn't listening to Emily's chatter about the wine bar. Her knickers felt wet and she needed to talk to someone about her problem. Emily moved about on the bed, her legs parting further as she giggled and talked of the time when she'd had too much wine. Charlotte stared at the girl's bulging panties, strangely enchanted by the blonde curls sprouting either side of the tight material running between her thighs.

An unfamiliar feeling welling from the pit of her stomach, Charlotte crossed her legs. Uncharacteristic thoughts surfacing from the depths of her mind, she wondered whether Emily's crack was the same as hers. It would be, she knew as she watched the girl move about on the bed, her thighs opening wide as she talked about a lad who worked in the ironmonger's. The strip of red material too narrow to conceal fully her most private place, the rise of her outer lips becoming visible, she was unaware of Charlotte's longing gaze.

'Emily,' Charlotte finally murmured. 'Have you ever . . . What I mean is . . .'

'What?' Emily smiled, her blue eyes sparkling. 'Have I ever what?'

'I feel wet. You know, down there,' Charlotte confessed, her face reddening as she hung her head.

'So do I,' the girl grinned impishly as she sat up and rested her back against the quilted headboard.

'*You* feel wet?' Charlotte asked surprisedly.

'I always do when I think about that good-looking lad. When I saw him the other day—'

SCHOOLGIRL LUST

'No, you don't understand. I woke up this morning and the sheet was wet with a sort of creamy liquid.'

'That's perfectly normal,' Emily breathed. 'Surely you've noticed it before?'

'No. Well, not like this.'

'Don't you cream your panties?'

'Cream them?' Charlotte echoed, puzzled by the girl's words.

'The white starch in your panties. It's pussy cream. You must get very wet when you come.'

'Come?'

'An orgasm,' Emily frowned, beginning to wonder whether Charlotte was on the same planet. 'When you have an orgasm.'

'I've never—'

'You've never come? Never had an orgasm?'

'No, I haven't. How would I?'

'How would you? You *are* having me on, aren't you?'

'I'm serious, Emily. How could I have an orgasm?'

'Don't you ever . . . Obviously not.'

'Ever what?'

'Masturbate.'

'Goodness me, no. It's wrong to—'

'Wrong?' the other girl said, shaking her head. 'It's *wonderful*.'

'*You* do it?' Charlotte asked, her dark eyes widening. 'I mean, you masturbate?'

'Yes, of course. *Everyone* does. You're seventeen, Charlotte. You must have . . . I don't know. You must have rubbed yourself off. I started when I was twelve. And I've never stopped.'

'Twelve?' Charlotte gasped. 'What made you do it? Why did you start?'

'I was in bed one morning fiddling between my legs. You know, rubbing and stroking my crack. I found my clitoris and . . . Well, I came.'

'Your clitoris?'

'You *are* having me on, Charlotte!' Emily giggled, her long blonde hair falling over her fresh face. 'You're not going to tell me that you don't know where your clitoris is.'

'I've never heard of it.'

'Don't be daft, of course you have.'

'I mean it. I've never heard of the word.'

Wishing she'd never broached the subject, Charlotte dragged her eyes away from her friend's bulging panties and stared at the carpet. *Clitoris?* She pondered on the word. How was she expected to know what it was, let alone *where* it was? She wanted to take her dictionary from her school bag, but decided against it. She reckoned that it sounded like a medical term. Greek? Latin? She couldn't work out its meaning. She knew of her vagina, although she couldn't remember how she'd learned the word. She'd also heard of an orgasm, but didn't know what it was. Clitoris. She'd have to ask her friend, embarrassing though it was.

'I've never heard of the word,' she repeated dolefully, brushing her long back hair away from her dark eyes. 'What is it?'

'It's between your pussy lips,' Emily said, realizing that the girl was serious. 'Feel between your lips, at the top of your crack, and you'll find a little hard spot.'

'What does it . . . What's it for?'

'God, Charlotte. You really are naive. If you rub it, you'll come. You'll have an orgasm. You do know what an orgasm is, don't you?'

'Yes, no. Well . . .'

'Put your hand down your panties and find your clit.'

SCHOOLGIRL LUST

'No, I can't.'

'Go on, for God's sake. You can't go through life not knowing what or where your clitoris is.'

Sighing, Charlotte stood up and wandered to the window. Gazing at the back garden, she again wished she'd never mentioned her problem. She felt stupid, ignorant, as she thought about rubbing between the soft lips of her vagina. When washing in the bath, she'd been aware of a pleasant feeling within her girl crack, but had never deliberately rubbed herself there. Before that morning, she'd never peeled her vaginal cushions apart and examined her inner flesh. She'd had dark thoughts at times, it was true, thoughts about the private slit between her thighs, but she had successfully forced them back down into the deepest, most secret regions of her mind.

'Do you want me to show you?' Emily asked, unashamedly lifting her firm buttocks clear of the bed and tugging her skirt up over the smooth plateau of her stomach.

'No,' Charlotte gasped, turning and staring at her friend's tight panties.

'It's better that *I* show you rather than some fumbling boy. Mind you, most boys don't know about the clitoris.'

Emily's blue eyes sparkled as she peeled her red panties away from her pubic mound. Charlotte gazed at the rise of her friend's sparsely fleeced mons, the alluring divide of her swollen outer lips. She watched in amazement as Emily ran her fingers up the creases between her fleshy sex pads and the tops of her firm thighs. This wasn't happening, she thought, holding her hand to her pretty mouth. This had to be a crazy dream. What had come over Emily? she wondered. She'd never behaved like this before.

'There,' Emily said, peeling the swollen lips of her pussy

wide apart and displaying her pinken girl flesh. 'See, it's just there.'

'Emily!' Charlotte gasped.

'Come and take a look, for God's sake. You can't be seventeen years old and not know where your clitty is.'

'Show me, then,' Charlotte conceded, sitting on the edge of the bed.

'There, that little pink lump.' Emily pulled her inner lips wider apart. 'That's my clitoris. If I rub it for long enough, I'll come.'

The sight of her friend's blatantly exposed inner sex flesh sending a quiver through her young womb, Charlotte felt her face flush. Never had she examined inside her own sex valley, let alone seen another girl's blatantly exposed secret folds. To her horror, she realized that she wanted to reach out and touch Emily there, feel the hard nodule of her ripe clitoris. Focusing on the girl's yawning sex valley, the milky liquid oozing from the open mouth of her vaginal throat, she felt her young womb contract. Her mind aching with confusion, she finally managed to look away and rise to her feet.

This was so very wrong, Charlotte knew as she reached the window. Turning, she focused on Emily's young girl crack again. Her friend was still holding her swollen sex pads wide apart and examining the intricate petals within her yawning valley. Charlotte felt her knickers wetting as her stomach somersaulted. Her consciousness was narrowing, filling her awareness with overpowering impulses to explore forbidden worlds of lust. This was wrong, she repeatedly tried to convince herself.

'Come and lie on the bed,' Emily smiled, pulling her panties back up and lowering her skirt. 'I'll show you where your clitoris is.'

SCHOOLGIRL LUST

'No,' Charlotte gasped. Her hands trembling, she sighed. 'Emily, it's wrong to—'

'Wrong to show you where your clitoris is?'

'No, I mean . . . You know what I mean.'

'Come here and lie next to me.'

Tentatively sitting on the edge of the bed, Charlotte swung her legs up and reclined. Her head resting on the pillow, she stared upwards. Trying to remove herself from this disturbing new reality, she focused on the cracks in the ceiling above her bed. Fanning out in zigzags, they'd been there since she was young. They'd grown as she had grown, the ceiling cracks bigger, her sex crack fuller. Closing her eyes as she felt her friend tugging her skirt up, she thought of school, the homework she should be doing. Desperately trying to drag her thoughts away from her girl slit, she shuddered as she became aware of Emily's hands on her knees. Her clothing was moving, the heavy material of her long skirt crawling up her thighs and over the rise of her pubic mound. The other girl's fingers slid between the tight elastic of her knickers and the smooth skin of her warm stomach and Charlotte involuntarily raised her buttocks as her mons veil was slowly removed.

Her knickers now down around her knees, Charlotte could feel fingers stroking her naked sex lips, tracing the gentle contours of her cream-drenched valley. She shouldn't be allowing this violation of her most private place, she knew as her fleshy pads were parted, the hot ravine of her young vagina opening wide. She should never have agreed to this. She *hadn't* agreed. It had just happened. She should never have mentioned her problem. They should have gone out, to Ravensbrook, anywhere away from the privacy of her bedroom. The walls were watching, the cracks in the ceiling spying.

Her head turning to one side, Charlotte opened her dark eyes and gazed out of the window. A bird hovered in the blue sky, a cotton-wool cloud drifted, aimless in its drifting. Why wasn't she outside, enjoying the warm weather? Why was she lying on her bed with her knickers pulled down and another girl's finger delving into her secret crack? *Clitoris*. A new and powerful word. A word she'd never forget. She had to stop Emily, she knew as her stomach rose and fell with her quickening breathing. If her mother came in and witnessed the disgusting act . . . Was *God* a witness to this illicit violation of her young body?

'*That*'s your clitoris,' Emily murmured, her fingers massaging the sensitive tip of the hard nodule nestling within the top of Charlotte's sex valley. 'Is that nice?'

'Yes, no . . .' Charlotte sighed as her clitoris swelled and throbbed. 'I don't know.'

'You like me rubbing it, don't you?'

'I . . . I . . .'

'Of course you do. Are you going to come for me?'

'No, Emily. You mustn't—'

'Lie still and relax.'

Her body trembling uncontrollably as unfamiliar sensations of sex transmitted deep into her contracting womb, Charlotte began to gasp in her new-found pleasure. She could smell the heady scent of her young friend's perfume, hear the other girl's deep breathing, feel the sensual touch of her slender fingers working expertly within her drenched sex slit. This was wrong, she again tried to convince herself. Her mind was a mess, her thoughts screaming at her as her girl-pleasure gradually built.

'You're going to come,' Emily whispered huskily. Charlotte could feel the tip of the girl's finger between the pink petals of her inner lips. She was trying to gain entry to her inner sanctuary, her virginal sex sheath. A woman's voice echoed in Charlotte's head. Her mother was calling in the shimmering distance of her mind. Her head lolling from side to side, her mind seemingly leaving her body, she whimpered as her friend's finger glided into the creamy hot sheath of her vagina. She tried to protest as her mind drowned in confusion, but the words wouldn't come.

Her erect clitoris pulsating, her vaginal sheath rhythmically contracting, Charlotte lay in a dreamlike state as her illicit pleasure heightened. She could feel the wetness of her vagina, hear the squelching of her creamy juices as her friend fingered her private duct. Her clitoris pulsating, she dug her fingernails into the eiderdown and arched her back. She instinctively knew that she was about to have an orgasm. The thought worried her. What would it be like? Would it hurt?

'No, Emily,' Charlotte breathed as another finger slipped into her hot sex sheath. Her body shaking wildly, her eyes rolling, she tossed her head back and clung to the eiderdown as her juices of sex issued from the gaping mouth of her vagina. 'No,' she murmured again as fear gripped her. She didn't want this. It was wrong, immoral. If her mother happened to walk in . . . 'Oh, oh,' she whimpered, trying desperately to deny the incredible pleasure Emily was bringing her. Her vaginal muscles rhythmically contracting, gripping the girl's pistoning fingers, her clitoris swelling beneath Emily's intimate caress, she cried out as her first orgasm erupted within her pulsating budlette and ripped through her convulsing body.

'No, no,' Charlotte gasped, her knuckles whitening as she gripped the eiderdown. Her nostrils flaring, her eyes wide, her body convulsed wildly as her frenzied pleasure peaked. The sound of her squelching juices resounding around the room, she sang out in her pioneering climax, her wails of female pleasure reverberating throughout the cottage. Again, she could hear her mother calling in the distance. Were there footsteps on the stairs? Slipping her fingers out of Charlotte's spasming vaginal duct, Emily leaped off the bed and moved to the door.

'Quickly,' she said, staring at Charlotte's convulsing body. 'Your mum's coming up.' Dragging her knickers up and lowering her skirt, Emily rolled off the bed and clambered to her feet. Trembling like a leaf, she brushed her dark hair away from her sex-flushed face and stood with her back to the window as her mother entered the room. The woman gazed first at Emily and then at Charlotte. There was suspicion mirrored in her beady eyes as she looked at the bed, the ruffled eiderdown. Evidence of lesbian sex.

'What are you two up to?' she asked, moving to the bed and straightening the eiderdown.

'Er . . . Nothing, mother,' Charlotte breathed, flattening her skirt with her palms as Emily announced that she needed the loo and left the room.

'I've been calling you, Charlotte. Didn't you hear me?'

'No, no, I—'

'What have you been up to? Your face is flushed and you look as if . . . Are you feeling all right, Charlotte?'

'Yes, I'm fine,' the girl replied, forcing a smile. 'We were talking about . . . about school work. Our English projects.'

'Well, I suggest you get on with it. I'm going to the post office now. Do something with your hair, girl. You look like you've been dragged through a bush.'

As her mother left the room, Charlotte tossed her hair back over her shoulder. The elastic band had slipped off, her ponytail loosening and her dark hair flailing as she'd writhed in the grip of her orgasm. Her knickers soaked, her hands still trembling, she sat on the end of the bed. Guilt engulfing her as her young body calmed, she stared blankly at the wall. The room had witnessed her wanton vulgarity. Her tight vagina sullied, the veil of virginity torn aside, she hung her head as tears streamed from her eyes.

'You OK?' Emily asked, trotting into the room and closing the door.

'Yes, I think so,' Charlotte sobbed.

'Well, what did you think?'

'Think?'

'Your orgasm, your first ever orgasm.'

'It was . . .'

'Now you know how to do it, you'll never stop.'

'No . . . Emily, we shouldn't have . . .'

'Don't be so silly. So, shall we go to Ravensbrook?'

'No, I don't want to go out.'

'Why not?'

'I just want to stay here. I have to think. Think about what we did.'

'Think about it?' the girl giggled. 'What do you want to think about it for?'

'I don't know. I feel guilty. It's not right to do what we did.'

'OK. While you're wallowing in your guilt, I'm going to Ravensbrook to check out the new wine bar.'

'I'll see you later. This afternoon, perhaps.'

'All right,' Emily sighed, leaving the room. 'I'll call round after lunch.'

Wandering to the window as Emily trotted down the stairs, Charlotte again thought about her crude act of lesbian sex. Her life had changed now, she knew as she gazed at the back garden. Never would she be the same after experiencing illicit sex with another girl. The flimsy gown of her innocence had fallen away, never to clothe her again. Slipping her hands up her skirt, she pulled her wet knickers down and stepped out of them. Hiding them behind the ottoman, she went downstairs and out into the back garden. She was looking for solace, and thought she might find it at the bottom of the garden where she had played as a child.

The sun warming her, she wandered across the grass to the trees. Realizing that she hadn't put a clean pair of knickers on as the breeze waited up her skirt and cooled her inflamed vaginal lips, she smiled. If her mother knew that she was in the garden without knickers . . . Wandering behind the shed, she gazed at a patch of grass between the trees. She used to sit there and wonder what her father had been like. Now, she pondered on her womanhood, her clitoris – and orgasms.

Sitting with her back against a tree, Charlotte pulled her skirt up her long legs. Bringing her knees up and apart, she lowered her head and gazed at the open valley of her young vagina. She knew about sex, the penis entering the vagina and depositing the seed of life there. But she'd never seen a penis, didn't know what the seed looked like. Peeling the oily wings of her inner lips apart, she eyed the pink nubble of her ripe clitoris. Tentatively rubbing the sensitive protrusion, she gasped as ripples of sex flowed through her contracting womb.

'Oh,' she gasped, looking up to see a rabbit watching her. Lowering her legs and tugging her skirt down as the animal scurried off, she closed her eyes. She would never masturbate, she decided. It was *wrong* to touch and rub 'down there'. Watching a beetle clambering over a decaying leaf, she listened to the birds singing, a tractor's engine throbbing in the distance. Charlotte loved the countryside. Peace and tranquillity reigned among the trees.

SCHOOLGIRL LUST

But her mind was tormented. Uncharacteristic thoughts careered around the emotional wreckage caused by her guilt, wreaking havoc where there had once been quiet and calm. Why had she allowed Emily to rub her there? Why had she allowed the girl to . . . She'd taken the first step along the path to her sexual awakening. Her head lolling forward, Charlotte fell into a deep sleep and dreamed her dreams of masturbation and orgasm.

Chapter Two

Picking at her lunch, Charlotte gazed across the table at her mother. Was the woman aware of her own clitoris? she wondered. Did she know what it was for? Consumed by guilt, Charlotte sighed. She'd never forget the lewd incident, she was sure as she sipped her orange juice. Why had Emily behaved like that? she wondered again, acutely aware of her naked vulval flesh beneath her skirt. Would it happen again?

'Are you all right?' her mother asked.

'Yes, yes, I'm fine,' Charlotte smiled.

'You were miles away.'

'I was thinking about my school project.'

'How are you getting on with it?'

'Quite well.'

'I was talking to Mr Goodhugh earlier. You didn't tell me that he's offered you a Saturday job.'

'Oh, yes. I forgot all about it.'

'What's on your mind, Charlotte?'

'Nothing, apart from my project.'

'Well, I told Mr Goodhugh that you'd start next Saturday. He wants you there at eight o'clock.' Rising from her chair, the older woman began clearing the table. 'You're not going to finish that, are you?'

'I don't feel hungry,' Charlotte replied, pushing the plate of salad away. 'I'm going for a walk.'

'Where to?'

'Just around the village. I won't be long.'

'Call into the shop and see Mr Goodhugh while you're out. He wants to talk to you about the job.'

'Yes, I will.'

Leaving the cottage, Charlotte walked to the village hall and took the narrow path that went alongside the building and into the woods. Wandering through the trees, she stopped by the side of the small stream. The gentle sound of the running water calming her mind, she sat on the grassy bank by the wooden bridge. This was heaven to her. The birds, the breeze rustling the leaves high above her, the smell of pine . . . far removed from the stench and noise of the town. Watching a leaf floating down the stream, she wondered whether she was being carried away on the tide of illicit sex. Would she allow Emily to masturbate her again? Her mind wouldn't let go of the lewd incident, pictures of the girl sitting on the bed with her fingers delving into her sex sheath constantly intruding on her thoughts. Would Emily want Charlotte to massage the erect nub of her clitoris?

Reclining, Charlotte looked up at the foliage high above her. As the sun glistened through the leaves like a thousand twinkling stars, she turned her thoughts to Mr Goodhugh. She didn't really want to work in his shop. The weekends were for relaxing, roaming through the woods and emptying her mind. She'd have to go and see him, talk to him. He didn't close the shop until five so there was plenty of time. Wondering how much he intended to pay her, she sat upright as she heard twigs cracking underfoot. She didn't want to meet anyone. This was her secret place where she could hide from people, hide from the world.

'Your mother said that you'd gone for a walk so I

thought you'd probably be here.' Emily smiled as she approached.

'What's in the bag?' Charlotte asked as her friend sat beside her.

'I bought this in Ravensbrook,' Emily said, pulling a red skirt from the bag. 'It's for you, Charlotte. It's about time you dressed properly.'

'How much was it?' Charlotte asked, holding the miniskirt up. 'Goodness, it's very short.'

'Don't worry about the money. Try it on.'

'What, here?'

'Why not? There's no one around.'

Remembering that she wasn't wearing any knickers, Charlotte hesitated. But she then realized that Emily had seen more of her intimate place than she herself had. Standing up, she slipped her long skirt down and stepped out of the garment. She couldn't let her mother see the miniskirt, she knew as she tugged the small item of clothing up her long legs and veiled the wet crack of her vagina. Her mother would think her a harlot for wearing such a revealing garment.

'Well, what do you think?' she asked Emily.

'I think you don't have any panties on,' the girl grinned. 'Here, I also bought you these.' Pulling a pack of five pairs of panties from the bag, she passed them to Charlotte. 'You can't wear those awful woollen knickers beneath a miniskirt. Apart from looking hideous, they must have made you very hot.'

'Oh, thank you,' Charlotte beamed. 'But why did you buy me all these presents?'

'Because . . . because you need some clothes. Clothes suitable for a girl of seventeen, not an old granny.'

Turning this way and that, Charlotte grinned as she

looked down at her new skirt. Her legs appeared to be longer, and she felt feminine for the first time in her life. Taking a pair of panties from the pack and slipping into them, she felt good. She was a real teenage girl, a young female wearing female clothes. What her mother would say, she dreaded to think. She'd have to hide the miniskirt and panties, wearing them only when her mother wasn't around. Charlotte had never lied to her mother. Until today.

'Quite a transformation,' Emily smiled. 'You look really good.'

'Thanks, Emily. You'll have to tell me how much I owe you.'

'No way. If you've got any money, then buy yourself some decent tops.'

'I wish my mother . . .'

'Don't worry about your mum. Hey, I've got an idea. Why not keep the skirt at my house? When we go out, you can change in my bedroom. Your mum will never know.'

'That's a good idea. But I don't really want to lie to her.'

'You won't be lying.'

'No, I suppose not. Oh, I forgot to tell you. I've got a Saturday job.'

'Where?'

'Mr Goodhugh's shop.'

'Really? How much?'

'I don't know yet. I start next week.'

'Does your mum know?'

'Of course. He spoke to her about it this morning. I'm going to see him later today.' She looked down at the miniskirt again, her face beaming. 'I do like the skirt, Emily,' she grinned. 'You shouldn't have bought it. It must have cost . . .'

'I bought it with my birthday money. And it doesn't

matter what it cost. I'd better get home. I haven't had my lunch yet. I thought I'd give you the skirt before going home.'

'I'll see you later?'

'Yes. Come round.'

'OK, I'll bring the skirt with me.'

Watching Emily follow the path to the village hall, Charlotte looked down again at her new skirt and grinned. The skimpy garment *had* transformed her. But why had Emily spent money on her? Again pondering on her mother's reaction if she were to see the skirt, Charlotte wandered along the path by the stream. It was a good idea to keep the skirt at Emily's house, she decided. What her mother didn't know wouldn't worry her. Lies.

Walking for a hundred yards or so, Charlotte breathed in the heady scent of the undergrowth. A miniskirt was hardly suitable for walking in the woods, but she didn't want to take it off. The panties felt good – tight, hugging. The flesh of her vulva was cool beneath the soft silk. Unlike the woollen knickers she'd been used to. Thinking how pretty Emily was as her clitoris swelled within her moist sex valley, Charlotte wondered whether the girl would touch her again. Her mind flooding with thoughts of pushing her finger into her friend's tight vaginal sheath, she turned and headed back along the path. She knew how quickly the hours passed when she was in the woods, and she thought it best to go and see Mr Goodhugh before doing anything else.

'That's strange,' she murmured, scanning the ground for her skirt. Looking about her, she was sure she'd left the garment by the bridge. She hadn't seen Emily take it, so . . . Perhaps someone had passed by and picked it up. The carrier bag had gone, too. Her heart racing as she looked down at her miniskirt, she didn't know what to do. She dared not go home dressed like that. Unless she could creep into the cottage and sneak upstairs without her mother seeing her.

Hurriedly following the path deeper into the woods, she knew she'd eventually come out behind the cottage. If she could climb over the wall and slip in through the back door . . . Reaching the ivy-covered wall, she peered over the top. Her mother was in the kitchen. Not knowing what to do, she decided to go to Emily's house. Following the path, she finally came out into the street by Goodhugh's shop. A few people were milling around, but she had no choice other than to make a dash to her friend's house some two hundred yards up the hill.

'Ah, Charlotte,' Mr Goodhugh beamed as he stepped out of his shop. 'My, you look—' he began, gazing at her skirt. 'Er, I'm pleased that you've come to see me. Come in and we'll talk about the job.' Forcing a smile, Charlotte followed him into the shop. He'd tell her mother about her short skirt, she was sure as he stood by the counter gazing at her long legs, her naked thighs. 'We'll go through to the stockroom and . . . and I'll tell you about the job.'

Following him through a door at the rear of the shop, Charlotte prayed that he wouldn't mention the skirt to her mother. She should never have wandered off and left her old skirt by the bridge, she knew as the man closed the door and grinned at her. This was a mess, she thought, wondering who could have taken her skirt. Someone might have recognized the skirt as belonging to her, she thought fearfully. If they took it to the cottage and . . . How could she explain why she'd taken her skirt off and left it in the woods? And the pack of panties . . .

'I've never seen you dressed like that,' Mr Goodhugh smiled. 'Is this your new image?'

'No, I . . .'

SCHOOLGIRL LUST

'You look lovely, Charlotte,' he breathed, his stare locked to her inner thighs. 'It's been a joy watching you grow over the years. I remember when you used to trot into the shop with your mother and . . .' Rubbing his chin, he frowned at her. 'I must say I'm surprised that your mother allows you to wear so short a skirt. I know she's somewhat old-fashioned and I really can't see her allowing you out in the street dressed like that.'

'She . . . The thing is . . .' Charlotte stammered as the man gazed longingly at her youthful thighs.

'She doesn't know that you're out dressed like that, does she?' he asked accusingly. His tone was threatening. 'She *doesn't* know, does she?'

'Well . . .'

'Oh, dear. You've put me in quite a predicament, Charlotte. I wouldn't want to have to lie to her.'

'Lie to her?' Charlotte echoed, the pools of her dark eyes widening. 'You don't have to lie, Mr Goodhugh. Just don't mention it.'

'It wouldn't be right for me to keep this from her.' The shop bell tinkling, he smiled and moved to the door. 'I won't be a minute,' he said. 'We're going to have to talk about this, Charlotte.'

Looking about her as the shopkeeper left the room and closed the door, Charlotte sighed. The weekend had started so well – but now? Wishing she'd not gone to the woods, or allowed Emily to touch her, she realized what a terrible mess she was in. Not only was she going to have to explain the disappearance of her long skirt, but somehow she'd have to stop Mr Goodhugh telling her mother about her red miniskirt. It might be best to be honest with her mother, she thought. There again, knowing the woman's attitude towards Emily's skirts . . .

'I'm not one for telling tales,' Mr Goodhugh said as he re-entered the stockroom. 'But I do feel that your mother should know about this.' Charlotte looked at his balding head as he perched himself on the edge of his desk, the light from a solitary bulb shining on the round patch of perspiring skin. 'I really don't know what to do, Charlotte,' he sighed. 'Since your father passed away, I've tried to help your mother as best I can. Several people in the village have been supportive to her and . . . I really don't know what to do. You see, I feel somewhat responsible. Your mother trusts me and I wouldn't want to betray her trust.'

Her hands trembling as she watched the man shaking his head, she knew that she was going to be in real trouble. Her mother would disown her if she knew about the miniskirt and panties. Not only was Mr Goodhugh now a threat, but someone might have taken her long skirt home and . . . How could she explain that she'd taken her skirt off in the woods? It didn't bear thinking about, Charlotte knew as she sat on an old wooden chair. Her mind aching, she couldn't come to terms with her wanton behaviour. To allow Emily to rub her clitoris to orgasm, and then for her, Charlotte, to parade around in a miniskirt . . .

'I have an idea,' the shopkeeper grinned, his gaze transfixed by the firm flesh of Charlotte's shapely thighs as he thrust his hands into the pockets of his Harris Tweed jacket. 'I'm a bit of an amateur photographer. You might have seen some of my work exhibited in the village hall.'

'Yes, I have,' Charlotte murmured, wondering what he had in mind.

'How about if I take a few shots of you?'

'Why would you want pictures of me?' she asked naively.

'It's not easy to find models in a small village,' he chuckled, his stare darting between her thighs and the mounds of her young breasts. 'Would you like to be my photographic model, Charlotte?'

'What about my skirt? I thought . . .'

'The skirt will be our little secret.' Clapping his hands, Mr Goodhugh moved to the door. 'I've a feeling that we're going to work well together,' he smiled. 'Not only on Saturdays, in the shop, but during our photographic sessions.'

'*Sessions?*' She frowned.

'I'll go and get my camera and we'll start straight away.'

Nervously twisting her long black hair around her trembling fingers, Charlotte wished she'd stayed at home and worked on her school project. Lying on the bed with her knickers down and Emily's fingers in her vagina, and now in the stockroom at the local shop waiting for . . . But she had no choice, she knew. She was prepared to do whatever it took to prevent her mother discovering the truth. Besides, a few photographs wouldn't do any harm. Would they?

'Right,' the man beamed as he entered the room with an expensive-looking camera. 'I think we'll have you sitting on the desk.' Clearing some papers away as Charlotte stood up, he fiddled with the camera. 'OK, just sit on the edge of the desk and relax.' Complying, she tossed her long hair back over her shoulder and stared at him. 'Look over there,' he said, pointing to the filing cabinet as he knelt on the floor. 'That's it. Now, I want you to sit with your legs apart.'

Her stomach churning, Charlotte pressed her young thighs together as he moved closer. 'I'll sit like this,' she murmured, pulling her skirt down to conceal her naked thighs.

'No, no,' he mumbled with a note of irritability in his voice. 'You're a photographic model, Charlotte, not a tailor's dummy. Open your legs a little.'

Her hands trembling, she parted her thighs. 'Is that all right?' she asked shakily.

'A little further,' he ordered her, focusing the camera.

'Mr Goodhugh, I don't want—'

'OK, as wide as you can now.'

'I thought you wanted pictures of my face,' she said, parting her thighs further.

'Not *just* your face, Charlotte. I want photographs of your whole body.'

'But—'

'Charlotte, I don't want to have to tell your mother about your skirt,' he said threateningly, lowering the camera and scowling at the girl. 'No one else will see the photographs, so you needn't worry.'

'But this is wrong,' she sighed.

'And you think it's right to walk around the street in a skirt so short that people can see your panties?'

'Well, no . . .'

'Would your mother think it right?'

'No, she wouldn't.'

'OK, then. Now, I want some really good shots. Open your legs as wide as you can. Ah, that's more like it,' he beamed as she parted her legs to the extreme, the narrow strip of material between her thighs barely concealing the swell of her outer sex lips.

As he moved in, the camera now between her parted knees, Charlotte gazed at his shiny head. She shouldn't be doing this, she knew as he clicked the shutter. Wondering how she'd got herself into such a horrendous situation, she couldn't wait to get home and change into more familiar clothes. It had been nice of Emily to buy her the skirt, but it was causing nothing but trouble. Breathing a sigh of relief as the shop bell tinkled, she slipped off the desk and pulled her skirt down to cover her naked thighs.

'That will do for now,' the grinning man said, placing his camera on the desk. 'Er . . . what are you doing this evening?'

'I'm . . . I have to help my mother,' she lied, eyeing the door.

'I'd like you to come back at seven o'clock, Charlotte. We'll take a few more photographs and—'

'I can't. I have to—'

'I'm sure you'll be able to get out for an hour or so. Your skirt is our little secret – and we want it to *remain* our secret. Right, off you go and I'll see you this evening. Just ring the bell on the wall outside and I'll let you in.'

Leaving the stockroom, Charlotte crept around the back of the racking to avoid being seen by the customers who were standing at the counter. Leaving the shop, she breathed a sigh of relief as she looked up and down the deserted road. Deciding to go home rather than try to make it to Emily's house, she followed the path by the side of the shop into the woods. She'd just have to climb over the garden wall and pray that her mother wasn't around. If she was caught sneaking up to her room . . . Well, she'd face that nightmare when she came to it.

Walking through the trees, she wondered about Goodhugh and his camera. She didn't want to go back to the shop that evening, and wished again that she'd stayed at home and worked on her school project. Wondering what he was going to do with photographs of her panties as she scaled the wall, she almost fell into the back garden. Picking herself up, she stole across the lawn to the back door. She could hear the radio in the lounge as she stepped into the kitchen. If luck was on her side . . .

'Thank God,' she breathed, creeping up the stairs to her bedroom. Quietly closing the door and tugging her skirt down, she kicked it beneath the bed and opened the oak wardrobe. Slipping into a long skirt, she took a deep breath as she heard her mother climbing the stairs. What to say? she wondered, opening the door as if she was about to leave the room.

'I thought I heard you come in,' her mother said as she reached the landing.

'I needed the loo,' Charlotte smiled. 'That's why I came straight up here.'

'You were a long time. Where did you go?'

'For a walk and then to see Mr Goodhugh.'

'He's a nice man, Charlotte. You'll enjoy working for him. So, what did he say?'

'I was thinking . . . I might not take the job.'

'Why ever not, girl?'

'Because . . . I don't really want to work in a—'

'Don't talk nonsense, Charlotte. Of course you'll take the job. Mr Goodhugh has been kind enough to offer you a job, and you'll take it.'

'Yes, mother,' Charlotte sighed.

'I hope you're not thinking of going out again. You have your project to do and . . .

'I was going to call on Emily.'

'You saw her this morning, Charlotte. Besides, she's not the sort of person I want you mixing with. That skirt of hers is so short I don't know why she bothers to wear it. Why don't you get on with your project? Go and sit in the garden and work on your project. It's a lovely day.'

'Yes, I will.'

Shaking her head, Charlotte sat on the end of her bed as her mother trotted back down the stairs. Everything was a

SCHOOLGIRL LUST

mess, she reflected. Mr Goodhugh couldn't force her to go to his shop that evening. If she didn't arrive, would he really tell her mother about the skirt? Charlotte doubted it very much. After all, he'd have nothing to gain by getting her into trouble. But he'd sounded threatening, she reflected. He'd known her since she was a baby, and she was sure that he'd not say anything to upset her mother. Finally grabbing her school bag, she went out to the garden and sat on the bench beneath the laburnum tree.

She couldn't concentrate on her work. Continually disturbed by thoughts of Goodhugh's photo session and her new-found sexual relationship with Emily, she spent most of the time staring at the grass. It was pointless trying to work, she decided after two hours. Grabbing her bag, she was about to go into the cottage when her mother appeared at the back door with a tray of tea and biscuits. Charlotte smiled as the woman approached. Her mother meant well, she knew. But, at seventeen years old, Charlotte needed time and space to grow.

'Mr Goodhugh called to see me,' the woman said, placing the tray on the bench.

'Oh?' Charlotte frowned, her heart racing.

'He'd like you to go to his shop this evening.'

'Why? I thought he wanted me to—'

'He has some paperwork he needs a hand with. As I said to him, I'd far rather you were doing something useful than hanging about in the village with that Emily girl. He wants you there at seven o'clock.'

'But, mother—' Charlotte began.

'But mother, nothing. It's only for an hour or so. What's the matter with you, Charlotte? You seem different today. Has anything happened?'

'No, mother. Nothing's happened.'

Drinking her tea, Charlotte watched her mother return to the house. She was going to have to say something to the woman about Mr Goodhugh, she knew. To have the man taking photographs of her, Charlotte, blatantly displaying her underwear was horrifying. Perhaps he was harmless, she tried to convince herself, finishing her tea and lugging her bag up to her room. Pacing the floor, she wondered whether to take Emily with her as a chaperone. Deciding that Goodhugh was nothing more than a keen amateur photographer, she felt safe enough. And he was a long-standing friend of her mother's, so he wouldn't harm her. The time approaching seven, she said goodbye to her mother and walked the short distance to the shop. There was nothing to worry about, she was sure as she found the door ajar. Wandering inside, she called out for the shopkeeper. There was nothing to worry about.

'Ah, Charlotte,' he grinned, emerging from the stockroom and striding towards her. Bolting the door, he pulled the blind down and took her hand. 'I'm all ready for you,' he said, looking her up and down. 'I was hoping you'd wear your red skirt, but not to worry.' Leading her through the door at the rear of the shop, he waved his hand around the stockroom and smiled. 'As you can see, I've prepared for the shoot.'

Charlotte looked around the room, her dark eyes frowning. The filing cabinet had gone and the desk had been replaced by a chaise longue upholstered in pink velvet. Eyeing a white sheet hanging on the wall behind the chaise longue, Charlotte turned and gazed at the camera that had been set up on a tripod. Lighting equipment was propped against the back wall. The stockroom had been transformed into a photographic studio.

'The shop was quiet this afternoon,' Goodhugh said,

SCHOOLGIRL LUST

taking a pile of photographs from a shelf. 'Giving me time to develop these.' Charlotte gazed in horror at the close-up shots of her bulging red panties. 'Well, what do you think?' he asked.

'I . . . I don't know what to say,' she stammered, looking at a shot of her pretty face, her young thighs spread wide, exposing the tight material of her red panties straining to contain her full sex lips.

'Slip your skirt off and we'll get started,' he grinned, placing the photographs on the shelf. 'Oh, and your blouse.'

'Mr Goodhugh,' she said shakily. 'I'm not taking my clothes off. I thought you wanted pictures of—'

'Don't you like the photographs?' he frowned.

'Yes, no . . . I mean . . .'

'Oh, that's a shame. I thought they were rather—'

'They're photographs of my knickers,' she broke in. 'I don't want you to take—'

'Perhaps I'll show them to your mother and ask for her opinion.'

Her dark eyes widening, her breathing fast and shallow, Charlotte swayed on her sagging legs as she realized that he was as good as blackmailing her. The miniskirt had been bad enough, but if her mother were to see the photographs . . . She held her hand to her pretty mouth as he fiddled with the camera, wondering how to escape the dreadful situation. Moving to the door, she decided to leave. She'd be able to explain about the miniskirt. She'd tell her mother that Emily had bought it and . . . No, the woman would think the worst and disown her.

'Come on, Charlotte,' Goodhugh urged her, taking her hand. 'We only have an hour.'

'Mr Goodhugh,' she said as firmly as she could without appearing rude. 'I'm *not* going to take my clothes off.'

37

'Well, I'm very sorry to hear that,' he sighed. 'I didn't mean take *all* your clothes off, only down to your bra and panties. However, the choice is yours and I respect that.'

'May I go now?' she asked hopefully.

'Yes, yes, of course. Oh, er . . . is your mother at home?'

'Yes, she is,' Charlotte replied, opening the door.

'I'll bring your photographs along later,' he smiled.

'*My* photographs? I thought—'

'I'll be along to see your mother later,' Goodhugh said, taking the photos from the shelf. 'I'll explain that you left your prints in the shop and I thought it only right to return them.'

'But she'll know *you* took them,' Charlotte murmured, her stomach sinking as she closed the door and turned back to face the shopkeeper.

'If you look carefully at them, you'll notice that my desk isn't in frame and that there's a blank wall behind you. There's nothing to connect the photographs with me or my shop. Tell your mother that I'll be along to see her in about half an hour.'

'You know I can't do that,' Charlotte murmured solemnly, wringing her hands.

'Charlotte, all I'm asking is for you to be my photographic model. All I want are a few pictures for my private collection.'

'If that's all,' the girl said. 'I suppose it'll be all right.'

'Of course it will. Now, we've wasted enough time so slip your clothes off and lie down on the chaise longue.'

Pulling her shoes off, Charlotte tugged her long skirt down and stepped out of the garment. Unbuttoning her blouse, her face reddening, she turned away from Goodhugh. *First Emily, then the miniskirt, and now this*, she mused fearfully, releasing the last button. Slipping her blouse off her shoulders, she laid it on the floor beside her skirt. Looking down at her straining bra, the deep ravine of her cleavage, she again wondered how she'd got herself into this horrendous situation. It was blackmail, she knew as she sat on the chaise longue and crossed her legs. There was no other word for it. Her head spinning, she looked up at Goodhugh as he stood behind the camera.

'OK,' he smiled, peering over the top of the camera. 'Lie back and relax. That's it, that's good. Now keep your left foot on the floor and lay your right leg on the chaise longue.' Lifting her foot, Charlotte realized that her thighs were parting wide as she placed her leg on the chaise longue. Gazing at the narrow strip of her red panties running between her thighs, her face flushing with embarrassment when she saw her dark pubic curls sprouting either side of the tight material, she couldn't believe what she was doing.

This was Mr Goodhugh, the man who'd known her since she was a babe in her mother's arms. Recalling the times she'd skipped into the shop in her school uniform to ask for sweets, she watched as he focused the camera. He'd always been so friendly and polite. What had changed him? she wondered as he ordered her to rest her right arm on the back of the chaise longue. He'd often given her strange looks, his glazed stare scanning her young body, but he'd never behaved like this.

This was the beginning of a nightmare, she knew instinctively as he clicked the shutter. The more photographs he had of her, the more evidence he had to blackmail her. *Evidence?* she asked herself. *Evidence of what?* She'd worn a miniskirt, that was all. It was hardly a crime. There again, in her mother's eyes . . . Evidence of her wanton behaviour in front of a camera, she reflected fearfully. Evidence that she was clearly nothing more than a common harlot.

'Good, very good,' the man grinned, leaving the camera and kneeling by Charlotte's foot. 'I'm just going to adjust your bra,' he said, slipping the strap off her shoulder.

'No!' Charlotte protested as the cup fell away from the mound of her firm breast, revealing her elongated nipple, the chocolate-brown disc of her areola.

'Charlotte, we don't have a great deal of time.'

'You said I wouldn't have to—'

'Yes, I know what I *said*. But I really think it would make a lovely photograph if your bra cup was just low enough to expose—'

'I'm not going to do it,' she protested, pulling the strap back up over her shoulder. 'I am *not* going to allow you to—'

'I've just taken half a dozen shots of you on the chaise longue in your underwear, Charlotte. As well as your mother, what do you think your schoolteachers will say when they see them?'

'My schoolteachers?' she echoed fearfully. 'This is blackmail, Mr Goodhugh. Why are you—'

'Blackmail?' he chuckled. 'It's nothing of the sort. As I said earlier, I've watched you grow over the years, develop into a fine young woman. All I'm asking is for a few photographs of your beautiful body for my private collection.'

'No, I *won't* allow it,' she said firmly, grabbing her blouse and leaping to her feet. 'It's not right of you to do this to me. I'll tell my mother the truth about you and—'

'All right, Charlotte, all right. Have it your own way.'

'I will. I'm not going to be blackmailed into—'

'I understand how you feel. Get dressed and go home.'

'And you'll come and see my mother?'

'Yes. I have to return something.'

SCHOOLGIRL LUST

'Return what?' the girl asked as she dressed.

'I always close the shop for lunch. I don't go up to the flat. Not in the summer, anyway. I close for an hour and wander into the woods to eat my sandwiches. I was there this lunchtime, Charlotte. And I saw you with that young Emily.'

'Yes, we were there,' she said, wondering what he was getting at. 'What's wrong with that?'

'I have to return your skirt, Charlotte. Don't worry, I'll tell your mother the truth. I found it in the woods along with several pairs of skimpy red panties.'

'I . . . I don't care what you do,' she said softly, slipping her shoes on and leaving the room.

Racing through the shop, Charlotte dashed out into the street. Tears streaming down her face as she ran along the side of the shop and back into the woods, she only stopped when she reached the wall at the back of her garden. Gasping, out of breath, she leaned against the wall, her young body sliding down the ivy until she was sitting on the ground. Her long hair veiling her hands as her covered her face, she lowered her head and sobbed. She didn't know what was becoming of her young life, or understand what was happening and why. But whatever happened, she'd have to face her mother sooner or later, she knew. If Goodhugh called round . . . That was a nightmare she didn't want to face. Her life was becoming a nightmare that she *couldn't* face.

Chapter Three

Charlotte had mumbled goodnight to her mother and gone to bed early. Goodhugh hadn't been round, she was sure as she lay in her bed with the early-morning sun filtering through the window. Her mother would have stormed up the stairs in an uncontrollable rage had she learned the shocking truth about her daughter. Perhaps Goodhugh was biding his time, Charlotte mused, wondering what the day would bring as she kicked the eiderdown off the bed.

She was feeling vengeful, anger welling in her heart as she thought about Goodhugh and his threats. She'd cried behind the garden wall for half an hour before plucking up the courage to go into the cottage and face her mother. And it was all Goodhugh's fault. It was Emily's fault for showing her where her clitoris was and teaching her about masturbation and buying the miniskirt. It was Goodhugh's fault for . . . Sighing, Charlotte knew that she had no one to blame but herself. It was her life, and she had to take responsibility for her own actions.

Climbing out of bed, she stood at the window, looking out at the back garden. The sun bright in a clear blue sky, it was going to be another hot day. Was it too hot for thick woollen knickers and a long skirt? Recalling her miniskirt beneath the bed, she thought about wearing it in front of her mother. She turned and gazed at her long skirt draped over the ottoman. It seemed to beckon her like an old friend. But she'd made new friends, and she wondered whether she should try to move on. Looking down at the firm mounds of her young breasts, the sensitive protrusions of her elongated nipples, she jumped as her mother called out. Breakfast would be ready, Sunday breakfast. Eggs and bacon, fried bread, sausages, mushrooms, plum tomatoes . . . Her mother tried her best, Charlotte knew as she slipped her dressing gown on. She tried, in her own way.

'Morning, mother.' Charlotte smiled as she wandered into the kitchen and sat at the table. 'That smells good.'

'And so it should,' the older woman responded. 'I've been up for an hour preparing this for you.'

'I *do* appreciate it,' Charlotte said, wishing she'd woken earlier. And wondering why it had taken so long to cook a fried breakfast.

'I'm pleased to hear it. We need to have a good talk, young lady.'

'Do we?'

'Indeed we do.' The woman turned and scowled at Charlotte. 'Mr Goodhugh called round last night after you'd gone to bed.'

Charlotte's stomach sank, adrenalin coursing through her veins as she held her gown close to her breast. 'Oh?' she finally murmured, half expecting to see lewd photographs of herself propped up against the marmalade pot.

'We had quite a chat about you,' her mother said mysteriously.

'And?' Charlotte breathed, fearing the worst. Waiting for a reply, she realized that her parent wasn't fuming mad. 'What did he have to say?' It couldn't have been about the photographs, she was sure.

'We were talking about your visit to his shop last night.' Almost fainting, Charlotte leaned on the table and held her hand to her head. 'He's worried about you, Charlotte.'

'Worried?' she echoed, her hands trembling, her stomach churning. 'What . . . what do you mean, *worried*?'

'He reckons that you need a male figure in your life. As he was saying, you're growing into a woman, and you need a father figure.'

'You're going to *marry* him?' she gasped.

'Don't be ridiculous, Charlotte,' her mother returned. 'What he means is . . . He only offered you the Saturday job because he felt that you need the company of a male. It's not that he's trying to replace your father. It's just that you need to spend some time with a man of his age and . . . and you need a certain amount of responsibility. Hence, the job.'

'Mother, I don't *want* the job.'

'Of course you do. Don't start all that nonsense again. He's a good man, Charlotte. An upright man who will, in some ways, replace your father. I don't mean *replace*. I mean, he'll be able to take you under his wing.'

'How?'

'Just by being there. He's a regular churchgoer. He's a wholesome, decent man, Charlotte. A man of high morals and—'

'Morals?' the girl gasped in disbelief.

'Yes, morals. Unlike that Emily girl. Martin . . . Mr Goodhugh would like you to go and see him this morning.'

'But I have my school project to do.'

'I want you to get to know Mr Goodhugh, become friends with him.'

'Friends?'

'There's your breakfast.' The woman smiled, placing a plate before Charlotte. 'He's offered to teach you how to play chess. I think it might be an idea to visit him a couple of evenings a week.'

'But, mother—'

'There are no "buts" about it, girl. Eat your breakfast and then get ready for church. Later this morning, you can go and talk to Mr Goodhugh.'

Sighing, Charlotte prodded her bacon with the fork. Goodhugh was a clever man, she ruminated. Getting in with her mother like that, he was building a foundation. A foundation designed to support what? she wondered. He'd gained her mother's trust and confidence over the years, and now ... Perhaps he'd planned this long ago, she reflected. Perhaps, when she was very young, he'd planned for the day when ... She had to tell her mother what sort of man Goodhugh was, she decided.

'Mother,' she began hesitantly. 'Mr Goodhugh takes photographs.'

'Oh, yes, he's a keen photographer,' the woman smiled enthusiastically. 'I've seen his pictures exhibited in the village hall.'

'Yes, but he also takes pictures of—'

'You're letting your food go cold. What does he take pictures of?'

'Nothing,' Charlotte sighed, picking at her breakfast.

After she'd washed up, Charlotte got ready to go to church. She knew that Goodhugh would be there, watching her, grinning at her. Unable to face him, she feigned a stomach-ache. Not only to get out of going to church – she hoped she'd also be able to get out of meeting the man later that morning by pretending to be ill. The less she saw of him, the better. Although annoyed, her mother ordered her to stay at home.

Pacing her bedroom floor for almost two hours, Char-

SCHOOLGIRL LUST

lotte had tried to come up with a plan but had failed miserably. It seemed that there was no way out of the terrible situation. Goodhugh was well in with her mother, and Charlotte had to go along with their plans for her. A father figure? She laughed softly, bleakly. Goodhugh would never become a father figure. A monster figure, more like.

Writing a note to her mother, Charlotte placed it on the kitchen table and left the cottage. Walking to the woods, the sun warming her, she wished she could turn the clock back. Sitting by the stream, she reflected on her young life. Everything had changed for the worse, she ruminated, watching a frog watching her from the far side of the narrow stream. It was all right for frogs, she decided. No worries, no troubles. She was going to have to take a grip on the situation, she knew as she lay on her back and looked up at the trees. The sun sparkling through the foliage, she wished she could be a tree. *Trees don't hurt. Trees don't feel pain. Do they?*

'You here again?' Emily asked as she approached.

'Oh, hi,' Charlotte smiled, looking up at the silhouette of the girl leaning over her.

'I guessed you'd be here. By the way, I saw your mother. She wants you to go and see Goodhugh. She told me to tell you to—'

'Emily, has Mr Goodhugh ever—'

'Ever what?' the other girl asked, sitting down beside her friend.

'I don't know.'

'Why do you have to go and see him?'

'He . . . he's going to teach me to play chess.'

'What for?' Emily laughed. 'Chess is boring. My parents are going out this afternoon. Why don't you come round and we'll . . . You know.'

'What?'

'You can show me where *my* clitoris is this time.' The girl grinned salaciously.

Wincing, Charlotte bit her lip as she sat up. This was going to become a regular occurrence, she knew as she gazed at her friend's miniskirt, her naked thighs. But her thoughts told her that she needed the comfort, the physical contact, the . . . *Love?* she asked herself, her stomach somersaulting as she gazed at Emily's red glossed lips. Wondering what it would be like to kiss the girl, she moved closer. Was she in love? In love with another girl? No, it wasn't possible. She *hoped* it wasn't possible. If her mother discovered that . . . Goodhugh was the problem, not Emily.

'Will you come round, then?' Emily asked.

'Yes, after lunch,' Charlotte replied, hoping that she wasn't making a big mistake. *Love? What is love?* 'Emily, have you ever been in love?' she asked, immediately wishing she hadn't.

'I don't know. I suppose I've thought I've been in love but . . . I don't know. Why do you ask?'

'May I kiss you?' Charlotte asked.

'Like this?' Emily smiled, taking her friend's head in her hands and locking her full lips to hers.

Charlotte's heart leapt as she closed her eyes and breathed in the heady scent of Emily's perfume. Their inquisitive tongues meeting, warm saliva blending, they breathed heavily though their noses as their lesbian desire rose. Falling backwards, they lay on the ground, entwined in a passionate kiss that sent Charlotte's head spinning. She *was* in love, she knew as her friend's hands wandered over the firm mounds of her rounded breasts. Unbuttoning Charlotte's blouse and lifting her bra clear of her young melons, Emily moved down and sucked her erect nipple into her hot mouth.

SCHOOLGIRL LUST

'God,' Charlotte breathed, her teenage juices of arousal spewing from the mouth of her young vagina and flooding her panties. Writhing in her frenzied passion as Emily sucked her other nipple into her wet mouth, her eyes rolling, Charlotte lay quivering in the grip of her new-found emotion. As Emily's hands ran over the gentle swell of her stomach, Charlotte threw her head back and gasped in expectation. The girl's fingers beneath the waistband of her skirt, creeping over the fleecy-haired flesh of her mons, Emily delved into Charlotte's sex crack and massaged the swell of her ripening clitoris. Charlotte knew that she was going to have another orgasm as her passion spot pulsated. Squirming on the grass, her legs parted wide, she sang out in her lesbian pleasure as her climax erupted within the pulsating nubble of her young clitoris.

Her cries of ecstasy resounding through the trees as her friend fervently massaged the solid tip of her sensitive clitoris, her juices of orgasm soaking her panties, Charlotte grimaced as Emily sank her teeth into the elongated budlette of her nipple. On and on her teenage pleasure coursed through her convulsing body, reaching every nerve ending, tightening every muscle. She'd found her heaven, she knew as her nostrils flared. The smooth flesh of her stomach jerkily rising and falling, her thighs twitching uncontrollably, she whimpered in the velveteen grip of lesbian love. She'd found her heaven. And her soulmate.

The tide of her girl-pleasure finally ebbing, Charlotte lay on the soft grass with her blouse open, her heaving breasts bared, her young body shaking violently. Digging her fingernails into the soft grass, her head lolling from side to side, she drifted down gently from her climax like a leaf fluttering to the ground. Finally settling back into her quivering body, she opened her eyes and looked up at the sun sparkling through the leaves high above her. Did trees fall in love?

'All right?' Emily smiled, slipping her girl-scented fingers out of Charlotte's knickers and lying on the grass.

'Oh, yes,' Charlotte gasped, her trembling hands pulling her bra down, settling the cups back over the firm globes of her youthful breasts. 'God, yes.'

Listening to the rustling leaves, the singing birds, as she recovered, Charlotte turned her head and gazed at the alluring rise of Emily's teenage breasts. Her T-shirt outlining her elongated nipples, her long blonde hair fanning out over the grass like a golden lily, the girl was sensual in the extreme. Focusing on her friend's short skirt, Charlotte felt her stomach somersault as she thought of slipping her hand between the welcoming warmth of Emily's young thighs. The lesbian act was inevitable, she knew as she propped herself up on her elbow. Whether it happened now or later, the act of lesbian masturbation was inevitable.

Running her fingers up the smooth skin of the other girl's inner thighs, Charlotte pressed her fingertips into the warm cushion of her tight panties. Tugging the garment down her long legs and over her ankles, she slipped her hand beneath her skirt again and lovingly stroked the fleshy pads of her outer sex lips. Emily gasped, her eyes closing as her juices of lesbian lust seeped between the folded wings of her inner lips and trickled down the crevice of her young buttocks. As Charlotte's finger ran up and down the wet divide between her pouting lips, Emily arched her back, opening her legs wide and offering the sexual centre of her girl-body to her friend in lust.

Leaning over the girl's trembling body and pulling her red skirt up over her stomach, Charlotte examined her moist sex valley, scrutinizing the pink petals of her inner lips. Parting the warm hillocks of her outer labia, she gazed in awe at the intricate girl-folds nestling within her wet ravine. In search of the girl's clitoris, she eased her fleshy lips up and apart, grinning as the erect protrusion of pleasure emerged from beneath its pinken bonnet. Pressing on the glistening flesh surrounding the small sex nodule, she eased out its full length.

'That's nice,' Emily breathed as Charlotte encircled the small budlette of passion with her fingertip. Running her finger down the girl's drenched valley of desire, she slipped it between the petals of her inner lips and drove deep into her tightening vaginal sheath. Moving closer, she focused on the intimate flesh within Emily's sex crevice, gazing longingly at the creamy liquid clinging to her finger as she repeatedly withdrew and thrust back into her friend's young body. Lubricious, warm . . . What did it taste like?

Charlotte knew nothing of oral sex, the lesbian girl-licking of a swollen clitoris, the intimacy of pussy tonguing. She could only emulate her friend's act of masturbation, massage her nub of desire as Emily had massaged hers. Wondering whether she should experiment while in the privacy of her bed, massage her own clitoris and finger her vaginal sheath, she felt her young womb contract in expectation. She was embarking on a new road, she knew as she fervently rubbed the quivering girl's throbbing clitoris. An unmapped road to an unknown destination.

'Yes,' Emily cried, her body convulsing fiercely as her orgasm erupted within her pulsating clitoris. Charlotte grinned triumphantly as she fingered the tightening sheath of her friend's hot vagina and massaged her orgasm from her solid clitoris. She'd done it, she reflected happily. She'd given Emily an orgasm, fingered her sex duct and massaged her clitoris until she'd reached the height of her girl-pleasure. Writhing and squirming on the grass, Emily shuddered and sang out in her lesbian-induced climax. Charlotte watched in awe as her stomach rose and fell jerkily, her juices of arousal squelching with the illicit girl-pistoning.

Sustaining her friend's clitoral pleasure with her vibrating fingertip, Charlotte lowered her head and kissed the hot flesh of Emily's stomach. Licking her navel, pushing her tongue into the small indentation, she gasped as Emily grabbed her head and pushed it further down. Her mouth against the other girl's warm mons, she became confused. This wasn't what Emily had done, she reflected as the girl pushed her head down further still until her mouth pressed against the pink flesh of her friend's sex valley. Emily writhed and whimpered as her pleasure peaked, her juices of lust pouring from the bloated mouth of her young vagina. Breathing in the heady scent, the taste of girl-sex on her lips, Charlotte sat up and slipped her finger out of Emily's drenched love duct. Emily lay gasping, her fingers between the rise of her vaginal lips, bringing out her orgasm, as Charlotte looked on in bewilderment.

Finally sitting up and hurriedly pulling her panties up her long legs, Emily glared at Charlotte. Climbing to her feet, her pretty face flushed, she announced that she was going home and stormed off. Frowning, Charlotte didn't know what she'd done wrong. The girl had had an orgasm, she'd seemed to enjoy the intimate attention, so why was she in a bad mood? Standing up, Charlotte adjusted her clothing and ambled along the path to the village hall. Still wondering what was wrong with Emily, she emerged from the woods and walked along the road. Then she saw her mother standing outside the cottage.

'Where have you been?' the woman asked irritably as Charlotte stood before her.

'I went for a walk,' Charlotte replied, somewhat puzzled. 'I left you a note.'

'Yes, but I didn't think you'd be this long. How's your stomach now?'

'My . . . Oh, much better.'

'Look at the state of you, girl. I don't know about walking, you look as if you've been *rolling* about in the woods. But you've no time to change. Mr Goodhugh is waiting for you.'

'But—'

'He walked me home from church, hoping to have a word with you, but you'd gone out. Lunch will be in an hour, so you've plenty of time to go and see him. And be pleasant to him, Charlotte. Brush your hair away from your face and smile.'

'Mother, I really don't want to—'

'Now you listen to me, my girl. Mr Goodhugh has been very kind to us over the years. He's now offering to befriend you. Albeit in a small way, he's going to help with your upbringing. You might not feel that you need his friendship and help, but *I* do. God knows it's not been easy for me. Bringing you up alone . . . Just go and see him, Charlotte. You do want to learn how to play chess, don't you?'

'Well . . .'

'Had your father been alive . . . Lunch will be in an hour. Now, off you go.'

Walking towards the shop, Charlotte sighed. Her heart sinking, she didn't know what to do about Goodhugh. What with the incriminating photographs he had, and her mother's belief that he was a decent man of high moral standing, there wasn't a great deal she *could* do. She'd feign a stomach upset again, she decided, pausing outside the shop door. If she pretended to be ill, he'd send her home. At least she'd be safe for a while. The door opening, she jumped as the shopkeeper appeared.

'Come in, Charlotte,' he grinned. 'I'm all ready for you.'

'Listen—' she said firmly as she stepped into the shop.

'We'll go straight through to the back.' He smiled, locking the door.

'Mr Goodhugh, we have to talk about this,' Charlotte persisted, following him into the stockroom. 'You've convinced my mother—'

'She's a lovely woman,' he broke in, closing the door.

'The point is that you can't order me to come here whenever you want and—'

'But I *can*, Charlotte. Your mother wants me to help with your upbringing.'

'I'm seventeen. I don't need—'

'Charlotte, I don't want to go against your mother's wishes. I don't know why you're making all this fuss.'

'Because I don't want you taking rude photographs of me.'

'Rude? Oh, Charlotte. It's art, not . . . We're wasting time again. Slip your clothes off and we'll resume where we left off yesterday.'

'No. I'm sorry, but you're not going to get me here under false pretences and then order me to take my clothes off. Why don't you teach me to play chess? That's what you told my mother you were going to do.'

'Take your clothes off, Charlotte.'

'No, I won't. I'm leaving, Mr Goodhugh. I'm going home now.'

'All right, go home.'

'And?'

'And what?'

'Where are your threats? Why aren't you threatening to go and see my mother and—'

SCHOOLGIRL LUST

'I don't want to threaten you, Charlotte. I was hoping that we could be friends. I was hoping that you'd enjoy coming to see me.'

'I can go, then?'

'Yes, of course.'

'What will you say to my mother?'

'Well,' he sighed, shaking his head. 'I'll have to tell her about your visit to the woods with that Emily girl.'

'The woods?' Charlotte echoed fearfully, her stomach churning.

'I walked your mother home from church and then took a stroll through the woods. I'm interested in wildlife and had my camera at the ready.' He paused, his beady eyes grinning at her. 'The wildlife I photographed was . . . It was interesting, to say the least. I'll put a new roll of film in the camera while you slip out of your clothes.'

Her legs sagging beneath her, Charlotte held a trembling hand to her chest. Her dark eyes wide, her mind swirling with images of Emily masturbating her, pushing her finger into her wet vagina, she leaned against the wall to steady herself. Praying that Goodhugh was bluffing, she thought he might have seen her doing nothing more than talking to Emily. Yes, that was it. He'd seen her talking, and no more. He was bluffing.

'We were talking,' she said, forcing a giggle. 'Emily and I were just talking.'

'Of course you were,' he smiled, closing the back of the camera.

'There's nothing wrong with talking.'

'You're right there. There's nothing wrong with enjoying a chat with a friend.'

'No. So that's all right, then.'

'Yes, it is. Your mother will be pleased to see the

photographs of you and Emily enjoying a chat. As you said, there's nothing wrong with talking. These modern-day telephoto lenses are a marvel. I can take close-up shots from a good distance. Crystal-clear shots showing the smallest detail. Well, I'm ready. Take your clothes off and lie on the chaise longue and we'll get started.'

Her head aching, Charlotte tentatively unbuttoned her blouse. She couldn't believe that this was happening as the man gazed longingly at her straining bra, the alluring cleavage of her young breasts. He was evil, she knew as he licked his lips, his beady eyes widening. He'd tricked a trusting middle-aged woman in order to take lewd photographs of her young daughter. *A man of morals?* Charlotte reflected fearfully. *A wholesome, decent man?* He was the Devil, she knew. But it didn't matter what he was. Charlotte had to put an end to the nightmare before . . . before what, she dared not think.

'You have no morals,' she breathed, her blouse slipping off her shoulders and falling in a crumpled heap on the floor. 'You go to church every Sunday and then—'

'Wait a minute, Charlotte,' he snapped back angrily. '*You* were the one strutting around in a miniskirt like a common strumpet. *You* were the one in the woods with Emily. Don't talk to *me* about morals. Your mother has done her best to make a decent girl of you, and that's how you repay her. To behave the way you did after all your mother has done for you, after all she's tried to teach you . . . I think my taking a few photographs, in comparison with your own wanton behaviour, is perfectly innocent.'

'*Innocent*?' she echoed mockingly.

'In comparison with your lewd behaviour, yes. I feel so sorry for your poor mother.'

'Then why do this to her daughter?'

'Do *what*, Charlotte? What have I done, exactly?'

'You've blackmailed me and taken rude photographs of me.'

'There's been no blackmail, and the photographs aren't rude. I'm trying to help your mother to bring you up properly.'

'How can you say that?'

'You've misbehaved, Charlotte. If I were your father, I'd punish you severely. I'm sure your mother would want me to reprimand you for your despicable behaviour. However, I'm not going to punish you because I think you've realized the wickedness of your ways and won't do it again. Let's not talk about punishment, Charlotte. The time is running on and we haven't even started yet. Now, take your clothes off and lie on the chaise longue.'

Slipping her shoes off, she tugged her skirt down her naked legs and stepped out of the garment. Lying on the chaise longue, she bit her lip as she looked down and noticed the wet patch moistening the tight crotch of her red panties. Her face flushing, she wished her mother knew exactly what sort of man Goodhugh was. If only there was a way of letting her know of his ulterior motives. But she could see no way out of the mess, no way to put an end to the nightmare. And the nightmare was only just beginning.

'Your bra.' Goodhugh smiled. 'You remember yesterday just before you walked out?'

'No, I'm not doing that,' Charlotte replied firmly.

'Just slip the strap off your shoulder and lower the cup a little.'

'I am *not* going to—'

'Oh, forgive me,' he said, his lips furling into an evil smirk. 'I omitted to settle up with you yesterday.'

'Settle up with me?' she murmured, her dark eyes frowning.

'Your fee for yesterday's session.' Thrusting his hand into his pocket, he pulled out a five-pound note. 'There we are. I'll leave it on top of your clothes so you won't forget it. Now, where were we?'

Eyeing the money, Charlotte knew that it would come in useful. Her mother had struggled on next to nothing for years and, even though five pounds wasn't a great deal, it would certainly help her. Wondering why Goodhugh was paying her and blackmailing her at the same time, she looked down at the straining cup of her full bra as he again asked her to slip the strap off her shoulder. Would it be so bad? she wondered, looking again at the money. After all, it was only her nipple. And the photographs were for his private collection so no one would see them.

Tugging the strap down, her bra cup falling away from the firm roundness of her teenage breast, exposing the brown protrusion of her elongated milk teat, she closed her eyes. She could hear the camera shutter, Goodhugh breathing heavily as he took shot after shot of her young body. If he gave her five pounds for every session . . . But he wouldn't want to take hundreds of pictures of her, would he?

'Very good,' he smiled, changing the roll of film. 'Now I'd like you to sit with one leg on the chaise longue like you did yesterday,' he said. Charlotte obeyed, all too aware of her exposed nipple as her bra cup slid further down the unblemished flesh of her mammary sphere. 'That's good, Charlotte,' he praised her. 'You're learning fast. OK, a nice smile.'

As he took more photographs, she wondered again how she'd ended up in this awful situation. She recalled the wet patch on her sheet, talking to Emily about vaginal cream, the conversation moving on to her clitoris and then . . . It had started out as perfectly innocent, she reflected. The miniskirt had been a present from Emily, not something that should have led to blackmail. And now Goodhugh was paying her for posing for him. Everything had run away with her, she knew. One thing had led to another and now she'd lost all control.

'Pull your panties to one side,' Goodhugh said, focusing the camera on the tight strip of bulging material running between her splayed thighs.

'Mr Goodhugh,' Charlotte gasped in horror, placing her foot on the floor and sitting upright. 'I'm not going to . . . I have to go home now.'

'We've another twenty minutes,' he breathed, checking his watch.

'I don't mind how long we've got, I'm going home.'

'I'm becoming a little tired of your attitude,' he said sternly. 'Unless you do as you're told, I'll give the photographs to Father James.'

'You . . . you wouldn't dare,' she gasped.

'I'll say that I found them in an envelope in the street and I'll suggest that he talks to your mother about it. As I said, I'm becoming tired of your attitude. Take your panties and bra off and lie down.'

'You said pull them to one side,' she murmured shakily.

'I'm now ordering you to take your panties off. And your bra. I don't want to hear another word from you, Charlotte. You'll do exactly as I say – or you'll find yourself in serious trouble.'

Slipping her panties down her long legs, her hands trembling, Charlotte pressed her thighs tightly together. The triangular patch of her pubic curls now blatantly displayed below the gentle rise of her stomach, she unhooked her bra and dropped it to the floor. Her face turning scarlet as Goodhugh gazed at the brown budlettes of her erect nipples, she lay back – but with her thighs still pressed firmly together. As she'd expected, he ordered her to place her right leg on the chaise longue. She couldn't do it, she knew as she hung her head. Embarrassment and shame swamping her, she again wondered how she'd got herself into such a dreadful predicament. The crack of her vagina would gape, Goodhugh would see her feminine intimacy and . . .

'You're trying my patience, Charlotte,' he sighed. 'After all, I *am* paying you for this.'

'Please, I—' she whimpered, folding her arms to conceal her teenage breasts.

'All right, I'll develop the photographs and then give Father James a ring and ask him to come and see me. You get dressed and go home to your mother.'

'You wouldn't—'

'As an upright and decent man, I'd have no choice other than to expose a wanton harlot such as you. This is a respectable village, Charlotte. If people knew that their village was inhabited by a . . . a teenage slut . . .'

'I am *not* a slut,' she sobbed.

'Aren't you? I would have thought that anyone who saw the photographs of you in the woods with Emily would immediately come to the conclusion that you're nothing *but* a slut. The things you did with that girl were . . . They were despicable and obscene, to say the least.'

'All right, all right,' she cried. 'I'll do it and then I'm going home and never coming back.'

'That's more like it. Let's get this over with. The sooner we're finished, the sooner you can go home.'

SCHOOLGIRL LUST

Lying back again, Charlotte lifted her foot and rested her leg on the chaise longue. The crack of her vagina opening wide, her inner petals unfurling, she closed her eyes as the camera shutter clicked. This was worse than a nightmare, she reflected, her naked body trembling as her humiliation rose. This was a horror story. Swearing never to return, the stark reality of the situation filtered through her naivety and shook her very soul. Each time she'd visited Goodhugh, she'd given him more ammunition. Her every visit *had* armed and *would* arm him with more evidence of her wicked ways, her sluttish behaviour.

'Peel your pussy lips wide apart,' Goodhugh breathed, taking the camera from the tripod and kneeling by her foot.

'No . . . Please . . .' she sobbed.

'Just a few more shots and you can go home.'

Complying, Charlotte gripped her swollen outer sex lips between her fingers and thumbs and pulled them wide apart. Squeezing her eyes shut as the man moved forward and focused on the pinken flesh surrounding her exposed sex hole, she thought she was going to die of embarrassment. The camera shutter clicking, she heard him moving about, taking shots of her teenage body from every possible angle. Finally releasing the fleshy pads of her vaginal cushions, she leapt off the couch and grabbed her clothes.

'Very good,' the man grinned as she dressed hurriedly. 'There's a little something for today's session.' Passing her a ten-pound note, he removed the film from the camera and began packing his equipment away. Clutching the money, Charlotte finished dressing, wishing she could run away and hide from the world. Her trembling fingers brushing her long black hair away from her flushed face, she left the stockroom and fled the shop. Tears streaming down her cheeks as she ran to the safety of home, her world in pieces, she wondered what to do.

She'd been so stupid, she knew as she stood outside the cottage. Goodhugh now had enough evidence of her lewd behaviour to demand that she return to the stockroom again and again. It was too late to confess to her mother, she reflected as she wiped her eyes and entered the cottage. The aroma of Sunday lunch filling her nostrils, she heard her mother in the kitchen and took a deep breath, doing her best to compose herself.

'Hallo,' she said, forcing a smile.

'Ah, Charlotte,' the woman replied, placing roast potatoes on two dinner plates. 'How did you get on with Mr Goodhugh?'

'All right,' she murmured, clutching her fifteen pounds.

'Only all right? Tell me all about it. I hope you were friendly and polite.'

'Yes, mother. I was very friendly.'

'So, what happened? Did you play chess?'

'No, yes . . . He's teaching me.'

'That's good. He's such a pleasant man. You should think yourself lucky that he's taken such an interest in you, Charlotte. I've a feeling that this is going to work out very well. If nothing else, at least you'll be spending time with someone decent rather than with the likes of Emily. Now, have your lunch and then you can spend the afternoon working on your English project. How are you getting on with it?'

'All right, I suppose,' she replied, slipping the money beneath her thigh as she sat at the table.

'You only suppose? What's the matter, Charlotte? You seem to have changed over the last couple of days. You spend too much time with Emily, that's the problem. She's

SCHOOLGIRL LUST

not good company. Still, you have Mr Goodhugh now. Which reminds me. When we were walking back from the church, he kindly offered to spend Monday evenings here.'

'Monday evenings?' Charlotte gasped. 'But you go to see Mrs Langly on Monday evenings.'

'Exactly. That's the whole point, Charlotte. You won't have to sit here on your own.'

'But, mother . . . Emily comes round, so I'm not on my own.'

'It'll put a stop to her coming here. I can never relax when I'm with Mrs Langly because I'm wondering what dreadful ideas that girl is putting into your head. Knowing that you're in the safe hands of Mr Goodhugh, I'll be able to relax and enjoy a chat and a cup of tea with Mrs Langly.'

Chapter Four

Charlotte had spent the afternoon in her bedroom. Not working on her English project, as her mother had suggested, but lying on her bed, distraught with worry. Her young mind lurching between the photographs Goodhugh had taken and his Monday night visits, she'd driven herself into a state of frenzied anguish. To add to her problems, she couldn't stop wondering what she'd done to upset Emily. She was supposed to have visited the girl that afternoon, but what with her stomping off and the evil Mr Goodhugh's threats, she'd only felt able to lie on her bed, drowning in her misery.

Finally coming to a decision, she made her way downstairs. Her mother was sitting in the lounge listening to the radio. Charlotte hovered by the woman's armchair, her hands trembling, her stomach knotted with anxiety. If only Emily hadn't bought the miniskirt, if only she'd not let Goodhugh see her wearing it, if only she'd told her mother the truth . . . If only.

'I'm going out, mother,' Charlotte announced.

'Out? Where to?' the woman asked. 'You have school tomorrow.'

'Only for a walk. I'll be no more than half an hour. It's just that I've been working on my project all afternoon and I need some air.' Charlotte didn't like lying to her mother, but she felt she had no choice. 'I've got on really well with my project.'

'All right. But no longer than half an hour.'

Charlotte kissed the woman's head. 'I'll see you later,' she said softly, leaving the room.

Walking down the road, Charlotte knew that this was her only chance, albeit a slim one. There was no one she could talk to, no one she could pour her heart out to – not even Emily. Following the cobbled path through the gravestones, she pushed the heavy church door open and wandered into the cold stone building. She felt as if the eyes of God were upon her as she tentatively walked down the aisle. He'd be aware of her sins, she knew only too well as she noticed a light emanating from a side room. Perhaps Satan had goaded her to commit vile sexual acts. Would she be forgiven?

'Oh, Charlotte.' Father James smiled as she tapped on the office door. 'Come in, my child.'

'Father, I need to speak to you,' she whispered. 'I've . . . I've done something terrible. Two things terrible. I mean—'

'All right, calm down,' he said softly. Rising from his desk, he placed his hand on her shoulder. 'Go into the confessional and I'll be with you in a minute.'

'Before I do . . . Is it right that . . . Anything I tell you will be secret, won't it?'

'Between you and me, Charlotte. And God. No one else will hear a word of your confession.'

'Oh, right. Thank you.'

Leaving the priest's office, Charlotte made her way across the church to the confession box. Pulling the heavy velvet curtain across, she knelt on the soft cushion and waited. This was the right thing to do, she was sure. There was no one else she could speak to. Not Emily, her teacher, the village doctor . . . and certainly not her mother. Her breathing fast and shallow, she clenched her fists, wondering why

SCHOOLGIRL LUST

it was taking Father James so long. It had taken a mountain of courage to go to the church. The least he could do was . . . Finally hearing movements behind the grille, she took a deep breath.

'All right, Charlotte,' the priest said softly. 'You may begin.'

'Father, I . . . A man has taken photographs of me.'

'What sort of photographs?'

'Of me with . . . with no clothes on.'

'I see.'

'No, no, you don't see. He was blackmailing me. He still *is* blackmailing me.'

'Blackmailing you?' the priest gasped. 'You'd better start from the beginning, my child.'

'A friend bought me a short skirt and I tried it on. This man saw me wearing it and threatened to tell my mother. Knowing my mother, you'll understand why I didn't want her to know about the skirt.'

'Yes, I do understand.'

'Well, he said that he wouldn't tell her if I allowed him to take some photographs of me in the skirt. I sort of agreed and . . .'

'And it went from bad to worse?'

'Yes. Once he had photographs of me in the skirt, he had real evidence to show my mother. The photographs he took of me today were . . . were vulgar. And now he's—'

'All right, my child. Just relax. You've been to see this man more than once?'

'Yes. He took photographs of me yesterday and a lot more this morning.'

'How long have you known him?'

'All my life, Father.'

'So, I take it that he lives in the village?'

'Yes, he does.'

'In which case, I'll know him. How old is he? Is he the same age as you?'

'No, no. He's about my mother's age.'

'I see. So, let me get this right. The blackmail began with this short skirt of yours.'

'Yes, Father. It was very short and—'

'It would have been better to tell your mother about the skirt in the first place.'

'I couldn't. You know what she's like, Father.'

'It always pays to tell the truth, my child. Let that be a lesson to you.'

'Yes, Father.'

'So, this man now has these photographs with which to blackmail you.'

'Yes.'

'Are they really that bad, Charlotte? I mean, they'd probably be bad in the eyes of your mother, but—'

'They're extremely indecent, Father.'

'When you say indecent . . . Give me a rough idea of what they're like.'

'I have no clothes on and my legs are wide apart and I'm . . . I'm holding myself open.'

'I see.' The priest paused. 'You must tell me who this man is, Charlotte,' he finally said sternly.

'No, no, I can't do that.'

'Don't worry, I don't intend to confront him. As I said, not one word of your confession will be passed on to a soul. Tell me who he is and I'll talk to him.'

'But—'

'I have ways of talking to people, gleaning information without their realizing it. Place your trust in me, my child. And in Almighty God.'

SCHOOLGIRL LUST

'His name is . . . It's Mr Goodhugh.'

'Mr Goodhugh?' the priest echoed surprisedly. 'All right, Charlotte. Leave this with me. You did the right thing by coming here.'

'Yes, Father. Thank you, Father.'

'You are forgiven your sins, my child. Go now and make good your contrition.'

'Yes, Father. I will.'

'And, Charlotte.'

'Yes, Father?'

'Will you be able to come back in, say, an hour?'

'Well, my mother . . .'

'Tell your mother that you're coming to see me. Tell her the truth, Charlotte. You're coming to see me. I'm sure that we can sort this out, so don't worry.'

'No, Father, I won't.'

Leaving the confession box, Charlotte walked out of the church and wandered home. She felt positive. A terrible weight had been lifted from her sagging shoulders. If Father James spoke to Mr Goodhugh and . . . and what, she didn't know. All she could do was pray that the problem would go away so that she could lead a normal, carefree life again. But first, she had to get permission to go out again.

She found her mother in the kitchen filling the kettle.

'Mother . . .' she began hesitantly. 'I was wondering . . .'

'And *I've* been wondering, Charlotte,' the woman scowled as she turned and faced the girl.

'Oh? Wondering what?'

'Wondering why there was fifteen pounds beneath the table.'

'Oh, I . . .'

'Where did you get it from?'

'I . . . I found it.'

'Found it? Where?'

'In the street. I was going to give it to you. I forgot.'

'It seems odd that you should forget that you found fifteen pounds, Charlotte.'

'It was lunchtime. I'd tucked it in the waistband of my skirt and we were talking about Mr Goodhugh and . . . Mother, I bumped into Father James while I was out. He wants me to go and see him. Is that all right?'

'Of course you can see him. You don't have to ask me.'

'This evening – he wants me to go to the church this evening.'

'This evening? You have school tomorrow and . . . What's it about?'

'Just . . . just helping out in the church at the weekends. Flowers. That was it. Flower arranging.'

'All right. But don't be too long.'

'I'll walk over to the church now. I won't be long.'

'Charlotte, you wouldn't lie to me, would you?'

'No, I'm going to see Father—'

'I'm talking about the money.'

'Oh, no, I wouldn't lie. I found it.'

'All right, off you go.'

The situation with her mother was worsening, Charlotte knew as she walked down the road. More lies, she thought. The skirt, Mr Goodhugh, the money . . . Father James would help her, she was sure. How he'd help, she didn't know, but she'd placed her trust in him – and in God. Sitting on the wall outside the church, she worried about school the following morning while she waited for the priest. She'd done nothing on her project. She'd tell Miss Chambers – what? More lies, she supposed.

'Ah, Charlotte,' Father James called as he approached.

SCHOOLGIRL LUST

'Come into the church.' Following him, Charlotte wondered whether or not he'd spoken to Goodhugh. What could he have said? she wondered. Without mentioning her by name, how could he have discussed the problem? Sitting on an old swivel chair in the corner of the priest's office, she watched the man settle behind his desk and adjust his cassock. His elbows on the desk, his chin resting on his clasped hands, he frowned at her. There was suspicion lurking in the dark pools of his eyes, although she didn't know why. She was the aggrieved party, not the guilty one. But, somehow, guilt swamped her again.

'I saw Mr Goodhugh,' the priest began. His tone was accusing, menacing. 'I mentioned that I'd been talking to you. Not about this, you understand.' He pursed his lips and stared hard at the girl. 'He guessed that you'd been to see me about the photographs.'

'What did he say?' Charlotte asked, her wide eyes locked to his.

'His account differs from yours, Charlotte.'

'He's lying,' she gasped. 'He *did* take photographs of me.'

'He doesn't deny that.'

'Then, how—'

'He freely admitted taking nude photographs of you. He said that you'd removed your clothes and posed for him.'

'That's right.'

'Do you think that was wise, Charlotte?'

'No, no . . . He said that he'd tell my mother about the short skirt and—'

'Now, this is where his account differs from yours. He said that he'd paid you to pose for him.'

'Yes, he gave me money but—'

'Ah, now we're getting somewhere.' Father James smiled.

'Stop me if I get anything wrong. As I understand it, you went to Mr Goodhugh's shop for a pre-arranged meeting with him.'

'Yes, about a Saturday job.'

'Wearing your miniskirt, you entered the shop and went into the stockroom with Mr Goodhugh. You posed for photographs and he paid you.'

'No, he blackmailed me.'

'Did he pay you for posing in your short skirt or not?'

'Yes, the next time I saw him he gave me five pounds.'

'That's when you went back and allowed him to take several more photographs?'

'Yes, no . . .'

'Which is it, Charlotte? Yes or no?'

'Yes.'

'On your second visit, you removed all your clothes and allowed him to take lewd photographs of your naked body in exchange for money. Before you left—'

'Yes, but—'

'Allow me to finish, Charlotte. Before you left, he paid you for posing in lewd positions.'

'Yes.'

The man leaned back in his chair and rubbed his chin pensively. 'Blackmailers don't usually pay their victims, Charlotte,' he said accusingly.

'But—'

'Please, allow me to continue. I'm not taking Mr Goodhugh's side. I'm simply trying to establish the facts. The facts are, and correct me if I'm wrong, as follows. You wore an extremely short skirt when you went to visit Mr Goodhugh. You went into the stockroom with him where he took photographs of you and, in return, he paid you. On another occasion you went back to the shop and removed all your clothes and he took another series of photographs. Again, he paid you for posing in lewd positions.'

'You make it sound awful, Father,' Charlotte sighed.

'It *is* awful, Charlotte. I know next to nothing about the law but, as far as I can see, neither you nor Mr Goodhugh have broken it. You are above the age of consent and I can't see that any criminal act was committed. Did you remove your clothes of your own accord?'

'Yes.'

'He didn't touch you in any way?'

'No, he didn't.'

'As I understand it, this was a business arrangement between you and Mr Goodhugh. You posed for him, allowing him to take wholly indecent photographs of your naked body, and in return he paid you. In the eyes of the law, neither you nor Mr Goodhugh have committed an offence. Of course, in the eyes of God . . . That's another matter, Charlotte.'

'He only gave me the money afterwards. He blackmailed me, that's why I did it. It wasn't for the money. I didn't know he was going to pay me.'

'What have you done with the money?'

'My mother has it.'

'You gave it to your mother?'

'I . . . I told her that I'd found it in the street.'

'Do you normally lie to your mother?'

'No, never.'

'Never? You lied about the skirt and the money, Charlotte. I doubt that this would ever get to a court of law, but imagine for a moment that I'm a judge. You are telling me that you were blackmailed. All eyes are upon you in the court room. I'm watching you, as are the jury. You are accusing a man of blackmailing you and yet you say that your blackmailer paid you. I don't think any judge or jury in the land would believe that, Charlotte.'

'He paid me *after* he'd blackmailed me, Father. *After* he'd taken the pictures.'

'An attractive seventeen-year-old girl dressed in an extremely short skirt goes to see Mr Goodhugh and allows him to take indecent photographs of her. She takes money in exchange for posing. It doesn't matter when she takes the money. The point is that she takes it. At some other time, she returns and removes all her clothes and allows Mr Goodhugh to take photographs of her naked body in wholly indecent poses. Blackmail, Charlotte? Firstly, as I mentioned before, why would a blackmailer pay his victim? Secondly, a decent girl with proper morals wouldn't have gone into the stockroom wearing a skirt so short that—'

'So, you can't help me,' Charlotte murmured solemnly, realizing that she was getting nowhere.

'There's another aspect to this that you've not told me about, Charlotte.'

'I've told you everything, Father.'

'Have you? Firstly, you came here accusing Mr Goodhugh of blackmailing you, conveniently omitting to mention that he'd paid you for your services.'

'I forgot.'

'You forgot that he'd paid you? All right, what were you doing in the woods with Emily earlier today?'

'We . . . we were talking.'

'Talking? Not only do you parade yourself in the street wearing a short skirt, you take money in exchange for posing naked in a wholly disgusting manner, and you prove yourself to have no morals whatsoever by engaging in an indecent sexual act with another girl in a public place. Now that *is* against the law.'

'No, I—'

'What you did with Emily isn't against the law, but doing it in public—'

'We were in the woods, not in public. Besides, we were only talking.'

'Talking? Is that what you call it? A public place is where the public are free to roam. Children might have been playing nearby and witnessed your vulgar act. Anyone could have stumbled across your . . . your depraved act.'

'We were only talking about . . . What are you going to do, Father?'

'It's not what *I*'m going to do, Charlotte. What are *you* going to do?'

'I . . . I don't know.'

'It could be said that Mr Goodhugh took advantage of you, your youth and your naivety. All I can do is advise him as to what is right and wrong in the eyes of God. I can't *order* him to stop taking photographs. I can't order *you* to stop prostituting yourself.'

'Father!'

'That's what it is, Charlotte, You have prostituted your young body. You've taken money in return for—'

'Please, I don't want to hear any more. What shall I do, Father?'

'Begin by severing all contact with Emily, and don't pose for any more photographs.'

'But Mr Goodhugh will threaten me.'

'If he tries to blackmail you, which I doubt very much, then you'll have to call the police.'

'The police?'

'The problem there is that you have no proof. You can't accuse someone of blackmailing you without proof. Mr

Goodhugh would say that he'd paid you and . . . How much did he pay you?'

'Fifteen pounds altogether.'

'And how much did you give your mother?'

'Fifteen pounds.'

'Did you give the money to your mother on the same day Mr Goodhugh had given it to you?'

'Yes, Father. It was today.'

'Being an honest woman, your mother would say that you gave her fifteen pounds on Sunday. The very same day that Mr Goodhugh paid you fifteen pounds for . . . And there's something else that goes completely against you.'

'Isn't there enough already?'

'More than enough. I saw one or two of the photographs, Charlotte. Not only were you freely posing before the camera, but you were smiling. To me, it didn't look as if you were being forced, coerced or blackmailed in any way whatsoever. I really don't know what you're going to do, Charlotte. Take a walk around the church while I think about this.'

Rising to her feet, Charlotte left the office and wandered into the church. The situation had gone from bad to worse, she reflected as she walked up to the altar. The way Father James had put it . . . The whole business sounded terrible. *Prostitute?* Holding her head, she pondered on the dreadful word. There was no way out of her predicament, she knew. She didn't dare go to the police. She'd made matters worse by confiding in Father James. She'd now put him in a terrible dilemma and . . .

A tear rolling down her cheek, she thought back to Saturday morning when she'd woken to the sun streaming in through her window. She'd had no worries, no problems. Wondering how her life could have been turned upside

SCHOOLGIRL LUST

down and inside out between Saturday morning and Sunday evening, she hung her head and sighed. In one weekend, her life had been destroyed. She'd lost her innocence, lain on her bed and allowed Emily to masturbate her to orgasm. She'd masturbated Emily in the woods, strutted along the street in a miniskirt, posed naked before a camera and taken money in exchange for the disgusting photographs. She'd lied to her mother . . . Turning as she heard Father James approaching, she offered him a slight smile. His face frowning, he didn't return her smile as he leaned against the altar.

'It's getting late, Charlotte,' he murmured.

'My mother knows where I am,' she said. 'I don't have to be home yet.'

'All the same, I think you'd better go.'

'But . . . Can't you help me?'

'I don't believe I can. I'm going to give it some thought, but I really don't see what I can do.'

'Please, Father,' she gasped, holding her hand to her mouth. 'You don't know what I'm going through.'

'Putting the problem of you and Mr Goodhugh aside for a moment, there's this business of you in the woods with Emily. Are you going to tell me that Emily used blackmail to force you to commit disgusting sexual acts with her?'

'No, of course not. But we weren't . . .'

'An analogy, Charlotte. I'm the headmaster of a school and I can see that one of my pupils is having problems. What should I do?'

'Talk to the pupil's teacher about it?'

'Exactly. I'm a man of God and I can see that one of my children is going off the rails with another girl. What should I do?'

'I . . . I don't know.'

'Talk to the girl's mother about it.'

'But—'

'It would be a pretty poor headmaster who stood back and did nothing. And it would be a pretty poor man of God who stood back and did nothing.'

'That's it, then. You're going to talk to my mother.'

'The arrangement you have with Mr Goodhugh, the money he pays you, no doubt helps your mother.'

'No, it's not like that.'

'I know she's always struggled financially but . . . That aside, Mr Goodhugh found a skirt belonging to you in the woods, and four pairs of . . . He also found some underwear. You've been in the woods in a state of undress with Emily on more than one occasion, haven't you?'

'I was trying the skirt on, that was all.'

'I now know of two occasions and I dread to think how many more there have been. I feel that it's my duty to inform your mother of this, Charlotte. She has done her best to bring you up to be a wholesome and decent young woman. And she's failed miserably.'

'No, it's not her fault.'

'She brought you up, Charlotte. She has gone very wrong somewhere along the line and should be told of her failing. Look, I don't have a great deal of time. Go home now and I'll be in touch.'

'With my mother?'

'No, not until I've given this some serious thought and spoken to you again.'

'What about Mr Goodhugh?'

'It seems to me that you have this arrangement with him and, for some reason, you want to get out of it.'

'Of course I do. I never wanted to get into it.'

'I commend you for wanting out, for seeing sense. But to try to get him into trouble—'

SCHOOLGIRL LUST

'I don't want to get him into trouble.'

'Don't you?'

'No. I mean, yes. Yes, I *do* want to get him into trouble. He's blackmailing me.'

'Blackmail is a very ugly word, Charlotte. I wouldn't use it again if I were you.'

'But . . .'

'Don't get me wrong, I'm not condoning what he's done. What he's done is wicked and immoral, but not illegal. He's very worried, Charlotte.'

'*He*'s worried?'

'Your arrangement has worked so far. Immoral though it is, you've both kept it secret and it's worked. Now you've decided to say that he forced you to act in an indecent manner. You're accusing him of blackmail. It's wicked and immoral to take photographs of young girls in lewd poses. It's also wicked and immoral to accuse a man of blackmailing you when he's been paying you to undress and behave in such a disgusting manner. Go home now, Charlotte.'

'I'm not wicked and immoral,' she sobbed.

'This sort of thing is happening more and more these days. A young girl preys on a man's weakness, brings him down – and then cries rape.'

'No, I didn't say—'

'Go home, Charlotte. And think very carefully about Mr Goodhugh. It's one thing wanting to break the agreement you have with him, but it's another to accuse him of blackmail.'

'He *is*—'

'Just think very carefully, Charlotte. If word got round the village that you're accusing him of blackmail and it came to light that you'd been taking money in exchange for . . . well, just think very carefully. I'll be in touch with you.'

Leaving the church, Charlotte felt her stomach sink. She couldn't believe that Father James was blaming her for the way Goodhugh had behaved. Holding her aching head, she thought about school the following morning. and Mr Goodhugh's visit to the cottage tomorrow evening. Her life a complete mess, she'd turned to the church. But she'd made matters worse by confiding in Father James. He now thought her to be not only a harlot, but a liar and a troublemaker. *Prostitute*. She pondered again on the word as she walked home. The way he'd put it had been . . . He'd made the whole thing sound awful. He blamed her for the business with Goodhugh, and for the incidents in the woods with Emily. As she reached the cottage, she took and deep breath and opened the door. She supposed the episode with Emily had been her fault. But to blame her for Goodhugh's filthy photographs . . .

'Is that you, Charlotte?' her mother called.

'Yes, mother,' Emily replied, forcing a smile as she found the woman sitting in the lounge.

'There's an envelope on the side for you. Hand-delivered, but I didn't see who it was.'

Taking the large brown envelope, Charlotte read her name scrawled on the front. 'Oh, it's . . . it's from Emily,' she lied. 'It's to do with my project.'

'Aren't you going to open it?'

'Yes, upstairs. I'll get ready for bed and be down in a minute.'

Climbing the stairs, Charlotte instinctively knew who the envelope was from. Closing her bedroom door, she tore it open and gazed in horror at several photographs of her slender fingers holding the fleshy lips of her vagina wide open. She was smiling in a couple of the shots. But she'd only done as Goodhugh had asked, she reflected. He'd told her to smile and pose like that. And he now had all the

SCHOOLGIRL LUST

evidence he needed to blackmail her for life. Hearing the doorbell, she stuffed the photographs beneath the bed.

'Charlotte,' her mother called.

'Coming, mother,' she replied, wondering whether Emily had called to see her. Bounding down the stairs, she wandered into the lounge and found herself staring at Goodhugh. 'Oh,' she gasped, her heart banging hard against her chest.

'Good evening, Charlotte,' the man grinned.

'Er . . . Good evening, Mr Goodhugh.'

'I was just saying to your mother that I thought I'd bring this round for you.'

Taking the package, Charlotte's dark eyes darted between her mother and Goodhugh.

'Aren't you going to open it?' her mother asked.

'Er . . . yes, of course,' she smiled, tearing open the paper. 'Oh, thank you,' she said, gazing at a wooden chess set.

'Oh, that's lovely, Charlotte.' Her mother beamed. 'You're too kind, Mr Goodhugh.'

'As I'm teaching Charlotte to play chess, I thought it would help her if she had her very own set. There are one or two opening moves I'd like to show you, Charlotte,' he smiled, looking at his watch. 'But I suppose it's getting late.'

'It's not that late, Mr Goodhugh,' the girl's mother said. 'Charlotte, why don't you set the board up on the table?'

'Well, I was about to go to bed.'

'I'm sure it won't take long, Charlotte. I'm going to have a bath so I'll leave you to it.'

'But, mother—'

'Don't be so ungrateful, Charlotte. Mr Goodhugh has brought you a gift and you can't even spare him half an hour. I'm sorry, Mr Goodhugh. I just don't know what's got into her lately.'

'I'll set the board up,' Charlotte sighed as her mother left the room and closed the door.

Goodhugh sat in an armchair, watching Charlotte as she set up the chess pieces. She could feel his stare burning into her. Thoughts roiled in the mire of her racked mind. He'd seen her completely naked, posing with her vaginal lips crudely spread. Embarrassment welling, her face flushing, she inadvertently knocked a chess piece to the floor. Even her home wasn't a sanctuary, she reflected, kneeling and grabbing the piece. Was there nowhere she was safe from the evil man?

'I'm very disappointed, Charlotte,' he sighed. His voice was soft, deep — threatening. 'Very disappointed.'

'Oh?' she said, her heart leaping.

'You went running to Father James and told him a pack of lies.'

'Lies?' she gasped.

'You said that I was blackmailing you. You know very well that I've paid you for posing for me.'

'You . . . you said that you'd tell my mother about the skirt unless . . .'

'I was joking, Charlotte. I told you that your skirt would remain our little secret. It's hardly a secret now that you've told Father James.'

'You also said that you'd show my mother the photographs.'

'Again, I was joking. Do you really think that I'd upset your mother like that? Besides, I'd be incriminating myself. Everyone knows that photography is my hobby. They'd put two and two together and come up with me. As I said, I'm very disappointed. We had an arrangement that was working well, and now you've jeopardized that arrangement.'

'No, I haven't. All I did was—'

SCHOOLGIRL LUST

'All you did was tell Father James a pack of lies.'

'You sent me those photographs as a threat, didn't you?'

'A threat? I thought you might be pleased to have a few copies. I really don't know what I'm going to do. You see, now that Father James knows about our work—'

'*Work?* Is that what you call it?'

'As I was saying, now that Father James knows, I'm going to have to reassess the situation.'

'What do you mean?'

'If it became common knowledge that you're having a lesbian relationship with Emily, and that you sell your body—'

'I don't—'

'And that you sell your body by posing naked before a camera and taking money in return, and that you strut around in a miniskirt . . . I have an idea, Charlotte.'

'Blackmail?'

'If that's the attitude you're going to take, then I can't help you.'

'Help me?'

'I don't want people knowing the truth about you any more than you do. It would destroy your mother if she were to discover the sort of girl you are, and I don't want that. I can help you by telling Father James that you no longer pose for me and that I've destroyed all the photographs of you. That would help, wouldn't it?'

'Well, yes.'

'I can also help you by telling the Father that it turned out that the skirt I found in the woods wasn't yours after all. I could say that, when I developed the photographs I'd taken in the woods, I realized that I'd made a terrible mistake and it wasn't you with Emily. I can get you out of this trouble, Charlotte. And I promise that I won't mention a word of this to your mother. I would never be so cruel to your mother.'

'What do you want in return?'

'Nothing. As I said, I don't want your mother upset. You don't have to worry about me, Charlotte. You never did have to worry about me. But you *do* have to worry about Father James. I've known him for a long time. He'll talk to your mother about your lewd behaviour, believe me.'

Biting her lip, Charlotte again thought about her mistake. She should have never gone to see Father James. Eyeing Goodhugh, she began to wonder whether he was telling the truth and he really did want to help her. If he spoke to the priest, he could certainly put the man's mind at rest and probably stop him from talking to her mother. Once the priest was told that Emily was with another girl . . . But Goodhugh would want to take more photographs in return, she knew.

'Did you admit to Father James that you were in the woods with Emily?'

'Yes, I said that we were talking.'

'That's a pity. I'll have to tell him that I was mistaken, that I saw another girl with Emily. If I choose my words carefully, your problems will be over. He's seen a couple of the photographs of you naked on the chaise longue, but I'm sure that if I tell him there'll be no more, he'll be happy and drop the matter. We're going to have to work together on your problems, Charlotte. Without me, you're in real trouble. You do understand that, don't you? Without my help, you're going to be in serious trouble not only with your mother and Father James, but your school.'

'My school?'

'When word gets round, as I'm sure it will, you'll probably be hounded out of the village. Please, allow me to help you.'

Gazing at the chess set, Charlotte knew that she had no choice. Only Mr Goodhugh could save her from the most terrible public shaming and humiliation. Nervously toying with a chess piece as he stood up and moved to the door, her head aching, she felt tired. The weekend had been a horrendous nightmare, and she wanted everything and everyone to go away. If she could turn the clock back to Saturday morning . . . But that wasn't possible. There was no going back, only forward.

'I'll see you tomorrow evening, Charlotte,' Goodhugh said, placing his hand on her shoulder.

'Yes, all right,' she murmured, forcing a smile. 'Will you speak to Father James?'

'Of course I will. But there's something I want you to do in return.'

'Oh?' she breathed, her stomach churning, her hands trembling.

'I want you to stop running to people and telling lies. Forget the skirt and don't worry about the photographs. Between us, we'll make sure that your mother never learns the shocking truth about you. Go up to bed now. I'll see myself out. Oh, talking of the photographs, throw them away. Not tonight because you may rouse your mother's suspicion by going out to the garden. Throw them away in the morning. I'll destroy the ones I have when I get home. Good night, Charlotte.'

'Good night, Mr Goodhugh.'

Turning the lights out as the man left, Charlotte climbed the stairs to her room. Closing the door, she flopped onto her bed and closed her eyes. Feeling a little easier in her mind, she prayed for things to be all right, for everything to work out. Perhaps Mr Goodhugh wasn't so bad after all, she mused. He'd only taken a few photographs and not once had he tried to touch her. Perhaps everything would turn out all right. Perhaps.

Chapter Five

Feigning another stomach-ache, Charlotte managed to get the day off school. Her mind in turmoil, she couldn't have concentrated on her work, or faced Emily. Spending the day in bed, she could think of nothing other than Mr Goodhugh and Father James. Was everything all right? Had Goodhugh put the priest's mind at rest? It was unlike Charlotte to waste a beautiful summer day, but she found some solace beneath her eiderdown, hidden away from the world.

In the warmth of her bed, she ran her fingers up and down the moist crack of her vagina several times, but worry wouldn't allow her clitoris to swell. She slipped her fingers into the wet sheath of her tight vagina a dozen times, exploring her hot sex cavern, learning about her teenage body. Why did Mr Goodhugh want to take photographs of her inner flesh, the intricate folds within her girl crack? Did he really want to help her?

The evening came all too quickly. Charlotte had been desperate to talk to Goodhugh and discover her fate, but now she feared the worst. Finally leaving the comfort of her bed, she gazed at her naked body in the dressing-table mirror. The mounds of her young breasts perfectly symmetrical, the dark discs of her areolae topped with beautifully elongated milk teats, she realized for the first time that she was sexually attractive. Emily wanted to fondle her intimacy, Goodhugh had wanted photographs of her naked body . . . Her development, her womanhood, was attracting attention. Sighing, she dressed and trotted down the stairs where she met her mother in the hall.

'I'll be back at ten,' her mother smiled. 'You'll have three hours with Mr Goodhugh. Be sure to offer him tea and biscuits and, above all, be polite and ladylike.'

'Yes, mother,' Charlotte murmured as the woman opened the front door.

'Are you feeling any better?'

'Much better.'

'Good. If Emily calls, you're to send her away. Do you understand?'

'Yes.'

'Right, I'll see you later. And do make an effort to smile, Charlotte. You've been looking so sullen lately.'

Goodhugh arrived within minutes of her mother leaving, and Charlotte wondered whether he'd been lurking somewhere in the street waiting until the older woman had gone. Wearing an open-neck shirt and tight trousers, he followed Charlotte into the lounge and stood with his back to the mantelpiece. Rubbing his chin, he stared hard at her. He didn't appear to be at all happy, Charlotte observed as he frowned and shook his head negatively. Perhaps he'd not been able to convince Father James . . .

'I'm afraid I have some bad news,' he murmured.

'Did you speak to Father James?' Charlotte asked, her head aching with worry.

'Yes, but I'll tell you about that in a minute. Charlotte, the photographs I sent to you . . . Did you throw them away?'

'Yes, I did it this morning.'

'Where? Where did you put them?'

'I waited until my mother went out and then put them in the dustbin.'

'The dustbin? Why didn't you burn them?'

'Well, I . . . What's happened?'

'I've just had a phone call from a man. He said that he has photographs of you and he wants money.'

'Photographs of *me*? But—'

'I burned the copies I had, along with the negatives. Someone must have seen you go to the dustbin and, for some reason, taken a look after you'd gone back into the cottage. Did you tear them up?'

'Yes, I did. Not into small pieces but—'

'Have you told anyone else about the photographs? Apart from Father James, I mean.'

'No, no, I haven't. Anyone could have seen me go to the bin. It's at the side of the cottage, not far from the road. No one would search the dustbin, Mr Goodhugh.'

'Someone did. If only you'd burned them, Charlotte.'

'I'm sorry, I . . . I should have thought.'

'This man wants two hundred pounds in exchange for the photographs.'

'He's blackmailing you?' she gasped.

'He rang me at the shop, so he's obviously guessed that I took the photographs. It must be someone from the village. Everyone knows about my interest in photography. If someone had seen you entering or leaving my shop during closing hours they might have been suspicious.'

'What will you do?'

'No, no. You don't seem to understand, Charlotte. This man, whoever he is . . . He's blackmailing *you*.'

'*Me*? But—'

'They're photographs of *you*, not me. He has nothing to

blackmail me with, has he? He found indecent photographs of you in your dustbin. He's blackmailing *you*.'

'Oh, my God!' she cried, holding her hands to her face. 'What will my mother say?'

'All right, calm down. Do you have any savings?'

'Well, only a few pounds.'

'The shop gives me a living but . . . He said that the photographs will be made public unless he receives the money within four days. He obviously knows that you don't have a phone. Anyway, he's going to ring me back with instructions on Friday.'

'What shall I do?'

'Unless you can get two hundred pounds . . . Wait a minute, I've just had a thought. I might be able to help you. I'll nip back to the shop and make a phone call. There's a slim chance that I might be able to save your neck.'

Charlotte hung her head as he left the cottage. Her mind spinning, she couldn't believe that she'd been stupid enough to put the photographs in the dustbin without ripping them to shreds. There again, she'd not expected anyone to go rummaging through the rubbish. Riddled with anxiety as she paced the lounge floor, she wondered what to do. Two hundred pounds was a lot of money. There was no way she could raise fifty pounds, let alone two hundred. Hearing Goodhugh at the door, she dashed into the hall.

'Whoever this man is, he's watching us,' Goodhugh said mysteriously, following Charlotte into the lounge and dumping a leather bag on the floor.

'What do you mean?'

'The minute I stepped into the shop, the phone rang. It was him. He must have seen me go into the shop. He might live over the road or—'

SCHOOLGIRL LUST

'What did he say?'

'He saw you in the woods yesterday with Emily.'

'Oh, no.'

'This is a mess, Charlotte. You had sex with Emily in the woods and . . . Anyone could have seen you. Why did you do it?'

'I . . . I don't know.'

'You left your skirt there, you walked along the street in that short skirt, you told Father James everything, and then you put the photographs in the dustbin in broad daylight.'

'I'm sorry. I didn't mean to—'

'I might be able to get you out of this mess. I rang a friend of mine. He collects erotic photographs. I told him about you, that you're an attractive seventeen-year-old. As luck would have it, he's offered to pay two hundred pounds for a wad of photographs of you.'

'But we don't have any. You burned yours and mine have been—'

'I've brought my camera,' Goodhugh said, pointing to the bag. 'I'll just have to take some more photographs of you.'

'But . . . No, not more. I don't want any more.'

'All right, I understand.' Grabbing the bag, Goodhugh moved to the door. 'There's nothing I can do so I'll be going.'

'Going? But what about this man?'

'What about him?'

'He wants two hundred pounds.'

'I know he does, Charlotte. He knows where you live and he'll probably send copies of the photographs to your mother and—'

'What shall I do?'

'I don't know. You don't have any money so there's not a

great deal you *can* do. I've done my best to help you but . . . I'm sorry but I don't want to get involved. This is all your doing and I don't want any part of it.'

'*My* doing?'

'*You* told Father James everything. *You* took your clothes off in the woods, *you* left your skirt and those panties there for all to see, *you* had sex in the woods with Emily in broad daylight . . . Anyone could have seen you. *I* saw you, for goodness' sake. And so did this man who's now blackmailing you. You've caused so much trouble, Charlotte. The best thing I can do is keep well out of it.'

'But *you* took the photographs in the first place,' she returned, her face flushing as her anxiety welled. 'You said that you'd show my mother unless I—'

'You're confused, Charlotte.'

'I'm not. You said that no one would know that you had taken them because there was a blank wall behind me and . . . and you said you'd tell my mother that I left the photographs in the shop and you thought you'd better return them.'

'You're all mixed up,' he sighed, dumping the bag back on the floor. 'I said, if you remember, that no one would know where the pictures were taken because there was a blank wall behind you. I was trying to put your mind at rest. I also said that I wanted a few photographs of you for my private collection. Do you remember that?'

'Yes, yes, I do. But I don't remember . . .'

'This is getting us nowhere. Particularly as you don't seem to remember what was said. You dreamed up this blackmail thing and, along with everything else you've done, it's got you into trouble. I have to go, Charlotte. This man, whoever he is, might be watching the cottage. He'll know that I'm here and—'

SCHOOLGIRL LUST

'If you take some more photographs of me . . .'

'This friend of mine lives in Cornwall. He doesn't know you or anyone else in the village. You'd be quite safe. Unless, that is, you go running to everyone telling them . . .'

'No, I won't tell anyone. Two hundred pounds is a lot of money. What sort of photographs does he want?'

'I don't think this is a good idea, Charlotte.'

'Why not? If he's willing to pay two hundred . . .'

'I wanted a few photographs of you for my private collection, and look at the trouble you've caused me. I thought you were adult enough to—'

'I won't cause trouble, I promise.'

'Well, I . . .'

'Please, Mr Goodhugh. You have to help me.'

'I *have* helped you, Charlotte. I've spoken to Father James. I had a long chat with him. I lied to him, and I can't abide lying. I told him that it wasn't you I saw in the woods with Emily. I also said that the skirt wasn't yours after all. Fortunately for you, he's going to forget the matter.'

'Thank God for that.'

'I don't think I can help you out again.'

'I need two hundred pounds. Just take the photographs and . . .' Hanging her head, tears streaming down her cheeks, she sat on the arm of the sofa. 'Please, Mr Goodhugh,' she sobbed. 'Take the photographs and get me out of this.'

'All right. But this is the last time I'm going to help you. If you get yourself into trouble again, don't come running to me. You'd better take your clothes off.'

'In here?' she asked, standing before him.

'Where else?'

'I . . . I don't know.'

'When will your mother be back?'

'Ten, ten o'clock.'

'At least we have plenty of time. I'll get the camera ready while you undress.'

Hurriedly slipping her clothes off, Charlotte carefully laid them over the back of the armchair and stood before Goodhugh. He seemed to take little notice of her young breasts, the triangular patch of dark pubic fleece nestling below the plateau of her stomach as he adjusted his camera. Her nipples rising, she folded her arms and waited. She knew that he didn't want to do this as he shook his head and sighed. The last thing *she*'d wanted was to pose for more photographs, but it seemed that she had no choice. Praying that this would put an end to the nightmare, she was thankful that Father James wasn't going to talk to her mother. Once this man had the money and had returned the photographs, she'd be free to enjoy her life again.

'Right,' Goodhugh finally said, looking up from his camera. 'Stand with your feet wide apart and touch your toes.'

'But . . .'

'Stand over there, by the wall. It'll make a pleasing backdrop.'

'I thought you might want me to lie on the sofa,' she said softly.

'No, no. I want you to stand with your back to me with your feet as wide apart as you can and touch your toes.'

'No, I really don't think—'

'I knew this was a bad idea,' Goodhugh breathed angrily. 'I don't know why I'm wasting my time on you.'

'All right,' she conceded, moving to the wall. 'I'll do it.'

Bending over, her feet wide apart, Charlotte gazed between her legs at an upside-down Goodhugh as he focused the camera on her blatantly exposed femininity. She had a feeling that naivety was getting the better of her as she gazed at the swell of her vaginal lips between her firm thighs. This might well have been a trick just to take more pictures, she reflected. But she couldn't risk the blackmailer showing her mother the lewd photographs. There might not *be* a blackmailer, she mused as Goodhugh moved in and clicked the shutter. Perhaps Goodhugh had made the whole thing up and . . . She couldn't be sure. Her head aching, her mind spinning, she couldn't think straight.

The problem with Father James had been real enough, she reflected. Goodhugh hadn't caused that problem. And it wasn't his fault that she'd stripped off and had lesbian sex in the woods with Emily. Humiliated and degraded by the lewd pose as the man focused the camera on her protruding inner lips, she closed her eyes. Mr Goodhugh was right, this had all been her doing. She could only pray that, with his help, the end of the nightmare was now in sight.

'OK, reach behind your back and pull your buttocks wide apart,' Goodhugh ordered her, kneeling behind her naked body.

'No,' she gasped. 'I'm not going to—'

'Please, Charlotte,' he snapped. 'Let's just get this over with.'

Complying, she pulled the rounded melons of her young buttocks apart, exposing the brown inlet to her rectum as the man took several photographs. Her face flushed, her heart racing, she wondered again how on earth she'd ended up in such a terrible situation. This wasn't a nightmare or a horror story, it was a living hell. If this didn't work, if the man had made copies of the photographs and demanded more money, then there'd be no way out of the mess. All she could do would be to flee the village and . . . With no money, where could she go?

'OK, you can stand up straight now,' Goodhugh said.

'May I get dressed?' Charlotte asked softly, covering the swell of her firm breasts with her folded arms.

'Not yet. We'll need quite a few more shots before . . . OK, kneel on the floor.'

'Why?' she asked, kneeling and looking up at him with an angelic innocence shining from the dark pools of her eyes.

'My friend will want some oral shots.'

'Oral shots?' She frowned.

'My penis in your mouth.'

'No!' she cried, staring wide-eyed as he unzipped his trousers. 'No!'

'Can we just get this over with, Charlotte?' he breathed, pulling his erect organ out. 'I have better things to do than—'

'I'm not going to . . .' Her eyes almost popping out of her head, she stared in horror at the first penis she'd ever been confronted with. 'Please, I can't . . .'

'If you don't want my help, then we'll forget the whole thing.'

'I am *not* going to . . . to take that into my mouth. I don't care what happens, I'm not . . . The very thought is sickening.'

'All right,' he sighed. 'We'll forget it. I've wasted enough time as it is.'

'I thought your friend would want photographs of—'

'For two hundred pounds, he wants more than photographs of a naked girl sprawled on a sofa. He wants photographs of sex, Charlotte.'

'Sex? But my mouth . . . That's not sex.'

'You'd better put your clothes on.'

SCHOOLGIRL LUST

'I'm sorry, Mr Goodhugh,' she whimpered, grabbing her clothes. 'But I can't . . .'

'You don't have to apologize to me,' he smiled, zipping his trousers. 'If you don't want to do it, that's fine.'

'I . . . I'm a virgin, you see. I've never even seen a penis before, let alone—'

'It's all right, don't worry.'

'Why my mouth?'

'That's what people do, it's what men and women enjoy.'

'I can't believe it.'

'I can't believe the things you did with Emily.'

'That was . . . It was different.'

'That's a matter of opinion. I've wasted enough time this evening, so I'll be going now. I have some paperwork to catch up with and—'

'What shall I do about the money?'

'I'll send the few photographs I have to my friend. If we're lucky, he might pay ten or twenty pounds for them.'

'Is that all?'

'That's all they're worth, Charlotte. Can you borrow the money?'

'I don't know. Who would have two hundred pounds?'

'No one I know. Anyway, even if you *were* able to borrow it, how would you pay it back?'

Dropping to her knees, Charlotte sat back on her heels, sobbing as Goodhugh placed his camera in the leather bag. She felt that the end of her life had come as she heard him move towards the door. Her mother would discover the truth and disown her, throw her out onto the street. Father James would denounce her as a harlot, the villagers would hound her . . . Clutching her clothes, she buried her face in the bundle of material and wailed in her plight as she heard the lounge door open.

'I'm sorry, Charlotte,' Goodhugh said. 'I succeeded with Father James, but there's nothing I can do to help you with this problem.'

'I don't know how I got into this,' she sobbed, lifting her tear-streaked face and looking up at him.

'You got into this by having sex with that Emily girl. By wearing that miniskirt in the street for all to see and then lying to your mother. You got into this by leaving your clothes in the woods, by telling Father James a pack of lies about me, by allowing people to see you throwing the photographs into the dustbin . . .'

'I didn't mean to do any of it,' she wailed, leaning forward and hitting the floor with her fists. 'I didn't mean to do any of it.'

'Come and sit next to me,' he sighed, perching on the edge of the sofa.

Dragging herself up, she'd forgotten about her nudity as she sat next to Goodhugh. Pressing her face into the warmth of his chest as he put his arm around her, she cried uncontrollably. If only she could turn the clock back to Saturday morning, she reflected again. If only Emily hadn't bought that silly skirt and . . . If only she'd behaved in a decent and moral manner as a teenage girl should, none of this would have happened. Mother always knew best. Holding her close, Goodhugh kissed the top of her head, telling her that she should go to bed and try to get some sleep.

'How can I sleep?' she asked, lifting her head and looking up at him.

'I . . . I don't know, Charlotte,' he said softly, shaking his head. 'It seems that the end has come. Your life just won't be worth living when . . . You have until Friday. That's when the man will be phoning me for the money. Perhaps, between now and then, something will happen.'

'*What* will happen?' she snivelled. 'Do you think two hundred pounds will fall out of the sky?'

'No, I don't. You're right, nothing is going to change between now and Friday. You've made your bed, and now you have to lie on it. Charlotte, I want you to know that I wasn't blackmailing you. I don't blackmail people, for goodness' sake. When I saw you wearing that miniskirt, I was genuinely concerned. Your mother has done her best to bring you up properly and . . . I didn't want to see you going off the rails. And the obscene episode in the woods with Emily left me stunned.'

'I . . . I don't know why I did that.'

'You're young and naive. I wouldn't exploit your naivety. You became confused and thought I was threatening you. Believe me, Charlotte, there's no way I'd want you or your mother upset or distressed.'

'I know. I'm sorry.'

'I don't know what you're going to do. If you went to the police . . . No, you'd end up in prison if you did that.'

'Prison?' she gasped.

'After all you've done . . . Try not to think about it.'

'I'll do it,' she sighed, her dark eyes wide as she gazed at him.

'What, go to the police?'

'No, no. The photographs . . . I'll do the oral thing.'

'Are you sure?'

'Yes, I'm sure. I'll do anything to get out of this mess.'

'Only if you're sure. I don't want to force you to . . .'

'You're not forcing me. I *want* to do it.'

'All right. But you must do exactly as I say, Charlotte.' He smiled, rising to his feet and once more taking his camera from the bag. 'No arguments or time-wasting. Do exactly as I say.'

'Yes, I will,' she sobbed, kneeling back down on the floor.

'And you promise not to cause me any more trouble?'

'Yes, I promise. Let's get it over with as quickly as possible.'

'All right. As quickly as possible.'

Placing the camera on the sofa behind him, he unbuckled his belt and dropped his trousers to his ankles. Charlotte gazed in awe as his penis rose above his heavy balls, the fleshy shaft swelling, his foreskin-veiled knob pointing to the ceiling. Watching his full balls rolling, she bit her lip as he grabbed the camera and focused on her tear-streaked face. Moving closer, he positioned the solid shaft of his organ close to her pursed lips and clicked the camera shutter.

'Hold my penis,' Goodhugh ordered her. Tentatively reaching out, she gripped the warm hardness of his shaft in her small hand. 'Now pull the skin back.'

'Pull it back?' she murmured.

'Hold it at the top and move your hand down towards the base.'

'Like this?' she asked, gazing at his purple knob as it came into view.

'That's perfect,' he gasped. 'Now suck it into your mouth.'

The shutter clicking, Charlotte sucked his purple plum into her pretty mouth, her face grimacing as the salty flavour tantalized her taste buds. Goodhugh breathed heavily in his male ecstasy as her angelic dark eyes looked up at him. Taking a shot of her lips stretched tautly around the rim of his bulbous glans, he ordered her to use her tongue and lick his knob. Obeying, she gripped his rock-hard shaft harder and ran her tongue around his purple globe. He began to tremble, his legs sagging as he took another shot of her pretty face, her full lips enveloping his swollen glans.

'I'm . . . I'm going to . . .' he gasped, his hands trembling as he tried to steady the camera. His sperm jetting, filling her cheeks, he managed to click the shutter as she moved her head back. Coughing and spluttering, she grimaced as his sperm jetted from his knob and splattered her lovely face. Ordering her to massage his shaft as she looked up at him in bewilderment, he told her to smile. 'Stay there,' he gasped as she moved her head further back to avoid the white rain of male orgasm. Moving forward, his sperm showering her cheeks, running down her nose, she forced a smile.

Kneading the fleshy rod, her wide eyes focused on his huge organ as his sperm jetted from the slit in long white threads and landed on her face, she prayed for the crudity to end as he took several photographs of her enforced debauchery. His heavy balls finally draining, his flow of spunk ceasing, he managed to take another short of her cum-drenched face. Charlotte remained perfectly still as the male liquid ran in white rivers down her cheeks, dribbling from her chin to splatter the mounds of her teenage breasts. Goodhugh was trying to help her and she didn't want to cause trouble, make problems. Thankful that it was over, she offered him a slight smile as she looked up at him.

'That was perfect,' he breathed shakily. 'Just a couple more shots and we're done. I want you to lick the end of my penis, Charlotte. Lick the end and lap up the sperm.'

'But—'

'Do it, girl,' he snapped. 'Just do as you're told.'

'Sorry, I—'

'Lick the sperm off my knob.'

Lapping up the white liquid as she looked up at the camera, Charlotte cleansed the softening globe of his deflating glans. Taking several shots, Goodhugh finally tossed the camera onto the sofa and grabbed her head. Ramming his knob to the back of her throat, he shuddered his last shudder and finally withdrew his spent organ from her sperm-wet mouth. Sitting on the sofa, he lay gasping in the aftermath of his illicit coming as his wet penis snaked over his rolling balls. Charlotte started to wipe her face as she gazed down at the milky liquid running over the succulent protrusions of her elongated nipples. Instructing the girl to leave the sperm on her face and grin at him, Goodhugh took several shots of her cum-drenched face, her sex-matted black hair.

'Was that all right?' she asked as he adjusted the camera.

'Perfect,' he breathed. 'That was . . . that was perfect. Lick the sperm from your lips, Charlotte. I want a shot of my sperm hanging from your tongue.'

'No, I . . . I don't like the taste.'

'For God's sake, girl. Bloody well do it.'

'I'm sorry,' she murmured, licking the salty fluid from her lips and poking her tongue out as the shutter clicked. The white liquid hung in a long strand from the tip of her pink tongue and Goodhugh took several more shots.

'That was good,' he grinned. 'Now wipe your face and then suck the sperm off your fingers.'

'But I told you, I don't like the taste. It's—'

'Charlotte!'

'I'm sorry,' she whimpered, dragging the sperm from her cheeks and sucking her fingers clean as he took several more shots. 'I'm sorry.'

'You'd better get dressed now,' he said, standing and pulling his trousers up. 'I didn't mean to shout at you.'

'No, it was my fault,' she whispered, wiping her mouth on the back of her hand.

'You did very well, Charlotte. Look, I'd better be going. Clean yourself up before your mother gets home. I'll be in touch.'

'When will you—'

'I'll be in touch.' Grabbing his bag, he left the room. 'I'll see you soon,' he called from the hall.

'What about the—'

The front door closed as Charlotte looked down at the white liquid running over the swell of her firm breasts, hanging in long strands from the ripe teats of her mammary globes. Wondering why the man had left in such a hurry, she clambered to her feet and licked her lips again. Gazing at her reflection in the mirror above the fireplace, she noticed that the male fluid had sprayed over her dark hair. Her face glistening, her hair sticky with the product of orgasm, she was about to go up to the bathroom when the doorbell rang. Panicking, she grabbed her clothes and hurriedly dressed, trying to wipe her face and hair clean as she dashed into the hall. Taking a deep breath, she finally opened the front door.

'Hi,' Emily smiled, walking past Charlotte into the lounge.

'Oh,' Charlotte breathed, closing the door and following the girl. 'I thought you were cross with me.'

'Yes, I was annoyed,' Emily admitted, sitting on the sofa, her naked thighs revealed by her red miniskirt. 'What have you been up to? What's that in your hair?'

'It's . . . it's milk. It sprayed over me when I opened . . . Why were you annoyed with me?'

'Because, Charlotte, right in the middle of my orgasm, you stopped. That's the worst thing you can do.'

'I'm sorry, I . . . I didn't know.'

'I'll let you off this time. Why weren't you at school today?'

'I was feeling ill.'

'Is that why you didn't come round yesterday afternoon?'

'Yes, yes, that's right. I'm OK now, though.'

'Look at the state of you. What's happened to your clothes?'

'I was about to have a bath when you arrived. I had to put my clothes on quickly to get to the door.'

'I must say that I'm very annoyed with you, Charlotte.'

'I said I was sorry.'

'Not about that. I was talking to Marianne today.'

'Oh, I like Marianne,' Charlotte smiled. 'She's really nice.'

'That's why I'm annoyed.'

'What do you mean?'

'You like her more than me, don't you? Before you say anything, she told me that she often walks in the woods with you.'

'Well, yes, we have done that.'

'And she's spent time here with you.'

'Yes, but—'

'I thought you wanted to be with *me*, Charlotte.'

'Yes, I do. What are you getting at?'

'Why have you been seeing her?'

'She's a friend, Emily.'

'Would you rather be with her?'

'No, of course not. She's a good friend and—'

'Prove it.'

'Prove what? I don't know what you're talking about.'

'Prove that you like me more than you do her.'
'How?'
'Let's go up to your room. Come on, you said you were going to have a bath so I'll help you.'
'But, my mother will be—'
Watching as Emily left the room and climbed the stairs, Charlotte glanced at the mantelpiece clock. Eight-thirty. There was plenty of time to have a bath and . . . Suddenly realizing what Emily wanted, Charlotte bit her lip. Father James had told her to sever all contact with the girl. She'd as good as promised him that she wouldn't see her again. There had been enough trouble, she reflected. Mr Goodhugh had put things right with the priest. If he discovered that the girl had been to the cottage and . . . Recalling pushing her finger into Emily's vaginal sheath, her stomach somersaulting, she knew that she could keep this secret. No one would know, she mused. No one in the world would know. Besides, after her horrendous three-day ordeal, she needed someone to hold and comfort her. Climbing the stairs, she knew that she was about to make a big mistake as she wandered into her bedroom and gazed longingly at her young friend. But her teenage hormones were running wild. She needed to hold Emily close, kiss her, love her and . . .

'Slip out of your clothes and I'll wash you.' Emily smiled as she wandered into the bathroom.

'My mother might come home early,' Charlotte called from the bedroom, tugging her skirt down. 'You'd better wait in here for me.'

'Don't worry about your mother,' Emily said, filling the bath as Charlotte wandered into the room, her naked body glowing beneath the light. 'She'll be ages.'

'Yes, but if she comes home early . . .'

'You're beautiful,' Emily said softly, running her hands

over the swell of the girl's rounded breasts. 'Absolutely beautiful. OK, get into the bath and I'll wash you.'

No one would know about this, Charlotte again reflected, sinking into the hot water as Emily knelt beside the bath. As the other girl soaped her firm breasts, Charlotte closed her eyes and relaxed. This was what she needed after her three-day nightmare. Blackmail, photographs, Father James . . . and Mr Goodhugh, she mused, her sensitive nipples rising beneath Emily's massaging fingertips. She'd taken Goodhugh's penis into her mouth and sucked out his seed. She was disgusted with herself, sickened by her vulgar act. But it was over, that was the last photo session she'd ever have to endure. All her problems would be over once Goodhugh's friend had the photographs and the blackmailer had been paid.

Sighing as Emily slipped her hand between her thighs and massaged soap into the gaping valley of her fleshy vaginal lips, Charlotte felt completely relaxed. Serenity enveloping her, she slipped into a warm pool of tranquillity as her friend caressed her sensitive inner folds. Charlotte thought about her mother. Although the woman loved her, she wasn't demonstrative. Charlotte had never known physical affection, physical love. To feel Emily's finger slipping into the hot sheath of her vagina was heavenly. Having seen – and held, and sucked – Goodhugh's penis, the granite-hard rod of his masculinity, she now knew that it was the female form she craved. A second finger entering her tightening chamber of love, she breathed a deep sigh of satisfaction. Her clitoris swelling, she began to tremble as her friend expertly massaged the velveteen inner flesh of her spasming sex duct.

'Get on all fours,' Emily whispered huskily as she slipped her fingers out of the girl's rhythmically contracting love sheath. Complying, Charlotte knelt in the bath with the rounded orbs of her young bottom raised. Parting her friend's pert buttocks, Emily ran her fingertip up and down the girl's anal valley, paying particular attention to the sensitive brown tissue surrounding the inlet to her rectal duct. Grabbing the bar of soap, she lathered between the girl's buttocks, lubricating the tight hole to her hot sheath of illicit pleasure. Her fingertip gliding past the tight ring of her anal sphincter, slipping deep into the hot tube of her rectum, she caressed the velvety duct of her friend's bottom.

'No,' Charlotte murmured as Emily drove a second finger into her snug anal canal. Grinning, Emily managed to force a third finger into the girl's rectal tube. Charlotte's love lips bulging alluringly between her firm thighs, the milk of lust flowing from her gaping vaginal mouth, she gasped as Emily began her slow rectal pistoning. Her naked buttocks quivering as the sensations of illicit sex rolled through her pelvis, she thought about Father James. She'd disobeyed him, she mused as Emily reached between her thighs with her free hand and massaged the solid protrusion of her ripe clitoris. Her climax quickly approaching, Charlotte hung her head, her long black hair trailing in the water as she began to squirm in the grip of her lesbian pleasure. She shouldn't be doing this, she reflected. If Father James discovered—

'God,' she breathed, her clitoris exploding in orgasm, her rectal duct tightening around Emily's pistoning fingers. Her well-lathered bottom-hole stretched tautly around her friend's fingers, heavenly sensations coursing deep into her bowels, she shook violently in her girl-induced coming. On and on her pleasure rolled, taking her to hitherto unknown heights of sexual ecstasy as her young friend continued to finger her rectum and massage immense pleasure from her pulsating clitoris.

'Charlotte,' the girl's mother called up the stairs. 'Charlotte, are you there?' Yanking her fingers out of Charlotte's inflamed bottom-hole, Emily leaped to her feet.

'Charlotte,' the woman called again as she climbed the stairs. Sitting on the stool in the corner of the room, Emily composed herself. Charlotte lay on her back in the bath, her body shaking violently as her orgasm slowly faded. There would be trouble, the girls knew as the door swung open and hit the wall with a dull thud.

'What on *earth* . . .' the woman cried, standing in the doorway with her hands on her hips.

'I . . . I was just leaving,' Emily stammered, leaping to her feet.

'Charlotte, I have never—'

'It's all right, mother,' the girl breathed, folding her arms to conceal the rise of her teenage breasts. 'Emily was only—'

'I'll see you at school,' Emily said, dashing through the door and bounding down the stairs.

'Charlotte, what on earth do you think you're doing?'

'I needed a bath and Emily sat—'

'Have you no morals, girl? You do *not* have friends watching you bathe.'

'She wasn't watching me, she—'

'I'll speak to you about this in the morning. I have Mrs Langly downstairs. Get out of the bath and go straight to bed. You're in serious trouble, my girl. Make no mistake about it.'

Climbing out of the bath, Charlotte wrapped a towel around her curvaceous young body and wandered across the landing to her room. *Serious trouble?* she brooded, lying on her bed and looking up at the cracked ceiling. She was in enough serious trouble as it was. Hoping that her mother would have calmed down by the morning, she sighed. Calmed down? She doubted that very much. As long as Father James didn't get to hear about this . . . But Charlotte's mother was always talking to the priest. If there was going to be trouble – and Charlotte knew there was – it would be more than just serious.

Chapter Six

Charlotte donned her school uniform and crept out of the cottage before her mother had the chance to lecture her about bathing in front of Emily. Walking down the road, her head aching, she looked around her before slipping into Goodhugh's shop. She was desperate for news, but the man was busy serving customers. Not wanting to be seen by the locals, she wandered behind the shelving and crept into the stockroom. Had Goodhugh sent the photographs to his friend? she wondered. When would the money arrive? Finally joining her in the stockroom, the shopkeeper frowned at her.

'Bad news, I'm afraid,' he sighed, the light shining on his balding head as he looked down at the floor.

'I've had enough bad news,' Charlotte retorted, her stomach churning as she wondered what could have gone wrong now.

'The photographs . . .' he began.

'He still wants them, doesn't he?'

'Oh, yes. The problem is, they didn't come out. It must have been a faulty roll of film.'

'Oh, no,' she breathed, holding her hand to her head. 'Now what do we do?'

'All I can do is take another set of photographs. It's a bloody nuisance. I was up until midnight developing the film just to discover that—'

'No . . . no more photographs,' she murmured shakily. 'I can't go through all that again.'

'I quite understand, Charlotte. To be honest, I don't want to have to spend any more time taking photographs and developing film. Apart from time, it's costing me money. Your problems have kept me busy enough as it is.' He checked his watch. 'You're going to be late for school'

'I'm not going,' she said decisively. 'I've got so much on my mind, I can't go to school. I just don't know what I'm going to do. I thought, after last night, that it was all over.'

'So did I. Let me talk to your mother,' he suggested.

'Talk to my mother?' Charlotte breathed, her dark eyes wide with fear. 'What about?'

'I might be able to explain the photographs.'

'Explain? Explain what? That I took my clothes off and—'

'I don't know, Charlotte. It's Tuesday, and you have until Friday to come up with two hundred pounds. You either pay this man or tell your mother the truth.'

'I haven't *got* two hundred pounds.'

'He'll send the photographs to her, there's no doubt about that.' Looking up at the ceiling, Goodhugh rubbed his chin. 'As I see it, you have four problems,' he said pensively. 'One, your sexual escapade in the woods with Emily. Two, this business with the miniskirt. Three, the photographs and the blackmailer. Four, Father James might hear of this and—'

'I have another problem. Emily came round last night and—'

'Ah, that explains it,' Goodhugh said, gazing at Charlotte as she frowned.

'Explains what?'

'Father James was in this morning. He usually calls in for a paper and—'

'What did he say?' Charlotte broke in irritably.

'He said something about you having had a visitor last night and—'

'Oh, no. I promised him that I'd have nothing more to do with Emily.'

'And he saw her going into your cottage. No doubt he'll go and see your mother.'

'Would you speak to him? If you said that Emily—'

'No. I'm sorry but I've done enough, Charlotte. I've already lied to him about Emily being in the woods with another girl. He's not stupid, for God's sake. He'll realize that you and Emily have something going on. Apart from that, I'm trying to run a business. I can't spend any more time getting you out of trouble. I suggest you go to school now.'

'I can't.'

'Where will you go, then? You can't stay here all day.'

'Can I stay for a while?'

'All right. But don't go into the shop. The last thing I need is people seeing you in my shop when you're supposed to be at school. If Father James sees you in here . . . I dread to think of the consequences.'

As Goodhugh went to serve a customer, Charlotte perched her buttocks on the edge of the desk. This was a mess, she reflected, twisting her long black hair around her fingers. The priest didn't want her to see Emily, Emily didn't want her to see Marianne, the photographs hadn't come out, she was in trouble with her mother, and now she had to spend the day in hiding. Deciding to take a walk through the woods, she opened the door and scanned the shop. A customer was just leaving so she came out of the stockroom and walked to the counter.

'I'm going,' she said dolefully.

'I've just had another phone call,' Goodhugh sighed. 'The blackmailer saw you come in here.'

'He's still watching?' Charlotte asked.

'It looks that way. He must live nearby.'

'What did he say?'

'He wants the money by tomorrow.'

'But it's Wednesday tomorrow. He said Friday . . .'

'Yes, I know. Look, I'll call my friend and see whether he'll send the cash before he receives the photographs.'

'No, I don't want any more photographs taken.'

'In that case, you'd better prepare for your mother's wrath.'

'But—'

'It's up to you, Charlotte. This really is my last offer of help.'

'All right,' Charlotte finally conceded. 'Ring him now.'

Pacing the floor as Goodhugh picked up the phone, Charlotte prayed for his friend to send the cash before he received the photographs. It was unlikely, she knew as Goodhugh tapped his fingers on the counter. Her stomach churning, she bit her lip. This was getting out of hand. It was *already* out of hand. Taking another day off school wasn't a good idea, but she couldn't face lessons, or Miss Chambers who'd no doubt ask to see her English project. What with Emily seemingly jealous over Marianne and . . .

'What sort?' Goodhugh asked his friend. 'I don't know whether she'll agree to that. Yes, of course. And it'll be cash? Good. Yes, I'll call you back.' Replacing the receiver, he turned and faced Charlotte. 'He can put cash in the post today,' he said.

'That's great.' She beamed, a wave of relief rolling through her young body.

'There's a slight problem.'

'Oh?'

'Come through to the stockroom and we'll talk about it.'

Following the man, Charlotte decided that she didn't care what the problem was. As long as the cash turned up, nothing else mattered. If she called at the shop that evening and endured the ordeal of another photo shoot, the whole thing would be over. Watching Goodhugh as he closed the door, she wondered about the blackmailer. He might make copies of the pictures and demand more money. But she'd thought about that before. All she could do was hope that he was a man of his word.

'Right,' Goodhugh said, taking his camera from a shelf. 'This is the deal. The photographs are to be pornographic.'

'What do you mean, exactly?' she asked, nervously wringing her hands.

'I want you to go home and shave.'

'Shave? Shave what?'

'Down there, Charlotte. Shave your pubic hairs off.'

'No!' she gasped. 'I'm not going to—'

'All right, we'll forget the whole thing.'

'I can't do that. I can't shave.'

'Why not? The hair will soon grow back. Look, I've wasted enough time on this. You either do it or . . . On second thoughts, I'm washing my hands of this business. I've been through enough, what with this man watching my shop and ringing me.'

'All right, I'll do it,' Charlotte sighed.

'You'll have to find someone else to take the photographs. As I said, I've had enough of this.'

'Please help me,' she whimpered, watching him fiddle with the camera. 'I don't know anyone else with a camera, let alone someone who'd take photographs and develop the film.'

'Charlotte, you're always making problems. You won't do this, you won't do that . . . You either do this properly, without complaining, or we forget the whole damned business.'

'Yes, I'll do it properly. I'll do anything you say, but—'

'But what? *Now* what's the problem?'

'I haven't got a razor.'

'I can easily solve that.' He smiled, fiddling with his camera. 'Take a packet of razors and a can of foam from the shop. I want you to understand that the photographs are going to have to be pornographic. Hard-core sex, OK?'

'Hard-core?'

'Go and shave and I'll be ready for you at lunchtime.' Opening the door, he wandered into the shop and gazed out of the window. 'The coast is clear. I close at one, so be here then.'

'If my mother's in—' Charlotte began, grabbing a packet of razors and a can of foam from a shelf.

'Charlotte, you've put too many of your problems onto me as it is. If your mother's at home, that's your worry. By the way, do you have a radio?'

'A radio?' she frowned.

'They came in this morning,' he said, pointing to several small radios on a rack by the door.

'No, I haven't got a radio,' she sighed.

'They were on special offer so I bought a dozen. Take one, if you want.'

'I can't afford—'

'You don't have to pay me, Charlotte,' he chuckled, walking behind the counter. 'I know you don't have a television at home. Take a radio. And don't worry about your mother. I'll tell her that I gave it to you.'

'Thank you,' she smiled, taking one from the rack.

SCHOOLGIRL LUST

'I'll see you at one. Now, off you go.'

Charlotte left the shop. Walking home, she prayed that her mother was out. If she was in, she'd just have to say that she'd been sent home because her stomach was bad again. More lies, she thought, opening the front door. Fortunately, there was no sign of her mother. Bounding up the stairs, she went into her room and placed the radio on the windowsill. Slipping out of her school uniform, she stood in front of the dressing-table mirror and focused on the triangular patch of dark hair veiling her girl crack. To shave would be sacrilege, but she knew that she had no choice. The thought of defiling her young body was horrific, but today would bring an end to the nightmare.

Wandering into the bathroom with the razor and foam, Charlotte perched her naked buttocks on the edge of the bath. Parting her thighs wide, she massaged the white foam into the fleece of her vulval flesh. Taking a deep breath, she tentatively dragged the razor over the rise of her young mons, gazing in horror at the white strip of hairless flesh left in the razor's wake. Working between her thighs, the razor stripping her dark curls, shaving the swell of her vaginal lips, the soft flesh of her pubic mound, she removed every last vulval curl. Wiping the foam away with a flannel, she stood up and gazed at the fleshy hillocks of her naked vaginal lips, the exposed pinken valley of her girlhood.

Recalling the days before her pubic hair had veiled her young crack, a tear rolling down her cheek, she wondered what had become of her teenage life. From normality to depravity in a matter of days, she'd become something she'd never dreamed of. Lesbian sex with Emily, the girl's fingers pistoning her rectal sheath, lewd photographs of Goodhugh's penis sperming in her mouth, his orgasmic liquid running down her face . . .

'I have to get this over with,' she breathed, returning to her room. Catching sight of her naked vulva in the dressing table mirror, she focused on the rise of her sex lips, her inner petals of love protruding from the moist valley of her vagina. Years had been stripped, returning her to pre-pubescence. 'They'll grow again,' she sighed, wondering what to wear. Deciding on her school uniform, she quickly dressed and glanced at the bedside clock. Ten-fifteen. She had time to kill before the photo shoot, before the inevitable defiling of her youthful body. Time to think.

Leaving the cottage, Charlotte walked to the village hall and took the path to the woods. The sun shining, the birds singing, there was peace and tranquillity beneath the trees. Far removed from Goodhugh's shop or the cottage and her mother. Wandering aimlessly for a couple of hours, she finally sat down on a log. Acutely aware of her hairless vaginal flesh beneath the soft silk of her tight panties, she recalled her childhood days again. Innocence had reigned in those carefree days. What had gone so very wrong? she wondered. Remembering once more the previous Saturday morning when she'd woken to the sun warming her naked body, she couldn't wait to visit Goodhugh and then put the sordid affair behind her. She had to move on, she knew.

'I thought it was you.' Marianne smiled as she approached.

'Oh, hi,' Charlotte said, looking up at the girl. 'Why aren't you at school?'

'There is no school today. Oh, you weren't there yesterday, were you? We have the day off to work on our projects. Well, our class does.'

'Thank God for that.'

'Are you all right?'

'Yes, I'm OK.'

'So, what are you doing here?'

'Thinking.'

As the other girl sat on the grass by the log, Charlotte scrutinized the swell of Marianne's T-shirt. Her firm breasts straining against the tight material, her erect nipples clearly outlined, Charlotte wondered about the girl's teenage body. Did she masturbate? Did she slip her fingers into the wet sheath of her vagina? Perhaps she massaged her clitoris to orgasm as she lay in her bed at night. Eyeing the girl's naked thighs, Charlotte's own clitoris swelled as she fantasized about kissing the smooth skin of Marianne's young legs, licking the fleshy folds nestling between her thighs, breathing in the scent of her femininity. Recalling Emily's bad mood, and her jealousy, Charlotte prayed that her lesbian lover wouldn't discover her infidelity.

Infidelity? she mused, her juices of teenage arousal filling her tight panties. Father James had once said in a sermon that even sexual *thoughts* about another were deemed as infidelity in the eyes of God. But Emily would never know about Charlotte's thoughts. Wondering what was wrong with Emily, she gazed at Marianne's long blonde hair cascading over her shoulders, the alluring rise of her newly developed breasts. Mulling over her lewd impulses as she felt her clitoris pulsate, Charlotte sighed. She desperately wanted Marianne, to fondle and caress her naked body, but . . . but what? She was looking for love, she knew. She'd thought she'd found love with Emily until the girl had stormed off and then revealed her jealous streak.

'Are you all right?' Marianne asked, her blue eyes frowning.

'Yes, I . . . To be honest, I have problems,' she confessed.

'Anything I can help with?'

'No, I'm afraid not. No one can help me, Marianne – no one.'

'At least tell me about it.'

'I can't,' Charlotte sighed, checking her watch. 'What are you doing this afternoon?'

'Nothing. Why?'

'I'll meet you here.'

'OK.'

'Two o'clock. No, ten past.'

'Ten past?' The girl frowned. 'Why so precise?'

'I'll tell you about it later.' Slipping off the log, she checked her watch again. 'I'll tell you about my problems later. I have to go now.'

'Where to?'

'To . . . I'll see you here at ten past two.'

Goodhugh was hovering behind the shop door, putting up the 'closed' sign, when Charlotte arrived. Opening the door, he grinned at her, gazing at the swell of her young breasts thrusting against her school blouse as she wandered into the shop. Locking the door, he took her hand and led her through the shop to the stockroom. Her heart racing, she tried to blot out from her mind the stark reality of the situation. But with the chaise longue in place, the camera and lighting equipment set up, there was no blotting it out. She knew that she had to get this over with. When the sordid episode was over, she'd meet Marianne and they'd walk in the woods without a care in the world.

'I'll be using this,' Goodhugh said, taking a leather whip from the corner of the room.

'*Using* it?' Charlotte echoed fearfully.

'To whip your buttocks. I'll need a few shots of—'

SCHOOLGIRL LUST

'No!' she cried, backing away until she was against the door. 'You're *not* going to whip me!'

'Here we go again,' he sighed, dropping the whip to the floor. 'Problems, problems.'

'I am *not* going to allow you—'

'Charlotte, there's been a development. I wasn't going to say anything until we'd taken the photographs but . . . Father James came in just after you left earlier.'

'What did he want?'

'He was looking at the radios and asked how much they were. When I told him, he asked me how you could afford one. He saw you leaving the shop with a radio.'

'That doesn't matter, does it?'

'It matters very much. Where would you get the money from? They're nearly forty pounds each, Charlotte. He reckons that you got the money for posing naked again.'

'He said that?'

'Yes, he did. Not wanting to get you into more trouble, I said that we'd not taken any more photographs. He wondered again how you could afford a radio and then he suggested that you'd stolen it.'

'But I *didn't* steal it!'

'I know that, Charlotte. I was in a quandary. I either told him that you'd paid for it, or that you must have taken it. If you'd paid, then you'd obviously got the money for posing naked.'

'What did you say?'

'I said that I knew nothing about the radio.'

'Then he thinks I stole it?'

'Yes.'

'Why didn't you tell him that you'd given it to me?'

'Don't be silly, Charlotte. He knows about the photographs. He'd have immediately realized that I'd given it to you in return for sexual favours.'

'Oh, God,' she breathed, hanging her head. '*Now* what am I going to do?'

'He wants me to contact the police.'

'No!'

'If I don't, then he will. I can't get involved in this, you must understand that.'

'But—'

'If word gets round that I've given you an expensive radio and we've been having sex—'

'But we *haven't*.'

'Haven't we? Look what we did in your cottage. Because of you and your big mouth Father James knows about the photographs and—'

'I'll say that you gave me the radio. I'll tell the police everything.'

'What would they think of me if they discovered that I'd given a young schoolgirl a brand new radio?'

'I'll say I paid for it.'

'And they'd ask your mother where you got the money from. I'm a respected member of the community, Charlotte. And I am *not* going to risk my reputation for your sake.'

'The police will believe me. I'll tell them that I paid for it with money Emily lent me.'

'Then they'll check with Emily and *she*'ll be dragged into it.'

'I shall go to the police and tell them everything. I'll say that you—'

'My camera takes photographs in quick succession,' Goodhugh said, taking a pile of photographs from the shelf. 'I was playing about with the camera when you were here earlier. Take a look at these. This is one of you standing by the shop door. This one shows your hand reaching out to the rack. And this one shows you taking a radio. In this picture you can be seen holding the radio close to your body, as if you're trying to conceal it. You then left the shop and Father James saw you walking down the street with the radio.'

'I don't understand. Why did you take pictures—'

'As I said, I was playing about with the camera. It was more than a stroke of luck, in view of the latest development.'

'What do you mean?'

'These photographs show you stealing the radio, Charlotte.'

'But—'

'To save my neck, I'll have to tell the police that I saw you taking the radio.'

'They'll ask why you took photographs instead of following me into the street and—'

'I'll say that I was taking pictures of the shop for an advert I'm putting in the paper. I'll tell them that I didn't realize you'd stolen the radio until I'd developed the film.'

'Don't go to the police,' she gasped, leaning against the door to steady herself.

'If I don't, Father James will.'

'But you *gave* me the radio.'

'I don't have any choice, Charlotte. Can't you see that? I don't want the police to find out that I've been paying you for sexual favours. I'll have to say that you stole the radio. Fortunately, I have photographic evidence to prove it.'

'You planned all this from the beginning.'

'Of course I didn't. I didn't want any of this to happen. Last Saturday I saw you in the woods with Emily and . . . Well, I was shocked. Did I *plan* that? Did I *plan* for you to be in the woods having lesbian sex with that girl?'

'Well, no.'

'I wasn't going to say anything, but when you came in here wearing that miniskirt . . . All I wanted was a few photographs for my private collection and you spoiled everything by running to Father James.'

'You threatened me, blackmailed me and—'

'We've been through all this nonsense. Had you kept your mouth shut, things would have been fine. None of this would have happened. You do nothing but cause me problems, Charlotte. I give you a radio and it lands me in trouble. We're wasting time. I want you to strip off.'

'No, I . . . You can't do this.'

'I'm not doing anything, Charlotte. *You*'ve done all this, not me. I might be able to talk Father James out of going to the police but . . . The first thing to do is take the photographs and pay the blackmailer. He wants the money tomorrow, for God's sake.'

'Yes, yes, you're right. That's the first problem to deal with,' Charlotte agreed in her confusion. 'Then you'll talk to Father James?'

'If you behave and do exactly as I tell you, I'll speak to him about it. He asked me to go and see him this evening to discuss the matter. I'll try to persuade him to let me deal with you rather than go to the police. But you must behave yourself.'

'Yes, yes – I'll behave.'

'Good. Now hurry up. We don't have a great deal of time.'

As her trembling fingers fumbled with the buttons of her blouse, Charlotte slid her shoes off and kicked them aside. She was in more trouble than ever, she knew as her blouse dropped to the floor and she started to tug her skirt down. She could see Goodhugh's point. He could hardly say that he'd given her the radio. And he couldn't say that she'd bought it because everyone knew she couldn't afford it. Either way, she'd be subjected to searching questions not only by her mother but by the police.

Stepping out of her skirt, she unhooked her bra, her firm teenage breasts jutting out as the silk cups fell away, her succulent nipples rising. Slipping her panties down, her face flushing as the man gazed longingly at her shaved vulval flesh, she stood naked before him. At least this would put an end to the blackmailer's threats, she mused, noticing a bulge in Goodhugh's trousers as he continued to stare lustfully at her naked sex.

'Very nice,' Goodhugh grinned. 'There's nothing like a few close-up shots of a shaved cunt.'

'Please,' she murmured, placing one arm across her chest to conceal her young breasts, her erect milk teats and cupping her other hand over her bare pubic mound in the classic pose of threatened female modesty. 'Please, don't talk like that.'

'You've heard the word before, haven't you?' he asked.

'Yes, and I—'

'Where? Where did you first hear it?'

'I don't know. At school, I think.'

'You pushed your fingers into Emily's wet cunt, didn't you?'

'No, I—'

'Didn't you?'

'Yes!'

'Lie on the chaise longue with your legs open and push your fingers into your cunt. It looks like they're nearly there already.' Goodhugh chuckled coarsely.

'No! I thought we were going to—'

'Do you want my help or not?'

'Please . . .'

'Do it, Charlotte! You've caused me enough trouble as it is, so do as you're bloody well told!'

Obediently stretching out on the chaise longue, tears streaming down her flushed face, Charlotte parted her legs and gazed down at the yawning crack of her hairless vulva. Hovering with his camera, Goodhugh took several shots of her blatantly exposed girl flesh, the pink wings of her inner labia. Wondering why he'd suddenly changed, become annoyed, she felt humiliation engulf her as he moved in and took several close-up shots. The degradation would be over in less than an hour, she reflected. He had to open the shop at two and . . . But she now had the police to worry about. She'd be in real trouble, she knew as she gazed at the light shining on his balding head.

'Pull your cunt lips wide open,' Goodhugh ordered her. Gripping the fleshy pads of her vagina between her fingers and thumbs, she parted the soft hillocks, exposing her rubicund inner folds to the camera lens. The miniskirt, the episode with Emily in the woods, the photographs, the priest, and now the radio . . . Goodhugh knew everything, she thought fearfully. He had so much on her that she'd be a slave for ever to his every perverted whim. She dared not argue with him or cross him, protest or even try to reason with him. To make matters worse, if that was possible, Goodhugh was in with her mother who thought him to be some sort of saint.

'We're running out of time,' he murmured, checking his watch. 'Sit with your buttocks over the edge of the chaise longue and open your thighs as wide as you can.'

'What . . . what are you . . .' Charlotte stammered as he placed the camera on the floor and unzipped his trousers. 'What are you going to do?'

SCHOOLGIRL LUST

'I'm going to push my penis into your cunt and take some more photographs.'

'No! You're not going to—'

'Do as you're told, girl!' he hissed, kneeling between her feet as she slid her buttocks forward. 'I told you that the photographs had to be pornographic, and now you're complaining.'

'I don't *want* you to put that awful thing in me,' she whimpered, eyeing the swollen purple globe of his erect penis. 'I don't want—'

'I didn't ask you what you wanted, Charlotte. Unless you behave, I'll have to go to the police and let them deal with this business. Can't you see that you'll leave me no choice unless you cooperate?'

'Father James will go to the police, so—'

'Not if I tell him that I'm dealing with the matter. I'll have to lie again to save your neck. I'll do my best to help you, but this will be the last time.'

Running the silky bulb of his cockhead up and down Charlotte's creamy sex slit, lubricating his weapon tip in readiness for vaginal penetration, Goodhugh positioned his bulging glans between the petals of her dripping inner lips. Charlotte lowered her head, moaning in protest at this crude violation, gazing wide-eyed as his purple plum slipped into the tight sheath of her virgin vagina. Her hairless outer lips parting, stretching as his huge shaft glided along her vaginal passage, she suppressed her impulse to scream and struggle and focused instead on the pinken tip of her clitoris as it popped out from beneath its protective hood. Feeling as if her pelvic cavity was inflating, she watched with appalled fascination the naked flesh of her outer labia hugging the base of his huge penis.

'God, you're tight,' Goodhugh breathed, withdrawing his

pussy-slimed cock and driving it back into her young body. The sensitive tip of her clitoris massaged by his girl-wet shaft as he repeatedly withdrew and thrust into her hot quim, she lay back and closed her eyes. This wasn't so bad, she thought, her naked body rocking with the crude fucking. Gasping as he squeezed and kneaded the firm mounds of her teenage breasts, pinched and twisted her sensitive nipples, she knew that she was going to come. Her young body shaking violently as she listened to the squelching of her vaginal juices, she could feel the man's heavy balls battering the roundness of her pert buttocks.

Her first time wasn't meant to be like this, Charlotte thought dolefully. The act was supposed in be enveloped in a velvety blanket of love, not in cold, brutal lust. But this had to be done. Lifting her legs and placing them over his shoulders, Goodhugh increased his fucking rhythm, his swollen knob battering the girl's ripe cervix as she tossed her head from side to side in her new-found sexual pleasure. Her eyes rolling, she dug her fingernails into the velvet covering of the chaise longue as the birth of her orgasm stirred deep within her contracting womb.

Wondering why Goodhugh wasn't taking any photographs as she whimpered in her preorgasmic pleasure, Charlotte felt her vaginal sheath tighten still further around his thrusting penis. The squelching sounds growing louder as her vaginal juices gushed from her bloated sex sheath, her clitoris swelling, her naked body convulsed wildly as her orgasm erupted within the solid nub of her sensitive pleasure spot.

'Oh, yes!' she cried as Goodhugh breathed deeply, his penis swelling within the tight tube of her vagina. His sperm jetting from his swollen plum, bathing her young cervix, lubricating the illicit union, he repeatedly rammed his bulbous cockhead deep into her teenage body. Withdrawing his pussy-wet penis, he ran his orgasming knob up and down her sex valley, massaging her pulsating clitoris with his purple plum as his sperm gushed. The white liquid lubricating the clitoral massaging, jetting over the rise of her stomach, he crudely fucked the wet divide of her teenage labia until his swinging balls had drained.

Shuddering as his purple knob massaged the last of her pleasure from her swollen clitoris, Charlotte opened her eyes and gazed at the male sex liquid pooling in her navel, running in rivers of milk down the sides of her naked body. Her hairless vaginal lips inflamed, glistening in the light, she watched Goodhugh grab his cock by the base and run his hand up the deflating shaft. The remnants of his spunk oozing from his knob-slit, hanging in a long white thread and finally pooling within her gaping valley, she wondered again why he'd not taken any photographs.

'You did well,' he praised her, moving back and zipping his trousers. Taking his camera, careful to get her flushed face in frame, he took several photographs of her spermed body – her fucked body. Quivering in the aftermath of her coming, she wasn't listening to his lewd comments, his commentary about the spunked valley of her cunt. But when he mentioned her coming back to the shop that evening for another photographic session, she sat bolt upright.

'No . . .' she began. 'It's over, isn't it? I mean, you've taken the photographs so there's no need for me to come here again.'

'You're forgetting,' he smiled, standing and placing the camera on the shelf. 'I have to see Father James.'

'Yes, but—'

'You'll want to know the outcome, won't you?'

'Of course. But it's not necessary to take any more photographs.'

'I'm afraid it is, Charlotte. I have to open the shop in ten minutes and I've only taken a few shots. I'm seeing Father James at six, so get here about seven and we'll finish off.'

'I can't come back this evening,' she murmured, climbing to her feet. 'I have to help my mother with something.'

'It's up to you. No photographs, no money. No money and . . . It won't take long. Say, an hour or so. You'd better dress and get out of here.'

Grabbing her clothes, Charlotte veiled her spermed body, wishing she didn't have to return yet again to the stockroom. Eyeing the whip where it lay on the floor, she bit her lip. He was going to want photographs of her naked buttocks, she knew as she finished dressing. But it would be the last session, she was sure as the man straightened his tie and adjusted his trousers. One last session, and she'd have the money to pay off the blackmailer. The radio and Father James . . . That was another matter, she reflected fearfully as she followed Goodhugh into the shop.

'I'm sure that I can talk Father James into allowing me to deal with the stolen radio rather than going to the police,' he said, opening the shop door.

'I hope so,' Charlotte murmured, her blouse sticking to her stomach, her vaginal valley drenched with sperm.

'I'll see you at seven. And don't worry. With my help, I'm certain you'll soon be out of trouble.'

Leaving the shop, Charlotte wondered whether to go home and face the wrath of her mother or go to the woods and see Marianne. Deciding to go home as sperm oozed from her inflamed vagina and soaked into her tight panties, she realized that she'd have to have a bath and change. If Marianne had gone by the time she got to the woods, she'd go to the girl's house. Noticing her mother hovering by the front door, she took a deep breath and tried to compose herself. Her hair was a mess, her clothes soaked with Goodhugh's sperm . . . But that was the least of her worries, she knew as she approached the woman and thought again about Father James. If Goodhugh couldn't persuade the priest to drop the matter, then the nightmare would really begin.

Chapter Seven

Charlotte's mother had lectured her for half an hour. Morals, right and wrong, etiquette . . . All hell would have been let loose had the woman known that her daughter had been crudely fucked by Goodhugh. Finally managing to convince her mother that she had to visit Marianne to work on their English projects together, Charlotte explained that she'd been sent home from school for that very reason. Far from happy, the woman agreed but demanded that Charlotte return home before five o'clock.

Leaving the cottage, her panties soaked with a blend of sperm and girl juice, Charlotte made her way to the sanctuary of the woods. Marianne would have gone by now, she was sure as she followed the winding path to the stream. Praying for the girl to be there, she knew that she had to confide in someone about her predicament, talk to someone so as to take at least some of the weight off her shoulders. Father James did nothing but condemn her, her mother wouldn't understand, Emily . . . There was only Marianne.

'Thank God you're here.' Charlotte smiled as she approached the girl.

'I wasn't going to wait much longer. Where have you been?'

'Talking to my mother,' Charlotte sighed, sitting on the grass next to her friend. 'And now I need to talk to you.'

'Oh?'

'I'm going to tell you things that you must never breathe a word of. Promise me you'll not say anything to anyone.'

'Yes, I promise,' the girl said, her blue eyes quizzical.

'I really don't know where to start.'

'At the beginning?' Marianne proffered.

'No, I'll start with the radio. Mr Goodhugh gave me a new radio from his shop and he's now saying that I stole it. As I left the shop with the radio—'

'Charlotte,' Marianne broke in excitedly. 'You know that new leather bag of mine?'

'Yes.'

'Mr Goodhugh gave it to me a few weeks ago.'

'He *gave* it to you?'

'He said that I could pay him whenever I had the money. Even if it was a month or two, it didn't matter. I was in his shop a few days later and he said that I'd put him in a terrible predicament because I'd stolen the bag. He didn't know whether to go to the police or not.'

'And he has photographs of you taking the bag?' Charlotte sighed knowingly.

'Yes.'

'Oh, God. That's exactly . . . I've been such a fool. There were times when I thought I was being naive, but he seemed to be genuinely trying to help me. He made me believe that the trouble I was in was my fault. The way he put it, it seemed that I'd got myself into serious trouble and he was doing his best to help me.'

'What kind of trouble?'

'All sorts.'

'He's a clever man,' Marianne sighed. 'And an evil one.'

'When I think back . . . He's well in with my mother, making out that he's some kind of saintly man who's trying to help with my upbringing. Father James has—'

SCHOOLGIRL LUST

'You do know that Goodhugh and the priest are the best of friends, don't you?'

'They've known each other for a long time,' Charlotte said. 'But they're not—'

'They've known each other since they were at school. Has Father James turned up at Goodhugh's yet?'

'Turned up? What do you mean?'

'The trick is that he turns up and discovers you naked. He goes on about God and starts to lecture you. Goodhugh then leaves the room and the priest . . . Well, he has his way with you.'

'Father James . . . I can't believe it,' Charlotte gasped.

'It's true. I have to visit the church and have sex with him.'

'*What?* You have sex with Father James in the church?'

'Yes. And so will you before long.'

Stunned by the girl's revelation, Charlotte stared blankly at the ground. Realizing how stupid she'd been, she recalled the priest condemning her for her wickedness. All along, he'd been in cahoots with Goodhugh, probably laughing together as they'd looked at the photographs and made their evil plans. Her life had been made hell by the wicked pair. But at least now she knew the shocking truth.

'What will happen if you stop visiting the church?' she finally asked, knowing what the answer would be.

'He'll show photographs to my parents. Photographs of me naked and—'

'We have to do something,' Charlotte breathed. 'Now we know that we're not alone, now that we have each other, we must do something to stop them.'

'I agree. But what?'

'I've got to go and see Goodhugh this evening. He's going

to speak to Father James about . . . It's such a long and complicated story.'

'If I turn up,' Marianne breathed. 'Yes, that's it. I'll turn up and—'

'No,' Charlotte smiled. 'I have a better idea. I'll tell Goodhugh that I saw the police talking to Father James.'

'What for? How will that help?'

'We have to set them against each other. Once they're suspicious of each other, distrust will set in. I don't know what good it will do, but it's a start.'

'I'm just wondering how many other girls there are,' Marianne breathed. 'All along, I've thought I was the only one. There might be a dozen or more girls.'

'Leather bags, radios, offering them money in return for a few photographs . . . He'd have no trouble blackmailing gullible teenage girls. God, *I* was gullible. Now I know that the whole thing's a trick, I feel much better. There's no way Goodhugh would show the photographs to my mother.'

'What makes you say that?'

'He'd jeopardize everything. If word got out about me and there are other girls he's using for sex, they'll all come out of hiding.'

'Yes, I see your point.'

'I'm going to start the ball rolling by telling Father James that there's a rumour going around school about Goodhugh having sex with several girls. In fact, I'll go to the church now.'

'I'll wait here for you,' Marianne said, reclining on the grass.

'OK, I won't be long.'

Feeling positive as she made her way to the church, Charlotte reckoned that she could set Goodhugh and the priest against other without too much trouble. But putting

SCHOOLGIRL LUST

an end to the nightmare wouldn't be enough. She wanted revenge for all she'd been forced to endure. Meeting the priest by the altar, she hung her head as if embarrassed and asked whether she could speak to him.

'Of course.' He smiled, looking around the church. 'There's something I want to talk to you about first.'

'Oh?'

'Stealing, Charlotte. Stealing a radio.'

'Who stole a radio?' she asked, feigning puzzlement.

'*You* did. You stole a radio from Mr Goodhugh's shop.'

'I *bought* a radio,' she frowned. 'I didn't steal it.'

'Charlotte, it's no good lying to me. Look at the way you've behaved already. Taking money in return for posing naked, trying to get Mr Goodhugh into trouble, lying to your mother . . .'

'But I didn't steal the radio.'

'How could you afford it, then? They're nearly forty pounds, Charlotte.'

'I've been saving. It's my mother's birthday soon and I thought she might like a new radio.'

'According to Mr Goodhugh—'

'That's what I wanted to talk to you about. There's a rumour going around my school that . . . I don't know how to tell you this, Father.'

'A rumour?' he echoed, his eyes frowning as he stared at her. 'What about?'

'There was a policeman at our school. Apparently, he wanted to speak to one of the girls. No one knew what it was about but then a rumour started going round.'

'And?'

'Mr Goodhugh has been having sex with girls from my school.'

'*What?*' The priest gasped, his hands visibly shaking. 'Er . . . tell me what people are saying.'

'They're saying that Mr Goodhugh has girls visiting his shop and he . . . he has sex with them.'

'And that's why the police were there?'

'I suppose so. Apparently, there's also another man who goes to the shop and has sex with the girls.'

'Who?' Father James asked, a tone of urgency in his voice. 'Who is this other man?'

'I don't know his name. One of the girls reckons that she knows who he is but she won't say.'

'I see,' he murmured, leaning on the altar. 'Who is this girl?'

'I don't know. She's not in my class.'

'Why are you telling me all this, Charlotte?'

'Because rumour has it that Mr Goodhugh blackmails girls. That's what he did to me – not that you'd believe me.'

'You did the right thing by coming to me. I'll . . . I'll be speaking to Mr Goodhugh later. No doubt there's been some mistake that can be easily rectified. Don't mention this to anyone, Charlotte. See if you can find out who the girl is that knows the identity of this other man and let me know.'

'Yes, I will.'

'This business with the radio . . . Not to worry. I'll be seeing Mr Goodhugh later so I'll ask him about it then.'

'I'd better be going,' Charlotte said.

'If you hear any more, let me know.'

'I will, Father.'

Leaving the church, Charlotte grinned. She'd certainly caused some confusion, but what would happen next? she wondered as she headed for the woods. Now that Father James thought the police had been questioning a girl, he'd tell Goodhugh and they'd have to be very careful. Although the business was becoming a game, she didn't forget the danger involved. Goodhugh might well devise a counter plan, she reflected. Once he'd spoken to the priest, he might come up with a scheme to . . . All she could do was wait and see what developed.

Finding Marianne by the stream, Charlotte sat by the girl's side and told her what she'd said to the priest. Marianne seemed jittery, not really listening as she fidgeted and fiddled with her blonde hair. Charlotte sensed that something was bothering her, but put it down to the problems that they'd been having with Goodhugh. Marianne must have had sleepless nights, Charlotte mused. Forced to have sex with Goodhugh *and* with Father James, she must have been through hell.

'Are you all right?' Charlotte finally asked.

'No, I . . . I've just seen Emily.'

'Oh?'

'She was looking for you. I said that I didn't know where you were and she had a go at me.'

'Had a go at you?'

'She told me to keep away from you. I don't know what her problem is, but she doesn't want me to see you.'

'She can be funny like that.'

'Funny? She went mad when I said that I'd not seen you. She didn't believe me and asked again where you were.'

'Emily is the least of our problems.'

'I don't want to stay here in case she comes back. Shall we walk through the woods?'

'OK,' Charlotte replied, pondering on Emily. 'You prefer the countryside to the town, don't you?' she asked.

'Yes, any day,' the girl smiled, her blue eyes sparkling. 'I hate the town. The people and the traffic . . . The town's no place for me.'

'Nor me,' Charlotte sighed. 'I hate people. I don't mean you . . . I mean people in general. They all rush around interfering in each other's business and destroying the peace and . . .' Goodhugh and the priest had interfered and caused destruction, Charlotte reflected. And now Emily was doing her best to cause trouble. 'What I'd like is to live in the middle of the woods, surrounded by trees rather than people.'

'And me. Charlotte, do you mind if I ask you something?'

'No, of course not.'

'Have you got a boyfriend?'

'No, I haven't. Why?'

'I just wondered. A few boys have asked me out but I've not felt comfortable with the idea. I'd rather be walking in the woods with someone like you than going into town with a boy. I don't just mean that I don't like the town – I don't want to be with a boy. They like loud music and are always trying to show off. With you, I feel calm, peaceful. We've not gone for a walk in a long time, have we?'

'No,' Charlotte murmured abstractedly. 'I suppose we've been busy, what with the English project and everything. Not to mention the nightmare of Goodhugh and that evil priest. Let's sit here for a while.'

Dropping to her knees, Marianne settled next to Charlotte on the soft grass in a small clearing. After her lesbian experiences with Emily, Charlotte now looked at Marianne in a different light. She was thinking about the girl's clitoris, the firm roundness of her young breasts. Her eyes focused on Marianne's naked thighs rather on than her pretty face, she wondered about her own uncharacteristic thoughts, her true sexual identity. Sex with Emily, and then taking Goodhugh's penis into her mouth, his sperm raining over her face . . . And having to endure the humiliation of his erect penis driving in and out of her vagina. She didn't know what she was becoming.

Charlotte took a deep breath as she thought about kissing Marianne. How would she react? It wasn't the done thing to kiss another girl out of the blue, she knew as she again imagined caressing the moist valley of her young vagina. But her teenage hormones were running wild, and she was having difficulty controlling her rising passion. Placing her hand on her friend's knee, she felt her stomach somersault. She eyed again the smooth flesh of the girl's inner thighs and thought of the alluring crack of her vagina as she stroked her knee. Running her fingers over the milk-white skin of Marianne's thigh, she realized that she'd never felt like this about anyone before. With Emily, it had been . . . She wasn't sure what it had been. Her heart racing, her hands trembling, she licked her full red lips as she wondered about tasting the warm cream within Marianne's sex valley.

If Emily knew what she was doing, if Father James discovered her in the woods with Marianne, caressing the girl's naked thigh . . . But there was no one else this deep in the woods. Off the main path, Charlotte and Marianne were safe from the prying eyes of the interfering and judgemental world. Safe from the eyes of God? But God would understand. He'd know that Charlotte sought comfort from loving physical contact. Had her mother been able to hold her, cuddle her and show her some affection . . . Perhaps then Satan wouldn't have come into her life.

'Charlotte,' Marianne breathed as the other girl's fingers tickled her inner thigh. 'What are you *doing*?'

'Touching you,' Charlotte murmured, her fingers dangerously close to the swell of her young friend's panties.

'Charlotte, you . . . you shouldn't do that.'

'I know I shouldn't. It's just that I . . .' She realized that she hadn't lost control at all as she smiled at the girl. She knew what she was doing – she had complete control over her actions. 'I shouldn't do it,' she breathed. 'But I *want* to do it.'

'No, don't,' Marianne protested as Charlotte pressed her fingertips into the soft warmth of her panties. 'This is wrong.'

'It's not wrong to . . . to love you. Lie down, Marianne. Let me love you properly.'

As Marianne lay back on the grass and parted her long legs, Charlotte tugged the girl's knee-length skirt up over her stomach and gazed longingly at the red silk of her tight panties. The veil concealing the girl's sex lips was flimsy, easily torn down. Only a thin layer of silk lay between her mouth and the girl's wet vaginal valley. Slipping her inquisitive fingers beneath the material, she massaged the swell of Marianne's fleshy love lips, kneaded the warm cushions rising either side of her crack. The warm moisture within her valley of desire lubricating her fingers, Charlotte grinned as the girl closed her eyes and let out a long sigh of satisfaction. Marianne had succumbed to her sensual touch, Charlotte knew as she slipped her fingertip between the wet petals of her inner labia. She was putty in her hands.

But the thought of Goodhugh loomed in Charlotte's mind, spoiling her intimate time with her young friend. At least she now knew of the man's treachery, and was sure that she could put an end to his evil games. Father James wouldn't present a problem, she was sure. A man in his position couldn't afford trouble and would be sure to back off now that he thought the police were sniffing around. Feeling positive as she thrust her finger deep into the wet heat of Marianne's sex sheath, Charlotte decided to see less of Emily. Everything was going to work out, she was sure as she slipped her finger out of her friend's vaginal sheath. Watching as the girl lifted her buttocks and pulled her panties off, she smiled. Everything was going to work out.

'That's nice,' Marianne breathed, opening her thighs wide as Charlotte thrust two fingers into the tightening duct of her vagina. The squelching of the girl's juices was music to Charlotte's ears as she pistoned her tight sex cavern. Gasping, writhing, the girl arched her back and pulled her T-shirt up. Watching wide-eyed as she lifted her bra clear of her firm breasts, Charlotte knew that she'd found her real soulmate as she focused on the dark discs of Marianne's areolae, the sensitive protrusions of her succulent milk teats. Marianne was offering her body in the name of love, and Charlotte was eager to show the girl all the love she had. But still the thought of Goodhugh nagged her, gnawed at her. And the thought of her mother's wrath should she discover . . . She'd talk to the woman, tell her that she was never going to see Emily again. Everything was going to work out.

Encircling Marianne's erect nipple with her fingertip, Charlotte continued to massage the girl's inner vaginal flesh, inducing her sex milk to flow in torrents over her thrusting fingers. Marianne gasped and writhed, her breathing deep and heavy as her pleasure rose from her contracting womb. The girl's long blonde hair veiling her flushed face, Charlotte was fascinated by her quivering, her whimpers of delight as she tossed her head from side to side. Both of them were learning in their new-found lesbianism, their illicit loving, and Charlotte knew that they'd meet again in the woods and discover all there was to know about sex and loving.

'Oh, yes,' Marianne breathed as Charlotte left her sensitive nipple alone and massaged the hard nubble of her clitoris. 'Don't stop,' she murmured, parting her legs further as her body began to shake violently. Charlotte could feel her own juices of lesbian arousal pouring into her tight panties as she drove a third finger deep into her wailing friend's vaginal cavern. To masturbate each other simultaneously would be wondrous, she knew as she rubbed the girl's clitoris faster. Recalling Emily trying to force her mouth against her swollen clitoris, she leaned over and parted Marianne's vaginal lips, opening wide her valley of desire.

'God,' Marianne gasped as Charlotte swept her wet tongue over the solid protrusion of pleasure nestling within her yawning sex crack. Lapping up her lubricious juices, Charlotte breathed in the heady fragrance of Marianne's sex-scent, her own arousal soaring as she sucked and mouthed her friend's pulsating clitoris. Lost in her sexual delirium, she fingered the girl's fiery vaginal shaft, her juices of lust squelching as she sucked and licked her clitoris until her body became rigid. Crying out as her orgasm erupted within the pulsating nodule of her clitoris, Marianne threw her head back and gritted her teeth as the agonizing pleasure gripped her very soul. Her juices of desire gushing from her bloated vaginal sheath, splattering her inner thighs as she thrashed about on the grass, she screamed as her orgasm peaked. Her breasts heaving, her stomach jerkily rising and falling, she parted her thighs to the extreme, opening the sexual centre of her teenage body to Charlotte's pink tongue.

Withdrawing her fingers from the girl's rhythmically contracting sex sheath, Charlotte yanked her swollen outer labia wide apart and locked her mouth to her open hole of desire. Sucking out the girl's orgasmic cream, tonguing the deep shaft of her fiery vagina, she drank from her trembling body, swallowing the lubricious product of her incredible orgasm. The taste of girl-sex driving her wild, Charlotte forced her lips hard against the pink funnel of flesh surrounding the portal to her inner sheath, pushing her tongue deep into her writhing body.

'Oh, Charlotte,' Marianne breathed, her fingernails digging into the soft grass as she arched her back. Lost in her sexual delirium, Charlotte forced the girl's thighs wider apart, burying her head between her legs and pushing her tongue deep into her spasming vagina. 'God, no,' the trembling girl gasped as her orgasm intensified, her juices of lust spewing from her vaginal throat and filling Charlotte's mouth. On and on her pleasure coursed through her young body, her breasts undulating, her eyes rolling as she cried out in her lesbian lust. Her vaginal duct draining, her clitoris deflating, she shuddered her last orgasmic shudder and curled up into a ball.

'Are you all right?' Charlotte asked, licking the girl-juice from her lips. 'Marianne, are you OK?' Writhing, gasping for breath, the girl rolled this way and that, the creamy fluid of orgasm pouring from her gaping vaginal mouth and running in torrents over the milk-white flesh of her thighs. Charlotte glimpsed the brown star of her bottom-hole as she rolled onto her stomach and spread her legs. Her sex-drenched vaginal lips bulging between her shapely thighs, her buttocks parted, Marianne's young body invited Charlotte's fingers, her tongue. Pushing her legs wide apart, Charlotte parted her buttocks and buried her face between the warm globes of flesh.

Quivering as Charlotte's tongue encircled the brown tissue nestling within her anal crease, Marianne whimpered incoherent words of love. Pushing her tongue into the tight hole, tasting the inner flesh of her rectum, Charlotte finally lost all control of her senses and forced the girl's bottom orbs painfully further apart. Fervently mouthing and sucking at her friend's anal inlet, she groped between the girl's thighs and forced three fingers into the drenched sheath of her tight vagina.

'Oh, yes!' Marianne cried as Charlotte slipped her tongue out of her bottom-hole and drove two fingers into her private duct. 'God, that's wonderful.'

'It's disgusting!' Father James gasped, emerging from the bushes with Goodhugh following hard on his heels.

'I have the evidence right here,' Goodhugh chortled, brandishing a camera as Charlotte yanked her fingers out of her friend's hot anal canal and stared wide-eyed at the leering men.

'Charlotte, remove your clothes,' the priest ordered the girl.

'No, I . . .' she stammered, huddling close to Marianne.

'In that case, we'll develop the film and your mother will be shown the photographs. Your parents, too, Marianne. They will see exactly what kind of dirty little whore of a daughter they have.'

'Please,' Marianne cried, tugging her T-shirt down to conceal the firm mounds of her young breasts. 'I was only—'

'Never have I witnessed such vulgarity. You're nothing but sluts. Dirty, filthy, debased, wanton sluts.'

'From now on, you'll both do exactly as you're told,' Goodhugh grinned. 'We have enough on both of you not only to have you expelled from your school and disowned by your parents, but prosecuted for shoplifting as well. Your clothes, Charlotte. Now, please.'

Unbuttoning her blouse as Marianne sobbed, Charlotte knew that there was no way out of the nightmare now.

SCHOOLGIRL LUST

Goodhugh was right, he had more than enough evidence to destroy her young life. Revealing her teenage breasts as she unhooked her bra, she clambered to her feet and tugged her skirt down her long legs. Her feeling of humiliation rising as she pulled her wet panties down, exposing the shaved lips of her vagina, she gazed at the priest's wide eyes, the evil reflected there.

'And you, Marianne,' Goodhugh snapped. 'We want you naked, too.'

'No, I'm not going to—'

'You'll do as you're bloody well told,' the man hissed. 'You're already half naked, you filthy slut. Now remove the rest of your clothes. Unless, that is, you want *me* to strip you.'

'Charlotte has a beautiful cunt.' Father James grinned in his devilry, staring at the girl's naked vulval flesh. 'A cunt I'm looking forward to fucking and spunking.'

'You're supposed to be a *priest!*' Charlotte gasped, her heart banging hard against her chest as the man stared at her girl crack.

'And you're supposed to be a decent young woman. Not a filthy lesbian tramp.'

'Before we fuck her, she should be punished,' Goodhugh murmured. 'The trouble she's caused me, and now the lies she's been telling you about the police . . .' Snapping a branch off a nearby bush, he grinned. 'Severely punished for her lies, her thieving, her sluttish behaviour with another girl, her wickedness . . .'

'No!' Charlotte screamed as Goodhugh slapped the palm of his hand with the branch.

'You're a slut, Charlotte. A filthy, lying, thieving slut.'

'Both get on all fours,' the priest ordered his victims. 'You came running to me with your lies, Charlotte. The police haven't been to the school, I've checked. No one's been spreading rumours about girls having sex in the shop. Now get on all fours and stick your bums out.'

Complying, Charlotte rested her head on the ground and projected the firm globes of her naked bottom as Marianne removed the rest of her clothes. This really was the end, she knew. The end of a normal life and the beginning of a living hell. She'd been stupid to believe that she could get away with causing trouble between the evil pair, she knew as she grimaced in readiness for the inevitable thrashing. Even if she *did* go to the police, they'd never believe that a man of God and a respected shopkeeper would behave in such despicable ways.

'This is for opening your mouth,' Goodhugh said, bringing the branch down across the pale flesh of Charlotte's firm buttocks.

'Please!' she screamed as the rough branch lashed her milk-white flesh.

'And this, Marianne, is for opening *your* mouth.'

'*No!*' the girl cried as the branch bit into her twitching anal orbs.

'The Lord would want these slags punished most severely for their wickedness,' Father James said. 'They have used their bodies purely for their own sexual satisfaction. They have committed vile and debased sins of the flesh. Masturbating each other, going with men . . .'

'You made us do it!' Charlotte cried.

'We didn't make you push your fingers into another girl's arse,' the man of God returned. 'You are both common, vile harlots. I have never met such disgusting little whores as you.' Turning to Goodhugh, he grinned. 'They should punish each other,' he said. 'They should thrash each other for their sins.'

SCHOOLGIRL LUST

'I agree,' Goodhugh replied. 'Marianne, you'll take the branch and thrash this little whore-slag until she screams for mercy. If you don't, then *I'll* thrash *you* to within an inch of your life.'

Clambering to her feet, the girl took the branch from Goodhugh and stood behind Charlotte's naked buttocks. They both knew that, unless they obeyed their masters, they'd be severely thrashed. Either way, they'd have their naked buttocks cruelly lashed. But it was better to punish each other than to have the men beat them. Turning her head, Charlotte looked up at Marianne as she raised the branch high above her head. The thrashing would be followed by crude sex, Charlotte knew as she rested her head on the ground and squeezed her eyes shut. Both men would take her, crudely fuck and use her teenage body again and again.

'No!' she screamed as the branch swished through the still summer air and landed across the twitching globes of her pert bottom. Again, the rough twigs of the branch bit into her anal spheres, the stinging pain permeating the flesh of her young bottom. Threatened by the cruel men, Marianne continued the gruelling beating, repeatedly bringing the branch down across Charlotte's crimsoned buttocks. The thrashing numbing Charlotte's bottom, she pushed her face hard against the grass, breathing in the scent of decaying leaves. Her twitching buttocks burning, her naked body shaking uncontrollably, she screamed as the coarse bark caught the rise of her hairless vaginal lips bulging between her young thighs. Again, the branch flailed her swollen sex pads, the agonizing pain permeating her vulval flesh as she dug her fingernails into the grass.

'That will do for now,' the priest said, taking the branch from Marianne as Charlotte rolled onto her side, writhing on the ground like a snake in agony. 'For your evil ways, Charlotte, you shall receive your just reward. The Lord has charged me to punish you for your blasphemy. He has—'

'I have not blasphemed!' the girl cried.

'You have used the temple of your body for the sole purpose of sexual pleasure. You have wilfully desecrated the shrine of your naked body and brought shame upon the Lord.'

'No, I haven't! I was forced to—'

'The Lord has bestowed upon me the power to punish you in whichever way I think fit. Get on all fours again.'

Obediently taking her position again as Marianne watched in horror, Charlotte buried her face in the grass. Goodhugh would visit the cottage every Monday, she'd be forced to go to the church and give her body to the priest . . . And there was nothing she could do to save herself from her terrible fate. There was no need for lies and trickery now. Goodhugh only needed to snap his fingers and she'd have to obey his every perverted command. Father James would only have to beckon her with his finger, and she'd have to fall to her knees before the man of God and attend his every sexual need.

'Marianne, part the girl's buttocks and push your index fingers into her arsehole,' Father James ordered the terrified girl.

'No, I—'

'Do it!'

Kneeling behind her friend, Marianne slipped her fingers into the tight sheath of Charlotte's bottom, tears streaming down her flushed cheeks as she gazed into the dank portal to the girl's bowels. Her blue eyes staring in horror at the priest as he ordered her to push her tongue deep into Charlotte's open anal inlet, she knew that she'd have to commit the debased act. Leaning forward, her cheeks sandwiched between the other girl's warm buttocks, she pushed her tongue out and tasted the brown tissue of her anus. The priest ordering her to stretch the girl's bottom-hole wide open, she closed her eyes and took a deep breath. Her tongue entering the gaping, hot duct as she stretched the girl's private hole wide open, she savoured the bitter-sweet taste of her friend's anal tube.

'Tongue-fuck her arse,' Goodhugh instructed her, chuckling wickedly as he watched the girl commit the crude act. Her lips pressed hard against Charlotte's brown tissue, her tongue embedded deep within her dank anal shaft, Marianne knew that she'd regularly be forced to perform crude sexual acts with her friend. On her visits to the church to have sex with the priest, she'd be accompanied by Charlotte. They'd both be forced to attend his perverted sexual needs.

Marianne's naked body jolted as her own firm buttocks were yanked apart. She closed her eyes as she felt a bulbous knob pressing hard against her anal iris. It was Father James, she knew as he forced her buttocks further apart, opening the inlet to her rectal duct. She'd endured anal sex with him many times during her visits to the church. This was nothing new, but to have her bottom fucked while she tongue-fucked Charlotte's bottom . . . This was only the beginning.

Her tongue driving deeper into Charlotte's rectum as the priest's solid penis thrust into her anal canal, Marianne felt her pelvic cavity inflate to capacity. As he began his vulgar anal fucking, his swinging balls battering the swell of her vaginal lips, she opened her eyes and watched Goodhugh sit with his thighs either side of Charlotte's head, his erect penis pointing skyward.

'Suck it, bitch,' the man breathed, yanking the girl's head

up by her hair. 'Suck the spunk out of my knob.' Raising her head, Charlotte opened her mouth and sucked on Goodhugh's purple knob as Marianne's tongue explored the inner flesh of her rectal sheath. The priest gasping in his anal fucking, Marianne knew that she was about to have her bowels pumped full of sperm. She'd become used to the debauchery, the anal abuse, but knew that Charlotte had only just embarked on the road to sexual degradation. There was more in store for the young girl, particularly when the priest had her naked body tied over the altar.

'Yes!' Father James cried, his lower belly slapping Marianne's anal orbs as his knob swelled and his spunk gushed into the tight duct of her young arse. Goodhugh's knob throbbing as he gasped in his own debased pleasure, he clutched Charlotte's head and pumped his sperm into her gobbling mouth. As the men drained their balls, the girls both taking their share of gushing spunk, Charlotte felt her juices of arousal spewing from the gaping entrance to her young vagina. But this was enforced arousal, she tried to convince herself as she sucked on Goodhugh's throbbing knob and swallowed his salty sperm. Her clitoris swelling, pulsating, she did her best to not to think of Marianne's tongue teasing the inner flesh of her tight bottom-hole. She wasn't enjoying her lesbian lover's anal tonguing. Was she?

'Christ,' Goodhugh whispered as voices echoed through the trees. 'Someone's coming this way.' His spent cock slipping out of Charlotte's mouth as he leaped to his feet and zipped his trousers, he ordered the girls to be at the church at seven that evening. 'Be there, or be in real trouble,' he hissed as the priest yanked his deflating cock out of Marianne's spermed bottom-hole and clambered to his feet. Leaving the girls' naked bodies sprawled on the grass, the men adjusted their clothing and left the clearing.

Tears streaming down her face, sperm dribbling from her mouth, Charlotte grabbed her clothes and began dressing.

'I don't want to go to the church,' she whimpered as Marianne tugged her panties up, veiling her sperm-oozing bottom-hole.

'We have no choice,' the girl sighed. 'We have to go.'

'But . . .'

'Don't worry. I'll think of a way out of this if it's the last thing I do. We'll have to go to the church this evening, but—'

'And tomorrow and the next day,' Charlotte sobbed.

'Not if I can help it. Hurry up and we'll get out of here. The last thing we need is to be caught half naked in the woods.'

'I'm not going, Marianne. I don't care what happens, I am not going to the church.' Slipping into the bushes, Charlotte turned and smiled at her friend. 'I'm running away,' she said, disappearing into the undergrowth.

Shaking her head, Marianne finished dressing and brushed her long blonde hair away from her flushed face. She knew that, if Charlotte didn't turn up, she'd be severely punished. There again, perhaps running away was the best thing to do, she reflected. Running away might not be such a bad idea after all.

Chapter Eight

Not knowing what to do or where to go, Charlotte finally went home and told her mother that she was feeling unwell again. Lying on her bed, her mind racked with confusion, she glanced at the clock. One hour before she had to be at the church. One hour before she was to endure sexual abuse at the hands – and penises – of two men. Her world seemingly falling apart, her thrashed buttocks stinging like hell, she again contemplated running away. But it wouldn't solve anything. Wondering whether to call Goodhugh's bluff, she thought about telling him and his perverted friend to go to hell.

The doorbell rang and she leaped off the bed and dashed across the room. It was Father James. She could hear his deep voice. Friendly, slimy, evil. Had he come to expose her? she wondered. Was he displaying the photographs of Goodhugh's penis in her mouth, sperming over her face? Perhaps he was showing her mother the pictures of Marianne in the woods, Charlotte's finger embedded deep within the girl's anal tract. Opening the door, Charlotte listened to the conversation.

'I'm sorry to hear that she's not well,' the priest said sympathetically.

'She's resting on her bed,' her mother said. 'Why don't you go up and see her?'

'Well, I'm not sure that it would be right to—'

'Don't be so silly, Father,' the woman chuckled. 'She'll be delighted to see you.'

'In that case, I will.'

'Would you like a cup of tea? I was about to make some anyway.'

'That would be lovely. I'll be down shortly.'

Her whole body trembling as she heard the priest climbing the stairs, Charlotte looked about the room. There was no escape, nowhere to hide. Coming to the cottage like that, he was as bad as Goodhugh, she reflected – if not worse. Her mother had to be told the truth about the evil men, but Charlotte knew that she'd be implicated. She was heavily involved and would appear to have been a willing participant in the lewd sex sessions. As the priest tapped on the door and entered the room, she sat on the edge of the bed and prayed that he'd believe she wasn't feeling well.

'I hope you're coming to the church later,' he said, pressing his back against the door to close it.

'No, I don't feel well,' she replied softly as the catch clicked. 'I have a bad stomach.'

'In that case, you'd better stay here and rest.'

'What . . . what are you going to do? I mean, if I don't go . . .'

'I have ten minutes or so,' he smiled. 'Time enough.'

'Time enough for what?'

'Time enough to enjoy your pretty mouth, your wet tongue. There's no need for you to go to the church, Charlotte. You can suck me here, in your room.'

'No, I—'

'I'm not prepared to tolerate any nonsense, Charlotte. You will do exactly as you're told, when you're told. Do you understand?'

'You can't come here and—'

SCHOOLGIRL LUST

'I'm warning you, my girl.'

'Not here, in my bedroom. For God's sake . . .'

'The choice is yours,' he grinned, lifting his cassock and exposing his erect penis as he stood before the pale-faced girl. 'You can either suck the spunk out of my cock here, or come over to the church later.'

'No, I won't do it,' she gasped, eyeing the solid shaft of his penis, his heavy balls. 'My mother's downstairs and—'

'And I'll show her the photographs unless you suck my cock.'

'Please, you can't come here and do this,' she whimpered as he retracted his foreskin, exposing the swollen globe of his glistening knob.

'Suck my cock and swallow my spunk or you'll find yourself in real trouble.'

Gazing at the man's ballooning knob, his sperm slit, Charlotte felt her stomach churning as she again thought of her mother downstairs. If the woman knew, if she could see how Father James was behaving . . . But even if she *did* walk into the room, the priest would turn the situation round and Charlotte would be accused of whoredom. Watching the man knead his heavy balls, she decided to get the sordid act over with. At least she wouldn't have to go to the church and endure Goodhugh's sexual abuse, she mused.

Moving her head forward, she parted her full red lips and sucked his glans into her wet mouth. Gasping, the priest clutched her head, rocking his hips and fucking her pretty mouth as she moaned through her nose. She could hear her mother making the tea, the cups and saucers rattling as the man of God fucked her mouth. There was no escaping the wicked man, she knew as his swinging balls repeatedly battered her chin. What with Goodhugh regularly visiting the cottage, and now the priest . . .

'Use your tongue, you filthy whore-slut,' he hissed in his wickedness, withdrawing his solid organ until her wet lips enveloped just the swollen crown of his penis. Snaking her tongue over the silky-smooth surface of his glans, she wondered whether the nightmare would ever end. Unless she could get her hands on the photographs, the evidence, this wanton abuse might continue for years. Even if she married and had children, Goodhugh and the priest would still have a hold over her.

'Get your tits out,' the man breathed, watching the girl's lips rolling along his salivated shaft. 'Undo your blouse and get your tits out.' Her trembling fingers unbuttoning her blouse as she sucked and mouthed his throbbing knob, she looked up at him. Her dark eyes wide, she watched him gasping in his male pleasure as his swollen knob once more repeatedly drove to the back of her throat. He *was* evil, she reflected, lifting her bra clear of her pert mammary spheres. After all he'd said to her in the church about prostituting herself . . . She couldn't believe that this was the same man. He was a hypocrite. He was the Devil's advocate.

Recalling Marianne's words, Charlotte wondered how many other girls were being blackmailed, threatened and sexually abused by Father James and his vile friend. There might be a dozen or more, she thought fearfully, his pubic curls tickling her nose as he thrust his bulbous knob deep into her hot mouth. The photographs would be in Goodhugh's flat above his shop, she was sure as the priest positioned his purple glans again between the softness of her full lips and ordered her to lick and suck his knob. If she could break into the flat and—

'Coming,' the cleric finally gasped, clutching Charlotte's head tighter to ensure that she didn't escape swallowing the liquid fruits of male orgasm. His sperm jetting from his

SCHOOLGIRL LUST

knob-slit, bathing her tongue, dribbling down her chin and splattering the elongated teats of her teenage breasts, he gasped as his heavy balls drained. Charlotte did her best to swallow the evidence of oral sex, but her mouth overflowed, the white fluid running over the mounds of her breasts and dripping onto her skirt. She'd have to change before her mother saw her, she reflected as the priest's knob throbbed and pumped out his spunk. Deciding to have a bath and go to bed when the evil man had satisfied his base desires, she looked up at him as her mother called out.

'The tea's ready, Father,' the woman called.

'I won't be a minute,' he replied as Charlotte sucked the last of his spunk from his deflating knob. 'You did well,' he whispered, withdrawing his saliva-slick penis from the girl's spermed mouth and lowering his cassock. 'I'll expect you at the church at seven.'

'No,' she gasped, licking her wet lips and wiping the sperm from the mounds of her young breasts. 'You said—'

'I've changed my mind,' he grinned, moving to the door. 'Be there at seven or . . . I don't think I need tell you what will happen if you don't turn up.'

As he left the room, Charlotte hung her head and cried. Her gracious femininity stripped, the temple of her once unsullied body crudely desecrated, she was for ever a slave to the priest and his wicked accomplice. Easing her bra over her sperm-starched breasts, she buttoned her blouse. Again wondering if she could get her hands on the photographic evidence, she also wondered whether she could get into Goodhugh's flat. If Marianne kept the man busy in the church, it might be possible to retrieve the photographs.

'Father James has just left,' Charlotte's mother announced as she entered the room. 'Look at the state of you, girl. Tidy yourself up and do something with your hair. You're to go to the church and help Father James with—'

'I don't feel well,' Charlotte broke in.

'You've taken time off school and . . . You've been feigning a stomach-ache for too long, Charlotte. Now get yourself ready and go to the church. Apart from anything else, the fresh air will do you good.'

'But—'

'Not another word. What's that white stuff all down your skirt?'

'Er . . . it's toothpaste.'

'Clean yourself up and go to the church. When you get back . . . What's that radio doing there?'

Charlotte followed her mother's gaze to the windowsill. 'Mr Goodhugh gave it to me,' she replied, wishing she'd hidden it beneath the bed along with her red miniskirt.

'He's a kind man, Charlotte. A decent, upright man. I just hope you appreciate all he's doing for you. And you should be grateful for the interest Father James is taking in you, too. Now, get ready.'

As the older woman left the room, Charlotte sighed. The priest was a clever man, she reflected, tugging her sperm-stained skirt down her long legs and gazing at the swell of her wet panties. Both men were not only clever but wicked, a dangerous combination. Changing into a long skirt and clean blouse, Charlotte decided to get to the church early. She might learn something, possibly where the photographs were hidden. If she hid and listened to the men talking, she might learn a lot. With luck, they'd discuss other girls they were blackmailing and using for perverted sex.

Leaving the cottage, she made her way to the church and crept through the graveyard. Squatting below the open office window, she could hear the evil pair talking but

SCHOOLGIRL LUST

couldn't work out what they were saying. Goodhugh was saying something about a young girl, but who? Catching the odd word – photographs, whip – she wondered whether Marianne had arrived. Realizing that she was going to get nowhere like this, she decided to slip into the church and hide in the shadows. She had to discover more about their sordid scam, she knew as she walked around the building to the main door.

The cold air hitting her as she entered the church, she shuddered. Where was God now? she wondered, gazing at the crucifix above the altar. Where was Lucifer? The murmur of the men's voices was coming from the office so she crept down the aisle and squatted behind the pews. Goodhugh was talking about Sharon, a girl Charlotte didn't know. From what he was saying, Sharon was another victim of their cruel sexual abuse. Deciding to try to locate the girl, and any others who had fallen prey to the depraved pair, she wondered again where Marianne had got to.

'Ah, there you are,' the priest grinned, towering above Charlotte. 'It's no good hiding. Take all your clothes off and stand by the altar.'

'I think we should talk about—' she began shakily.

'We'll talk about nothing. Do as I tell you, or else.'

'I'll get the rope,' Goodhugh called from the office doorway.

'Hurry up, Charlotte,' the priest snapped. 'You don't want to be here all night, do you? I wouldn't want to have to tell your mother that you didn't turn up and I saw you in the graveyard having sex with some young lad.'

Walking to the altar, Charlotte unbuttoned her blouse and dropped the garment to the floor. This was becoming rather too regular, she reflected, unhooking her bra and peeling the silk cups away from the delicious mounds of her sperm-starched breasts. Tugging her skirt down as Goodhugh emerged from the office with several lengths of rope, she stepped out of the garment and stood before the altar in her wet panties. As she watched Goodhugh throw the ropes over the altar, she knew instinctively that she was about to endure the worst sexual abuse yet.

'Take your panties off and lean over the altar,' Father James ordered her. Obediently slipping her panties down and kicking them aside, exposing the fleshy cushions of her hairless vaginal lips, she leaned over the altar and closed her eyes. Trembling as ropes were tied around her ankles, holding her feet wide apart, her arms pulled across the altar and her wrists secured, she jumped as fingers ran over the firm moons of her thrashed buttocks. There was no point in complaining, she knew as her tensed anal spheres were rudely parted, exposing the brown eye of her tightly closed anus. She was a slave to her captors, her body theirs for the taking – the crude defiling.

Shaking as a finger slipped past her anal sphincter and drove deep into the dank heat of her rectum, she grimaced. First a finger, and then . . . She knew only too well what she was going to be forced to endure as fingers groped between her parted thighs, massaging the swell of her naked vaginal lips. Wondering for the umpteenth time how she'd ever got herself into such a horrendous situation, she breathed in the musky smell of the altar cloth and again thought back to that fateful Saturday morning. If only she'd not talked to Emily about the creamy substance between her legs, if only Emily hadn't bought the miniskirt . . . If only.

'She needs to be punished most severely,' the priest said sternly. 'Lock the door and I'll get the whip.'

'Please!' Charlotte whimpered as the finger withdrew

SCHOOLGIRL LUST

from her tight anal sheath with a loud sucking sound. 'Please don't—'

'And gagged, if she's going to start complaining.'

'No, no, I won't complain,' she said softly, squeezing the smooth globes of her buttocks together in readiness for the whip.

The first lash of the cat-of-nine-tails jolting her naked body, she bit her lip and tried not to scream. The deafening crack of the whip resounding around the church as the leather tails swished through the air again and bit into her weal-lined buttocks, she clung to the altar in desperation as the men chuckled in their wickedness. Finally crying out as the agonizing pain permeated her crimsoned buttocks, her tethered body convulsing wildly, she begged for mercy. Her head lifted and her wet panties stuffed into her mouth, she knew she was going to have to endure at least an hour of sexual torture as the tails repeatedly swished through the air and flailed the stinging flesh of her firm buttocks.

Again wondering where Marianne was as the thrashing ceased and a heavy blanket was thrown over her head, she wondered what was going on. There were movements behind her, more than two people, she was sure as she listened to feet scuffing on the stone floor. In the dark beneath the blanket, she listened intently to whispers, male whispers. She heard a belt buckle, a zip, clothing rustling. She knew that she was about to be crudely taken, her teenage body fucked and pumped full of sperm.

A bulbous knob slid up and down the yawning valley of her vagina and she gasped as the swollen glans slipped between the slippery-wet petals of her inner lips and drove deep into her tightening sex sheath. Sure that there were several voices whispering, she wondered whether Goodhugh and the priest had invited other men to use and abuse her naked body. Hoping that she was wrong, she moaned through her nose as the penis within her tight vaginal duct withdrew and then thrust back into her naked body. Again and again, the massive organ drove into the hugging sheath of her teenage pussy, repeatedly inflating her pelvic cavity as gasps of male pleasure reverberated around the church. Heavy balls pummelling the hairless lips of her vagina, a swollen glans battering the soft hardness of her ripe cervix, she froze as the organ slipped out of her girl-sheath and the ballooning knob pressed hard against the brown tissue of her anal orifice.

Her naked body shaking violently as the bulbous knob pressed harder against her tightly closed anal inlet, she knew that the portal to her bowels would soon open to accommodate the man's erect organ. This was the most vile degradation possible, she thought as she imagined the solid penile shaft thrusting deep into her bowels, completely impaling her teenage body. Moaning through her nose as she bit on her panties-gag, she thought she was going to split open as her brown ring began to yield, her rectal throat swallowing the invading cock-head. The solid penile shaft gliding along the dank passage of her rectal canal, painfully stretching her brown ring wide open, she couldn't believe what was happening to her.

To be treated like this without even being able to see her abuser was horrendous. It could be anyone, she reflected as the rock-hard organ withdrew and thrust back into her hot rectum, the swinging balls slapping the swollen lips rising either side of her sex-drenched vaginal ravine. She pictured the village doctor standing behind her, fucking her bottom. The postman, a schoolteacher . . . The man's lower belly repeatedly meeting her rounded buttocks as he crudely thrust his penis in and out of her inflamed bottom-hole, low whispers and chuckles resounding around the church, she found herself wondering what her mother was doing. Was she making tea? Perhaps she was listening to the radio while her daughter was enduring enforced anal sex.

'Yes,' the man breathed, his solid shaft swelling, his knob ballooning as he pumped his spunk deep into Charlotte's hot bowels. Increasing his fucking rhythm as his sperm gushed from his orgasming glans, he gripped her hips and drove his rock-hard member into her rectum with such force that her head bobbed with the crude fucking. She could feel the gushing liquid of male orgasm filling her tight anal cylinder, lubricating the pistoning cock-head as the man grunted in his coming. This was something she'd never dreamed of, an act she'd had no knowledge of. But it was now an act she was to endure on a regular basis, she knew as the man's penis began deflating in the aftermath of its anal sperming.

The spent penis finally withdrawing, the spermed knob leaving the inflamed entrance to her rectum with a squelching sound, she breathed deeply through her nose and tried to relax. Sperm oozing from her anal eye, running over the small bridge of skin between her sex holes and trickling into her gaping vaginal entrance, she jumped as her buttocks were painfully yanked apart. Another swollen knob pressing against her burning anal iris, she prayed for the man to pump out his sperm quickly and leave her to recover from her ordeal. Was it Goodhugh or the priest? she pondered as a rock-hard penile shaft glided along her sperm-flooded rectal channel. Or was it yet another man?

'God, she's tight,' the man murmured, his heavy balls coming to rest against her naked pussy lips as he drove his cock fully home. Charlotte wasn't sure which man it was, but it didn't matter. Once the illicit act was over, she hoped she'd be allowed home. The evil pair wouldn't be able to take her again, would they? Once they'd drained their swinging balls, pumped out their sperm, they'd free her. Were there other men waiting in a queue? she wondered fearfully as warm hands grabbed her naked hips and the forceful penile shafting of her anal canal began. Who was the man grunting behind her, crudely arse-fucking her? In such a small village where everyone knew everyone, Goodhugh and the priest wouldn't risk allowing anyone in on their secret. Would they?

Her bowels filling with sperm again as the man gasped in his anal fucking, Charlotte bit hard on her panties, praying for freedom as her naked body rocked with the crude pistoning. The white lubricant oozing from her stretched bottom-hole and running down between her fleshy vaginal lips, rushes of air left her nostrils with each shafting of her tight arsehole. Again and again, the man's organ drove into her rectum, the bubbling sperm lubricating his screwing as he arse-fucked her teenage body. The spent cock finally gliding out of her inflamed duct, she grimaced as the leather whip again flailed the burning globes of her pert buttocks. Tears streaming from her eyes, she tensed her naked body as the leather tails repeatedly swished through the air, cracking loudly across the stinging flesh of her teenage bottom.

'I'd like some photographs of the candle,' Goodhugh said. Charlotte heard movements behind her as the cruel thrashing halted and someone rudely parted the stinging orbs of her buttocks. A cold object pressing against the inflamed tissue surrounding her anal eye, she knew that the evil pair were going to force a church candle deep into the well-oiled duct of her bottom. Beneath the blanket, she listened to the male whispers, the scuffing of feet. Sure that there were more than two men, she squeezed her eyes shut as the candle painfully stretched open the brown entrance to her bowels and glided into her once-private duct.

Believing that she was going to split open, Charlotte held her breath as the huge candle drove deeper into the restricted channel of her rectum. Her pelvic cavity inflating, the delicate brown tissue of her anal rosebud painfully stretched around the solid wax shaft, she knew that this was only the beginning of the sexual corruption of her naked body. Morning, noon and night, they'd call upon her to satisfy their vulgar desires, to suck the sperm out of their knobs, to open her arsehole to their rigid cocks. There was nothing the evil pair wouldn't do in the name of depraved sex. And there was nothing Charlotte could do to stop them.

'That's great,' Goodhugh murmured, the camera shutter clicking as he focused on the waxen phallus emerging from the girl's abused anal canal. Again wondering where Marianne had got to, Charlotte lifted her head as the blanket was removed and the gag yanked out of her mouth. Staring at a huge sheet of plywood standing on the altar only an inch from her flushed face, she frowned. A three-inch-diameter hole had been drilled in the wood and she knew what was expected of her as a solid penis slipped through the hole. Her tearful eyes gazing at the rock-hard shaft, the purple glans, she knew she was to drink the man's sperm. The bulbous knob pressing against her pursed lips, she wondered who the owner of the huge organ was as she breathed in the heady male scent of the swollen plum.

Instinctively parting her full lips and sucking the silky glans into her wet mouth, Charlotte wondered again whether there were other men in the church waiting to use and abuse her naked body. The candle pushed deeper into her dank bowels and she jolted as a solid glans slipped between the inflamed lips of her pussy and drove deep into the tight duct of her vagina. This was degradation beyond belief, she reflected as the knob bloating her mouth drove to the back of her throat. Her lips stretched tautly around the base of the huge cock, she breathed deeply through her nose as the man behind her began his fucking motions. Her tethered body rocking with the enforced double fucking, her forehead pressing against the plywood partition, the stark reality of her predicament hit her.

Half the men in the village might be queuing up to slip their cocks through the hole and sperm her wet mouth! Goodhugh and the perverted priest might be charging them for the pleasure of shooting their spunk down a young girl's throat. Were all men really that debased? Charlotte wondered as the knob within her hot mouth ballooned and sperm jetted over her pink tongue. Her cheeks filling with the white liquid, she swallowed hard as the unseen man rocked his hips, his huge cock fucking her bloated mouth as he gasped in his male pleasure behind the partition. Sperm running down her chin and pooling on the altar, she coughed and spluttered as her mouth overflowed. Again and again the swollen glans thrust to the back of her throat, her wet lips rolling along the veined shaft as the man drained his balls. Licking her spunked lips as the penis finally withdrew and disappeared through the hole, she gasped for breath.

Her contracting vagina filling with sperm as the man behind her moaned in his debased pleasure, Charlotte grimaced. The candle stretching her anal duct moving in and out of her inflamed bottom-hole, her vaginal sheath pistoned by a huge cock, she again thought she'd split open as her pelvic cavity ballooned. Another penis slipping through the hole in the partition, the swollen knob glistening in the light, she took the salty glans into her mouth and ran her wet tongue over the silky-smooth surface. Her young breasts pressing against the rough cloth of the altar, her nipples sore and erect, her vulval flesh devoid of pubic hair, she wondered whether her once-unblemished young body would ever be allowed to heal.

From shy virgin to cum-slut, Charlotte had evolved in her enforced evolution. Never again would the gracious curves and mounds of her teenage body glow in the light of innocence. Forever sullied, her virginity rudely plundered, her naked body was now a temple of lust. She should have been working on her English project, she mused in her confusion. Did Miss Chambers suck spunk from orgasming knobs? Did she fuck? Arse fuck?

Sperm gushing from the glans swelling her mouth, bathing her tongue and filling her cheeks, she again swallowed hard. The crude acts of mouth-fucking and spunk-drinking had become routine, as commonplace as any other bodily function. She knew that if she ever fell in love, sex would be an act committed in the name of cold lust, performed purely for the pleasure of her male partner. But did she want a man? she wondered as she drank the fruits of male orgasm from the throbbing glans. Where was Emily? Where was Marianne?

'Right,' the priest's voice echoed around the church as the deflating glans left her sperm-bubbling mouth. Another cock slipping through the hole in the partition, she took the glans into her mouth and listened to the movements behind her. 'While she's gobbling, we'll fix the belt around her,' he chuckled. Wondering what he was talking about as she sucked and mouthed on the bulbous glans, the deflating penis within her vaginal sheath withdrawing, she jolted as the candle was yanked out of her anal duct. She could feel a cold band encircling her waist, straps running between her legs, as the knob inside her mouth exploded in orgasm. Sperm filling her cheeks, she again swallowed hard, draining the unseen man's balls as hands fiddled with the straps. Wondering what horrendous sexually depraved act she'd be forced to perform next, she gasped for air as the sperm-dripping glans finally left her aching mouth and the penile shaft disappeared through the hole.

The straps running between her thighs on either side of her swollen vaginal lips biting into her soft flesh, Charlotte waited in fear and trepidation as the waist band was tightened. Wondering what the device was for, she instinctively parted her wet lips as another bulbous glans emerged through the hole in the wooden partition. Sucking the purple plum into her sperm-drenched mouth, she knew now that there were indeed several men in the church. Did they know who she was? she wondered as the man rocked his hips, fucking her bloated mouth. If the men who'd crudely spunked her knew her identity, they'd look at her in the street and think their dirty thoughts. She'd never know which of the men in the village had used her to satisfy their debased desires and had spunked her orifices.

'We don't have a great deal of time,' Goodhugh said.

'You're right,' the priest murmured. 'How many are still waiting?'

'The last one's fucking her mouth now.'

'OK. We'll release her as soon as he's finished.'

'Is the belt secure?'

'Yes. She'll never be able to remove it.'

Again wondering at the purpose of the belt, Charlotte sucked and licked the glans engulfed between her spermed lips, praying for the man to come quickly so she could go home and cleanse her teenage body, wash away the slime of

SCHOOLGIRL LUST

debauchery. Perhaps the belt was some kind of chastity device, she pondered. Although she couldn't think why they'd bother. The purple glans driving in and out of her mouth, she knew that she couldn't swallow any more male orgasmic fluid as sperm jetted from the swollen knob and bathed her snaking tongue. The white cream gushing from her gobbling mouth, hanging in long threads from her chin, she ran her tongue around the throbbing glans until the flow of salty semen stemmed.

Sighing with relief as the penis withdrew and she was released from her bonds, she managed to haul her abused body upright. Gazing at the priest and Goodhugh, she knew that the other men had made their escape. How many had there been? she wondered as sperm oozed from her anal hole, trickled from the inflamed entrance to her young vagina. Looking down at the leather belt around her waist, the straps running between her sagging legs, she wiped the sperm from her face and licked her lips as the priest unceremoniously threw her clothes at her.

'Get dressed and go home, slut,' he ordered her.

'What about this?' she asked, pulling on the leather waistband.

'That stays where it is.'

'But—'

'Along with this,' Goodhugh grinned, kneeling before her as the priest grabbed her arms and held her. Driving a massive wooden dildo deep into the tight sheath of her vagina, Goodhugh laughed. 'The belt serves two functions,' he said, fixing the end of the dildo to the straps with two thin chains. 'One, to keep the dildo in place. Two, it's our insurance.'

'Insurance?' she echoed, rubbing the stinging globes of her crimsoned bottom as she was released.

'If you're disobedient, then I'll have to tell your mother of your vile ways. Once she sees the belt and dildo, she'll realize that you're nothing more than a dirty little whore. By the way, the belt is reinforced with steel. You won't be able to cut through it. Oh, and there's an inscription on the back. "To Charlotte, from your lesbian lover, Emily".'

Finally allowed to dress, Charlotte thought again about running away. As she tugged her panties up her long legs, concealing the end of the dildo, she knew that she could either run or for ever be a slave not only to Goodhugh and Father James but to several other men in the village. Turned into a whore, she had no choice, she knew as she finished dressing and staggered up the aisle to the door. Her vagina bloated, the dildo massaging her creamy sex sheath as she walked, she opened the door and walked out into the evening sun.

'Hi,' Emily said, hurrying across the road.

'Oh, hi,' Charlotte murmured, eyeing the other girl's microskirt, the naked band of flesh below her short top.

'Are you all right?'

'Yes, I'm fine. Just a little tired.'

'Let's go for a walk in the woods,' the girl grinned, winking at Charlotte. 'It's a nice evening. I thought we might—'

'No, I have to be home to help my mother with something,' Charlotte lied, the leather straps biting into the soft flesh between her legs.

'You've been avoiding me, haven't you?' Emily said accusingly.

'No, of course not. Look, I must go.'

'If you've been seeing Marianne, I'll—'

'Emily, please. Just leave me alone.'

'You don't want me any more, do you?'

'It's not that. I'm just tired, Emily. I'll see you tomorrow.'

'No, you'll see me now. I'm going to the woods. If you don't turn up within half an hour, I'll come to your place and tell your mother that you're a lesbian.'

'For God's sake, Emily. Please don't do this to me.'

'I'll be waiting by the stream.'

Watching the girl strut off, Charlotte hung her head. Her shoulders slumped, she mooched along the road, dreading the thought of facing her mother. She couldn't take much more, she knew as she wondered whether Emily would turn up and carry out her threat. The wooden dildo massaging the spermed walls of her aching vagina, she decided to try to remove the belt. If anyone saw it, they'd believe her to be a nymphomaniac. She'd remove the belt, and then . . . She didn't know what she was going to do as she stood at her front door. Running away was the only option open to her.

Chapter Nine

Waking with a start, Charlotte looked around her bedroom. As the events of the previous evening drifted back into her racked mind, she pushed the eiderdown aside and gazed at the belt around her waist, the leather straps running between her thighs, the dildo emerging between the swollen lips of her vagina. She'd not managed to cut through the reinforced belt or slip the wooden phallus out of her aching pussy. But she had managed to evade her mother's questioning by feigning another stomach-ache.

Focusing on the fleshy swell of her hairless vaginal lips stretched tautly around the massive shaft of the protruding phallus, she hurriedly pulled the eiderdown back up as she heard her mother climbing the stairs. What the woman would say if she saw her daughter's body in bondage, Charlotte dreaded to think. Goodhugh and the priest had done their job well. Apart from the threats, Charlotte had to see the evil men again if she was going to have the belt removed.

'She's been like this for several days,' her mother said, leading the doctor into the room.

'Mother,' Charlotte gasped, holding her hand to her mouth. 'You didn't tell me that—'

'I called Doctor Johnson because you've been complaining of a stomach-ache, Charlotte.'

'Let's have a look at you,' the middle-aged man said, dumping his bag on the floor by the bed.

'I'll be downstairs,' Charlotte's mother smiled, closing the door behind her.

'I'm . . . I'm all right now,' Charlotte murmured as the doctor sat on the edge of the bed.

'I'll just take a look at your stomach, Charlotte. There's a nasty virus going round and if you've been like this for a few days . . .'

'No, no, I'm all right now,' she said firmly.

'There's no harm in my taking a look at you,' he persisted.

'All right,' she conceded, praying that he'd not notice the leather belt as he pulled the eiderdown back, exposing the firm mounds of her young breasts, the smooth plateau of her stomach.

'Does that hurt?' he asked, pressing his fingertips into the soft flesh of her abdomen.

'No, it doesn't. I told you, doctor. I'm all right now.'

'We have to be sure that . . . What's this?' he gasped, pulling the eiderdown further back and gazing at the leather belt.

'It's—'

'Charlotte, what have you done to yourself?' he asked, his dark eyes wide as the straps came into view. Yanking the eiderdown up before he noticed the dildo, her face flushing, Charlotte didn't know what to say. 'I think we need to have a talk,' the doctor murmured, shaking his head. 'Did *you* shave your pubic hair off?'

'I . . .'

'I know you're young and . . . You shouldn't do that to your body. I know that, at your age, your hormones will be running wild and—'

SCHOOLGIRL LUST

'No, you don't understand,' Charlotte broke in, her hands trembling, her heart thumping hard against her chest.

'I can't believe it, Charlotte. You've had a decent upbringing and you—'

'You're one of them, aren't you?' she said accusingly. 'You're part of it.'

'Part of what?' the man asked, perplexed.

'I know why you're here. I know what you want.'

'Charlotte, what are you talking about? I'm here because your mother—'

'Yes, I know. You'll tell my mother unless I—'

'I think you'd better tell me what's going on.'

'You *know* what's going on,' she returned, kicking the eiderdown off the bed. 'You're here for *that*, aren't you?' she snapped, opening her legs wide. 'You want my cunt, don't you?'

'Good God,' the man breathed, gazing at her swollen vaginal lips gripping the creamy shaft of the wooden dildo. 'Charlotte, what on earth . . .'

'You want me to suck your cock and swallow your spunk. That's why you're here, isn't it?'

'I'm going to speak to your mother,' he said, grabbing his bag and walking to the door. 'I have never known—'

'It's all right, you don't have to threaten me. I'll suck your knob and swallow your spunk and then you can fuck my arse. I know exactly . . .'

Her words tailing off as he left the room, she frowned. Grabbing the eiderdown and covering her naked body, she realized that she might have made a fatal mistake. If the doctor wasn't in on the scam and . . . 'God,' she breathed, hearing low murmurs downstairs. The horror story had now become worse than a living hell, she knew as she waited for the inevitable confrontation. But the doctor wouldn't say anything about the dildo, would he? There were codes of practice, Charlotte reflected. He had a duty to his patients and was forbidden to talk about them to others. All he could do was express his concern at . . . at what?

Leaping out of bed, she hurriedly dressed and brushed her hair. Whatever the doctor had said to her mother, she had to come across as happy, normal, and make out that she didn't know why he was concerned. Would he have told her mother about the dildo? she wondered again, slipping her shoes on. The front door finally closing, she took a deep breath and went downstairs.

'I need to speak to you,' her mother said as Charlotte wandered into the kitchen.

'I'm hungry,' Charlotte smiled. 'I'm feeling a lot better now.'

'Doctor Johnson is worried about you.'

'Oh? He seemed to think I was fine.'

'He was concerned about . . . Charlotte, have you done anything to yourself?'

'Done anything?' she echoed, forcing a bright smile. 'What do you mean?'

'He wouldn't tell me what, but he said that you'd done something to your body.'

'I haven't done anything to my body,' Charlotte chuckled. 'What did he say, exactly?'

'He wants you to go to the surgery this morning at eleven.'

'I don't understand. He said that I was fine. I'd had a stomach bug and—'

'Now what?' the older woman breathed as the front doorbell rang.

'I'll go,' Charlotte said, praying that it wasn't Goodhugh or Father James.

Opening the door to find Emily standing on the step, Charlotte knew that there was more trouble ahead. This was all becoming too much, she reflected, staring at a large brown envelope as the girl thrust it into her hand. Opening it, she frowned as she peered inside. Realizing that the envelope contained photographs, she feared the worst as she pulled them out. Gazing at pictures of herself in the woods, her fingers thrust deep into Marianne's anal duct, she held her trembling hand to her head.

'Well?' Emily said accusingly.

'Where did you get these from?' Charlotte asked shakily, slipping them back into the envelope.

'They were put through my front door, addressed to me. I don't think it's very nice of you to send me pictures of you naked in the woods with that cow. Especially with your fingers up her—'

'I didn't send them to you,' Charlotte gasped.

'Who took them?'

'I . . . I don't know.'

'Meet me in the woods by the stream in half an hour.'

'No, I . . .'

'In that case, I'll show these to your mum.'

'For God's sake, Emily.'

'Half an hour,' the girl snapped, grabbing the envelope and walking off.

Deciding to put an end to the nightmare, Charlotte closed the front door and walked to the church. Enough was enough, she fumed silently, striding through the graveyard to the main doors. What the hell did the evil bastards hope to achieve by sending Emily the photographs? Unless Emily was lying. But where else would she have got them from? Blackmailed by Goodhugh, sexually abused by God only knew how many men, and now Emily threatening to show the photographs to her mother . . . Enough was a damned sight *more* than enough.

Entering the church, Charlotte headed straight for the office, clenching her fists as her heart raced and adrenalin coursed through her veins. Kicking the door open, she looked around the empty room. There was no sign of the priest, and she knew that this was her chance to search his office for evidence. She doubted that he'd have photographs hidden there, but it was worth looking.

Rummaging through the desk drawers, she pulled out a red folder. She couldn't believe her eyes as she opened it and found a list of girls' names. They must be victims of the evil men, she thought, reading down the list. Hearing movements in the main part of the church, she thrust the folder into the drawer and looked around the office for somewhere to hide. Diving into the corner, she crouched behind the filing cabinet and held her breath as Father James entered the room and sat at his desk. Frozen to the spot, she listened intently as he picked up the phone and punched the buttons.

'Pink peaches,' he said softly. Wondering what he meant, Charlotte frowned. 'We've got a major problem,' the man continued. 'No, I am *not* becoming paranoid. If you'll listen for a minute, I'll tell you why I'm concerned. Marianne has disappeared. That's right. Apparently, she didn't go home last night. No, not yet. You'd better put everything in the safe. Yes, I will. All right, I'll see you soon.'

Watching the priest take the folder from the desk drawer, Charlotte emerged from her hide as he left the office. *The safe?* she mused, wondering where Marianne had got to. Slipping out of the office, she watched the cleric leave the church with the folder tucked under his arm. Wherever he was taking it, she was sure that the photographs would also

SCHOOLGIRL LUST

be there. Leaving the church, she noticed him walk round the corner of the stone building. Following, she peered around the wall to see him entering a dilapidated shed almost completely concealed by shrubs and brambles. That was the safe, she knew instinctively as she took cover behind a bush.

Watching Father James return to the church empty-handed, she stole through the long grass to the shed and slipped inside. This was risky, she knew. But she had to get her hands on the photographs and any other evidence that might be hidden there. Noticing a wooden trunk in the far corner, she gazed at the padlock and sighed. The trunk was too heavy to move and, without the key, there was no way she'd be able to open it. Sure that Goodhugh would soon arrive to stash the photographs in the trunk, she wondered whether both men had keys. Looking about the shed, she grinned as she moved an old coat aside and discovered a key hanging on a hook.

Unable to believe her luck, she took the key and opened the trunk. 'God,' she gasped, staring at piles of pornographic photographs and papers. This could well be the end of the horror story, she thought happily, gazing at photographs of a girl she recognized from school. Her naked body tied over the fallen truck of a tree, her vaginal lips shaved, she was sucking a man's erect penis. Another photograph showed the girl with a solid penis embedded deep within her young bottom-hole. Charlotte wondered whether she ought to go and see her. Deciding to round up all the victims and confront the priest, she grabbed several handfuls of photographs and closed the trunk. Snapping the padlock shut as she heard someone approaching, she hung the key back on the hook and dived behind a pile of cardboard boxes as the door opened.

'I hope that bloody girl turns up,' Goodhugh hissed.

'Put everything in the trunk and I'll move it tonight,' Father James whispered. 'If the police are called in, we're going to be in the shit.'

'They'll have no reason to come here.'

'That may be so, but I'm not taking any risks.'

'I reckon the girl will turn up and that'll be that. She's probably with a friend or . . .'

'We'll have to cancel tonight's session,' the priest said as Goodhugh opened the trunk.

'You must be joking,' Goodhugh returned. 'Mary's paid fifty pounds for—'

'We'll have to give her the money back. We can't risk—'

'No way,' Goodhugh snapped, slamming the trunk shut. 'She's a damned good client and she wants Charlotte.'

'All right, but we must be careful. I'll go and see Charlotte and tell her to be here at seven.'

'OK. I'll get back to the shop. I'll see you this evening.'

As the men left the shed, Charlotte wondered who Mary was. Racking her brains, she went through just about everyone she knew in the village. The only Mary that came to mind was a teacher at her school, the gym mistress. But, surely the woman wasn't . . . The way things were going, Charlotte wouldn't have been at all surprised to discover that one of her teachers was in on the scam. Deciding to sneak back later and grab the rest of the photographs and papers, she left the shed. Hiding the evidence she'd so far collected beneath a bush in the corner of the graveyard, she made her way to the teacher's house. It would really put the cat among the pigeons if she confronted the woman, she reflected.

She was about to walk up the path and knock on the door

when she had a better idea. Crossing the road to the phone box, she asked Directory Enquiries for the woman's number. Wondering what she was going to say, she knew that she'd have to play it by ear. Finally dialling the number, she remembered that Emily was waiting in the woods. Things were coming to a head, she thought as the teacher answered the phone.

'Sorry to trouble you,' Charlotte whispered, trying to disguise her voice. 'I have a message from Father James.'

'Father James?' the woman breathed. 'Who is this?'

'It's about tonight.'

'What did he say?'

'He'll be busy but, if it's all right with you, the girl will call at your house.'

'Girl? Er . . . what girl?' she asked, obviously worried. 'Who is this? What are you talking about?'

Fearing that she was making another grave mistake, Charlotte wondered what to say as the woman asked her again what she was talking about. There might well be another Mary in the village, she mused. Or perhaps from another village or town. The wooden dildo massaging her inner vaginal flesh as she crossed her legs, she recalled the priest's words. It was worth a try, she knew as she slipped her hand between her thighs and adjusted the dildo.

'Pink peaches,' Charlotte murmured, waiting eagerly for the woman's response.

'Ripe for the picking,' the woman breathed. 'Look, I can't have sex with the girl here. It'll have to be at the church or—'

Hanging up, Charlotte grinned. Now she knew the code word, she reckoned that she could track down all those involved in the sordid scam. Dashing home, she decided to tell her mother that she wasn't going to visit the doctor at eleven. There were more important things to do than listen to a lecture on morals. She might be involved in something far bigger than she'd at first realized, she knew as she thought about the doctor and wondered whether he was involved. There might be dozens of men from all over the area involved in the crude defiling of teenage girls. She had to be very careful, she thought as she entered the cottage and found her mother sitting in the lounge, listening to the radio.

'Charlotte, where have you been?' the woman asked irritably.

'Walking,' Charlotte smiled, sitting in the armchair opposite her. The dildo pressing against her cervix, she grimaced. 'I went for a walk in the woods.'

'Are you all right?'

'Yes, I'm fine,' Charlotte replied, wondering how to cut through the belt.

'I want to talk to you,' her mother said, rising from her chair. 'Wait there and I'll turn the oven off.'

'Talk to me?'

'Yes. That Emily girl came round.'

'Emily?' Charlotte echoed as her mother left the room. Praying that the girl hadn't carried out her threat, she wondered whether she was another victim of the scam. 'Pink peaches,' she murmured abstractedly as her mother returned.

'*What* did you say?' the older woman gasped, her face turning pale.

'I was just thinking aloud,' Charlotte replied.

'Pink peaches? Is that what you said?' her mother asked angrily.

'Yes, why?'

'Where did you hear that?'

'I . . . Someone mentioned it.'

'Who? Who was it?'

'What's wrong, mother?'

'It's something that happened long ago,' she sighed pensively.

'To do with pink peaches?'

'I . . . I don't want to talk about it.'

'Please, tell me.'

'You don't need to know, Charlotte.'

'I *do* need to know,' she insisted, the dildo pressing hard against the softness of her creamy cervix. 'Mother, I'm seventeen. I'm not a child any more.'

'All right,' the woman conceded, flopping onto the sofa. 'There was a . . . a group of people in the village. It's been over for years, thank God. It all came to light just before you were born.'

'What came to light?'

'Some men formed a secret society. They . . . they committed disgusting sexual acts. They blackmailed and exploited young girls and . . . I won't go into the sordid details. Who mentioned it to you?'

'I overheard some people talking, that was all. I thought it might make a good title for the story I'm writing for my English project. Pink Peaches.'

'Don't ever utter those words in this village, Charlotte.'

'Is there anyone still living in the village who was involved?'

'No. The village was cleared of the evil men. Who was talking about it?'

'A man and a woman,' Charlotte lied. 'I'd never seen them before.'

'I pray to God that it's not going to start up again. Has anyone approached you or threatened you in any way?'

'No,' Charlotte murmured, realizing that this was the time to tell her mother the truth. Deciding against it, she changed the subject. 'By the way, I won't be going to the doctor. I really do feel all right now.'

'I'd like to know what he was so concerned about. You should go and see him.'

'No, I'm fine.'

'He seemed very worried, almost shocked.'

'I can't think why. I'm going out for a while.'

'Where to, Charlotte? You've been out half the morning as it is.'

'I won't be long. I'm just going to the woods to look at a bird's nest I found the other day.'

Leaving the cottage, Charlotte hoped that Emily would still be waiting by the stream. She had to tell the girl the truth. Emily had to know about the priest and Goodhugh. Hoping that Marianne was all right, she followed the path through the trees, pondering on her mother's revelation. Goodhugh and the priest had lived in the village all their lives. Perhaps their fathers had been involved in the scam, she reflected. Whatever had happened in the past, it was the present that she had to think about. Seeing Emily sitting by the stream, Charlotte called out as she approached.

'Where have you been?' Emily asked irritably.

'I got held up,' Charlotte smiled. 'Where did you get the photographs from?'

'I told you, they were put through my letter box. What I want to know is . . .'

'I don't believe you. Who would have put them through your letter box?'

'You, or Marianne. Just to make me jealous, I would imagine.'

'That's ridiculous. Emily, I have to tell you something.'

SCHOOLGIRL LUST

'No, I'm going to tell *you* something. If you see Marianne again, I'll—'

'Emily, you must listen to me.'

'I'll show your mother the photographs if you're unfaithful to me again.'

'What's wrong with you?' Charlotte snapped. 'You can't expect me to do as you say. You don't own me, Emily. If I want to have other friends, I will.'

'Friends? You were naked with that cow. You had your fingers stuck up her arse. You're mine, Charlotte. Remember that.'

'I am *not* . . . By the way—' Charlotte smiled, deciding that Emily needed to be taught a lesson '—Mr Goodhugh gave me a radio. I was looking at them in his shop, and he gave me one.'

'Why tell me?'

'I just thought that he might give you one if you showed an interest. They're really good. Why don't you go there and look at them? I'll bet anything he'll let you have one.'

'I don't want a bloody radio,' Emily murmured. 'You're not going to see Marianne again, are you?'

'No, I promise.'

'Who took the photographs?'

'Marianne's camera has a timer. She took them.'

'She's a cow. Why on earth did you allow her to take pictures of—'

'To be honest, I didn't realize she was taking photos until it was too late.'

'More to the point, what the hell were you doing with your fingers stuck up—'

'What are you going to do with the photographs?'

'Keep them so I've got something on you. If ever you—'

'Go and see Goodhugh. Even if you don't want a radio, you could sell it. I'll wait here for you.'

'All right.'

'I'll be waiting.'

As the girl wandered away, Charlotte realized that she'd done a terrible thing by involving her. Goodhugh would no doubt allow her to take a radio and then blackmail her, threaten her and . . . But Emily was now using photographs to threaten Charlotte. A taste of her own medicine would do her good. Wondering why the girl had been sent the photographs, she thought about Goodhugh's plan. What was the idea? What was he hoping to achieve by sending the photographs to Emily? He obviously wanted to cause trouble, but why? Unless Emily was lying, she mused again.

The wooden dildo stretching her inner vaginal flesh, Charlotte lay on the grass to make herself more comfortable. Looking up at the sun sparkling through the trees, wondering what had happened to her young life, she thought about the future. Even if Goodhugh and the priest were dealt with, where would that leave her? There were other men in the village. Other men who'd spunked her mouth, fucked her tight bottom. Even if they were all locked up, where would that leave Charlotte? Having experienced perverted sex in the extreme, what sort of person would she now be? Whipped, her anal canal spermed, her mouth flooded with the liquid of male orgasm . . . What sort of person was she becoming?

Her vaginal muscles tightening around the smooth shaft of the dildo, she lifted her skirt and slipped her hand down the front of her wet panties. Desperate for sexual gratification, she felt an overwhelming need to come. She used to enjoy walking in the woods, watching the birds and breathing in the pine-scented air. But now her thoughts were concentrated on her young body, the sex-drenched crack of her teenage vagina, the erect bud of her yearning clitoris.

Massaging the soft cushions of her swollen vaginal lips, Charlotte closed her eyes and breathed heavily. Her clitoris emerging from beneath its pinken hood, she caressed the sensitive protrusion, trembling as wondrous sensations of sex rippled through her young body. She'd changed beyond all belief, she knew as she lay on the soft grass with her legs spread. Massaging the swollen nub of her clitoris, her juices of lust seeping past the dildo and running down to her tightly closed bottom-hole, she whimpered in her self-loving. The sensations driving her wild as her sex nodule pulsated, she threw her head back and massaged her ripening clitoris faster.

Masturbation was going to become a way of life, she thought, her breathing quickening as she neared her climax. Whether in bed or in the woods, she'd slip her hand between the warmth of her thighs and masturbate. But was that so bad? Recalling her first lesbian experience with Emily on that fateful Saturday morning, she imagined that the girl was with her in the woods. Emily's tongue entering the wet sheath of her young pussy, sucking out her juices of desire . . . Was it a male or a female she wanted? Did she prefer the hard shaft of a penis thrusting in and out of her tight pussy, sperming her ripe cervix, or a wet female tongue lapping up her flowing juices of orgasm? As she neared her climax she didn't know. Emily or Marianne? Male or female? Perhaps she wanted both men and women. She wanted Marianne.

Her cries of pleasure resounding through the woods as her orgasm exploded within the pulsating nodule of her solid clitoris, Charlotte shook violently. The birds fluttering from the trees, she lay writhing on the grass as her orgasm peaked, sending waves of pure sexual bliss rolling through her teenage body. Her vaginal muscles gripping the wooden phallus, her creamy juices of girl-desire spraying from her bloated sex sheath, she convulsed wildly as her multiple orgasm gripped her very soul. On and on her pleasure rode as she masturbated faster. Her clitoris pulsating, painfully swelling, she massaged her pleasure spot faster, sustaining the incredible sensations of orgasmic bliss as her vaginal sheath spewed out its love cream.

The branch of a bush lashed the soft flesh of her inner thighs. She screamed out and looked up in horror. Goodhugh was towering above her, his face scowling as he brought the branch down again and once more lashed her inner thighs. Rolling over in an effort to escape the evil man, Charlotte dug her fingernails into the soft grass as the branch swished through the air and flailed the already weal-lined melons of her rounded buttocks. Again and again the branch flogged her stinging bottom as she tried desperately to crawl away. Deafening cracks resounding throughout the woods, the agonizing pain permeating the soft flesh of her anal orbs, she dragged her young body across the grass.

'You filthy bitch,' Goodhugh breathed, ripping her panties off and exposing the crimsoned flesh of her young bottom. 'Where are the bloody photographs?' he asked, whipping her naked buttocks as her young body contorted and writhed like a tortured snake. 'Where are the bloody photographs?'

'I don't know!' she screamed, praying for someone to come to her rescue.

'I'll get the truth out of her,' the priest said, joining Goodhugh. 'Strip her naked and I'll thrash the truth out of the filthy little slut.'

Her skirt ripped off, her blouse torn from her young

body, Charlotte knew that she was in for a severe thrashing as the priest yanked her bra clear of her firm breasts. It had been a mistake to steal the photographs, she thought fearfully. She should have waited until she'd been able to remove all the evidence. Or perhaps it would have been better to burn the shed to the ground. Hindsight was useless, she knew as she lay naked on the ground. Watching in horror as Goodhugh threw her clothes into the stream, she wondered how she'd get home. She could hardly walk the streets naked. But she would have to endure a gruelling punishment before she could even think about going home.

The men stood over her as she prayed for Emily to come back. They'd run if they heard someone approaching. As they dragged her up by her arms and frogmarched her along the path, the dildo thrusting in and out of her teenage pussy, she knew that she'd never find freedom. Not knowing who was in on the evil scam, not knowing who was friend or foe, there was no way she could beat her abusers. Her naked body dragged deeper into the woods, she heard a dog barking somewhere in the distance. The world was unaware of her plight, she thought as she wondered again how she'd get home. People were shopping, working, pottering in their gardens . . .

'What are you going to do to me?' Charlotte sobbed as they dragged her into a small clearing in the undergrowth. Throwing her naked body to the ground, they hurriedly removed their clothes and ordered her to kneel before them. Complying, she gazed at their full balls, the veined shafts of their erect penises hovering only inches from her pretty mouth. She knew what she had to do as they pressed their solid knobs against her pursed lips. This was her duty now. Opening her mouth, she sucked one of the swollen plums inside and ran her tongue over its velveteen surface.

'Suck both at once,' Goodhugh ordered her. Parting her full lips wider, she managed to take both massive organs into her wet mouth. Grabbing her head, the men began their fucking motions, driving their purple knobs deep into her hot mouth as she moaned through her nose. She'd choke on their sperm, she knew as their heavy balls battered her chin. If they both came at once, filling her mouth with their salty spunk . . . Perhaps she'd manage to swallow all their male liquid, she mused as they crudely mouth-fucked her.

Her lips stretched tautly around their huge shafts, her vaginal muscles gripping the wooden phallus, Charlotte was grateful not to have received another thrashing as she sucked and licked the bulbous knobs. She could endure anything but a severe thrashing. Perhaps, if she behaved herself, eagerly complied with every crude instruction . . . All she'd been put through so far hadn't been too horrendous. Anal sex, oral, vaginal . . . She could endure just about anything, but not another gruelling whipping.

'Spunk the tart's mouth,' the priest gasped in his debauchery as both men shuddered in their soaring arousal. Her mouth suddenly filling with sperm as the men gasped in their debased pleasure, she did her best to swallow all their gushing orgasmic fluid. The white liquid overflowing, bubbling from her bloated mouth, streaming down her chin and dripping onto the elongated nipples of her pert breasts, she swallowed hard again. At least they'd come, she found herself thinking as they rammed their knobs to the back of her throat. At least they'd satisfied their depraved craving and drained their balls.

As they withdrew their spent organs, Charlotte gave up trying to gulp down all their jism, spat out the remnants of their spunk and licked her lips. This was the last time she'd

SCHOOLGIRL LUST

go to the woods alone, she decided as they pushed her to the ground. Once the dildo was removed, if it was ever removed, she'd leave the village. She had no money, nowhere to go . . . But that didn't matter. All that mattered was escaping the evil men and the village of crude sex.

Watching as they stood either side of her, their flaccid cocks in their hands, she wondered what they intended to do with her. Focusing on their purple knobs, the sperm dripping from their slits as they asked her again where the photographs were, she decided to say nothing. Even if she told them, they'd still use and abuse her. The blackmail would never end, she ruminated. The sexual abuse, the degradation of her teenage body . . . Unless she fled the village, she'd have no life.

Wishing again that she'd set fire to the shed, Charlotte jumped as warm liquid rained over her naked body. Unable to believe the humiliation, she looked up in horror at the men's purple knobs, the golden liquid spraying from their slits. Writhing, her body drenched, she tried to crawl into the undergrowth to save herself. But she knew there was no escape as Goodhugh pinned her down with his foot. With no clothes to veil her spunked and pissed body, she not only wondered how she was going to get home but *if* she'd ever get home.

'Please,' Charlotte sobbed, their hot urine showering the firm orbs of her young breasts, splattering her pretty face. 'Please, stop.' Ignoring her, they sprayed her teenage body, the hot liquid running between her thighs, raining over her swollen vaginal lips. Their bladders finally drained, they laughed as she wiped her face on the back of her hand. Never had she been so humiliated and degraded, she thought as the priest snapped a branch off a nearby bush. Never had she known such vile and sick depravity. They were the Devil's agents, she thought as she eyed the branch hovering ominously above her naked body.

The branch swishing through the air, its rough twigs and leaves lashing the firm spheres of her teenage breasts, she cried out and tried again to escape. She couldn't take another beating, she knew as the wooden phallus massaged the inflamed sheath of her inflamed pussy. Her body abused in the extreme, spunked on, pissed over, exhausted, she fell writhing to the ground and the jagged branch now repeatedly flailed the fleshy swell of her vaginal lips as they bulged around the protruding end of the dildo.

'Where are the photographs?' the priest asked, placing his knees either side of her head and squatting over her face. Lowering his body, his hairy balls settling over her mouth as the branch again lashed her naked vaginal lips, he wanked the huge shaft of his stiffening penis. Manoeuvring his hips and aligning the brown ring of his anus with her wet mouth, he ordered her to tongue his arsehole. She couldn't bring herself to commit the vulgar act. His warm buttocks pressing against her cheeks, his anal crevice yawning, she breathed in his male scent as he again ordered her to tongue-fuck his arse. Grimacing, she realized that she had no choice. The branch lashing her naked vulval flesh again, she finally complied and pushed her tongue between the warm globes of his buttocks.

'Lick it,' he instructed her. 'Lick my arsehole.' Pushing her tongue into his tight hole as her pussy lips received another lash from the rough branch, she knew she'd reached the bottom of the pit of debauched sex. There was no vile act she'd not committed, nothing more she could be forced to endure in the name of crude lust. Hearing the dog barking in the distance again, she wondered, lost in

SCHOOLGIRL LUST

her wondering. Was there nothing more she'd be forced to endure?

Tonguing the cleric's bottom-hole, Charlotte savoured the bitter-sweet taste as he wanked the fleshy shaft of his erect penis faster. The cruel vulval thrashing finally halting, she felt fingers delving between the moons of her pert buttocks, stretching open the delicate brown entrance to her dank bowels. The priest's balls bouncing, battering her forehead as he wanked his cock, she felt his spunk landing in her hair, running down her temples as he gasped and writhed in his coming. His anal entrance spasming, tightening around her darting tongue as he brought out his spunk, she squeezed her eyes shut and dug her fingernails into the grass. There was nothing more they could do to her. Was there?

She'd never be able to return home like this, she thought as her tongue slipped deeper into the man's hot anal canal. Breathing in the scent of his maleness as his sperm rained over her head, her rectal duct opening wide to accommodate Goodhugh's thrusting fingers, she again prayed for her freedom. But her prayers had always gone unheard, she reflected. She must have been bad when she was young. This was God's punishment. Or was it Satan's doing?

'Where are the photographs?' the priest again asked her as he moved away from her flushed face and sat by her side. 'If you don't tell us . . .'

'I didn't steal any photographs,' Charlotte replied, licking her anal-scented lips as Goodhugh's fingers slipped out her inflamed rectal duct.

'We know you stole them,' Goodhugh said, lifting her feet high in the air. Pressing her knees against her firm breasts, exposing the brown eye of her tight bottom-hole, he slipped his purple plum into her gaping anal valley. 'Where are they?' he asked again.

'I don't know,' she breathed, his glans slipping past her defeated sphincter muscles and driving into the tight sheath of her hot arse.

'I'll piss in your mouth unless you tell us,' Father James threatened her, kneeling with his flaccid cock hanging over her face.

'I don't know anything about—'

Goodhugh's massive shaft thrusting deep into her rectal tract, she gasped as he completely impaled her on his rock-hard cock. His hairy balls pressing against her burning buttocks, he withdrew briefly and rammed his cock deep into her anal canal with such force that she glided across the grass. Eyeing the priest's knob as he grabbed his solid cock, she closed her mouth as golden liquid dribbled from his slit and trickled down her cheeks. This wasn't happening, she tried to convince herself as her rectal sheath repeatedly stretched to accommodate Goodhugh's pistoning cock. Hot liquid running over her pursed lips, she relaxed her naked body and lay still. Sperm pumping deep into her bowels as hot liquid continued to rain over her flushed face, she resigned herself to the fact that she was nothing more than a lump of female flesh to be used and abused.

'Let's get out of here,' Father James said as Goodhugh drained his swinging balls, filling Charlotte's bowels with his sperm. 'We'll be back,' he said, scowling at the girl as he rose to his feet and dressed.

'Unless you return the photographs by this evening, we'll show you what *real* hard-core sex is all about,' Goodhugh warned her as he slipped his spent cock out of her inflamed anal channel.

Watching the evil pair dress, Charlotte rolled over onto

her side and closed her eyes. There was no point in living, she thought as she heard them stealing through the undergrowth. There was no point in anything any more. Her home, her school, her friends . . . All had gone, all had been taken away from her. Even Emily had shown her true colours, she thought sadly as she drifted into a deep sleep. There was no point any more.

Chapter Ten

The moon shone through the trees as Charlotte left the clearing and made her way along the woodland path to the stream. Her naked body shining in the silvery light, her nipples erect in the cool night air, she grinned as she walked into the village street and headed for the church. The village was deserted. People were in their homes, families watching television, unaware of the naked girl passing their houses. Walking through the graveyard, she stopped and looked up at the church. The steeple climbed up to the star-speckled sky like a phallic symbol. Erect. An emblem of the male species. Why was God male?

Pushing the oak door open, Charlotte walked down the aisle. The plush red carpet soft beneath her naked feet, this was supposed to be a sanctuary where one found comfort and protection from the evil ways of the world. But hypocrisy and illicit sex flourished in God's house. Where was the evil priest? she wondered, noticing a light emanating from the office. Where *was* the wretched bastard? Grabbing a wooden staff from the pulpit, she stood before the altar and laughed.

'I am the daughter of Satan!' she cried, swinging the staff with all her might and knocking the huge candles off the altar. 'I am the daughter of Satan! And I have risen from the depths of hell!'

'What the—' Father James gasped as he emerged from the office. 'Charlotte, what do you think you're—'

'Satan, my father! I offer thee my naked body. I offer thee my cunt.'

'For God's sake, get into the office,' the priest whispered through gritted teeth, grabbing her arm as she swung the staff and just missed a vase of flowers standing on a pedestal at the end of the altar. 'You'll have half the bloody village in here.'

'Leave me!' she screamed, breaking free and swinging the staff again. This time the vase smashed loudly on the stone floor and she raised the staff above her head again. 'This is the village of the damned!'

'Charlotte!' he yelled, backing away. 'Put that bloody thing down and get into the office.'

'You have opened my body, my mind and my soul. And allowed the father of my being to enter my flesh.'

'You don't know what you're saying, girl. For Christ's sake—'

'You have stirred my father, roused him and called him here to this house of sin. Demons of hell! Angels of Lucifer! Awake and come unto me!'

'For fuck's sake, Charlotte! Will you stop this and—'

'You will remove the belt of chastity,' she ordered the priest, her glazed eyes staring at him as she held the staff threateningly above her head. 'You will remove the belt now or I shall strike you down.'

'All right,' the cleric conceded shakily, dashing into the office and returning with a key. 'But you must be quiet. If people come in here and see you like this . . .'

'I am the goddess of sex!' Charlotte cried as he unlocked the belt and the wooden dildo slipped out of her drenched pussy, dropping to the floor. Dashing to the pulpit, she climbed the stone steps, wielding the staff as she flung her head back and looked up at the roof. 'Come unto me, Satan, the father of my being!'

Dashing back to the office, Father James grabbed the phone and dialled Goodhugh's number. The girl had gone mad, he was sure as the sound of breaking glass resounded through the church. As her blood-curdling screams echoed all around the stone building, he tapped his fingers on the desk, waiting for the man to answer. 'Come on, come on,' he breathed, wondering where his friend had got to as the noise of shattering glass again reverberated around the church.

'She's possessed,' he whispered loudly as Goodhugh finally answered.

'Who is?' the man asked. 'What are you talking about?'

'Charlotte. She's here, smashing up the church. Get here as quickly as you can.'

'What do you mean, *possessed*?'

'She's yelling things about the Devil and . . . Just get over here now.'

Banging the phone down, the priest stood in the office doorway and watched the girl as she clambered up onto the altar. Forcing a huge candle deep into the tight sheath of her drenched vagina, she looked up at the roof and once more called upon Satan. Unable to believe his eyes as the girl raised her hands high above her head, he stared at the candle as it began to move up and down, slowly pistoning her sex duct. Terror reflecting in his dark eyes, he turned as the main door flew open and a blast of icy wind whistled through the building.

'Jesus Christ,' he breathed, backing into the office as an eerie blue light bathed Charlotte's naked body. He'd gone too far with the sexual abuse, he knew as he spied through the crack in the door. Was this really the Devil? he wondered, watching the candle gliding in and out of the girl's vaginal sheath as she threw her head back. Enforced sex over the altar, the whipping and bondage . . . Had Satan been roused?

'In here,' he called as Goodhugh dashed into the church and stared open-mouthed at Charlotte.

'What the hell is she doing?' the shopkeeper asked as he entered the office.

'She's possessed,' the priest breathed, cringing as the girl's orgasmic screams echoed around the church.

'Don't be ridiculous,' Goodhugh laughed mockingly. 'Possessed?'

'How do you explain the candle, then?'

'What about the candle?' Goodhugh asked, watching the girl from the doorway. 'Bloody hell. It's . . . it's . . .'

'It's fucking her.'

'It must be a trick. She must be using her muscles to . . . Where's that blue light coming from?'

'Where's the cold coming from?' Father James murmured as he shivered.

'I'm going to get her. We can't leave her on the altar shouting and screaming like that. She'll attract attention and—'

'I wouldn't go near her, if I were you,' the priest warned his friend. 'If Satan's got her . . .'

'Don't talk crap. Come and give me a hand.'

Leaving the office, Goodhugh dashed up to the altar and grabbed Charlotte's feet. Pulling her down, the candle shooting out of her vaginal tube like a bullet, he dragged her off the altar and carried her naked body to the office. Kicking and screaming, her juices of lust spewing from

SCHOOLGIRL LUST

her vaginal duct, she finally managed to break free and stood in the corner of the office. Her eyes glazed, she stared hard at the priest as he closed the door. Her long black hair matted with sperm, urine and perspiration, her face flushed, she stood with her feet apart and bent her knees.

'Fuck me,' Charlotte breathed huskily, peeling the weal-lined lips of her juice-dripping vagina wide apart. 'Fuck my hot cunt.'

'Charlotte,' Father James began, gazing at the pinken folds of her wet inner flesh.

'Fuck my wet cunt,' she spat. 'That's what you wanted, isn't it? You both wanted to fuck my schoolgirl cunt. Now do it.'

'I'll fuck her cunt,' Goodhugh grinned, eyeing the pink nodule of her exposed clitoris.

'Smell the sperm on me,' she hissed. 'Breathe in the scent of my piss-drenched body. Breathe in the stench of depraved sex. I am the daughter of Satan. Take me, if you dare!'

'The stupid little bitch is trying to frighten us,' Goodhugh sneered. 'The daughter of Satan, my arse. I'll give her a damned good spanking.'

Grabbing the girl and forcing her to bend over the desk, Goodhugh spanked her naked buttocks as hard as he could. The slaps resounding around the office as he repeatedly thrashed her crimsoned flesh, he ordered the priest to get some rope and tie her naked body to the desk. Opening the bottom drawer of the filing cabinet, the cleric pulled out several lengths of rope. His eyes frowning as he bound the girl's wrists, he wasn't sure that this was a good idea. He didn't believe that the girl was possessed by the Devil, but he did wonder why she didn't struggle as he secured her ankles to the legs of the desk. The gruelling spanking continued – and she seemed to be enjoying the agonizing pain. Was Satan near? Father James wondered fearfully as Goodhugh finally stepped back and admired his handiwork.

'Right, now I'll fuck the cum-slut's arsehole,' Goodhugh grinned, unzipping his trousers and hauling his erect penis out. 'I'll give her Satan's bloody daughter.'

'I'm not sure that we should . . .' Father James began pensively.

'*I*'m sure,' Goodhugh chuckled, yanking the girl's fire-red buttocks wide apart and pressing the purple bulb of his penis hard against her inflamed brown ring. 'I'll fuck her tight arse until she begs for mercy.'

His bulbous glans slipping past her defeated sphincter muscles, he drove the full length of his solid shaft deep into the heat of Charlotte's tight rectum. The girl's anal tissue gripping the root of his broad cock, he grabbed her hips and began his fucking motions as the priest watched. Goodhugh grinned as the purple crown of his rock-hard penis repeatedly emerged and thrust back into her anal canal. His heavy balls battering her crimsoned vaginal lips, his lower belly slapping the weal-lined orbs of her firm buttocks, he took her with a cruel vengeance.

Standing at the other side of the desk, Father James finally succumbed to his base desires and slipped out of his cassock. Lifting the girl's head by her hair, he pressed the silky globe of his purple knob against her wet lips. Frowning as she eagerly sucked half his solid shaft into the wet heat of her mouth, he again pondered on the Devil. The girl had changed, he reflected as she gobbled on his ballooning glans and moaned through her nose. She'd become an insatiable nymphomaniac, but it was nothing to do with the Devil. Was it?

Her naked body rocking back and forth with the double fucking, she continued to moan her obvious pleasure through her nose as she mouthed and licked the priest's ballooning knob. The man looked down at her full lips rolling along the saliva-glistening shaft of his cock as he mouth-fucked her. She was eagerly sucking, tonguing and mouthing his purple plum, obviously desperate for his spunk to gush from his slit and jet to the back of her throat. Satan's daughter? The thought wouldn't leave his head, continually surfacing from the foul swamp of his mind to torment him.

Goodhugh grinned, his mind brimming with wicked ideas as his stilled his erect penis within the girl's anal hot canal. Forcing his left index finger into her inflamed anus, her brown tissue painfully stretching as he managed to drive his right finger too into her tight duct, he pulled the delicate tissue of her rectal sheath wide open. Resuming his forbidden anal fucking, he watched his cock shaft driving in and out of her gaping brown hole, his purple knob repeatedly appearing and disappearing as he crudely arse-fucked the young girl.

'Coming,' the priest murmured, his face grimacing as the girl sucked hard on his throbbing glans. His spunk gushing from his slit, bathing her snaking tongue and filling her cheeks, he held her head tight and rocked his hips. Goodhugh's sperm jetting from his pulsating knob, pumping deep into the dank heat of the girl's bowels, both men gasped in their debauchery. Charlotte swallowed hard, sucking the salty sperm out of the priest's knob as her anal throat swallowed Goodhugh's gushing spunk. Her clitoris swelling, her vaginal juices spewing from her gaping sex hole, she writhed in her lewd pleasure as her own orgasm exploded within the pulsating crown of her ripe clitoris.

'She's amazing,' Goodhugh gasped, pumping the last of his sperm deep into her rectal cylinder as she shuddered in her coming. His penis embedded deep within her bottom-hole, her brown tissue gripping the root of his deflating organ, his index fingers, he panted for breath as his purple knob absorbed the heat of her inner core. Focusing on her tight brown ring stretched tautly around his cock as he slipped his fingers out of her sex hole, he slapped her naked buttocks with his palm as she trembled in the grip of her climax.

Finally withdrawing his deflating penis from her tight tube of illicit pleasure, he stood back and watched the male liquid oozing from the gaping mouth of her anal canal and trickling down to the valley of her teenage cunt. 'I'll give her a bloody good whipping,' he murmured, grabbing a length of rope as the priest rammed his purple crown to the back of the girl's throat. Her orgasm receding as the priest's swinging balls drained, Charlotte gasped for breath as his spent organ slipped out of her spunked mouth.

Raising the rope above his head, Goodhugh brought it down across the girl's naked buttocks with a loud crack. Father James wandered out of the office and stood by the altar as Charlotte's cries of pain and ecstasy echoed round the old building. Pondering on the girl's words, he leaned against the altar and rubbed his chin. Her fear had gone, he reflected. Walking boldly into the church, wielding the staff and talking of the Devil, she'd changed beyond belief. Where was the innocent little schoolgirlie now? Wondering whether the crude sex had transformed her, he recalled the candle, the eerie blue light. His eyes might have been playing tricks on him, he mused as her screams again echoed from the office.

'Christ,' Goodhugh gasped as he fled the office and joined the priest.

'What is it?'

'The girl . . . She mentioned the code word and . . .'

'Then it *was* her who rang Mary.'

'No, no, that's not all. She said something about the basement.'

'What basement?'

'Here, in the church. She said something about the stench of death, and the dead victims of our fathers rising.'

'I . . . I think we'd better let her go. She's already smashed—'

'I'll release her,' Goodhugh broke in as she called out, her vile expletives resounding around the church. 'We'll get her out of here and then talk about this. We've got to decide what we're going to do about her.'

'Do?' Father James frowned.

'We can't have her roaming around the village. God only knows who she'll go blabbing to. I'll free her and then we'll make our plans.'

Releasing the girl, Goodhugh stood back as she rose from the desk and glared at him. There was evil reflected in the black pools of her glazed eyes, he was sure as she flashed him a salacious grin. Leaving the office, she walked to the main door and turned. Holding her hands above her head, she stared hard at Father James as he stood by the altar.

'I shall return!' she screamed. 'The daughter of Satan shall return when the dead rise.' Fleeing the church, she dashed across the road and stood outside her cottage. The street was no place to be without clothes, she thought, gazing at her mother through the lounge window. Sure that the woman was asleep in the armchair, she slipped around the side of the cottage and tried the back door. The door swung open and she crept into the kitchen and stole through the hall, praying that her mother wouldn't hear her. She climbed the stairs and breathed a sigh of relief as she entered her bedroom and closed the door.

'I wondered when you'd be back.' Marianne smiled as she emerged from the shadows.

'God,' Charlotte breathed, switching the light on. 'You made me jump.'

'Sorry.'

'What on earth are you doing, hiding in the dark?'

'I was waiting for you. Where are your clothes?' The girl frowned, gazing at Charlotte's naked body as she clasped her hands over herself to conceal her naked vaginal lips. 'You've been out in the street like that?'

'Yes, I . . .'

'I was watching you in the church,' Marianne said, perching her rounded buttocks on the edge of the bed.

'You were there?' Charlotte asked surprisedly.

'Hiding outside. Why did you leave your clothes in the church?'

'I didn't. It's a long story. Where have you been? I heard that you'd gone missing.'

'I've been at home. When Father James rang, I pretended to be my mother and told him that Marianne had been out all night.'

'He thinks that you've run off because of the things he's been doing to you. He's really worried.'

'And so he should be. So, what's all this nonsense about Satan's daughter?'

'I . . . I thought I'd frighten them,' Charlotte began

pensively, turning and taking a skirt from the wardrobe. 'But, then . . . I'm not sure what happened. It was as if . . . I don't know how to describe it.'

'As if you were possessed, from what I saw.'

'Yes, no . . .' Charlotte murmured, clutching the folded skirt against her stomach.

'God, you went mad. You completely lost control.'

'I felt as if I wasn't in my body. I know it sounds silly, but I felt that I had no control over my body. I was sort of standing back, looking at myself.'

'I watched you until you went into the church office and then I decided to come here and wait for you. I told your mother that we'd arranged to work on our projects and she said that I could wait here for you. My mum thinks I'm staying here the night, so there's no rush to get back.'

'You *can* stay, if you want to,' Charlotte smiled, thoughts of lesbian sex surfacing from the dark depths of her young mind.

'I'd better not. Charlotte, when you were in the church . . . Why did you smash the place up?'

'As I said, the idea was to frighten the priest. But things got out of hand. I'm not sure whether it was a rush of adrenalin or . . . or something else. I don't quite know what happened.'

'Do you think you really were possessed?'

'I don't know. If I *was* possessed, then . . . It doesn't bear thinking about. I'm pleased that you're here, Marianne. Emily has been threatening me and—'

'Don't talk about Emily.'

'I'd better put some clothes on. If my mother comes up . . .'

'I don't want you to dress,' Marianne whispered huskily.

'My mother's downstairs,' Charlotte protested, placing the skirt on the ottoman. 'If she . . .'

'What happened to your pussy?' Marianne asked, gazing at her friend's crimsoned vulval flesh.

'They whipped me there,' Charlotte confessed, lowering her head and gazing at the swollen pads of her vulva. 'It looks awful, doesn't it?'

'It's . . . God, you've shaved,' Marianne breathed, focusing on the other girl's hairless vaginal lips.

'I . . . It's another long story.'

'You look beautiful.'

'Do you think so?'

'God, yes. You look . . . absolutely gorgeous.'

Reclining on the bed, Marianne parted her long legs and smiled. She wanted sex, Charlotte knew as she settled beside her and pulled her skirt up over her stomach. Focusing longingly on the red silk of her tight panties, she realized just how much she wanted Marianne – needed her. Her own juices of arousal seeping between the swollen pads of her girl slit, she felt a delightful quiver run through her rhythmically contracting womb. She desperately craved the girl's lubricious juices of desire, longed to drink from her young cunt, suck on her solid clitoris and take her to her sexual heaven.

Tugging her friend's wet panties down her long legs and pulling them off her feet, Charlotte caressed the gentle rise of her wet love lips and massaged the warm flesh of her firm mons. Planting a kiss on the dividing cushions of her deep ravine, she breathed in her heady girl-scent, the aroma driving her wild as she pushed her face hard against her soft vulval flesh. Again breathing in the perfume of her sex valley, she hoped that her mother wouldn't come upstairs. All she wanted was a little time to love Marianne, lick and

SCHOOLGIRL LUST

finger her to orgasm, drink her hot girl milk from the sheath of her tight cunt. Just a little time to be alone and love her new lesbian lover was all she asked.

Slipping her finger between the wet petals of the girl's inner love-lips, she drove it deep into her creamy-hot vaginal duct, massaging the spasming walls of her tight vagina as the girl writhed in her lesbian ecstasy. Slipping a second finger deep into the girl's creamy love mouth, Charlotte was desperate for her friend to reciprocate. To finger and massage each other simultaneously would be heaven, she knew as she forced a third finger into the tightening sheath of Marianne's pussy. And to lick each other, suck their clitorises into each other's hot mouths and take each other to orgasm would be sheer bliss. Sliding her wet fingers out of Marianne's vaginal duct, Charlotte turned round and lay on the bed with the shaved lips of her pussy close to the girl's face, her mouth close to her moist sex crack.

No words of instruction were needed as she spread Marianne's long legs and buried her face between the warmth of her firm thighs. As Charlotte licked the full length of her friend's sex slit, the girl propped herself up on her elbow and reciprocated. Their tongues tasting each other's vaginal juices, lapping at each other's girl slits, they shuddered in their new-found lesbian coupling. The slurping sounds of female tongues filling Charlotte's ears, she again thought about her mother. If the woman woke up . . .

'I don't fucking care,' she breathed, parting Marianne's fleshy sex pads and exposing the nub of her erect clitoris to her dark eyes.

'What about?' her friend asked, her tongue running up and down Charlotte's sex-dripping girl slit. 'Why are you swearing?'

'I don't care whether or not my mother catches us loving.'

'I do,' Marianne replied, lifting her head and frowning at Charlotte.

'OK, I'll lock the door,' Charlotte mumbled, leaping off the bed. 'I want you to turn over,' she whispered. 'Lie on your stomach with your legs apart.'

Rolling over, Marianne parted her long legs, her young womb fluttering expectantly as Charlotte lay on her stomach with her head between Marianne's thighs. Breathing heavily as Charlotte kissed and nibbled the moons of her firm buttocks, Marianne closed her eyes. Her anal globes parted by her lover's slender fingers, she gasped as the other girl's tongue repeatedly ran up and down the secret flesh within her anal crease. She quivered as the girl licked the dank gully between her rounded buttocks, let out low moans of pleasure as her tongue swept over the sensitive brown tissue encircling the tight inlet to her rectal channel.

'You taste wonderful,' Charlotte murmured, pushing her tongue into the bitter-sweet tube of her lover's bottom-hole. As she sucked and mouthed the girl's anal portal, she pondered on the crude words surfacing from the mire of her young mind. Anilingus, anal tongue-fuck, arse-lick . . . Where the unfamiliar words were coming from, she didn't know. But the crude act excited her – the aphrodisiacal taste of Marianne's anal canal was driving her into a sexual frenzy. Pushing her tongue deeper into the girl's tight anal tube, she felt her clitoris swell and throb as she locked her lips to her anus and sucked hard.

'Keep doing that,' Marianne murmured, reaching behind her back and yanking the firm orbs of her bottom wide apart. Placing her fingers either side of her anal inlet, she pulled on her delicate flesh, opening the gateway to her illicit sheath of sexual gratification, offering the very core of

SCHOOLGIRL LUST

her young body to her friend's wet tongue. Charlotte pressed her mouth harder against the girl's ring of delicious chestnut skin, sucking out the tangy flavour of her intoxicating rectal glands. Her tongue aching as she drove it deeper into Marianne's anal duct, she licked the inner walls of her moist shaft, delighting in her wanton perversion as her clitoris ripened and pulsated in anticipation. Never had Charlotte known that such immense gratification could be got from pleasuring another girl's naked body. Her conception of love and sex had been rooted in the notion of the natural coupling of male and female. Never had she imagined that sexual satisfaction could be derived from a female tongue teasing a female bottom.

'Oh, my God,' Marianne sang in her sexual delirium as Charlotte slipped her tongue out of her hot bottom-hole and drove two fingers into her private sheath. Again praying that her mother wouldn't burst into the room, Charlotte forced a third finger deep into the other girl's anal canal. Licking the brown flesh stretched tautly around her fingers, she savoured the taste of the girl's duct of illicit pleasure. Sucking and mouthing Marianne's tight hole as she pistoned her rectal duct, Charlotte felt an overwhelming desire to commit the most debased sexual acts imaginable. Sliding her fingers out of Marianne's spasming anal channel, she leaped off the bed and moved to the dressing table.

'What are you doing?' Marianne asked, lifting and turning her head.

'You'll like this,' Charlotte grinned, taking a candle from the dressing table.

'I hope your mother doesn't—'

'Don't worry, the door's locked. Take all your clothes off.'

'I'd better not. If your mother comes up and knocks on the door—'

'I'll tell her that you went home and that I'm in bed. Take everything off.'

Grinning as the girl clambered off the bed and slipped out of the rest of her clothes, Charlotte ran her fingers up and down the smooth shaft of the candle. Her mind awash with thoughts of perverted lesbian sex, she again ordered her friend to lie on her stomach with her legs wide apart. Eyeing the girl's pouting vaginal lips nestling between her inner thighs, the dark divide of her naked buttocks, she settled on the bed between her legs. Kissing the pert globes of her bottom, she ran the tip of the candle up and down the girl's anal valley.

Parting Marianne's firm buttocks, Charlotte pressed the tip of the candle against the girl's anal rosebud and drove the waxen shaft deep into her tight rectum. Marianne gasped as the phallus impaled her, waking sleeping nerve endings deep within her anal core. Writhing, she spread her limbs further as Charlotte pistoned and twisted the candle, sending delightful ripples of illicit sex through her quivering pelvis. Pushing the waxen phallus deeper into Marianne's rectal channel, Charlotte sat back on her heels as a wicked idea sidled stealthily into her mind.

'Roll over onto your back,' she murmured, moving further back as the girl obediently complied. 'Now raise your knees and open your legs wide.' Lying on the bed with her buttocks close to Marianne's anal orbs, Charlotte reached beneath her thigh and grabbed the protruding end of the candle. Manoeuvring her hips, aligning the end of the candle with her tightly closed anal inlet, she moved closer to her friend. The shaft driving into her contracting anal duct, she gasped as the moons of her buttocks pressed against Marianne's, the candle embedded deep within both their anal shafts. As they writhed on the bed, the candle massaging their inner rectal flesh, the girls closed their eyes and let out long low moans of illicit pleasure.

This was heaven, Charlotte thought as she gently rocked her hips, the waxen dildo gliding in and out of each other's tight bottom-holes. Running her fingers over the smooth plateau of her stomach, Charlotte massaged the swell of her pouting vaginal lips, breathing deeply as the beautiful sensations permeated her quivering womb. Vibrating her fingertip over the solid protrusion of her ripe clitoris, she arched her back, the candle sending electrifying sensations deep into the dank cavern of her bowels as she gasped in her self-lusting.

'Are you there, Charlotte?' her mother called from outside the door.

'I'm . . . I'm in bed,' she managed to reply.

'I didn't hear you come in.'

'You were asleep in the chair.'

'Has Marianne gone?'

'Yes, she has.'

'All right. I'll see you in the morning.'

Breathing a sigh of relief, Charlotte moved closer to Marianne, the warm globes of their firm buttocks pressing firmly together in debased lesbian passion, the candle linking them in depraved lust. The bed gently rocking as they moved back and forth, the candle simultaneously fucking the tight shafts of their dank rectal sheaths, they breathed heavily in their decadence, trembled in their wanton teenage desire. Caressing her erect clitoris, Charlotte closed her eyes as the sensations crept over her naked flesh, reaching out to the extremities of her young body.

Recalling the events in the church as her clitoris painfully swelled within the wet valley of her cunt, Charlotte hoped again that she'd put an end to the predatory activities of Goodhugh and his priestly accomplice in debauchery. If they believed that Satan had risen, they'd think twice about ordering Charlotte to the church for crude sex sessions. And once she'd retrieved the photographs, she could turn the tables and, with luck, threaten the wicked pair. But, whatever happened, she knew that she'd never be the same again. A candle forced deep into her rectum, the other end thrust up Marianne's anal duct . . . Never would Charlotte be the same again.

Slipping the candle out of her bottom-hole, Charlotte leaped on top of Marianne and buried her face between the swollen outer lips of her vagina. Their naked girl cracks pressed against each other's faces, their mouths locked to each other's pussies, they began their lesbian licking. Grabbing the protruding end of the candle, Charlotte pistoned her friend's anal canal, sucking hard on her clitoris as she took the girl closer to her orgasm. Almost tearing her pussy lips apart, she gazed longingly at the girl's rubicund inner flesh, the lubricious juices of her desire oozing from her bared cunt hole. Pressing her mouth over the portal to her sex sheath, she sucked hard, bringing out the girl's creamy lubricant, sucking the pleasure from her writhing body. As Marianne's tongue entered her vaginal cavern, Charlotte lost herself in her wanton lechery, pistoning the girl's bottom-hole with the candle and fervently tongue-fucking her cunt as her naked body shook violently.

'Bite me,' she ordered Marianne as her clitoris swelled and pulsated, her preorgasmic juices flooding the girl's face. 'Bite my cunt hard.' Wondering at her crudity, Charlotte realized that she'd been through a transformation. She'd thought she'd found love with Marianne, but it was crude lust that had gripped her. Her friend's teeth sinking into the fleshy cushions of her outer labia, she gasped through a mouthful of vaginal flesh as the beautiful pain permeated the very core of her young womb.

'Push your fingers up my arse,' she breathed, her crude words sending her arousal soaring, her lust juices gushing from her gaping cunt. Three fingers forced into the spasming sheath of her tight bottom, Charlotte gasped for breath, her eyes rolling as the lewd sensations immersed her quivering body in a murky pool of decadence. 'Bite my cunt again,' she breathed, sinking her own teeth into the fleshy swell of Marianne's vaginal lips. 'Bite my cunt hard.' Wailing in her perversity, her pulsating clitoris massaged by the girl's chin as she nibbled on her vaginal flesh, Charlotte finally reached her shuddering climax.

'Yes,' she gasped, her pussy-wet face buried deep within the drenched ravine of Marianne's young cunt. 'More fingers,' she ordered the girl, her naked body rigid as her anal tube stretched open to accommodate half the girl's hand. 'More,' she breathed. 'More!' Lost in her arousal, she sucked on Marianne's solid clitoris until the girl shook fiercely in her coming. Her juices spewing from the gaping mouth of her vaginal throat, she cried out as Charlotte pistoned the contracting shaft of her arse with the hot candle. Both girls floating up to their sexual heavens, their clitorises pulsating in orgasm, their juices of lesbian lust gushing from their tight cunts, they screamed out in their agonized pleasure.

'Charlotte,' the girl's mother called, tapping on the door. 'Charlotte, are you all right?'

'Yes,' she panted, her vaginal muscles rhythmically contracting, squeezing out her juices of orgasm. 'I . . . I was dreaming.'

'Let me in, Charlotte. I want to—'

'No, no . . . I'm all right.'

'I'll see you in the morning. Goodnight.'

'Goodnight, mother.'

Panting quietly, the girls lay trembling in the wake of their massive orgasms, their faces flushed, their cunts burning like fire. Charlotte slid the candle out of Marianne's anal canal as Marianne withdrew her fingers from Charlotte's bottom-hole and they quieted their sated bodies. The smell of sex filling Charlotte's nostrils, she rolled off Marianne's naked body and onto her own stomach. Her face buried in the eiderdown, she hoped that her mother would return. All she needed was to be caught naked with another girl, their faces flushed with sex, their cunts dripping with the juices of orgasm.

'I'd better go home,' Marianne whispered, sitting upright.

'No,' Charlotte grinned, her dark eyes mirroring an almost evil inner lust. 'You'll stay here until—'

'Charlotte, it's very late.'

'Too late to go home. Besides, your mother thinks that you're staying here.'

'I know, but—'

'Sleep here, in my bed with me.'

'All right. But I'll have to go early, before your mum gets up.'

As Marianne lay back down in the bed, Charlotte moved to the dressing table and brushed her long black hair. They'd have a good night's sleep and wake early, she decided. They'd enjoy at least an hour of crude lesbian sex before Marianne left the cottage. Slipping into bed

SCHOOLGIRL LUST

alongside the girl, Charlotte pulled the sheets up and pressed her naked body close to her lover's. She was tired after a day of crude sex and whipping. Closing her eyes, she cupped the swell of Marianne's sex lips in her hand. In the morning, she'd lick the girl's vulval slit, suck her clitoris to orgasm, tongue her sweet bottom-hole, drink her juices of desire . . . In the morning.

Chapter Eleven

'You can see the predicament you've put me in,' Goodhugh said, rubbing his lined forehead as he stared hard at Emily. 'I turned my back for a few seconds and you took a radio and left the shop without paying for it.'

'You *gave* it to me,' the girl responded.

'Emily, I don't *give* my stock away. I happened to see you leave the shop with it tucked under your arm. Why would I have gone outside and apprehended you if I'd given you the radio?'

'You gave Charlotte a radio. She told me about it.'

'What did she say, exactly?'

'Just that you'd given her a radio.'

'Was that all she said?'

'Yes.'

'Charlotte did have a radio but, unlike you, she paid for it.'

'She told me that . . . I thought . . .' the girl stammered, brushing her long blonde hair away from her flushed face. 'You said that I could take one.'

'Yes, I did say that you could take one. I meant take one from the shelf so that you could have a look at it. I didn't mean take a radio and walk out of the shop without paying for it.'

'I just thought, seeing as Charlotte had one, you meant that I could—'

'I'm afraid that I have no option other than to call the police.'

'*What*?' Emily gasped.

'You've admitted that you left the shop without paying for it.'

'Look, you have the radio so there's no harm done.'

'No harm done? You walked out of my shop with . . . I'm sorry, Emily. I'm going to have to report this.'

'No, please. My parents will go mad. I honestly thought that you meant I could have one for nothing.'

'I really don't think the police will believe a story like that. Why on earth would I tell my customers that they can take my stock for nothing?'

'Look, it was a mistake. I thought—'

'Emily, it doesn't matter what you *thought*. The point is that you *stole* a radio.'

'I . . . I was in trouble with the police a while ago,' the girl confessed, hanging her head. 'I was in a bar and . . . If they think that I've now stolen a radio . . .'

'I can see your predicament, but you must be able to see mine.'

'Surely we can sort this out,' she sighed, nervously wringing her hands. 'We don't have to involve the police.'

'Well, I suppose we could talk about it.' Goodhugh smiled. 'Come though to the stockroom with me.'

Following the man, Emily couldn't understand why Charlotte had said that Goodhugh had given her a radio when she'd paid for it. But that didn't matter, she reflected, entering the stockroom and standing by the desk. Wondering what he had in mind, she watched him take his camera from the shelf. Saying nothing, he opened the back and slipped a new roll of film inside. Why he was fiddling with his camera at a time like this, she had no idea. Noticing the

SCHOOLGIRL LUST

wall clock, she sighed. Eight-thirty. She had to get to school. Having already taken time off, she dared not be late.

'You really are photogenic,' Goodhugh smiled. 'A complete natural. Let's have a big smile.'

'You said that we were going to talk,' she breathed as he clicked the shutter.

'Indeed we are. Tell me, have you ever done any photographic work?'

'No, no, I haven't. Look, about the radio—'

'Ah, yes. The radio. I have an idea,' he said, placing his camera on the desk and standing before the girl. 'You look lovely in your school uniform. You're a very pretty girl, Emily. Developing into a fine young lady. I've watched you grow and mature over the years. I remember when you were—'

'The radio, Mr Goodhugh,' she broke in. 'You said that you had an idea.'

'Yes, I have. I'd like to take a few photographs of you.'

'Photographs?' she echoed, shaking her head and glancing at the clock again. 'What about the radio?'

'I was coming to that. To involve the police would be disastrous for you and your parents. I have a proposition, Emily.'

'Oh?'

'I'll forget about the radio if—'

'Thank God,' the girl breathed, her shoulders sagging as a wave of relief rolled through her young body.

'If you'll be my photographic model.'

'Model?' She frowned.

'As I said, I'd like to take some photographs of you for my private collection.'

'Is that all?' She smiled.

'That's all.'

'OK.'

'I knew we could work this out,' he grinned, grabbing his camera. 'Er . . . unbutton your blouse and—'

'What sort of photographs?' Emily asked, noticing lechery reflected in his beady eyes as he focused on the deep ravine between her firm mammary spheres.

'Sexy photographs.'

'Sexy?'

'You're a very attractive young girl, Emily. Unbutton your blouse and I'll take a few shots of your breasts.'

Wondering whether she could turn the situation round, Emily decided to go along with anything he asked of her. Believing that she could threaten to expose him as a dirty old man, she realized that he'd want her to do more than unbutton her blouse. But she had a plan. Parting the white silk of her blouse and projecting the firm melons of her teenage breasts as they strained against her bra, she decided to allow him to take his sexy photographs. Once she had a few copies of the pictures, she'd have him over a barrel. She'd say that he'd forced her into the stockroom and threatened her. Realizing that the business with the radio was a ploy, she knew that he'd had no intention of calling the police. He was just a dirty old man who couldn't keep his eyes off schoolgirls.

'That's very good,' he smiled, clicking the shutter. 'You have lovely legs, Emily. Lift your skirt up a little.'

'I shouldn't be doing this,' she said softly, pulling her skirt up and exposing the triangular patch of her bulging red panties nestling at the tops of her firm thighs.

'Yes, that's perfect.'

As he knelt on the floor and focused the camera on the strip of silk taut between her parted thighs, Emily grinned. She wasn't averse to displaying her tight panties to a dirty old man. In fact, she was quite enjoying turning him on like this. His penis would be stiffening, she thought, aware of her clitoris swelling within her moist vaginal slit. Deciding to tease him, she parted her thighs wider and lifted her skirt up over her firm stomach. Placing her hands on the desk behind her, she leaned back, pushing her sexual centre forward as the man moved in with his camera.

'You're very good,' he praised her.

'I've often thought about becoming a model,' she smiled, deciding to miss school.

'I might be able to help you,' he said, lowering the camera and looking up at her pretty face. 'A friend of mine is an agent. If it's all right with you, I'll send him a few photographs.'

'That would be great,' she beamed enthusiastically.

'Mind you, the photographs would have to be . . . What I'm trying to say is . . .'

'There's someone in the shop,' Emily said as the bell rang.

'I won't be a minute. Don't go away.'

She knew exactly what he wanted as he left the room and closed the door. Slipping off the desk, she paced the floor. Recalling the photographs of Charlotte and Marianne, she frowned. She'd found the envelope pinned to Charlotte's front door and curiosity had got the better of her. Not wanting to tell Charlotte the truth, she'd told her that the photographs had been sent to her house. Perhaps Goodhugh had something to do with the photographs, she mused. Wondering whether he was in some way blackmailing Charlotte, she swung round on her heels as he returned to the stockroom.

'You were saying?' Emily smiled.

'This friend of mine, the agent . . . He deals with men's magazines. Now I'm not saying that he'd want photos of you in lewd poses.'

'I'm pleased to hear it,' she said, feigning shock.

'But he would want photographs of you in your underwear.'

'Oh, I see,' she murmured. 'I really don't think—'

'Nothing sordid, you understand. Just sexy shots of you in your underwear.'

'I'm not sure, Mr Goodhugh. I really don't want to take my clothes off.'

'It was just a thought. Mind you, he does pay very well,' he added pensively. 'But, if you don't want to do it, that's fine. Right, I'd like a few more shots of you sitting on the desk.'

Perching her buttocks on the desk, Emily again pulled her skirt up and exposed the tight material of her red panties. She could almost feel Goodhugh's arousal as he mopped his brow with a handkerchief. His heavy balls would be rolling, she knew. Once she'd gone, he'd probably get his cock out and wank. Picturing her tight panties, imagining her sweet sex crack, he'd shoot his spunk over the floor. He was quite normal, she mused, recalling her next-door neighbour spying through the bushes as she'd sunbathed in her bikini. All men were desperate for a glimpse of schoolgirls' knickers.

The light shining on his balding head, Goodhugh took several more shots of her damp panties before standing upright and rubbing his chin. He was trying to think of a way to convince her to remove her clothes, she knew as she noticed the bulge in his trousers. She'd tease him, she again decided, parting her thighs wider. Work him into a state of sexual frenzy and then leave him alone with his rock-hard cock.

Gazing longingly at her swelling panties, he frowned as the shop bell rang. Leaving the stock room, he closed the door as Emily slipped off the desk. Pulling her panties up,

SCHOOLGIRL LUST

the red material slipping into the wet divide between her fleshy outer labia, she looked down and grinned. That would send his libido through the roof, she mused, lowering her skirt. Wondering how far she should go as she waited for him to return, she thought again about the photographs of Charlotte with Marianne in the woods. Convinced that Goodhugh had something to do with the lewd pictures, she decided to talk to Charlotte about it. And question her about the radio she'd said Goodhugh had given her.

'I'm sorry,' Goodhugh smiled as he entered the room and closed the door. 'It looks as though it's going to be a busy morning.'

'You've got your photos, so I'll be going,' Emily said, brushing her blonde hair away from her pretty face.

'Just a few more shots,' he virtually begged, taking his camera.

'All right,' she conceded, sitting on the desk again.

Pulling her skirt up, she parted her thighs wide, feigning oblivion to the swollen lips of her pussy bulging either side of her red panties. Goodhugh's eyes were almost popping out of his head as he knelt on the floor and took several shots of the young girl's blatantly exhibited intimacy. Concealing a grin, Emily knew that the man was putty in her hands. His threats about the radio counted for nothing now that he'd seen the delights she had to offer. This was better than going to school, she thought as the shop bell rang again.

'I'll be going now,' Emily said, sliding off the desk and pulling her skirt down as he muttered something under his breath.

Silently fuming, Goodhugh bit his lip. 'Er . . . perhaps you could come back this evening,' he said, placing the camera on the shelf.

'Well, I . . . I don't know,' she stammered.

'Come back at six,' he persisted. 'I'll be waiting for you.'

'If I can,' she replied, leaving the room. 'You have your photographs, so—'

'Just a few more,' he broke in urgently. 'I just need a few more.'

'I'll see.'

Leaving the shop, Emily decided to call on Charlotte. As she approached the cottage, she doubted that the girl had gone to school. Charlotte had taken most of the week off, so probably wouldn't go back until the following Monday. Knocking on the door, aware of her panties nestling within the wet ravine of her vagina, Emily decided to lure her young friend to the woods and have sex with her. After displaying her bulging pussy lips to Goodhugh, she needed sex. Charlotte's wet tongue darting in and out of her tight cunt, snaking over the sensitive nub of her erect clitoris and—

'Oh, it's you.' Charlotte's mother scowled as she opened the door. 'Charlotte isn't here,' she said, folding her arms. 'She's at school. And that's where you should be.'

'I'm going to school now,' Emily replied, forcing a smile. 'I'll see her there.'

As she walked down the road, the sun warming her back, Emily wondered whether Charlotte was in the woods. She had to talk to the girl, ask her about the photographs. And the radio. If Goodhugh *was* involved, if he was blackmailing Charlotte and Marianne . . . No, she mused. The man was harmless enough. He was a dirty old bastard, but harmless enough. Wandering along the path to the bridge over the stream, she sat on the grass and thought about Goodhugh. He'd obviously conned her over the radio, ensuring that he had a hold over her. He'd demand that she remove all her clothes the next time she was in the stockroom, she was sure. But she'd play her games, tease him until his cock was granite-hard and he spunked in his trousers.

Hearing someone approaching, Emily slid down the bank to the stream and crept beneath the wooden bridge. Skipping school wasn't a good idea, she reflected as the sound of twigs cracking underfoot grew louder. Holding her breath as someone crossed the bridge, she clambered up the bank to see Charlotte and Marianne following the path into the woods. Silently fuming, Emily waited for a few minutes before trailing them, keeping her distance as they slipped into the undergrowth. Peering through the bushes into a clearing, Emily watched the girls.

'You'll have to stay again,' Charlotte said, smiling at her lesbian lover.

'We should have gone to school,' Marianne sighed. 'We'll be in real trouble if we're not careful.'

'I've been off with a bad stomach all week so I'm not worried. And the doctor came out, so I'm covered. Mind you, I did tell my mother that I was going in today. It looks as though it's all gone quiet on a certain front.'

'Thank God,' Marianne murmured. 'But for how long?'

'That's a good question. At least we've got the evidence. They'll never find the bag.'

Emily wasn't going to learn anything, she was sure as she listened to the girls chatting. But she'd seen and heard enough to know that Charlotte had defied her and been unfaithful again. She'd talk to her later, she decided as she heard someone approaching. Not wanting to be caught missing school, she backtracked through the undergrowth and made her way through the woods. There was no point in spending the day swanning around and then having to lie to her parents, she knew. Although she'd be late, school was the best option.

'Who's there?' Charlotte called, leaping to her feet as the bushes rustled.

'I definitely heard someone,' Marianne said, looking around the clearing. 'I hope it's not Emily.'

'It might have been a rabbit,' Charlotte smiled, settling next to her friend.

'So, the runaway has returned,' Father James said as he emerged from the bushes and scowled at Marianne. 'I knew you'd be back.'

'Leave me alone,' the girl whimpered as he stood in the clearing, towering above her.

'What do *you* want?' Charlotte snapped.

'Well, if it's not the Devil's daughter,' the priest grinned. 'You both need to be severely punished for your wicked ways. You, Marianne. Running off like that when you'd been ordered to come to the church. And you, Charlotte. Wrecking the church and—'

'What are you going to do about it?' she interrupted him. 'Goodhugh isn't here, and there are two of us, so—'

'Oh, I see,' he laughed. 'So you're both going to . . . What *are* you going to do, exactly?'

'Just fuck off,' Charlotte hissed.

'That's the sort of language I'd expect from a slut like you. I do believe that it's high time you were dealt with most severely. You've wrecked the church, you've caused no end of trouble—'

'Fuck off, pervert,' Charlotte snapped.

'Let's go,' Marianne said softly, rising to her feet.

'You're not going anywhere,' the priest grinned. 'OK, lads,' he called.

Staring open-mouthed as four teenage boys emerged

from the bushes, Charlotte gasped. She knew only too well what was going to happen. Even the threat of Satan hadn't deterred the perverted priest, she reflected. Turning as Marianne dashed across the clearing and slipped into the bushes, Charlotte was about to follow her when Father James grabbed her arm and pulled her to her feet.

'Leave her,' he said as two young men dashed across the clearing after Marianne. 'This is the one I want. OK, Charlotte. You know what to do. You know what's expected of you. Take all your clothes off.'

Hanging her head, Charlotte began unbuttoning her blouse. There was no point in trying to escape the inevitable, she knew as she slipped the garment off her shoulders and let it fall to the ground. The young men eagerly watching as she tugged her skirt down her long legs, she kicked the garment aside and unhooked her bra. The whispering of male desire echoing around the clearing as the silk cups fell away from her firm breasts, the brown teats of her sensitive nipples elongating in the relatively cool air of the woods, she felt a wave of despondency roll through her. She was nothing more than a sex doll, an object of desire, a naked body to be fucked and spunked.

Slipping her wet panties down, Charlotte stood before her audience and obediently awaited her instructions. Nothing seemed to matter any more. She was to be fucked, her orifices pumped full of spunk . . . It really didn't matter any more. Gazing at the young men as they removed their clothes, their huge cocks snapping to attention, she wondered who they were, where they'd come from. She'd never seen them in the village and could only assume that the priest had rounded them up from another village or town.

Watching as one man lay on his back on the ground, the purple head of his massive cock-shaft pointing to the sky, his hairy balls rolling, Charlotte took a deep breath as the priest ordered her to straddle his naked body. Kneeling either side of his hips, she leaned on her hands as he grabbed the base of his solid organ and slipped his swollen glans into the gaping ravine of her teenage cunt. His shaft driving into the hot creamy sheath of her tight vagina, she closed her eyes as he completely impaled her young body on his male hardness.

This wasn't happening, Charlotte tried to convince herself as another man knelt behind her and rudely yanked the globes of her firm buttocks wide apart. She could feel the bulbous knob of his penis stabbing at her vaginal entrance as the other young man slowly withdrew his girl-wet shaft until her girl lips hugged the rim of his male crown. It *was* happening, but it didn't matter. She was sure that they weren't both going to try to push their huge members into the wet shaft of her tight pussy. There was no way they could achieve such a degrading act, she knew.

'No,' she gasped as the man kneeling behind her managed to force his ballooning knob past the taut inner lips of her bloated pussy. Grimacing as he drove his shaft deep into her painfully stretched cunt, the two knobs pressing against the hard softness of her young cervix, Charlotte believed that she'd tear open. Her sex sheath wasn't designed to accommodate two erect penises, she found herself thinking. The inner lips of her vaginal mouth stretched tautly around the massive shafts, she again thought that she'd split open. A finger slipping into the dank shaft of her tight anal canal, she cried out as someone lifted her head by her hair. Opening her eyes, she gazed in awe at the purple knob hovering before her flushed face. Wondering whether Marianne would return with help, she parted her full lips and sucked the silky-smooth glans into her wet mouth.

Chuckles filling the air as her audience watched the three-way fucking, her naked body rocking, Charlotte knew that she was in for a good hour – at least – of debauchery. Her vaginal cavern painfully stretched as the two penises thrust in and out of her tight sex duct, she ran her tongue over the silky glans bloating her pretty mouth. The sooner the men had pumped their sperm into her young body, the sooner they'd leave her, she reflected, bobbing her head back and forth to bring out the white liquid of the man who was fucking her mouth. The sooner she'd been crudely fucked and spunked . . .

'Right,' the priest said, painfully slapping the firm flesh of her rounded buttocks. 'I'll be going to get your mother shortly so that she can see what a little slut her daughter really is.' Her eyes wide, Charlotte was sure that he was bluffing. He wouldn't jeopardize the sordid scam by bringing her mother to the clearing. Or would he? Sperm suddenly bathing her pink tongue, filling her cheeks, she repeatedly swallowed hard. The salty liquid dribbling down her chin as the man's swinging balls battered her neck, a thousand thoughts swimming in the mire of her mind, she came to a decision.

She'd for ever be a sex slave to Goodhugh and the priest. There was no way out of the horror. But there might be a way to live a half-normal life, she mused, swallowing the gushing spunk as the unknown man crudely mouth-fucked her. If she couldn't beat them, she could join them. It was an idea that had only just come to her. With no money, running away was out of the question. And living with constant blackmail threats was impossible. If she joined forces with the evil pair, life would become a lot easier. And she might even be given a share of the money they were making.

The inflamed sheath of her vagina filling with sperm as both men grunted, the spent penis leaving her spunked mouth, she gasped for breath. She could take anything, she knew as the double pussy-fucking rocked her naked body. Anything but the leather whip. She could hardly believe that, only five days previously, she'd woken to the sun streaming in through her bedroom window, warming her virginal body. In such a short space of time, she'd had every orifice fucked and spunked, her buttocks thrashed, she'd shaved her pubic hair, had her vulval flesh whipped, her naked body pissed over . . .

'It's time to get your mother,' Father James grinned, kneeling and lifting her head.

'I'll join you,' she said softly.

'Come with me?' he chuckled. 'Oh, no, you—'

'No, I mean that I'll join you in . . . You won't have to blackmail me any more. I'll be a willing participant in the sex.'

'Really?' he grinned as the two cocks slid out of her double-spunked vaginal duct. 'You do realize that, in order to become a member of our little club, you'll have to undergo a test?'

'Anything,' she gasped, her burning vaginal lips closing over the rubicund portal to her sex sheath.

'Anything?' he murmured as she rolled to one side and lay on the grass. 'I'll tell you what I'll do. You prove yourself to be a true slag-whore, and then I'll have a chat with you about joining us.'

'All right,' she gasped, massaging the sore lips of her vagina.

'OK, we'll begin with a double arse-fucking.'

Staring at the priest as he rose to his feet, Charlotte couldn't believe what he'd said. A double arse-fucking? It wasn't possible, she thought fearfully as a young man lay on the ground, his erect cock standing proudly to attention. She'd just about managed to take two solid penises into the tight shaft of her pussy, but the narrow sheath of her rectum? But, like it or not, she was to endure a double bum-fucking, she knew. Either she willingly took two huge cocks deep into her anal canal, or she was forced. The choice was hers.

Kneeling astride the man's hips, Charlotte leaned forward, placing her hands on the ground and resting her weight on her arms. Closing her eyes as the man beneath her grinned, she knew that the swell of her puffy vaginal lips was blatantly displayed to her eager audience. Her feeling of humiliation rising, she could hear movements behind her naked body, feel warm hands groping the pert orbs of her young bottom. Her buttocks rudely yanked wide apart, the bulbous head of the man's cock pressing against the once-private portal to her rectum, she breathed faster as her anxiety rose. His purple glans slipping past the brown tissue of her anus, she let out a rush of breath as his swollen cock-head entered her hot rectal sheath. More movements – another man behind her, kneeling with his solid weapon poised for anal penetration. They'd never accomplish the illicit act, she was sure as the second glans pressed hard gainst her already taut anal ring. It wasn't physically possible to thrust two huge penises into the restricted tube of her anal canal.

As more hands groped her naked buttocks, pulling her tensed globes wide apart, she felt fingers exploring within her anal gully. Her already stretched anus forced to open further, she whimpered as the second solid knob pressed harder against her delicate tissue. Her face flushed, her breathing fast, she squeezed her eyes shut as the purple crown slipped into her rectum alongside the first penile plum. Picturing the sensitive tissue of her anus, she imagined the brown flesh stretched tautly around the two ballooning knobs, the two veined shafts about to force their way deep into the tight tube of her hot rectum.

As two men knelt before her and pulled her head up, Charlotte focused on their erect organs, their swollen knobs hovering only inches from her gasping mouth. Four penises? she pondered fearfully as the two organs within her rectal duct drove further into the heat of her bowels. Taking the silky knobs into her wet mouth, tasting the maleness of the salty sex globes, she prayed that the priest would allow her to join him in his debauchery and put an end to the continual threats. If she could at least live without the fear of Goodhugh calling at the cottage and fucking her mouth, without having to worry every time the doorbell rang . . . But she knew in her heart that the nightmare would never end. The penises would thrust into her young orifices, the knobs swell and the spunk gush – no matter what happened.

'Yes,' the man behind her gasped as the two penises drove deeper into her rectal duct, bloating her pelvic cavity.

'That's four cocks,' Father James chuckled. 'If we can find a way to force another cock up the slag's tight cunt . . .'

'I'll push this right up her cunt,' a male voice laughed.

Shuddering as something was slipped between the wet wings of her inner lips, Charlotte moaned through her nose as a cold, cylindrical shaft was forced into the constricted sheath of her sex-wet vagina. The dildo suddenly bursting into life, transmitting powerful vibrations deep into her rhythmically contracting womb, she quivered in her arousal. Her exposed clitoris pressed against the buzzing shaft, the sensations driving her wild as the double arse-fucking rocked her young body, she thought she was going to pass out. Her mind blown away on the wind of lust, she gobbled on the knobs bloating her hot mouth, running her tongue over the silky globes, desperate to drink the spunk from the men's full balls.

The vibrator thrusting in and out of the drenched sheath of her teenage cunt, her juices of desire spewing from the gaping mouth of her burning duct, Charlotte shuddered uncontrollably as her swollen clitoris exploded in orgasm. Her mouth filling with the double sperming, the men kneeling before her gasping in their coming, she swallowed the fruits of their debauchery as her anal sheath overflowed with sperm. Perspiration matted her long black hair as she writhed and gasped, her eyes rolling, her naked body quivering. Never had she known that such immense pleasure was to be had from the debased combination of four sperming cocks and a huge vibrator. Never had she dreamed that her young body would be simultaneously fucked by four young men.

Again wondering whether it was the rough hardness of the male or the delicate juiciness of the female that she really craved as she rode the crest of her enforced climax, Charlotte drank from the orgasming knobs, swallowing as much spunk as she could before the two pairs of heavy balls ran dry. The squelching sounds of her double-cock-pistoned arse filling her ears as she slurped on the throbbing purple knobs, her own juices of orgasm bubbling within her spasming cunt as she was crudely fucked by the buzzing vibrator, she knew that she'd reached the pinnacle of sexual deviancy. From the angelic innocence of virginity to the crude vulgarity of a common whore . . .

The deflating penises finally withdrawing from the sperm-bubbling sheath of her bottom as the vibrator shot out of her young cunt, the spent knobs slipping out of her sperm-dripping mouth, Charlotte rolled over onto the grass and lay quivering uncontrollably in the aftermath of her incredible coming. Had she passed the test? she wondered, the white liquid of male orgasm oozing from the burning eye of her anus. Would she now be allowed at least some freedom to live her young life? Watching the priest through her eyelashes as he ordered the young men to dress, she hoped that her ordeal was over. She had to rest, she knew as her naked body shuddered and the muscles of her cunt tightened, squeezing out the cream of her orgasm. She needed to wash and then sleep.

'You'll always be ready for sex,' Father James said, towering over the girl as she lay panting on the grass. 'You'll obey me without question or hesitation. Do you understand?'

'Yes,' she breathed. 'Whatever you say.'

'And you'll return the photographs.'

'I don't have them,' she lied. 'I've never had the photographs.'

'We'll discuss that when you come to the church this evening.'

'This evening? But—'

'You'll be there at six o'clock for your initiation ceremony. By the way, shave your cunt. I don't like stubble.'

'May I go now?' Charlotte asked as the men began to leave the clearing.

'There's one more thing I want you to do.' The cleric grinned, lifting his cassock and kneeling astride her head. 'Lick my balls.'

His hairy scrotum settling over her mouth, Charlotte looked up at the veined shaft of the priest's erect penis standing to attention above her dark eyes. Pushing her

SCHOOLGIRL LUST

tongue out, she tasted his scrotal sac, licked his full balls as he ordered her to wank him. Grabbing his solid penis, she moved the loose skin back and forth, his purple knob appearing and disappearing as he breathed heavily in his male pleasure. He was going to spray his sperm over her face and hair, she knew as she licked and nibbled the soft skin of his balls. His male scent filling her nostrils, she savoured the heady taste of his genitalia as she moved her hand up and down his solid flesh-pole.

'You'll do this every day,' he gasped. 'Cleansing me with your tongue and wanking me will be a daily occurrence.' Moving the warm skin of his shaft up and down, Charlotte continued to lick and nibble his ball sac as he trembled in his male ecstasy. Wondering what other sexual acts would become a daily occurrence, she thought about shaving the stubble from her vulval flesh. She reckoned that, what with keeping her pussy lips smooth and cleansing the priest with her tongue every day, she might find that she had to endure more crude sexual acts as a member of the so-called club than were demanded of her before. But she'd do anything to put an end to the blackmail, the constant threats to reveal her sordid secret to her mother.

'God,' Father James breathed as his white spunk shot from his purple knob. Splattering her hair, running down her hand and dripping onto her pretty face, the orgasmic rain drenched Charlotte as she licked the man's bouncing balls. On and on the flow of sperm pumped from his knob-slit as he shuddered and gasped in his sexual euphoria. The liquid running down his balls, trickling over her tongue, she slowed her wanking rhythm as he grabbed her arm. Moving her hand aside, he grabbed his deflating cock, forced the purple plum into her mouth and ordered her to suck out the last of his sperm. At least he was satisfied, for the time being. Now, she could go home and wash – and sleep.

'The church,' he breathed, clambering to his feet. 'Be there at six o'clock.' Adjusting his cassock, the priest moved to the edge of the clearing and turned. 'The initiation ceremony will take at least two hours,' he grinned. 'You'd better lie to your mother. Tell her you're going to see a friend or something.' As he disappeared into the bushes, Charlotte licked her spunked lips and sat up. Rivers of testicular liquid running down her cheeks, she wiped her flushed face on the back of her hand and stood up.

She wondered as she dressed. Wondered about the future, her mother, Marianne, Emily . . . and her defiled young body. She'd become strangely numb to the horrendous events of the past few days, she knew as she veiled her spunked curves. Her cunt was nothing more than a hot wet hole for men to shove their cocks up and shoot their spunk into. Her mouth, too, was purely a fuck-hole, as was her tight anal sheath. Her teenage body finally clothed, she sat on the grass and listened to the birds singing, the gentle summer breeze wafting through the trees above.

She'd go home later, she decided, twisting her sperm-matted hair around her fingers. Go home, pretend to her mother that she was fine, have a bath and shave her vulval flesh . . . and then visit the church for the initiation. Shaking her head, she smiled wryly. Initiation? Hardly the right word for a quadruple fucking, an arse-sperming, a mouth-spunking, a vulval thrashing, a . . . Perhaps Satan would call on the church.

Chapter Twelve

Sitting on her bed, Charlotte wondered where her mother had got to. Five o'clock. There'd been no sign of the woman since Charlotte had got home several hours previously. Her mother might have gone into Ravensbrook, Charlotte thought, humming softly to herself as she gazed down at her naked body. She'd had a bath and shaved her mons, removed the stubble from the fleshy pads of her vaginal lips. She'd washed and brushed her hair, cleansed her sex holes and . . .

'Ready for several men to use and abuse me,' Charlotte sighed despondently. 'If I'd known last week what this week would bring,' she murmured, wandering through her memory as she stared out of the window at the blue sky. 'Look at the state of you, Charlotte,' she snapped. 'You haven't even dressed, girl. It's slovenly to mooch around the cottage like that.' She grinned as she pictured her mother standing with her hands on her hips. '*Mr Goodhugh is a decent, upright man. You should think yourself lucky that he's taken such an interest in you.*'

'He's taken more than an interest in me, mother,' she chuckled, reclining on her bed. 'He's fucked my cunt and my mouth. Oh, and he's been so kind to me. So very kind that he pushed his huge cock right up my bottom and pumped out his sperm. He was very good to me in the woods the other day. He knelt over my face and pissed in my mouth. You're right, mother. He really is an upright, decent man of high moral standing. I honestly don't know how to thank him for all he's done for me.'

Eyeing her new radio, she thought about Goodhugh's accomplice in perverted sex. 'Father James has been very good, too,' she murmured. 'Why, he has gone out of his way to make sure that he satisfies his disgusting male desires. He brought four young men to the woods this morning and they all fucked me at once. Two forced their cocks up my arse and the other two wanked in my mouth. And to help in my upbringing, he forced a vibrator up my wet cunt and fucked me to orgasm. Oh, and then he made me lick his balls and wank him off all over my face and hair. What a good, decent man of God he is.'

Leaping off her bed as she heard the front door shut, Charlotte hurriedly slipped into her skirt and blouse and stood by the window. She could hear her mother coming up the stairs. Perhaps she should tell the woman what she'd been doing in the woods, she mused. Perhaps it was time to reveal the evil ways of the priest and the shopkeeper. Was there to be a lecture? she wondered as the door opened. Perhaps she'd been talking to Goodhugh and he'd convinced her that it would be best if he tucked Charlotte into her bed at night.

'Are you all right, Charlotte?' the woman asked. 'You look tired.'

'No, I'm fine, Charlotte smiled. 'I wondered where you were.'

'I went into town. I had to go to the bank and do one or two other things. How was school?'

'Fine,' Charlotte said, realizing that lies didn't matter any more. 'Mother, I went for a walk in the woods after school. I saw something that shocked me.'

SCHOOLGIRL LUST

'Oh?' the woman frowned. 'What was that?'

'I saw a man standing by some bushes with his thing out.'

'*What?* Did you recognize him?'

'He was rubbing his hand up and down his thing.'

'My God,' she gasped. 'Charlotte, I want you to keep away from the—'

'It was Father James.'

'Father . . . I can't believe that. You must be mistaken, Charlotte. Father James wouldn't dream of—'

'He'd taken his cassock off, but I recognized him. He was with a young girl. She was kneeling on the ground and she . . . Well, she grabbed his thing and licked and sucked it. White stuff shot out of the end and went all over her face and in her mouth.'

'My God,' the woman gasped again, holding her hand to her head.

'The girl was naked and she—'

'I don't want to hear any more, Charlotte. I'll . . . I'll have to speak to someone about this. Who was the girl?'

'I don't know. I didn't recognize her. By the way, I'm going to Marianne's soon. We're going to work on our projects.'

'Yes, yes, all right.'

'Who will you speak to?'

'I . . . I don't know yet. I think I'll go and see Mrs Langly. I'll talk to her about it. You are sure that it was Father James, aren't you?'

'Definitely.'

'All right. Don't spend too long at Marianne's.'

'No, I won't.' Charlotte smiled.

'I'll see you later. And don't you go anywhere near the wood, my girl.'

'Or the church, mother?'

'No, yes . . . Go directly to Marianne's and then come directly home.'

Leaving the room, Charlotte's mother shut the door and bounded down the stairs. Charlotte grinned as she felt her warm vaginal juices seeping between the inflamed petals of her inner lips. There was nothing better than causing trouble for the man of the Devil, she reflected, wondering whether to tell her mother that she'd seen Goodhugh wanking in the woods. Hearing the front door slam shut, she gazed out of the window at the back garden. Recalling her younger days when she used to play on the lawn, she massaged her firm breasts through her flimsy blouse.

'I went to the church without wearing a bra or knickers, mother,' she grinned. 'Father James laid me on the altar and fucked my tight cunt. He spunked up my wet cunt. And then he forced his cock down my throat and fucked my mouth. And he thrashed my bottom, and whipped my shaved cunt and then . . . Being such a decent man, being such a kindly man of morals, a man of great integrity and honesty and ethics . . . he held his wet cock in his hand and pissed all over me. Did he really, Charlotte? Yes, mother, he did. Well, you should be thankful. Oh, I am, mother. How can I ever repay him for fucking every hole in my young body and whipping me and pissing all over me?'

Leaving her bedroom, Charlotte bounded down the stairs and opened the back door. Stepping out into the garden, the sun warming her, she looked around her. The garden was completely secluded, no prying eyes, no one to judge. Taking a hand-fork her mother had left in the flower bed, she ran her fingertips up and down the smooth wooden handle. Kneeling, she dug the fork into the lawn and lifted her skirt. The crimsoned lips of her pussy swelling as her arousal rose, she ran her fingertip up her creamy sex valley.

SCHOOLGIRL LUST

'And then Father James forced a piece of wood right up my wet cunt,' she breathed, squatting over the fork and aligning the rounded end of the handle with her gaping vaginal entrance. Lowering her trembling body, the wooden shaft parting the petals of her vagina, driving slowly into the hot sheath of her young cunt, she completely impaled herself on the makeshift dildo. Her long skirt settling around her feet, she rested her arms on her knees, breathing heavily as her sex muscles tightened around the invading phallus.

Gently bouncing up and down, her teenage juices squelching as the handle fucked her, Charlotte chuckled impishly. 'And then he fucked me with the piece of wood, a dildo. He pushed it in and out of my wet cunt, my creamy wet pussy squelching as he fucked me hard.' She shuddered as her inner labia rolled along the thick shaft, the stretching sensation sending quivers through her young womb. Lifting her skirt and placing her head between her parted knees, she gazed at the inflamed outer lips of her pussy lovingly hugging the wooden handle. The creamy-white liquid of her arousal running down the shaft of the dildo, she smiled as she recalled waking in her bed and discovering her wet crack, her sticky inner thighs.

That fateful day seemed like a lifetime ago, she mused, focusing on the pink nodule of her solid clitoris peeping out from her yawning girl crack. She'd experienced more in a few days than in her entire previous life. The anxiety of blackmail, the pain of the whip, the pleasure of orgasm, the taste of sperm, the fucking of her arsehole and the spunking of her hot bowels . . . Was there anything left? she wondered, the rounded end of the dildo massaging the creamy mound of her cervix. Undoubtedly.

Raising her young body, the wooden shaft gliding out of

the heat of her young cunt, Charlotte swivelled her hips and aligned the end of the wet handle with the brown eye of her rectal inlet. 'And then,' she gasped, the pussy-wet handle forcing the delicate tissue of her anal ring wide open. 'And then he pushed . . . he pushed the handle deep into my bottom-hole and . . .' Her tight rectal portal stretching to accommodate the wooden handle, gripping the huge shaft, she lowered her quivering body further. 'And then he . . .' She gasped in her self-abuse, the handle fully embedded within the tight canal of her rectum. 'And then he made me walk around the church with the thing stuck up my tight arse.'

Reaching beneath her young body, Charlotte grabbed the fork and pulled it out of the lawn. Tentatively rising to her feet, the handle massaging the dank flesh deep within her anal sheath, she stood upright and swayed on her sagging legs. The incredible sensations transmitting deep into her quivering pelvis, she managed to stagger to the end of the garden. The fork lifting the back of her skirt, she imagined a candle embedded deep within her anal tract, caressing the inner flesh of her rectum as she talked to her mother. No one would ever know of her lewdness, she mused. No one would guess that she was being anally fucked as she walked down the street.

'God,' she gasped as the lewd sensations permeated her hot bowels, rippled through her contracting womb. This was self-abuse in the extreme, she thought happily, tightening her anal sphincter muscles around the broad shaft. Abuse of her young bottom-hole, but not abuse enough. Walking across the lawn, she wondered what other act of crudity she could commit. Confused by her lewd thoughts, she eyed the bench beneath the laburnum tree, the wooden knobs topping the ends of the armrests.

SCHOOLGIRL LUST

'And then he forced a huge wooden ball up my cunt,' Charlotte breathed, standing with her feet apart, the wooden knob between her firm thighs. Her young body trembling, she bent her knees, pressing the huge ball between the swelling flesh of her vaginal cushions, bending her knees further, the knob painfully parting the engorged flaps of her wet inner lips. She gasped as it was suddenly sucked deep into the tube of her hot cunt. Gyrating her hips, the fork handle massaging her stretched rectal walls, the wooden ball bloating her drenched cunt, she thrust her hand up her skirt and massaged the solid protrusion of her exposed clitoris.

'Yes,' she gasped, the sensations rippling throughout her quivering body as she caressed her erect pleasure spot, her mind floating on clouds of pure sexual bliss. Her pelvic cavity bloated, her sex holes stretched to capacity, she massaged her clitoris faster. Her breathing quickening, her heart racing, she closed her eyes as her orgasm exploded within the rock-hard nub of her clitoris. 'God,' she breathed, her squelching pussy gripping the wooden ball, her anal canal tightening around the smooth shaft.

Sustaining her multiple orgasm as she cried out in the euphoria of her self-lusting, Charlotte listened to the satisfying sound of her squelching juices of orgasm as she bounced up and down and rubbed her pulsating clitoris. The wooden knob grinding against the soft hardness of her ripe cervix, her anal canal spasming, she shuddered in her lewdness as her pleasure peaked again and rocked her teenage body. 'Ah, my cunt,' she whimpered, the velveteen tube of her sex duct rhythmically contracting, her juices of crude sex spewing from her bloated cavern and running over the bench.

'Charlotte,' her mother called from the back door. 'Charlotte, what are you doing there?'

'I'm . . . I'm just resting,' she managed to reply, stilling her quivering body.

'Mrs Langly is here. Come and say hallo to her.'

'Yes, yes, I will,' Charlotte breathed, realizing that she was desperate for the loo.

'Come on, then.'

'I'll be right with you,' she said as the wooden ball pressed against her bladder, hot urine flowing from her urethral opening and gushing over the arm of the bench.

'I thought you were going to Marianne's?' the older woman persisted, stepping out into the garden.

'Yes, yes, I am,' Charlotte replied, almost angrily, as she eased her body up, the urine-flooded wooden knob leaving the fiery sheath of her young cunt with a loud sucking noise.

'Are you all right?' her mother asked as the girl staggered across the lawn, the fork billowing the back of her skirt, the handle embedded deep within her spasming anal duct.

'For goodness' sake, mother, I'm fine.'

'There's no need to snap. I only asked. What's that wet patch . . . Your skirt is soaked. Charlotte, have you—'

'I was watering the garden and got wet. I'll be in shortly.'

Discreetly easing the fork handle out of her bottom hole as her mother went into the kitchen, Charlotte gasped as the shaft popped out of her inflamed anal inlet. Her skirt and shoes soaked with urine, vaginal juice coursing down the smooth skin of her inner thighs, she tossed the fork onto the flower bed and stepped into the cottage. She had to get upstairs and wash and change, she knew as her mother called her from the lounge. The golden liquid cooling her long legs, she grinned as she walked through the hall to the lounge. Another experience, she mused, smiling at Mrs Langly as she popped her head round the door.

'Come in, Charlotte,' her mother said, looking up from the armchair.

'No, I have to go and change,' Charlotte replied. 'Hallo, Mrs Langly.'

'How are you?' the elderly woman asked.

'Very well, thank you.'

'I hear that you've had an upset stomach.'

'Yes, but I'm fine now. You will excuse me, won't you?'

'Of course, dear.'

'I'll see you before I go out.'

Running upstairs, Charlotte dashed into her room and slipped out of her wet skirt. Removing her blouse, she gazed at the reflection of her urine-soaked legs, the cream of desire smeared over the swollen lips of her cunt. Deciding not to wash, she grabbed her miniskirt from beneath the bed and tugged the garment up her long legs. 'Fuck it,' she breathed, not caring what her mother would say as she slipped into a tight T-shirt. Her shoes wet with urine, she brushed her long black hair back and left the room. Nothing mattered any more, she reflected as she bounded down the stairs and called goodbye. Opening the front door, she left the cottage before her mother could question her, rebuke her for dressing like a common strumpet. A breeze wafting up her short skirt as she walked to the church, cooling her hairless vaginal labia, she marched through the graveyard with her head held high.

Quietly opening the oak door, Charlotte crept into the stone building. Wondering where the perverts were lurking as she walked down the aisle, she noticed a shadowy figure sitting in the pews. His head down, his hands clasped in his lap, he didn't notice her as she sat on the bench and slid her naked buttocks along the polished wood until she was beside him. He was murmuring to himself, to God. That would do no good, Charlotte reflected, eyeing the naked flesh of her shapely thighs.

'Hallo, doctor,' she murmured as he raised his head.

'Oh, Charlotte,' he breathed surprisedly, his eyes widening as he glanced at her naked legs. 'What are you doing here?'

'I . . . I've just come in to . . . I'm sorry about the other day.'

'No, *I'm* sorry. I should have tried to understand rather than lecture you. I was hoping you'd call in at the surgery.'

'I should have done, but I couldn't face you.'

'What did you mean when you said that I was *one of them*?' he asked.

'I thought you were . . . It doesn't matter. Were you praying?'

'I often come here and sit alone with my thoughts. Maybe I'm not alone, I don't know. How's your mother?'

'The same as usual. Have you seen Father James?'

'He went out about ten minutes ago. No doubt he'll be back soon.'

'No doubt. Doctor . . .'

'Yes?'

'Nothing. It doesn't matter.'

'Talk about it, Charlotte,' he smiled. 'It's your . . . It's what you showed me, isn't it? What you've done to your body.'

Looking around the deserted church as wicked thoughts flooded her mind, Charlotte grinned. Her inner thighs, the swollen lips of her hairless cunt crack . . . She had power over men, she thought. Even the doctor couldn't resist temptation, she was sure. A teenage girl displaying her cream-dripping sex slit, begging to be finger-fucked, licked and cock-fucked . . . No normal man could resist Charlotte, the temptress of Satan.

'Done to my body?' she echoed, frowning at the man.

'Yes, the leather belt and—'

'Oh, you mean my cunt.' She grinned, tugging her miniskirt up over her stomach and opening her thighs.

'Charlotte,' the doctor gasped, his stare locked to her hairless vaginal lips. 'Please . . . this is a church.'

'This is the house of my father,' she whispered, moving her naked buttocks forward on the bench and parting her legs wider. 'This is the house of Satan. Feel me, feel my wet cunt.'

'For God's sake. Pull your skirt down and—'

'Don't you find me attractive?'

'Why are you doing this? Why are you talking about the Devil?'

'I'm the Devil's daughter,' she chortled impishly, slipping her hand between his legs and massaging his penis through his trousers.

'Charlotte, no.'

'Yes,' she hissed, groping for his zip. 'Let me suck you. I want to suck the spunk out of your knob and swallow it.'

The doctor was a mere man, Charlotte reflected as she tugged his zip down and pulled out his stiffening penis. A mere mortal with a cock who'd love to come in her mouth and spurt his cream to the back of her throat. He was married, but did his wife allow him to mouth-fuck her? Did she drink the spunk from his purple knob? Pulling his foreskin back, she leaned over and sucked his swollen plum into her hot mouth. Running her wet tongue over the silky globe, she listened to his protests as he gripped her head and gasped.

'Charlotte, no,' he breathed as she bobbed her head up

and down, his bulbous plum battering the back of her throat as she breathed in the heady aroma of his male scent. His pubic curls tickling her nose, she rolled her wet tongue around his glans, giggling inwardly as he shuddered and breathed heavily in his male lechery. Again, he murmured his protests as she sank her teeth into the veined shaft of his solid cock. But his complaints were perfunctory, uttered only for the ears of God. Was God watching? Charlotte wondered as she hugged the glans of the doctor's shaft between her succulent lips and snaked her tongue over his sperm-slit. Or was Satan, the proud father, lurking in the dark shadows of his daughter's soul?

The doctor was about to come, Charlotte knew as his body shuddered and grew rigid. Gasping, he held her head tighter as he neared his sexual heaven. It was a shame that he hadn't fingered her cunt, she mused. To heighten his arousal, it would have been nice if he'd tongue-fucked her cunt and sucked out her lubricious juices of teenage desire. But there'd always be another time. Perhaps she'd make an appointment to see him. In his surgery, she'd lie on the examination couch and he could finger and lick her beautiful cunt, suck orgasms out of her ripe clitoris. She might become a regular patient.

'Oh, God,' he breathed as his spunk jetted from his knob-slit, bathing Charlotte's snaking tongue, filling her pretty mouth. Moving her head up and down faster, her wet lips rolling along the solid shaft of his cock, she sucked and swallowed, bringing out his male seed as he writhed in his ecstasy. Her hot mouth overflowing, sperm running down his shaft and soaking into his trousers, he shook in his coming as the teenage temptress drained his rolling balls. He was done, finished in his coming, she knew as he pulled her head up and shuddered his last orgasmic shudder.

'There.' Charlotte grinned, deliberately allowing him to see the white spunk running down her chin. 'You enjoyed that, didn't you?'

'Charlotte . . .' he murmured, stuffing his saliva-wet cock into his trousers and tugging his zip up.

'What?' she smiled.

'Charlotte . . .'

'I'll be coming to see you in your surgery,' she whispered as Father James opened the door and walked down the aisle. 'I'll come and see you, and you can come up my wet cunt.'

'Ah, Charlotte,' the priest smiled. 'How are you, my child?'

'I was just going,' the doctor said, rising to his feet and concealing the wet patch at the crotch of his spermed trousers as he walked up the aisle. 'Goodbye, Father.'

'Goodbye,' the priest called. 'I'll be seeing you again.' Turning to Charlotte, he scowled. 'What were you doing?' he asked.

'Mind your own business,' she snapped.

'But you *are* my business,' he returned. 'You belong to me, Charlotte.'

'I belong to Satan,' she countered. 'And don't you ever forget it.'

'Don't start that crap again. Right, let's get down to the initiation ceremony.'

'I've changed my mind. You can fuck yourself.'

'Charlotte . . . All right, I'll go and see your mother and—'

'I told her that I saw you wanking in the woods,' she smiled. 'I said that a naked girl sucked and licked your thing and white stuff went all over her face and in her mouth.'

'Yes, of course you did,' he chuckled. 'OK, clothes off and lie on the altar.'

Walking to the altar, Charlotte looked up at the church roof and pondered on the Devil. In the woods, she'd been afraid of the priest, obediently complying with his every perverted request. But in the church . . . Where was her inner strength coming from? she wondered. Why had her fear turned to bravery? Where were her lewd thoughts coming from? The priest was no threat to her in the church. If anything, she felt that *she* was a threat to *him*.

Slipping her skirt down, she pulled her T-shirt over her head and kicked her shoes off. Running her hands over the smooth plateau of her stomach and down to the bulge of her outer sex cushions, she stood with her feet wide apart and turned to the priest as he cast his eyes over the mounds and crevices of her teenage body. Wondering what he was thinking as she peeled her sex lips apart, exposing the creamy-wet inner folds of her hot cunt, Charlotte laughed.

'Come unto me, the daughter of Satan,' she hissed, her dark eyes mirroring the fire of her passion.

'Lie on the altar,' he instructed her irritably.

'When I'm ready,' she returned, thrusting two fingers into the tight duct of her vagina.

'Charlotte, you'll do as I tell you when I tell you. If you want to join us, then—'

'No,' she spat, slipping her wet fingers out of her cunt and licking them clean. 'If *you* want to join *me*, then you'll do as *I* say *when* I say.'

'Now you listen to me, my girl. Any more of your nonsense about the Devil, any more insolence or—'

'Lick my cunt out. Kneel before me, your mistress, and lick the juice out of my cunt.'

Grinning as the man dropped to his knees, Charlotte parted the soft hillocks of her vagina and exposed her ripe clitoris, the pinken mouth of her vaginal throat, to the man

SCHOOLGIRL LUST

of God. His tongue running up and down her gaping valley of desire, she let out a long low moan of pleasure as her womb rhythmically contracted. He had no hold over her, she knew as he lapped fervently at her open cunt, slurping up her creamy lubricant. His threats meant nothing any more. She had more than enough photographs to identify his victims and expose him and his accomplice.

Wondering where Goodhugh was as she stretched her inflamed sex hillocks further apart, she looked down at the priest. He was a pathetic man, she thought. The men who had queued to have their cocks sucked to orgasm and their spunk swallowed were all pathetic. *Man, the weaker sex*, she giggled inwardly. There was another way to beat the wicked pair, she mused. Take control, become the ringleader, and use *them* for debased and perverted sex. Watching the man lapping up the cream of her vagina, her mind brimming with ideas, Charlotte decided to take the first step along the road to becoming the priestess, the goddess of sex.

'Not good enough,' she hissed. 'Use your tongue properly and lick my clitoris and make me come in your mouth.' Looking up, his eyes briefly catching hers, he forced his mouth hard against her shaved vulval flesh and fervently licked and sucked her pleasure nodule. Writhing, Charlotte tossed her head back, revelling in the beautiful sensations emanating from her pulsating clitoris as the man obediently pleasured her sexual centre.

He had to use blackmail to have his evil way with young girls. Even before he laid eyes on the tightly closed crack of a young schoolgirl's vagina, he had to prepare and make his plans, spend time ensuring that he had photographs, building the evidence against her. All Charlotte had to do was flash a salacious grin, and her tight wet panties, and any man was hers for the fucking.

'Yes,' she breathed, the birth of her climax welling within her contracting pelvis. The juices of her cunt spewing over the priest's face, running down his neck as he slurped at her clitoris, she sang out in her sexual euphoria as her climax erupted. Her naked body shaking violently as her mind left her body, her cries of debased ecstasy resounded through the stone building. Her climax peaking, she leaned against the altar, her head thrown back as her mind-blowing pleasure rocked her very soul. Delirious in the grip of her multiple orgasm, a flood of cunt milk gushing from her spasming vaginal duct, Charlotte finally sagged on her trembling legs, crumpling in a heap on the floor as the priest moved back.

'Fuck,' she gasped, rolling on the floor as her pleasure began to wane. 'That was . . . that was incredible.'

'Now get onto the altar,' Father James said, rising to his feet and grabbing her arm. 'Come on, it's time for the initiation ceremony.'

'I have the photographs,' she told the man as he pulled her up.

'Where are they?'

'You'll never find them. I know exactly who you've been blackmailing and abusing.'

'I can see that I'll have to thrash the truth out of you,' he grinned, pushing her naked body over the altar. 'I have a long, thin bamboo cane in the office. You either tell me where you've hidden the—'

'You dare to threaten me?' she hissed, escaping his grip and standing back.

'Charlotte, I've had enough of your childish games.'

'Go and see my mother, then. Go on. Go and show her the evidence and tell her what a wicked whore I really am.'

'I will, if that's the way you want it.'

'She's at home now. Go on. You've been threatening me for long enough. Or would you rather I went to get her?'

'Right, that's it,' the priest snarled, walking down the aisle. 'I'll be back – with your mother.'

Laughing as he left the church, Charlotte grabbed her clothes and hurriedly dressed. If he dared to bring her mother to the church, she wasn't going to be around. Having an idea, she slipped beneath the heavy altar cloth and hid. The priest would believe that she'd run off, she mused, making herself comfortable. Again wondering where Goodhugh was, she froze as she heard voices.

'What's this all about?' her mother's voice echoed around the church.

'Sit down,' Father James said softly. 'I'm very concerned about Charlotte.'

'What's she been up to now?'

'I saw her in the woods today. I don't know how to tell you this. She was naked.'

'What? But she said that—'

'She's been lying, I'm afraid. She's told me terrible things that I know aren't true. She was here just now. That's why I came to get you. She's obviously gone now, probably to the woods to meet some boy or other.'

'That doesn't sound like Charlotte,' the woman breathed.

'I know it doesn't. She came here and . . . I really don't know how to tell you. I watched her from the office doorway. She didn't realize that I was there, of course. She removed her clothes and lay on the altar.'

'Good God,' the woman gasped. 'I can't believe . . . Are you sure that it was Charlotte?'

'There's no doubt about it, I'm afraid. I've noticed that she'd been behaving strangely of late.'

'Yes, so have I. I thought something was bothering her. But now . . .'

'Only the other day I saw her walking along the path to the woods. She dropped something, an envelope. I picked it up and was about to go after her when a photograph fell out. It was a photograph of Charlotte. She was naked and—'

'Naked?'

'She had a man's penis in her mouth.'

'Oh, my God!'

'I have it here,' he said, pulling a photograph from his cassock.

'Oh, my . . . There's no mistaking the girl. Wait a minute. That's my lounge carpet she's kneeling on. My God! She must have . . . When I was out, she—'

'Come into the office. I'll make you some tea. I was hoping to deal with this myself, but . . .'

'I'll deal with her when I get hold of her! My God!'

Cringing, Charlotte slipped out from beneath the altar and left the church. She really hadn't thought that the priest was going to reveal all to her mother. Now the woman had photographic evidence, there wasn't a lie in the world that would get Charlotte out of the horrendous mess. Making her way to the woods, she wondered what on earth she was going to do. She shouldn't have worn her miniskirt, she reflected, looking down at her long legs. She'd have to go home at some stage and face her mother, and the miniskirt would only make her predicament worse. If that was possible.

'Pink peaches,' she murmured, sitting on the grass by the stream. Perhaps it was best to tell her mother the truth, she mused. Tell her the whole story about the scam and admit to being a victim. Recalling the photographs Goodhugh had taken, she knew that she appeared to be a willing participant in the debauchery. Her smiling face covered with sperm, her eyes grinning as she sucked on a bulbous knob, licked spunk off her fingers . . . There was no way her mother would believe that she'd been forced to commit the sexual acts. And as for the photographs of Charlotte enjoying lesbian sex with Emily in the woods, and the pictures of her naked with Marianne . . .

This really was the end, Charlotte knew as she sighed and gazed down at the grass. She needed somewhere to stay for a while, she decided. Rather than go home, she thought it might be an idea to lie low until the dust had settled. Stay where? she mused. Apart from her aunt, she had no relations. And as for money . . . Leaping to her feet, she grinned. There *was* a way to earn some money. Not just a few pounds, but real money. If she followed the path into the woods, the walk would take an hour or so, but the trip would be well worth it, she was sure.

Chapter Thirteen

Charlotte looked up at the huge Victorian building as she made her way through the grounds. With parents paying several thousand pounds per term for their sons to attend the public school, she was sure that the lads would have plenty of pocket money. Certainly enough to spend a few pounds on a blow job. *Mouth-fuck*, she mused. *Mouth-spunking*. Was it worth ten pounds? Twenty, maybe? There were rich pickings within the school, she knew as she slipped around the side of the building.

She was far removed from the shy reserved girl who had woken in bed that fateful Saturday morning, she reflected. A timid, virginal, schoolgirl working hard on her English project and living a sheltered life in a small village community . . . The change couldn't have been more dramatic, Charlotte thought, looking down at her miniskirt, her long naked legs. Walking along a path running between well-kept flower beds, she wondered where she was going to sleep that night. Her mother would soon realize that she wasn't going home, she mused. The woman would become frantic, distraught with worry. And furious. But the cottage wasn't home to Charlotte any more. If only she could turn the clock back.

Noticing a young man sitting on a bench beneath a tree, she wondered how she was going to broach the subject of selling her young body for crude sex. *Want a blow job?*

Twenty pounds for a mouth-fuck. You can fuck my arse and spunk my bowels for fifty pounds. Never had she been so desperate for money. Nowhere to sleep, no food . . . She had no choice, she concluded. But it was only sex. Her body was young, firm and curvaceous. Why not sell it to young men for their pleasure? No harm would come from having her mouth and cunt fucked and spunked. There was nothing wrong with allowing men to push their cocks up her cunt and fuck her. Taking a deep breath as she gazed at the young man, she decided to play it by ear.

'Excuse me.' She smiled as she approached from behind.

'Oh, hi.' He beamed, turning and gazing longingly at her miniskirt, her naked thighs. 'How can I help you?'

'I seem to have got lost,' she replied. 'I was on my way to visit a friend and—'

'Where does your friend live?'

'Nepcote Down.'

'I'm afraid I don't know the area very well. We're not allowed out of the prison, you see.'

'Prison?'

'That's what we call it. I'm leaving at the end of this term. I'll be glad to be out of here.' Again focusing on the naked flesh of her inner thighs, he frowned. 'You're rather young to be roaming around on your own. How old are you?'

'Sixteen,' she lied, sitting beside him. 'Is there anywhere we can go? Somewhere private?'

'Private?' he echoed, obviously perplexed.

'You do want my body, don't you?'

'Er . . . Well, I . . .' he stammered, looking about him.

'Don't you fancy me?'

'Yes, of course.'

'So, what's the problem?'

'Nothing.'

'If you want sex with me, then we'll have to find somewhere private.'

'Right. Come with me.' He grinned eagerly as he leaped to his feet. He obviously couldn't believe his luck. 'I've never been approached like this before.'

'By the way, I charge.'

'Charge? You mean you're a—'

'A prostitute, that's right.' The word rolled off her tongue with ease. 'A mouth-fuck, twenty pounds.'

'Oh, er . . . Right.'

Following the bewildered lad, Charlotte reckoned that he was about eighteen. His cock would be fresh, unblemished, rock-hard. His balls were probably full, in dire need of draining. He'd no doubt have plenty of friends who'd also be keen to hand over money in return for fucking and spunking her pretty wet mouth. Twenty pounds, she thought happily. A couple of blow jobs, or perhaps five, would bring enough money to pay for a room for several nights. Although this was wrong, she didn't see that it mattered. A cock was a cock, she reflected. She'd been mouth-fucked by so many men that a few more would make no difference. It only took a few minutes to suck a cock to orgasm and swallow the sperm as it gushed from the throbbing knob. *Easy money*, she thought as he led her into a shed.

'Cash first,' Charlotte said, lifting her miniskirt and displaying the hairless crack of her young pussy.

'God,' he breathed, passing her a twenty-pound note. 'You really are—'

'Fuckable?' she grinned, kneeling before him as he leaned against a wooden bench. She couldn't remember where she'd heard the term. The priest, perhaps? 'Spunkable?'

'I've never known anyone like you,' he murmured, looking down and watching in amazement as she unzipped his trousers and hauled his stiffening penis out.

'There's a first time for everything. Ever been sucked before?'

'No, no, I haven't.'

'Ever fucked a girl?'

'Well, no . . .'

'That's good. There's nothing I like more than a virgin.'

Easing his heavy balls out, Charlotte gazed at the spermspheres clearly outlined by the thin sac of his hairy scrotum. This really was easy money, she reflected again, gently retracting his foreskin and focusing on his purple globe. Sucking two or three cocks a day would earn more than enough money to cover rent, food, clothes . . . Wondering why her mother had spent a lifetime of impoverishment when she could have used her mouth to earn money, Charlotte tried to imagine the woman with a knob bloating her mouth, spunk running down her chin. She could have had several regular clients and . . . Perhaps not.

The young lad's penis twitching expectantly, Charlotte moved her head forward and sucked his swollen glans into the wet heat of her pretty mouth. Breathing in the heady scent of his pubes, she rolled her wet tongue over the velveteen globe of his penis and wondered whether he wanked. He probably slipped his cock out and thought of young girls as he massaged his knob to orgasm. She pictured him shooting his spunk over the floor, gasping as he gazed longingly at naked girls in a men's magazine. Clutching the money, she took half the length of his solid shaft into her hot mouth and moaned through her nose as he quivered in his arousal. From now on, he'd picture Charlotte sucking his cock as he wanked, picture her full lips enveloping the purple globe of his solid penis.

Her tongue repeatedly snaking over his silky glans, Charlotte wondered how many young men she could suck to orgasm in one day. Several hundred? She chuckled inwardly, stroking the lad's heavy balls. Men of all ages would be only too eager to hand over cash in return for her sexual favours. If she had a dozen or so regular clients, she'd be comparatively well off. But it was Marianne she really wanted. The soft fleshy folds of her young vagina, her lubricious juices of desire . . . If only they could run away together, she thought as she sucked and mouthed the twitching penis-head.

They were too young, she knew as the young man gasped and trembled. Marianne wouldn't be able to leave home, would she? Perhaps, if Charlotte accumulated enough cash and found a decent flat . . . But she'd end up a prostitute, she knew. Stark reality hitting her, she realized that she *was* a prostitute. But no one would know. Her conscience nagged her but she could see that she had no other option. Apart from her clients, no one would ever know of her secret life, she consoled herself. She'd have to write to her mother, she decided as the man's solid knob swelled, bloating her pretty mouth. Kneading his rolling balls, she sucked and mouthed his bulbous glans. She'd write to her mother and rent a flat and—

'Coming,' he finally breathed, sperm jetting from his slit and bathing her sweeping tongue. Swallowing his male fruits, Charlotte moved her head back and forth and breathed heavily through her nose. The salty taste of his gushing spunk driving her wild, she knew that she had to concentrate on his pleasure rather than hers. Clinging to the bench as his balls drained, he let out his low moans of ecstasy as she expertly brought out the flood of his seed. If he was satisfied with her services, if word got round that she was an expert knob-sucker, then his friends would be queuing to hand over their money. Licking his veined shaft as his orgasm receded, she lapped up the spilled sperm from his balls before sitting back on her heels. Money would soon be no object.

'All right?' she asked as he pushed his saliva-wet cock into his trousers and yanked his zip up.

'God, yes,' he grinned. 'Who are you? Where the hell did you come from?'

'Call me Sandy,' she said, rising to her feet. 'I come from . . . not far. Have you any friends who would pay for my services?' she asked unashamedly as she licked the spunk off her glistening lips.

'Er . . . yes, definitely.'

'Then you'd better go and get them. I have an hour or so,' she said as he opened the shed door. 'Bring one at a time and make sure they have cash with them.'

As he left, Charlotte licked her spunked lips again and leaned against the bench. If her mother knew what she was doing . . . There again, her mother no doubt thought her a slag as it was. The day would come when she'd visit the woman, she thought dolefully. She'd have money and be in a position to help her mother financially. In the meantime, she'd miss her. The cottage, her bedroom, the garden . . . She had to look ahead, she knew as she waited for the next young man to arrive. It was no good looking back and pondering on the past and what might have been.

Wondering what Goodhugh and the priest would do when they heard that she'd gone missing, Charlotte hoped that they'd be questioned by the police. Perhaps the scam would come to light. Marianne knew where the bag of photographs was hidden and would be only too eager to help put the evil men behind bars. What was the offence? she wondered. Blackmail? There'd be no proving that Goodhugh had blackmailed anyone. All the girls were over the age of consent and the photographs showed them grinning as they sucked spunk from erect penises. There was nothing in writing that could be used as evidence of blackmail. Knowing the evil pair's luck, they'd get away with their debauchery. But, if it hadn't been for Goodhugh, Charlotte might never have discovered the pleasures her young body had to offer. She might have met a young man and fallen in love rather than fallen in lust. Why had her mother never remarried? she wondered. Did the woman masturbate in her bed at night?

'There she is,' the young man grinned as he showed a friend into the shed.

'Hi.' Charlotte smiled, licking her lips provocatively as the new youngster pulled a twenty-pound note from his blazer pocket. Taking the money as the first lad left the shed, she lifted her miniskirt and displayed her hairless vaginal crack to his bulging eyes. He grinned, his trousers bulging as he locked his stare to her teenage vulva. She reckoned that he was younger than the first lad. Younger, fresher, virginal.

'If you want that,' she breathed huskily, projecting her hips, her naked pussy crack seemingly smiling at the trembling lad, 'it'll be another twenty pounds.'

'OK,' he replied, pulling another note from his pocket.

'Have you ever seen a girl's cunt?' she asked, grabbing the money.

'I . . . No, I haven't.'

'Then this is your lucky day.'

Clutching her spoils, Charlotte leaned over the bench and tugged her skirt up over her back. She could hear her client behind her, his belt buckle, his zip. A cock was a cock, she mused again. It didn't matter who the owner was, cocks were all the same. His ballooning knob slipping between the wet petals of her inner lips, she grinned as he pushed his plum into the tight sheath of her teenage cunt. Her outer labia stretching tautly around the base of his rock-hard shaft, his silky globe pressing hard against her creamy cervix, she closed her eyes as he parted the full moons of her young buttocks and exposed the entrance to her sheath of illicit sex.

'It looks as if you've been whipped,' he said, slowly withdrawing his male hardness and again thrusting his glans deep into the fiery heat of her cunt.

'I have.' She giggled. 'Many times.'

'You're something else, you really are.'

'Fuck me harder,' Charlotte gasped in her decadence. 'I want to feel your spunk filling my tight cunt.'

'God, you're beautiful. How old are you?'

'Just fourteen,' she lied, realizing that men loved young girls. 'I might have to pay the school another visit. I think it best to keep you boys happy, don't you?'

'Definitely,' he breathed, all too soon nearing his climax. 'Any time you like.'

Listening to his grunting and heavy breathing as he fucked the tightening duct of her young cunt, Charlotte realized that she should have got into prostitution before Goodhugh had got a hold on her. Walking through the woods looking for wildlife had been fun, but fucking young lads in return for cash was what life was really all about. The best of both worlds, she reflected as her vaginal juices squelched, his heavy balls battering her shaved pussy lips. As much crude sex as she desired, and plenty of cash with it. To have continued with her schooling and then found a mundane job would have led to a life of boredom. Struggling to survive, as her mother had, was needless. With her curvaceous body, her wet cunt, there was no need to want for anything.

'I'm going to come,' the boy announced, grabbing her hips and thrusting his rock-hard cock into her young cunt with a vengeance. Charlotte waited in anticipation as his purple knob glided in and out of her hugging sex duct. His sperm would gush and ... 'Yes,' he cried, repeatedly ramming his huge knob hard against her ripe cervix. She could feel his spunk jetting into her young cunt, lubricating his pistoning shaft, dripping from her bloated sex hole and running down the soft skin of her inner thighs. He was a man now, she thought happily. He could tell his friends that he'd done it, fucked and spunked a girl's cunt. He was a man.

'Oh, my cunt,' Charlotte gasped, her head resting on the bench as his pussy-wet shaft massaged her pulsating clitoris. Her orgasm exploding within her solid cumbud, her vaginal muscles spasming, she wailed her appreciation for the man's granite-hard cock, his gushing spunk. Her cuntal juices mingling with his white sperm, squelching as he shafted her tight duct of lust, she shook uncontrollably as her climax ripped through her young body. Again and again he rammed his cock-head deep into her burning vaginal cavern, his balls pummelling her hairless mons, his knob battering her creamy-soft cervix. Spunk running down her thighs, she squeezed her eyes shut, gasping as her pleasure rocked her to her inner core, reached out to every nerve ending. Would he be able to restiffen his beautiful cock and arse-fuck her? she wondered hopefully. She was that desperate to feel his spunk flowing into the dank cavern of her bowels that she'd pay *him* for the pleasure. No, that wasn't the plan, she reflected as he slid his pussy-slimed cock shaft in and out of her brimming love tube.

Again wondering whether she wanted wet pussy or a man's solid organ, Charlotte decided to have both. She could live with Marianne and screw men on the side. The girl would never know of her wanton infidelity – she'd believe the white liquid oozing from Charlotte's cunt was the juice of love. Marianne would suck the sperm out of Charlotte's love tube, thinking that her lesbian lover was wet with desire in her girl-loving. *Lies*, Charlotte mused, her climax peaking and rocking the inner core of her pelvis. *More lies*.

The tight duct of her anal canal sadly neglected, she wondered whether to order her client to finger-fuck her hot arse. But no. He was paying for the delights of her cunt. Perhaps the next lad would pay fifty pounds to fuck her arsehole, to drive the solid shaft of his organ deep into her rectum and spunk her bowels. The more she thought about anal sex as her vaginal cavern bloated with sperm, the more she wanted a cock fucking her there.

Finally slipping his spent cock out of her spunked vagina, the lad staggered back and zipped his trousers. Lifting her trembling body off the bench, Charlotte stuffed her earnings into her shoe. *Sixty pounds*, she mused happily as she rose to her feet and grinned at the young man. This really was easy money. Wondering how many more cocks were waiting for her intimate attention, she asked the lad what it felt like to be a man.

'Great,' he said, brushing his black hair back with his fingers. 'I hope I'll see you again.'

'*Fuck* me again, don't you mean?'

'Yes, I suppose so.'

'You will, don't worry. You'd better send the next one in.

SCHOOLGIRL LUST

I have nowhere to sleep tonight so I'd better start looking . . .'

'Sleep here,' he suggested.

'I'm not sleeping in a shed,' she returned indignantly.

'No, I don't mean in the shed. There's plenty of room in our dorm if you're stuck.'

'I just might do that,' she smiled, imagining spending the night with a dozen or more teenage boys.

'Meet me down by the pond when you're done here. I'll be waiting.'

'OK, thanks.'

'I'll sneak you into the dorm later. There's a side door and . . . I'll see you by the pond.'

As he left the shed, Charlotte slipped her hand between her firm thighs and ran her finger up and down her sperm-dripping girl-crack. There was more sperm to come, she mused, wondering whether the next lad would want her hot mouth or her tight cunt. Although it had been a long day, she wasn't tired. She could suck the spunk out of swollen knobs and have her cunt and arse fucked all night, if necessary. As the door opened, she turned and smiled at a young lad as he entered the shed and stared at her as if he'd never seen a girl before.

Charlotte was becoming used to having sex with strangers. There was no embarrassment any more, no shame or guilt. Ordering him to drop his trousers as he passed her a twenty-pound note, she stuffed the money into her shoe. His penis was flaccid, snaking over his hairy ball-bag like a dead slug. He was obviously shy, but she'd soon stiffen his organ and bring out his sperm. He said nothing as he stepped out of his trousers and waited for her to make the first move. *A little virgin*, she thought happily.

'Sit on the edge of the bench,' she said, desperate to take

his salty cock-plum into her thirsty mouth and suck out his spunk. Complying, the boy sat with his thighs wide apart, his heavy scrotum hanging freely over the edge of the wooden bench. Charlotte knelt before him, focusing on his hairy sac as he leaned back on his hands. Watching her pink tongue snaking over his balls, his penile shaft rolling up to his stomach, he let out little gasps of pleasure. He was going to come quickly, she knew as she licked his balls, her wet tongue exploring every inch of his genital flesh. Licking in the creases between his scrotum and his thighs, she breathed in his male scent, her clitoris swelling as her arousal soared. His cock finally solid, pointing to the roof, she pulled his foreskin back and ran her tongue up his veined shaft to his exposed glans.

Engulfing his purple knob in her wet mouth, Charlotte gently sucked and tongued his sex globe. The boy shuddered and gasped as she lowered her head, taking his bulbous glans to the back of her throat. Without warning, his sperm jetted from his slit, filling her mouth as she raised her head and engulfed his throbbing knob between her wet lips. Tonguing his sperm-slit, she sucked and licked his young cock as his orgasmic fluid pumped into her gobbling mouth. His balls heaving, he thrust his hips forward, driving his glans to the back of her throat, obviously delighting in his first mouth-fuck.

Charlotte drank from the youngster's throbbing fountainhead, swallowing his gushing spunk as he held her head and shuddered in his male pleasure. She wondered how many more lads were waiting – as she sucked the remnants of his sperm from his deflating knob, she thought she might earn several hundred pounds from her young body in her very first session as a tart. Sperm dribbling down her chin as she slipped his cock out of her mouth, she was about to order him to send the next client in when she heard a commotion outside the shed.

Leaping to his feet, the lad yanked his trousers on and fled the shed, his school uniform in a state of disarray. Perhaps the boys were arguing, Charlotte mused, wiping her spunked mouth on the back of her hand as shouting filled the evening air. There was probably a dispute over who should be next to fuck and sperm her hot mouth. Wondering whether to suck two cocks to orgasm at once, she decided to allow three boys to fuck her. Her mouth, her cunt and her arse, she thought. The money was going to pour into her purse as fast as the spunk poured into her mouth. The floor flew open and she grinned as her vaginal muscles contracted. *More sperm*, she thought happily. Another young knob to suck to orgasm and—

'My God!' a man in his sixties bellowed as he burst into the shed and gazed at Charlotte. 'What on earth is going on in here?'

'I was just—' Charlotte began, wondering who he was as she adjusted her skirt.

'I've been watching from my study window. Why was there a group of boys queuing to come in here?'

'I . . . I got lost and—'

'Got lost?' he growled. 'You'd better come with me, young lady.'

Assuming that he was one of the teachers, Charlotte followed him out of the shed and looked about. The boys had gone. Scattered, more than likely. She was going to be in serious trouble, she knew as the man led her up some stone steps and into the huge Victorian building. Following him through an oak door, she glimpsed the sign: *Headmaster*. This was all she needed, she reflected fearfully, wondering whether to run for it.

'This is a very serious matter,' the headmaster said as he turned to face her, his grey moustache twitching as he eyed her long legs. 'As you'll appreciate, the boys at this school are in my care. I'm responsible not only for their education and welfare but for the reputation of the school. What, exactly, were you doing in the shed?'

'Talking,' Charlotte replied, feigning an air of confidence.

'I saw Gibson-Brown leave the shed. Do you know him?'

'I do now. I mean—'

'I know what was going on, Miss . . .?'

'Evans, Sandy Evans,' she lied.

'Miss Evans. Which school do you attend?'

'I don't.'

'You don't go to school?'

'I work,' she murmured.

'Do you, indeed? How old are you?'

'Sixteen.'

'*Sixteen?* My, God. I'll need your address and—'

'Wait a minute,' Charlotte broke in. 'I was only talking to a boy. Is that a crime?'

'You were doing more than talking to him, Miss Evans. I'm not stupid. Look at your legs. Look what's running down your thighs. Apart from anything else, you were trespassing. I'll have to call the police. This is a matter to be dealt with—'

'No, don't call the police,' she murmured, realizing that she'd be taken home.

'The school's reputation is at stake, Miss Evans. I simply cannot allow this sort of behaviour on its premises.'

'Look, I'll go and never come back. No one will know.'

'I can't risk that. If it came to light that you'd been here and . . . I'll have to call the police.'

'Please,' she whimpered. 'Do anything, but—'

'There *is* another way we can sort this out,' the headmaster said sternly, eyeing her naked thighs.

'Oh?'

'What you were doing in the shed was despicable,' he said, walking across the room and locking the door. 'I have never known such disgusting behaviour. You'll have to be punished for your wicked ways.' Standing before her, his beady eyes focused on the cleavage of her young breasts. 'The choice is yours.'

'Choice?' She frowned.

'The police – or the cane.'

The cane? she pondered. Now that was a punishment she'd love to endure. But Charlotte didn't want the ageing man to know of the pleasure she derived from a naked-buttock thrashing. She'd feign horror, she decided, grimacing as he waited for her reply. Holding her hand to her pretty mouth, her dark eyes wide, she finally hung her head. Sobbing incoherent words, she concealed a wicked grin as he took a long cane from a cupboard. She could almost feel his arousal soaring as he turned and faced her. He'd be picturing her young buttocks, no doubt believing her to be wearing tight, skimpy panties. He'd probably come in his trousers once he saw that her anal globes were naked. Her clitoris swelling expectantly, she realized again that all men were the same. They fell prey easily to the delights of young girls' bodies. She had power over men, she knew. His penis would be stiffening, his purple knob swelling, his heavy balls rolling . . . She had power.

'Well?' he asked. 'What's it to be?'

'The cane,' she said softly, raising her head and wiping her eyes.

'Good. Bend over the desk and lift your skirt up.'

'Not . . . not too hard,' she whimpered.

'You'll be punished according to your crime, young lady. Ten lashes.'

Walking to the desk, Charlotte leaned over the polished oak top and reached behind her back. Her feet wide apart, she lifted her skirt up over her back, the rounded moons of her naked buttocks jutting out, her dark anal crease opening. She could hear the headmaster standing behind her, his breathing deep as he swished the cane through the air as if to test its flexibility. He'd be gazing longingly at the globes of her young bottom, she knew as her juices of arousal seeped between the pinken wings of her inner labia. He'd be eyeing the swollen hillocks of her hairless vaginal lips, his penis twitching, his balls rolling as he imagined fucking the tight, wet shaft of her teenage cunt.

'Why aren't you wearing knickers?' he asked her.

'I . . . I forgot to put them on,' she replied.

'Forgot, or didn't bother?' His tone was accusing. 'I believe that you came here with the sole intention of seducing my boys.'

'No, no, I—'

'Don't lie to me. You came here with no knickers on because you intended to seduce my boys. That's true, isn't it?'

'Yes,' she confessed, her arousal heightening.

'Yes, *sir*.'

'Yes, sir.'

'A sixteen-year-old girl strutting about in a short skirt with no knickers on underneath . . . Do you often do this sort of thing?'

'Yes. Yes, sir.'

The cane swished through the air and landed squarely across her twitching buttocks. Charlotte let out a yelp. Again, the thin bamboo bit into the tensed flesh of her anal orbs, the pain permeating her rounded bottom as she quivered in her delight. Her juices of lust streaming from her gaping vaginal valley and running in rivers down her inner thighs, she grimaced as the third stroke of the cane jolted her young body. Another seven strokes, and she'd be free to leave. Or would she? she thought as the fourth lash cracked loudly across her trembling bum cheeks.

'Five,' the headmaster breathed, bringing the cane down again. Clutching the far edge of the desk, Charlotte parted her feet further, imagining her dripping vaginal crack yawning as she stuck out her weal-lined buttocks. 'Six.' The stinging sensation sending quivers of ecstasy through her contracting womb, she decided to give the pervert a thrill. Squeezing her muscles, she grinned as hot liquid coursed down her legs and splashed on the floor between her feet. Wondering whether the old man interfered with the boys, wanked and sucked their fresh young cocks, she yelped again as the seventh lash of the thin bamboo cracked across the crimsoned orbs of her pert bottom.

'Eight,' the man breathed, obviously delighting in what he thought to be Charlotte's plight as she drained her bladder. As the last of the hot liquid splashed onto the floor, he raised the cane above his head, 'Nine,' he gasped, flailing the girl's naked bottom so hard that her young body bucked. Feigning tears as she clung to the desk, Charlotte cried out as the tenth stroke of the headmaster's cane swished through the air and struck her quivering bottom. Listening to movements behind her, she wondered whether the pervert was going to touch her, if he'd stroke the wet cushions of her gaping sex slit, push his fingers deep into the tight duct of her teenage cunt. Could he resist?

'Let that be a lesson to you,' he said sternly as Charlotte placed her hands on the desk and raised her body. 'Don't stand up yet,' he ordered her.

'But—' she whimpered, resting her head on the desk again.

'I haven't finished with you. I want to know *exactly* what you were doing to those boys.'

'We were just talking.'

'Sir.'

'Sir.'

'Then what was running down your legs?'

'I don't know, sir.'

'Tell me the truth, girl.'

'I sucked them, sir.'

'Sucked them? Sucked what?'

'The boys' penises, sir. I licked and sucked their penises.'

'My God. You're a wicked harlot.'

'Yes, sir.'

Moving around the desk, the headmaster lifted Charlotte's head and gazed into the dark pools of her tear-filled eyes. Wondering what he was thinking, she looked at the bulge in his trousers, picturing his stiff penis, his ballooning knob. Was he married? she wondered. She doubted that his wife sucked him off, took his knob into her mouth and sucked out his semen. Had he screwed her arsehole? The poor man probably stuck his cock up her fanny and loosed his sperm once a month, she concluded.

'I want you to show me exactly what you did to the boys,' he breathed, unzipping his trousers and hauling his solid penis out. Fully retracting his foreskin, he exposed his swollen knob, his sperm-slit, to the girl's wide eyes as he moved forward. Easing his full balls out of his trousers as she gazed wide-eyed at his huge shaft, he ordered her again to show him what she'd done to the boys.

Opening her wet mouth as his knob moved forward, Charlotte engulfed his penile crown and sucked hard. The old man gasped, his body visibly shaking, and she knew that she had him just where she wanted him. He was weak in his desire, she knew as he moved his hips forward, sinking his purple globe deep into the wet heat of her pretty mouth. After caning her and watching her piss run down her long legs, he'd be desperate to pump out his spunk. Didn't he want to fuck her wet cunt? she wondered as he gasped in his perverted pleasure.

'Use your tongue,' he murmured, taking her head in his hands and slowly rocking his hips. Breathing heavily through her nose, Charlotte snaked her tongue around his silky knob. Wondering whether she'd be a regular visitor to the headmaster's study, her succulent lips enveloped his velveteen glans and she thought about charging him for the debased pleasure she was giving him. He was obviously into caning schoolgirls' naked bottoms and would surely hand over twenty pounds in exchange for being allowed to administer the gruelling punishment. There was money at this school, she knew as she breathed in the aroma of his pubic hair. Money for the taking.

His sperm jetting from his throbbing knob, the pedagogue gasped as she rolled her tongue over his silky-smooth glans and sucked hard. He was a dirty old man, Charlotte reflected, swallowing his orgasmic fluid. Would he finger-fuck her cunt after he'd drained his swinging balls? Perhaps he'd force his cock-head deep into her tight arsehole and spunk her. But, at his age, she doubted that he'd manage to come twice. Thinking about her next visit to the school, she wondered how many boys there were. Several hundred, she imagined, drinking the gushing spunk as the headmaster quivered in his orgasm. Several hundred fresh knobs ripe for the sucking.

'And let that be a lesson to you,' the man breathed,

slipping his shrinking cock out of Charlotte's sperm-flooded mouth and zipping his trousers. 'You may go now,' he said as she hauled her body up and staggered on her sagging legs. 'But I want you back here tomorrow.'

'Yes, sir.' She smiled, licking her wet lips.

'Tomorrow evening. Now, off you go.'

Leaving the study, Charlotte walked down the corridor and left the building. The grounds were deserted, she noticed as she crossed the grass to the pond. The boys had no doubt gone into hiding after the headmaster had discovered their lewd antics. Sitting behind some bushes close to the pond, she wondered where the young man who'd offered her accommodation in a dormitory had got to. Perhaps he'd had a change of mind now that the headmaster was on the warpath. All she could do was wait, and hope, she knew as she reclined on the soft grass and closed her eyes. If he didn't turn up . . . She didn't know what she was going to do. She could hardly sleep beneath the sky. As sleep engulfed her, she dreamed of her mother, the homely cottage and her comfy bed. And Marianne.

Chapter Fourteen

Waking at six in the morning, Charlotte lifted her aching body off the grass and looked about her. As the sun rose above the trees, she ambled around the pond and made her way through the grounds to the woods. She'd have to go home, she knew. The money in her shoe pressing against her foot, reminding her of her evening of debauchery, she thought about her plans. Hungry and in need of a bath, she realized in the cold light of day that her idea about finding a flat wasn't so brilliant. At seventeen and with no change of clothes or other belongings, she doubted that anyone would rent her a flat. Besides, she still hadn't got enough money for a deposit and rent in advance. There really was no choice other than to go home. But could she face her mother? She walked on slowly, taking her time. The sun climbed higher in the sky. Finally reaching the wooden bridge, she sat by the stream and wondered what to do.

'God,' Charlotte sighed, shaking her head despondently as her stomach rumbled. Everything was such a bloody mess. The police were probably searching for her. Her mother would be hysterical with worry . . . She had to come to a decision, she knew as she listened to the water trickling in the stream. Peace and tranquillity reigned in the woods, but her mind was in turmoil. She could go into Ravensbrook and buy some clothes and have a decent breakfast. If she then returned to the boys' school and earned some more money . . . But it might take several days to find a flat. It all seemed so hopeless.

'I thought I'd find you here,' Marianne said as she approached. 'Where have you been?'

Charlotte looked up and smiled at the girl. Wearing a short skirt and loose-fitting blouse, her long blonde hair cascading over the swell of her young breasts, she was looking, as always, extremely attractive. Staring at her shapely thighs, Charlotte felt her stomach somersault as she pictured Marianne's sex crack, the inner petals of her vagina protruding alluringly from her girl-slit.

'Hi,' Charlotte said as the other girl sat beside her. 'I've been out all night. I expect the police are looking for me and—'

'I saw your mum last night. She told me what happened in the church. She mentioned the photograph and—'

'Oh, God. What did she say?'

'Not a lot, funnily enough. She just said that she'd talk to you about it when you get home. She was worried because she didn't know where you were. I said that you were staying at my house.'

'Thank God for that.'

'She wasn't angry or anything.'

'I'll have to go home,' Charlotte sighed. 'What are *you* doing up this early?'

'Looking for you. I knew you'd be here, like I said. Anyway, it's just gone seven. It's not that early.'

'No, I suppose not.'

'So, what are you going to do?'

'Go and see my mother. I have no choice. Well, I do but . . . She saw a photograph of me sucking Goodhugh's penis. What she must think of me, I can't begin to imagine.'

'You'll never know unless you go and talk to her.'

SCHOOLGIRL LUST

'That's true. Whatever happens, can I meet you here later?'

'Of course.'

'If it all goes wrong, would you consider . . . No, it doesn't matter.'

'Consider what?'

'I might have to rent a flat.'

'I'd come with you, if that's what you were about to ask.'

'Great. That's what I wanted to hear. OK, I'll see you here in, say, an hour?'

'I'll be here. Charlotte, I'll *always* be here for you.'

'OK.' She grinned, leaping to her feet. 'Wish me luck.'

'Yes, good luck.'

Walking along the path, Charlotte emerged from the woods and looked up and down the road. The village was deserted. No one would see her miniskirt, her spunked thighs, her dishevelled hair. But what would her mother say? But it didn't really matter what the woman said. Charlotte had nothing to lose. If she was thrown out, then she'd go back to the school and earn enough money to rent a flat. Reaching the cottage, she took the key from beneath the flowerpot and let herself in. Taking a deep breath as she heard the woman in the kitchen, she crept upstairs and changed into a long skirt. Brushing her long black hair, she grimaced as her mother called her. This was it, she thought fearfully, leaving her bedroom.

'Oh, I didn't think you were up,' Charlotte said, bounding down the stairs and finding her mother in the hall.

'You're back early. Have you had breakfast?'

'No, I haven't,' Charlotte replied as she followed her mother into the kitchen, wondering why she'd not been lectured.

'I was talking to Father James last night.'

'Oh?'

'He showed me a photograph.'

Her stomach churning, Charlotte sat at the table. 'Really?' she smiled, her heart racing as she watched the woman fill the kettle.

'A photograph of you, he claimed. He said that he'd found it in the street. He thought it was you. I must admit that, initially, *I* thought it was you, too. When I looked closer, I could see that it wasn't.'

'What sort of photograph was it?' Charlotte asked, her dark eyes frowning.

'Just a girl kneeling down. There's your tea. Would you like toast or a cooked breakfast?'

'Er . . . a cooked breakfast would be nice.'

Wondering why her mother hadn't recognized her own daughter in the photograph, Charlotte thought that she was in denial, unable to face the shocking truth. Surely, she'd have to say *something* about her daughter's despicable behaviour? She'd said in the church that she recognized the lounge carpet, so she must have known the truth. Whatever was in the woman's mind, Charlotte was thankful to be home. Sleeping beneath the stars wasn't a way of life that appealed to her.

'When you've eaten that, you'd better have a bath,' the older woman said, placing a plate of eggs and bacon on the table.

'Thank you,' Charlotte smiled, wondering whether the subject of Father James wanking in the woods with a naked girl had cropped up in the church.

'Seeing as it's Friday, I don't suppose you'll be going to school.'

'Er . . . no, I won't. I'll go back on Monday.'

'Is your stomach better now?'

'Yes, yes, it is.'

'Right, I'll leave you to eat your breakfast. I have to go and see someone.'

'Isn't it rather early?' Charlotte asked.

'It is, but this is very important. I'll see you later.'

As her mother left the cottage, Charlotte again wondered why she seemed to be blotting out the horrendous truth. As she ate her breakfast, she also wondered who she'd gone to see. Father James? she mused. Or Goodhugh? Unable to comprehend her mother's reaction, Charlotte finished her breakfast and washed up. Climbing the stairs to her room, she thought about Marianne. She didn't want to keep the girl waiting, and hurriedly slipped out of her clothes. Stuffing the money behind the ottoman, she grabbed a towel and ran a bath. Immersing her abused young body beneath the hot soapy water, she wondered what the day would bring. Sex? Would she return to the boy's school? she wondered, massaging soap into the soft valley of her vagina. If things were all right at home, which they seemed to be, there'd be no need to return to the school. There again, there was a need within her valley of desire. An urgent need.

Finally leaving the cottage, the morning sun warming her as she made her way to the woods, Charlotte felt positive. The boy's school looming in her thoughts, she wondered whether to visit the shed once a week. She'd do well financially, and would derive immense sexual satisfaction from her sordid exploits. And a weekly caning from the headmaster? Marianne would know nothing of her clandestine visits, neither would her mother. A secret life, she thought happily as she neared the wooden bridge.

Looking about her, she wondered where Marianne had gone. Goodhugh wouldn't have nabbed her, would he? Perhaps the priest had . . . Deciding to visit the church,

Charlotte followed the path back to the road. If she was going to remain living in the cottage, she didn't want the evil pair hounding and threatening her. It was high time to put an end to the blackmail. Feeling confident as she walked through the graveyard, she pushed the oak door open and entered the stone building. Gazing at the altar, she smiled. She'd been crudely used and abused by many a man, she reflected. Wandering down the aisle, she thought about Satan. Was he lurking in the shadows of her mind?

'Ah, Charlotte.' Father James grinned as he emerged from his office. 'I didn't expect to see you here again.'

'Why's that?' she asked, standing before the evil man.

'Well, after . . . How is your poor mother coping? Now that she knows that her daughter is a slag and—'

'She's about to discover that the local priest is a sad pervert,' Charlotte broke in. 'I'll be showing her the photographs later.'

'I think you're forgetting one or two things, Charlotte. Mr Goodhugh has many photographs of you. Not only having sex with men but with Emily and Marianne. Any photographs you might show people will only incriminate you further – and the other girls involved.'

'There's been a lot of talk about photographs.' Charlotte grinned, taking a prayer book from a pew. 'Pictures of me in Goodhugh's office,' she said, ripping a page out of the book. 'Photographs of me sucking his cock in my lounge.' Another page fluttered to the floor. 'Emily in the woods with me. Marianne in the woods with me.'

'Do you mind putting the book down?' the priest asked as she ripped several more pages out and dropped them to the floor.

'There are one or two things that you don't know,' she continued.

'Such as?'

'I too have photographs. Photographs of you and Goodhugh sexually abusing young girls.'

'Of course you haven't.'

'Goodhugh isn't the only one who has a camera.'

'You'd better be very careful, young lady. You've caused enough trouble as it is. You've upset people in high places. It's not just Goodhugh and me.'

'And it's not just me,' Charlotte shot back, ripping up what was left of the book. 'I'm not alone in this. There are other girls who have come forward. There's a large group of us now. By the way, you can tell the gym mistress that she's about to lose her job.'

'Now you listen to me, Charlotte. There are more people involved in this than you realize. And remember *this* before you go showing photographs to people: the girls are all willing participants. Anyone can see that from the photographs. They're smiling, laughing, loving every minute of the sex. The girls are old enough to have sex. You might think you have something on me but, in reality, it's *you* who will end up in serious trouble. You stole a radio, for starters.'

'Rubbish. That won't wash with the police.'

'Won't it? Of course, there's the other business.'

'What other business?'

'Many years ago, a man was questioned by the police about the sexual abuse of young girls in the village. He wasn't arrested because, like me, he'd not committed an actual offence. The girls were seen as willing participants in the sexual acts and they were old enough. The police had to keep quiet about the matter, otherwise he'd have sued them for libel. So no one knew of his secret sex life with teenage girls, and they still don't. He fled the village, believing that word would get round, despite the police being legally gagged, and he'd be disgraced. As it happened, word *didn't* get round.'

'What has all this to do with—'

'Have you ever wondered where your father is?'

'He's . . . he's dead.'

'He is the man I'm talking about, Charlotte.'

Collapsing into a pew, Charlotte held her head in her hands. This wasn't true, it couldn't be. Her father had died when she was a baby, her mother had said. He'd have made contact if . . . Her head spinning, she didn't know what to think as the priest stood before her and raised his cassock. Gazing at his erect penis, his swollen glans, she couldn't believe that this was happening. The man's balls rolling, he thrust his hips forward. What was his threat this time? she wondered. He'd tell her mother the awful truth about her husband? Charlotte couldn't stand back and allow that to happen. No matter what, she couldn't . . .

'You'd better do exactly as I tell you,' the priest laughed, wanking the solid shaft of his huge penis. 'Your mother has had a big enough shock as it is. We'll start with an early-morning blow job. This evening, I'll fuck your arsehole. In fact, every day I'll fuck your mouth, your cunt and your arse. You're in for a lifetime of bondage and spanking, whipping, dildos, nipple clamps, tongue-fucking, tit caning, cunt thrashing . . . And there's nothing you can do about it.'

Dashing out of the church in a flood of tears, Charlotte ran to the woods. Flopping onto the grass by the bridge, she couldn't believe the priest's cruel words. Her mother had said that pneumonia had taken her father. He couldn't be living, she was sure. In her confusion, she wondered again why her mother hadn't gone mad over the photographs and thrown her out onto the street. *Something* was going on — but what?

Hauling herself up, she wandered along the path, deep into the woods. She should go and talk to her mother, she knew as she walked aimlessly through the trees. She should ask the woman about her father, what sort of person he'd been. She'd never broached the subject before because she'd felt that her mother hadn't wanted to talk about it. There were unanswered questions, Charlotte mused. Why hadn't her mother mentioned Father James wanking in the woods with a naked girl? She'd talked to Mrs Langly about it, but hadn't mentioned it again.

Her mind in turmoil, Charlotte began to wonder whether Goodhugh was her father. Or the priest? Her thinking going haywire, she emerged eventually from the woods and stared at the boys' school, the huge building looming from its grounds and reaching up to the sky. She had to get her mind off her father, drag her thoughts away from the priest's terrible words. Would crude sex with a dozen boys help? she wondered. Perhaps a good caning by the headmaster would take her mind off things.

Walking through the grounds, she sat by the pond and watched the ducks. She had to put an end to the priest's threats once and for all. It seemed that, whatever she threatened him with, he responded with a heavier threat. Again thinking about leaving the village and living in a flat, she knew that would end the nightmare. That was what it was going to take, she concluded. Running away was the only avenue open to her. She'd need to get her money and gather a few clothes, but at least she could go home without fearing the wrath of her mother.

Rising to her feet, she looked at the school. There was money there, plenty of money. Her mind set on leaving the cottage, she made her plans. A room would do to begin with, possibly a bed-and-breakfast item. Once the money was pouring in, she'd find a proper flat. Although Marianne had said that she'd go with her, Charlotte doubted that she'd leave home. There again, if the girl was really in love with her, she'd do anything to be with Charlotte.

'I need another hundred,' she murmured, walking towards the school. She knew that she'd be welcomed with open arms – and stiff pricks – by the boys, if she could find them. And their wallets would be bulging like the crotches of their trousers. Nearing the shed, she wondered what to do. Recalling one boy mentioning a side door to the dormitories, she stole round the side of the building. Praying that she wouldn't be caught by one of the teachers, or by the headmaster, she slipped through a small door and found herself at the foot of a narrow staircase.

She was going to get lost, Charlotte knew as she followed a labyrinth of corridors. This was a bad idea, she thought as she came across a small oak door. Her knickerless pussy dripping with her juices of desire, she was more than ready for crude sex. But where were her clients? Tentatively opening the door, she slipped into a small office and looked around her. A desk, chair and filing cabinet were the only items of furniture, and she wondered to whom the office belonged. Opening the cabinet, she was about to rummage through the files when she heard footsteps in the corridor.

With nowhere to hide, Charlotte stood motionless by the filing cabinet as the footsteps grew louder. She was going to have to come up with an instant lie. She was looking for the headmaster's office. She been given the wrong directions. She'd got lost. Taking a deep breath as the door handle turned, she waited in fear and trepidation as the door slowly opened.

'May I help you?' a middle-aged man asked as he stood in the doorway frowning at her.

'Sorry.' She smiled. 'I was looking for . . . I seem to have got lost.'

'I'm not surprised,' he said, closing the door. 'This building is a maze of corridors and passageways. Who were you looking for?'

'Er . . . Gibson-Brown.'

'Ah, Gibson-Brown,' he grinned, loosening his tie as he perched himself on the edge of the desk. 'And what would you be wanting with him?'

'I'm his sister.'

'Are you now? I didn't know he had a sister. There again, I don't know everything about every boy in the school. My name's Davis, by the way. Although I'm not dressed for the part at the moment, I'm the chaplain here.'

'Oh, right. Well, I'd better be going.'

'Young Gibson-Brown will be in lessons now. Why don't you wait in the visitors' lounge just inside the main entrance? If you can hang on for a few minutes, I'll take you there.'

'No, no . . . I'll find the way'

'You hang on a minute,' the chaplain said, lifting the telephone. 'I'll send for someone to escort you. You're bound to get yourself lost again.'

'No, it's all right,' she said firmly, moving to the door. 'I'll be all right, honestly.'

Replacing the receiver, he looked her up and down. 'How's your father?' he asked. 'I haven't seen him for a while.'

'He's . . . he's fine, thank you.'

'Still working hard in America?'

'Yes, yes, he is.'

'I think you'd better sit down,' the man said, slipping off the desk and waving his hand at the chair. 'Sit down and tell me what you're really doing here.'

Flopping into the swivel chair, Charlotte hung her head as the chaplain paced the floor. She'd have been better off saying that she'd been to see the headmaster yesterday and had come back to discuss a private matter. But it was too late to change her story now. She wasn't in trouble, she consoled herself. Yet.

'Well?' the man asked, standing in front of the desk.

'Gibson-Brown is a friend of mine,' she breathed.

'His Christian name?'

'I . . . I don't know. I only met him the other day.'

'And you thought you'd sneak around the school looking for him?'

'Yes, no . . . Look, I haven't done anything wrong. All I was doing was looking for—'

'I didn't say that you'd done anything wrong. What intrigues me is that I saw you creeping around the grounds yesterday, and now you're creeping around again today. On top of that, you told me that you're Gibson-Brown's sister. What's going on?'

'All right,' Charlotte sighed. 'I got lost yesterday and bumped into Gibson-Brown. I said that I'd come back and see him. It's as simple as that.'

'Then why didn't you say so in the first place?'

'I don't know.'

'I think the best thing you can do is go home. Why not write to the boy?'

'Yes, yes, I will,' she smiled, rising to her feet and moving to the door.

'Are you a local?'

'I'm from Nepcote Down.'

'Ah, a lovely village. Have you lived there long?'
'All my life.'
'Ah, then you must know Father James.'
'Yes, I do,' Charlotte said softly 'Do you know him well?'
'We've been friends for years,' he smiled. 'We go back—'
'Do you see much of him?'
'Not a great deal.'
'Tell me about him,' Charlotte said, retaking her seat.
'There's not much to tell. He went through a bad patch after the trouble with . . . I shouldn't say anything about that.'
'I know about his problems,' she lied.
'Do you?' he frowned. 'If that's the case, you're the only one in the village who does.'
'He's very good friends with my mother, you see. They have long chats over tea and I've overheard things. I'd never say anything, of course.'
'Oh, right. Well, after the trouble, he went downhill. Which isn't surprising. But he seems to be fine now.'
'I like him very much. He's been good to me.'
'He's done a lot for the community. I did think that, after the accusations, he'd leave the church. And the village.'
'The accusations were terrible,' Charlotte said, wondering what the priest had been accused of. 'I can't begin to imagine how he must have felt at the time.'
'Dreadful. We talked about it often. The awful thing was that, because a silly young girl accused him of that . . . Anyway, it's all in the past.'
'Where's the girl now?'
'She moved to Australia with her parents, thank goodness.'
'Oh, yes. I did hear something about that. Well, I'd better be going.'

'What did you say your name was?'

'Sandy, Sandy Evans.'

'OK, Sandy. Give my regards to Father James.'

'I will. Goodbye.'

Leaving the office, Charlotte couldn't stop grinning as she made her way through the corridors and finally emerged from the building. If she could discover the young girl's name, then the priest would believe that she knew about his sordid past. What was sordid about it, she didn't know. But, the way the man carried on, it wasn't difficult to hazard a guess. He'd threatened the girl, blackmailed her and sexually abused her. No doubt Goodhugh would have \been in on the act. This could be the break Charlotte was looking for, she thought happily as she walked back through the grounds and into the woods.

Finally emerging from the woods, she looked up and down the road. The coast clear, she walked briskly to the post office. The postmistress, Mrs Tiler, had lived in the village for ever and would be sure to know of the family who'd emigrated to Australia. Charlotte was right: the woman knew the Harringtons well. The daughter, Jenny Harrington, had been sixteen when she left the country. Thanking the postmistress, Charlotte left the post office and went directly to the church. Slipping into the building, she stood motionless as voices emerged from the office.

'What with you stealing the radio, and allowing sordid photographs to be taken of your naked body, I really don't see that I can help you,' the priest said as Charlotte stole around the pews and hid in the shadows by the office door. 'Mr Goodhugh has spoken to me about this.'

'Has he?' Emily asked surprisedly.

'He came to me and told me that you'd stolen a radio. He said that he wasn't sure what to do and asked whether I'd

SCHOOLGIRL LUST

talk to you. But, in view of your revelation . . . What your parents will say, I can't begin to think.'

'My parents must never find out,' Emily whimpered.

'I know your parents well,' the man continued. 'They'd be devastated if they discovered that their daughter was nothing more than a thief and a common whore.'

'Please, I—'

'To make matters worse, you come here telling me that Mr Goodhugh has been blackmailing you. The truth of the matter is that he *paid* you to strip naked before the camera. You told me that he paid you.'

'He paid me after . . . It was blackmail, Father. You must believe me.'

'Blackmailers don't usually pay their victims, Emily. There have been many other sordid incidents. In the woods with Charlotte, for example.'

'No, I've never—'

'The things you did with Charlotte were . . . I happened to see you while I was out walking. I wasn't going to say anything but, in view of your continued whoredom and stealing . . .'

'We were only—'

'I know what you were "only" doing, Emily. I know everything about you. I'm sorry, but it's my duty to inform your parents of your lewd behaviour.'

Seething with anger, Charlotte clenched her fists. She'd heard all this before, she reflected as Emily sobbed. Wishing she'd never suggested that the girl ask Goodhugh for a radio, she wondered what had happened with Emily. Had the man lured her into his stockroom and fucked her? The priest obviously hadn't got his hand up her skirt – yet.

'There might be a way out of this,' the priest said. 'I've

known Mr Goodhugh for a long time. I might be able to persuade him . . .'

'Please try,' Emily breathed pathetically.

'I'd like you to visit me now and then. Come to my office, say, three times a week.'

'What for?'

'You're a slut, Emily.'

'No, I—'

'A filthy, common slag who drops her knickers and opens her legs and has sordid sex with men and young girls. You use your body, your cunt—'

'Father!' Emily gasped.

'Don't feign shock, for God's sake. You're used to such words, and you know it. You're a dirty little whore, Emily.'

'I'm going,' she sobbed. 'I don't have to stay here and listen to—'

'To the truth? You're a dirty tart. A filthy whore-slag. Pull your knickers down and show me your dirty cunt.'

'No! You're as bad as—'

'In that case, I'll go straight to your parents' house and tell them that you're a slut. Lewd photographs, lesbian sex in the woods . . . The choice is yours, Emily. Drop your knickers and show me your dirty little cunt, or I go to your parents.'

Spying through the crack in the door, Charlotte watched the girl lift her short skirt and pull her panties down her long legs. Her sparse blonde pubes barely concealing the pinken crack of her pussy, she lowered her head as the priest knelt before her. Parting the pouting lips of her young vagina, he gazed longingly at her inner sex folds, the mother-of-pearl liquid hanging in globules from the wings of her unfurling inner lips.

'How many cocks have you had up your cunt?' he asked the girl unashamedly.

SCHOOLGIRL LUST

'I . . . I don't know,' Emily murmured.

'You've lost count, I would imagine. You're a dirty little slut. How many men have tongue-fucked your tight cunt?'

'Please, I . . .'

'Kneel down and suck this.' The man of God grinned, lifting his cassock and exposing his erect penis to the girl.

'Please . . .'

'Suck my knob and swallow my spunk, or I'll go to your parents.'

Kneeling before the cleric, Emily took his purple crown into her pretty mouth and sucked hard. Charlotte was in two minds about whether to burst into the office and confront the vulgar priest. But she decided to bide her time as Emily gobbled on the man's swollen glans. The spunk would soon gush from his slit and fill the girl's mouth. When the act was over, Emily would leave and Charlotte would make her entrance. And put her plan into action.

'Use your tongue, you fucking slag,' Father James gasped in his crudity as he rocked his hips, fucking the girl's wet mouth. His veined shaft driving in and out of the girl's bloated mouth, his purple glans gliding back and forth over her pink tongue, he looked up to the ceiling. His heavy balls swinging, battering her chin, he closed his eyes, lost in his sexual euphoria as he neared his climax.

Emily should never have threatened to reveal the photographs, Charlotte reflected. Had she not threatened to show her mother, Charlotte wouldn't have mentioned the radios and sent her to Goodhugh's shop. But the girl had enjoyed many a mouth-fuck. Sucking the priest to orgasm wouldn't bother her too much. If anything, she was probably enjoying the sordid coupling, looking forward to his sacred spunk gushing into her thirsty mouth. What *would* bother the girl was the threat of telling her parents about her sexual exploits. But Charlotte was about to put an end to the blackmail. What the priest would do, she had no idea. One mention of Jenny Harrington and he'd probably flee before he could be defrocked and hounded out of the village.

'Coming,' he breathed, rocking his hips faster, fucking Emily's mouth as if he was screwing her young cunt. 'Swallow my spunk,' he gasped, gripping the girl's head as he pumped his sperm into her gobbling mouth. Watching the white liquid dribbling down Emily's chin, Charlotte felt her own clitoris stir, her juices of desire seeping between the engorged lips of her vagina. But this was no time for pleasure, she knew as she watched the man of God draining his heavy balls. Coughing and spluttering, Emily drank from his solid cock, sucking out every last drop of sperm as the man of God shook uncontrollably in his coming.

'You did well,' he praised Emily, withdrawing his saliva-glistening penis from her sperm-bubbling mouth. 'This evening, I'll tie you over the altar and fuck your tight arsehole.'

'May I go now?' Emily murmured, rising to her feet and wiping the sperm from her mouth with the back of her hand.

'Yes, you can go. But I want you back here at seven o'clock. If you don't turn up, I shall go straight round to your house and speak to your parents.'

Slipping into the shadows as Emily emerged from the office. Charlotte watched her walk up the aisle and leave the church. The priest would be chuckling, she thought as she moved towards the office door. Believing he had conquered another teenage girl, he'd be rubbing his hands and looking forward to her returning that evening. Emily had wiped the man's sperm off her face, and now Charlotte was going to wipe the grin off his.

'Still abusing teenage girls?' Charlotte asked as she entered the office.

'Oh,' he breathed, spinning round on his heels. 'It's you.'

'Still enjoying mouth-fucking schoolgirls?'

'Yes, I'm enjoying young girls' naked bodies,' he replied. 'I think I'll enjoy yours, seeing as you're here. Take your clothes off and—'

'You can fuck yourself,' Charlotte hissed. 'Fuck your arse with your own cock.'

'It's a shame you've adopted that attitude, Charlotte. I wasn't going to mention your father to anyone but . . . Now, I suppose, I'll have to chat to a few people in the village. Mention your father and—'

'What a coincidence,' she grinned. '*I* was thinking about chatting to a few people about *you*.'

'Oh?'

'I've been talking to Jenny.'

'Jenny?'

'Jenny Harrington.'

'I . . . I've never heard of her,' Father James replied shakily, tidying a pile of papers on his desk.

'She's heard of *you*, all right.'

'Wait a minute. Harrington, Harrington,' he muttered, rubbing his chin. 'Wasn't that the family that went abroad several years ago?'

'That's right. Jenny has come back to the village.'

'Oh, that's nice,' he murmured, his hands trembling. 'So, what's she doing back here?'

'She has something to settle.'

'Settle?'

'A score to settle, as she put it. We had a long talk about

her past, about her school days. She's older now, of course. But she hasn't forgotten anything. She remembers how she was treated by certain people.'

'Where . . . where is she staying?' the cleric stammered. 'I'd like to see her again.'

'Funnily enough, she's very keen to see you, too. I told her that you're still here, and still enjoying the company of schoolgirls. Enjoying young girls' naked bodies, as you so aptly put it.'

'If girls want sex with me . . . I mean, there's nothing illegal about—'

'You're right, there's nothing illegal about having sex with consenting teenage girls, as long as they're sixteen or over. The police wouldn't be interested, so you have nothing to worry about.'

'No, I haven't.'

'Of course, the villagers would be extremely interested.'

'Yes, right. I think I'd better have a chat with Jenny.'

'It's not only Jenny you have to chat to. I might start blabbing about her and what happened when she was sixteen.'

'So, we'd better have a chat,' the priest said, forcing a smile.

'A long chat. But not now. I have things to do. I'll call back later.'

'I'd rather we sorted this out now,' he said, following her out of the office.

'Later, Father James. I wouldn't be at all surprised if that old shed burned down. You know what these vandals are like. I'm sure that, by the time I come back, the shed and its contents will have been destroyed by fire. I'll leave it to you.'

Leaving the church, Charlotte felt a wave of relief roll through her young body. The sun shone bright in a clear blue sky as she made her way home, deciding to spend some time relaxing in the garden before returning to the church. At last she was winning, she reflected happily. The end of the nightmare was in sight. Unless the priest and Goodhugh came up with a counterplan.

Chapter Fifteen

On entering the cottage, Charlotte was surprised to discover that her mother was still out. Wondering where she'd got to, she climbed the stairs to her bedroom. She knew that something was going on. Who had the woman gone to see? It had to have something to do with the photographs the priest had shown her of Charlotte sucking a cock-head and swallowing spunk. Perhaps Mrs Langly knew of the original Pink Peaches scam of two decades ago. The thought crossed Charlotte's mind that her own mother might have been a victim of sexual abuse in her younger days. Perhaps she'd known of Goodhugh's antics all along and had gone to speak to him? There were so many possibilities.

Opening the bedroom door, she gasped in horror at the sight of her gym mistress sitting on the end of the bed. The woman was wearing a skintight leather leotard and a studded collar around her neck. Horrified, Charlotte lowered her eyes and gazed in disbelief at the open crotch of the leotard, the woman's fleshy vaginal lips bulging through the hole in the leather. Charlotte stood motionless, frozen to the spot as she stared at the thigh-length leather boots, the fishnet stockings. This couldn't be happening, she thought fearfully as the woman rose to her feet. The gym mistress was wielding a riding crop and her dark eyes scowled at Charlotte.

'So, you're out to cause trouble,' she hissed, grabbing Charlotte's arm and throwing her young body across the bed.

'What . . . what are you doing here?' Charlotte asked, her heart banging hard against her chest as the gravity of the situation registered.

'I went to see Father James and happened to hear you talking to him, threatening him.'

'Get out of here,' Charlotte spat, gazing at the woman's black lipstick, her dark eyeshadow.

'I don't like the idea of you spoiling our fun.'

'Get out,' Charlotte repeated. 'How dare you come into my home and—'

'You've upset a lot of people, my girl. And now you're threatening Father James. I suggest you leave the village before—'

'Leave the village? I'll do nothing of the sort,' Charlotte retorted angrily. 'I suggest *you* leave this cottage before my mother returns.'

'I'll leave when I'm ready, and not before.'

Again eyeing the bulging flesh of the woman's vaginal lips, her inner sex petals protruding from the creamy ravine of her cunt, Charlotte shuddered. Perhaps the priest had been right and there were more people involved in the scam than she realized. How many other teachers at the school were members of the clandestine group? Then there were the priest, the local shopkeeper, the gym mistress . . . Why not the postman, the milkman . . . maybe half the men in the village?

'Remove your skirt,' the gym-mistress-turned-dominatrix growled.

'No, I—' Charlotte stammered, looking up from the bed.

'Remove your skirt or I'll rip it off you. I mean it,

SCHOOLGIRL LUST

Charlotte. I'm here to punish you, to correct your interfering ways.'

'You can go to—'

'That's for starters,' the woman grinned, knocking the alarm clock off the bedside table with the riding crop. 'Take your skirt off, or the ornaments go next. And then the window and then—'

Clambering off the bed, Charlotte tugged her skirt down, wondering what had possessed the gym mistress to behave like that. The woman was in her early thirties. Attractive and well dressed, she was usually quiet and reserved. But that was in school. Charlotte was discovering another side to her, an evil, sinister, side that she thought it best not to mess with. Dropping her skirt to the floor, she stood before the woman and eyed the riding crop. She was in for a thrashing, she knew as she was ordered to kneel on the floor and lean over the bed.

Obediently taking her position, Charlotte couldn't believe that the woman had entered the cottage dressed as a cruel dominatrix without being seen. How she'd got in, she had no idea. Unless Charlotte's mother had . . . No, surely not. But her mother had reacted strangely to the photograph of her daughter sucking a man's penis. And then she'd announced mysteriously that she was going to see someone. There seemed to be so many involved in the vulgar scam that Charlotte wasn't prepared to trust anyone. Emily? she thought, wondering whether the girl was in league with the priest.

'No!' Charlotte cried as the gym mistress knelt behind her and pressed the handle of the riding crop hard against her tightly closed anal inlet.

'You'll take this up your bottom,' the woman hissed, pushing the wooden shaft past the girl's anal sphincter muscles. 'I've wanted to get my hands on you for quite a while,' she chuckled, the girl's brown tissue expanding to accommodate the makeshift phallus. 'And now I have you.'

The gnarled wooden shaft of the riding-crop handle driving deeper into her anal canal, Charlotte grimaced as she realized that the abuse would never end. Even if Father James did flee the village, there'd be Goodhugh, the gym mistress and God only knew who else to carry on blackmailing and abusing teenage girls. To round up the entire gang of perverts would be impossible. A respected shopkeeper, the local priest . . . And to think that a teacher from her school, dressed in leather sadomasochistic gear had entered the cottage and was abusing her anal canal with a riding crop . . . There'd be no escape, Charlotte knew. Unless she left the village of sin. But even then, she might be hounded and—

'You've a tight little arse,' the woman breathed huskily, painfully parting the rounded cheeks of Charlotte's young bottom and gazing at her brown anal tissue gripping the wooden shaft. 'I've always watched you in the gym, thought how much I'd love to get my hands on your beautiful young body.' Charlotte said nothing as she felt a wet tongue slurping within her dank anal crease. A hand groping between the warmth of her inner thighs, she gasped as at least three fingers plunged into the wet depths of her hot cunt. The riding crop twisting within her spasming rectal cylinder, the lewd sensations permeating her quivering womb, she tried desperately to deny the immense pleasure the lesbian was bringing her as she writhed and whimpered on the bed.

The wooden shaft drove deeper into her stretched anal canal, penetrating the very core of her trembling body. The dominatrix's fingers twisting and thrusting in and out of her

SCHOOLGIRL LUST

inflamed cunt, massaging her inner vaginal flesh, Charlotte gasped and squirmed as the woman spanked her naked buttocks with her free hand. The squishing sound of her vaginal juices punctuated by loud slaps, Charlotte sank her teeth into the eiderdown as her young body convulsed wildly. She was going to come, she knew as the woman's thrusting fingers massaged the solid nubble of her pulsating clitoris.

'The times I've gazed at your beautiful young body when you've been playing netball,' the woman breathed. 'Your naked thighs below your pleated skirt, glimpsing your tight knickers bulging wonderfully over your teenage sex lips . . . I've dreamed of this, Charlotte. I've masturbated while fantasizing about finger-fucking your tight cunt and shafting your pert bottom. I've dreamed of this for a long time.'

Again unable to believe that this was her reserved, quiet gym mistress, Charlotte involuntarily jutted her naked buttocks out as her arousal rose. Her young thighs parting, her sex holes opening to accommodate the broad shaft of the wooden handle, stretching to take the pistoning fingers, she knew that she could no longer survive without crude lesbian sex. Lesbian or hetero? she pondered, her breathing fast and shallow as her body trembled. The beautiful sensation of sucking on a swollen knob, the heady aroma of male pubes, the intoxicating taste of gushing spunk . . . Or the fleshy, creamy-wet duct of a young girl's hot cunt? She desperately wanted both.

Gasping as her orgasm roused deep within her quivering womb, Charlotte wondered whether she'd be forced to attend the woman's base sexual needs. She'd probably be ordered to finger-fuck the tight shaft of her hot cunt, to tongue-fuck the dank sheath of her bottom, to bite her nipples, frig her clitoris to orgasm, swallow her girl-cum . . .

The very thought of pleasuring her abuser sent her juices of desire spewing from her young cunt and coursing down her inner thighs.

'Come,' the part-time dominatrix cried, her fingers thrusting in and out of Charlotte's contracting cuntal sheath. Grabbing the riding crop, she pistoned the girl's anal cylinder, delighting in her wanton act of lesbianism. Her clitoris painfully swelling, her anal muscles gripping the wooden dildo like a velvet-jawed vice, Charlotte trembled in her girl-desire as the woman's wet tongue snaked around the bloated hole that led to her rectal core. Licking the stretched brown tissue, tantalizing the sensitive nerve endings, she worked between the gasping girl's buttocks with expertise.

'God,' Charlotte breathed as the pulsating nodule of her clitoris exploded in a massive orgasm, shock waves of pure sexual bliss transmitting deep into her young pelvis. Her body shaking violently, she cried out, sinking her fingernails into the eiderdown as her illicit pleasure heightened. Praying that her mother wouldn't return and hear her orgasmic cries, Charlotte bit hard on the eiderdown to muffle her wails of pleasure. On and on her orgasm rolled, rocking the very core of her young body, her mind tossed on rip tides of lesbian lust as the woman attended the sexual core of her teenage body.

The dominatrix's fingers finally leaving Charlotte's inflamed vaginal throat, the riding crop yanked out of her tight anal duct, Charlotte jolted as the rounded cheeks of her buttocks were painfully wrenched apart. A wet tongue running up and down her yawning anal crease, licking the sensitive brown tissue surrounding the inlet to her hot rectum, she shuddered in her debauchery. Fingers entering the mouth of her tight arse and stretching open her anal canal, she sang out in her ecstasy as the woman pushed her tongue into her dank tube, licking the inner walls of her sheath of illicit sex. The sensations drove Charlotte wild and she squirmed on the bed, unable to believe the immense pleasure she was deriving from her abused rectum as her vaginal juices gushed from the spasming duct of her equally abused cunt.

'You taste beautiful,' the gym mistress breathed, her tongue darting in and out of the girl's hot rectal tube. Quivering as her clitoris sent wondrous ripples of sex throughout her young body, Charlotte lay dazed in the aftermath of her lesbian coming. Her eyes rolling as the arse-tonguing sent mind-blowing tingles of pleasure deep into her hot bowels, she parted her knees and pushed her rounded buttocks out further. She could feel the wet tongue delving further into her tight bottom-hole, massaging the moist tube of her rectum, waking the nerves of pleasure deep inside her fiery arse. Whimpering as the woman slipped her fingers out of her anus and pressed her lips hard against the sticky brown tissue, Charlotte let out a rush of breath as the tongue snaked its way to the core of her dank shaft.

This was sheer heavenly bliss, Charlotte thought in the mist of her sexual delirium. The heat of the woman's mouth against her sensitive brown ring, her wet tongue caressing the tube of her anal tract, Charlotte quivered uncontrollably as her clitoris swelled and her juices of lust issued in torrents from her gaping vaginal mouth. The wet tongue slipping out of her tight bottom-hole and driving deep into the steaming duct of her fiery cunt, Charlotte sang out again in her euphoria. The slurping sound of her tongue-fucked vagina was music to her ears as she reached behind her back and yanked the fleshy lips of her dripping cunt wide apart, opening her sexual core to the lesbian licking.

Painfully stretching the plump cushions of her sex-drenched pussy lips wider apart, opening the very centre of her young cunt to the woman's inquisitive tongue, Charlotte yelped as teeth sank into the soft folds of her vaginal flesh. Two fingers suddenly driving deep into the inflamed shaft of her arse, her body bucking wildly, she wailed her ecstasy into the billowing folds of the eiderdown. Her long black hair matted with the perspiration of lesbian sex, she held the swollen lips of her pussy wide apart as the woman's tongue lapped up her flowing juices of desire and she drank the milk of lust from her very womb. Her teenage body rocking back and forth as the woman thrust her sticky fingers in and out of her spasming bottom-hole, Charlotte knew that she couldn't take much more. Her sex sheaths aching, her mind spinning, she almost passed out as her second orgasm erupted within her erect clitoris and tore through her trembling body.

'God, no,' she breathed, her creamy ejaculate gushing from her mouth-fucked vagina. Her inner thighs splattered with her milky love juices, the hairless lips of her cunt-mouth inflamed, she finally fell limp, semiconscious in the swirling haze of her lesbian lust. Quivering, mouthing incoherent words of crude sex, she drifted gently down from her sexual heaven as her orgasm subsided. The fingers finally leaving the burning tube of her arse, her sex holes closing, Charlotte's dazed consciousness drifted through her exhausted body as she wondered what she was to endure next.

'We need to talk about your problems,' the woman said, stroking the bulging lips of Charlotte's well-juiced pussy. 'I think it best that you leave the village before—'

'No,' the girl gasped, clambering onto the bed and lying on her back. 'I'm not going anywhere.'

'I was afraid you'd say that,' the gym mistress murmured, moving to the door. 'I was hoping that I'd be able to make you see sense. You're a real threat to Father James. What happened in the past is history, and must stay that way. No one in the village knows what happened, and they never will.'

'Won't they? When Jenny—'

'I don't believe that Jenny Harrington has returned. You were lying, weren't you?'

'No, I wasn't,' Charlotte breathed. 'She's here, in the village.'

'If that's true, then she's made the biggest mistake of her life by coming back. Like you, she'll be dealt with.'

'What do you think you're in? The Mafia or something? This is a quiet country village and—'

'Yes, and that's the way we like it. Quiet, no one knowing what's going on behind closed doors . . .'

'Behind the church doors,' Charlotte murmured.

'We made a mistake by involving you, Charlotte. But mistakes can be rectified. As will Jenny's mistake, if she *has* made the mistake of coming back. But we're wasting time.' She grinned and left the room.

Wondering where the woman had gone, what she intended to do, Charlotte lay quivering on the bed, desperately trying to recover from her enforced orgasms as she heard voices outside her bedroom door. Had her mother returned? she wondered. Dressed in a skintight leather leotard with her vaginal lips bulging through the hole in the crotch, the gym mistress would hardly be speaking to her mother. Was it Goodhugh and the perverted priest? There were whispers coming from the landing, male mur-

murings, and Charlotte feared the worst as the door opened.

'Take her,' the dominatrix ordered four nude young men as they filed into the room and gazed longingly at Charlotte's teenage body. Watching through her eyelashes as the naked men surrounded the bed, Charlotte didn't care what happened to her. Her mind still swimming, her body trembling, she focused on the rolling balls, the solid shafts of the erect penises, the swollen purple knobs. She was going to be rudely fucked and spunked, she knew as her legs were spread, the crack of her teenage pussy opening wide to reveal the entrance to her tight cunt. The creamy mouth of her vagina crudely bared, she felt no humiliation, no degradation as fingers stroked the wet folds of her pinken sex valley. There were no emotions now, no feelings . . . Only cold, raw sex.

As the woman knelt on the bed, her knees on either side of Charlotte's head, the gaping ravine of her vagina hovering inches above the girl's flushed face, she ordered the men to fuck the girl. Instinctively opening her mouth as the dominatrix lowered her leather-clad body, Charlotte sucked on the wet flesh of her swollen vaginal lips, savouring her flowing juices of lust. The bed rocking, a solid knob slipping between Charlotte's splayed sex lips and driving deep into the hugging sheath of her cunt, she closed her eyes and resigned herself to the fact that she was nothing more than a rag doll to be used and abused. Pushing her tongue out, she breathed heavily through her nose as her vaginal cavern lovingly hugged the rock-hard penile shaft. The hot tube of the woman's pussy tasted of lesbian sex, the intoxicating aroma of her cunt filling Charlotte's nostrils, her warm juices of arousal flooding her mouth as she tongue-fucked her cruel mistress.

SCHOOLGIRL LUST

The solid penile shaft penetrating her tight cunt, its swollen knob pressing hard against her ripe cervix, Charlotte again wondered where her mother had got to and prayed that she wouldn't return and witness the debauchery. The gym mistress must have known that the woman was out. To bring four men into the cottage and have them hide upstairs and then enter Charlotte's room naked and fuck the girl . . . They either knew that the cottage would be empty all day or her mother knew of their plan and was keeping well away. Was her mother involved? Charlotte wondered. Nothing was impossible.

As the room lit up with a blue-white flash, Charlotte knew that they were taking photographs of her lewd entanglement. More blackmail threats, she thought angrily as the man between her legs thrust his massive penis in and out of her spasming cuntal duct. Her blouse torn open, her young breasts exposed, she jolted as what felt like a bamboo cane swished through the air and flailed the sensitive discs of her areolae. Screaming through a mouthful of pussy flesh, she tried to escape as the cane once more struck the sensitive spheres of her mammary glands, the agonizing pain permeating her young mounds. Again and again the cane lashed her crimsoned breasts as the penis within the sheath of her cunt repeatedly thrust into her. This was hell. This was heaven.

'Yes,' the gym mistress cried, her hot juices of orgasm flooding Charlotte's face as she reached her lesbian-induced climax. Listening to the vaginal squelching, the swishing cane, the loud cracks, the heavy breathing . . . now Charlotte prayed for her mother to come home and put an end to the debauchery. Perhaps the woman was downstairs? Perhaps she was waiting patiently while her daughter's wicked ways were corrected? Again trying to escape the gruelling thrashing as the man between her thighs gasped and pumped his spunk deep into her spasming cunt, she bit into the vaginal flesh filling her mouth. Her mother wouldn't allow this abuse, would she?

'More!' the gym mistress cried, grinding her open cunt hard against Charlotte's pussy-wet face, forcing her pulsating clitoris into the girl's wet mouth. Barely able to breathe as the woman swivelled her hips, her vaginal fluid gushing in torrents into her mouth, Charlotte repeatedly swallowed hard. The man fucking her teenage cunt grunting in his debauchery, her hot sex sheath overflowing with his copious sperm, her naked breasts stinging beneath the swishing cane, she reached her own mind-blowing climax. Squirming in the grip of her shuddering orgasm, her lashed breasts adding to her debased pleasure, she again bit into the wet folds of the woman's dripping cunt. Her pulsating clitoris massaged by the thrusting penis, her orgasm peaking, she sank her fingernails into the eiderdown and arched her back as she reached hitherto unknown heights of sexual elation.

Dizzy in her sexual euphoria, her weal-lined breasts stinging, Charlotte tossed her head from side to side as the woman finally slipped the drenched folds of her cunt out of her mouth and clambered off the bed. She was a slave, she thought, her body shaking violently as her clitoris pulsated in orgasm and her sore nipples grew erect beneath the cane. A slave, not only to her captors – but to herself. Having experienced crude and debased sex, never would she be able to lead a normal life. Her insatiable clitoris, her yearning cunt, the sensitive teats of her firm breasts, the tight tube of her bottom ... All brought her immense pleasure, great satisfaction. She was her own worst enemy, she knew.

'Suck it, bitch,' a man breathed, kneeling beside her head

with the solid shaft of his huge cock in his hand. Charlotte eyed his purple plum as her orgasm finally began to recede. His foreskin fully retracted, the slit of his glans seemingly smiling at her, she instinctively opened her pretty mouth and sucked on his male hardness. He gasped as his swinging balls brushed her face, his pubic curls tickling her nose as he forced his swollen glans deeper into her wet mouth. A second man kneeling the other side of her head, his huge shaft hovering ominously above her flushed face, his heavy balls rolling, she knew that she was to endure the beautifully decadent act of a double mouth-spunking.

The penis slipping out of her spunk-brimming vaginal sheath, the bed gently rocking, she arched her back as another man drove the solid shaft of his cock deep into her vaginal duct. *Seventeen years old*, Charlotte reflected as the second bulbous glans was forced into her already bloated mouth. And she'd endured more crude sex that most women do in a lifetime. The swollen knobs pressing against each other, her lips taut around the salty crowns, she rolled her tongue over the silky-smooth surfaces as the men gasped in their debased pleasure. As fingers delved between the pert cheeks of her bottom, she breathed heavily through her nose as her brown ring was forced wide open to expose the dank inner flesh of her arse. The fingers delving deep into her inflamed rectum, she closed her eyes as her naked body shook with the incredible abuse. More sex than most women get in a lifetime, and it had only just begun.

'Fill her mouth with spunk,' the gym mistress in her wickedness ordered the men as she slapped the firm mounds of Charlotte's swollen breasts. 'I want every hole fucked and spunked before I thrash her buttocks raw with the cane.' Gobbling on the two knobs as her body jolted with the cuntal fucking, Charlotte again wondered where her mother was. The woman didn't know what her daughter was being put through, did she? Perhaps the whole village was in on the scam, parents allowing their daughters to be blackmailed, blindfolded and fucked by neighbours. What with Emily now in the hands of the evil priest, Charlotte didn't know what she was going to do. The village of sin, she reflected as her mouth suddenly bubbled with sperm. Would she ever escape? Would she ever be free to leave the village of Satan?

Swallowing the gushing spunk, the white liquid overflowing from her bloated mouth and running down her cheeks, she thought about Jenny Harrington. If only she knew the whole story, she mused, the spunk running down to her temples and pooling on the eiderdown as the men fucked her hot mouth. It was probably the usual case of blackmail and crude sex, she concluded. The priest hadn't been arrested as no crime had been committed. The crime was taking a young girl's virginity and stripping her of her dignity. And that was crime enough. Determined to rid the village of Father James, Charlotte knew that she'd have to continue with her bluff, make out that Jenny had told her everything. And ensure that the man had no doubt that the girl was out for revenge. Wondering who the ringleader was, she pondered on Goodhugh's involvement. Perhaps he was the front man, initially selecting, luring, trapping and blackmailing the girls. Once he had photographic evidence of the girls' wanton promiscuity, they were then passed on to the perverted priest for further crude defiling.

The purple knobs sliding out of her spunked mouth, the deflating cock leaving her sperm-brimming cunt, Charlotte watched the men file out of the room. Now what? she wondered as the governess stood with her clenched fists on her hips, her lips furling into a salacious grin as she stared hard at her young victim. Another breasts-thrashing? A naked-buttock spanking? Whatever the woman did or threatened to do, Charlotte was determined to see the priest's downfall.

'You're a calculating little mare, aren't you?' the gym mistress grinned, slapping the palm of her hand with the riding crop as she paced the floor. 'A calculating, devious little bitch. You don't realize just what it is you're meddling with. You have no idea of the danger you're putting yourself in by interfering like you are. You've stolen photographs, brandished your futile threats about Jenny Harrington. You've pushed our patience to the limit, my girl. You've been warned and yet still you persist in your quest to put an end to our . . . our little club.'

'I *will* put an end to it,' Charlotte returned. 'No matter how long it takes, I'll—'

'One of the men who stood behind the partition in the church and fucked your sweet little mouth was a magistrate. Another was a policeman. Another was a councillor. Need I say more, Charlotte?'

'You're lying.'

'Am I? Can you be sure? We make money from the photographs. We make money by selling the girls for sex. For example, the men who fucked your mouth in the church each paid thirty pounds for the pleasure. They know who you are, but you don't know who they are. Here's a scenario for you. The police officer arrests you for stealing a radio and the magistrate sentences you. Even a silly teenage girl such as you must be able to see that—'

'I'm not interested in your threats,' Charlotte broke in. 'But you might be interested in this.'

'What lies are you going to come out with now?'

'Jenny's father is also here and he's going to—'

'Jenny's father, for your information, used to stand behind the partition in the church and fuck her mouth. He's fucked and spunked his daughter's sweet mouth a hundred times or more.'

'I don't believe a word of it.'

'Jenny didn't know who was behind the partition, but her father knew who he was mouth-fucking. You don't know who fucked your mouth, Charlotte. You have no idea who spunked in your pretty mouth, so why should Jenny have known? She had no idea who was fucking her arsehole while she was tied over the altar. Several men fucked her sweet bottom. One of the regulars was her father. You see, you know nothing. If Jenny has come back, then what does she hope to achieve?'

'I'm not telling you of her plans.'

'Plans?' the woman laughed. 'Jenny's in Australia with her family, and you know it. I'm going now. But I'll be back.' Moving to the door, she turned and grinned at Charlotte. 'I wouldn't want to have to tell you exactly who is involved in this. Don't make me tell you, Charlotte. Just be a good girl from now on, OK?'

Clambering off the bed and retrieving her skirt from the floor, Charlotte winced as the front door slammed shut. Whether she was telling the truth or not about Jenny and the magistrate and the police officer, the woman would be back. Walking to the bathroom and wiping the sperm off her pretty face with a flannel, Charlotte donned a blouse and brushed her hair. Tidying her bedroom, removing all signs of recent sex, she finally went out into the garden and sat on the wooden bench.

Her young breasts stinging like hell, sperm oozing from the inflamed shaft of her tight cunt, Charlotte tried to relax beneath the hot sun. The stark reality of her predicament wasn't going to go away, she knew as the brown ring of her anus burned and her abused rectal sheath ached. Her mind swirling with a thousand thoughts, she felt as if her head was going to explode. Lurching between her mother and the gym mistress, Goodhugh and the priest, Jenny, Marianne, Emily . . . She had to calm her mind, she knew as she took a deep breath and again tried to relax. Perhaps she should endure the sexual abuse and live as normal a life as possible in the village, she mused. Renting a flat was all very well, but becoming a prostitute?

'Ah, Charlotte,' her mother called from the kitchen. 'I thought you were out.'

'Oh, you're back,' the girl said, rising to her feet and trotting across the lawn. Spunk oozed between her inner love lips, reminding her of her wanton depravity. 'You were a long time.'

'As I said, I had to go and see someone.'

'Who? Who was it?'

'Never you mind, my girl.'

'Mother, I need to know something about my father,' Charlotte murmured.

'Oh?'

'Is there a possibility that he's alive?'

'What on earth makes you ask me that?'

'I need to know. I need to know whether there's a chance, no matter how slim, that he might be alive.'

'If you're asking me whether I saw him in the mortuary . . . No, I didn't. I wasn't with him when he died in the hospital.' She filled the kettle and turned to face Charlotte as the girl sat at the table. 'I can tell you this, Charlotte. Your father is dead.'

'Tell me about him, what he was like.'

'He was a quiet man. His passion was the garden. He

thought more of the garden than he did of me. That's why I do my best to maintain it. He loved walking in the woods. No doubt that's where you get it from. Why the sudden interest?'

'It's not sudden. I've often wondered about him. Did he know Mr Goodhugh?'

'They knew each other from school.'

'Were they good friends?'

'Not good friends, exactly. They got on all right but they didn't see a great deal of each other. Your father was like you, always wandering off to the woods. There were times when he'd be gone for hours.'

'And he was just walking in the woods?'

'Well, yes. Was that someone at the door?'

'I'll go,' Charlotte said, rising to her feet.

Noticing a brown envelope on the mat, she picked it up and read her name scrawled on the front. More trouble, she mused, tearing it open. Gazing at a house key and a slip of paper bearing an address, she frowned. Did Goodhugh or the priest want her to go to the address for crude sex? she wondered. Perhaps the gym mistress wanted to meet her there. There was only one way to find out, she thought.

'I'm going for a walk,' she said, popping her head round the kitchen door.

'Who called?' her mother asked.

'No one. It must have been the wind rattling the letter box. I'll see you later.'

'Don't be too long, Charlotte.'

'No, I won't.'

Leaving the cottage, Charlotte looked at the address again. The house or cottage was in the next village, about a mile down the lane. A pleasant enough walk, but what was this about? It might be a trap, she knew as she passed

Goodhugh's shop and headed up the hill. Wondering where Marianne was as she passed her house, she walked along the country lane and breathed in the scented summer air. It would be a week ago tomorrow when she'd woken in her bed and discovered her pussy cream, she reflected. A week of crude sex, whipping, caning, cunny licking, sperm swallowing . . . And now she was setting out on a journey to . . . the unknown.

Chapter Sixteen

The small cottage was idyllic, with a beautifully kept garden, roses arched over the door and leaded-light windows. This was definitely the right address, but who did the place belong to? Charlotte wondered. Slipping the key into the lock and opening the door, half expecting to find Goodhugh or the priest waiting for her, she tentatively walked inside. The lounge was tastefully furnished with antiques and a leather Chesterfield. A deep-pile Axminster carpet beneath her feet, paintings adorning the walls, wooden beams crossing the ceiling . . . Charlotte couldn't believe the luxury. The newly fitted kitchen was well equipped with all mod cons. The window over the sink looked out onto a large back garden. She wondered who the cottage belonged to.

Noticing an envelope lying on the pine table, she ripped it open and read the enclosed letter. 'I hope you like it here,' she began. 'It's not far from your mother but far enough from . . . from people. Make yourself at home. After all, this is your home now. As for money, I'm afraid I can't help you. But, as you're a resourceful young lady, you'll no doubt manage.' Placing the unsigned letter on the table, she frowned. Did the cottage belong to her? she wondered. Had someone given it to her?

Charlotte walked through the lounge and made her way upstairs. The two bedrooms were newly decorated and the bathroom had been completely renovated. Someone had spent a lot of money on the place, she observed. New fitted carpets, new curtains and beautiful furniture . . . But who? Did her mother know about this? she wondered. Had her mysterious meeting with someone been in connection with the cottage? Wandering back downstairs, she gazed at the telephone on the lounge table. Reading a card left by the phone company, she noticed that the new account was in her name. Someone had thought of everything. Perching her rounded buttocks on the edge of the Chesterfield, she grabbed the phone and dialled Marianne's number.

'I've just got in from school,' Marianne said. 'Where are you phoning from? Are you in the call box?'

'From . . . from a friend's place,' Charlotte replied. 'Have you seen Emily?'

'Briefly, at school. She didn't want to talk to me. Anyway, I don't care about her. Shall we meet somewhere?'

'Yes, come over to my . . . I'm in Hampton Vale.'

'I don't want to go to your friend's place. Who is it, anyway?'

'I'll explain everything when you get here. It's Thornycroft Cottage. As you come into the village, it's on the right. There's no one else here.'

'You'll have to give me a couple of hours.'

'OK, I'll see you later. You will turn up, won't you?'

'Yes, of course.'

What Marianne would say, Charlotte had no idea. To be given a cottage was incredible, and she wondered again whether her mother knew about it. Returning to the kitchen, she opened the cupboards. They were fully stocked with food. Opening the fridge, she took out a bottle of milk. Then she filled the kettle with water from the tap. She couldn't understand why someone would give her a cottage that was obviously worth tens of thousands of pounds. Unless she was expected to pay rent? she reflected. If so, to whom? The place was ready to move into. Telephone, TV, food . . . And even the bed was made up. Pouring a cup of coffee, she wondered what to do. She'd have to go home and tell her mother. And collect her things. But was it safe to stay in the cottage? Would Goodhugh turn up? Shaking her head and frowning again, she opened the back door and walked into the garden. Was her father still alive? she wondered, gazing at the neat flower beds. Had he done this for her?

Looking back over the past week, Charlotte wondered whether everything had been planned. Whoever had given her the cottage had obviously worked the whole thing out well in advance. Again thinking that her mother must have known something about it, she sat on the soft grass and gazed at the back of the cottage. Even the outside had been repainted, she observed. This was like a dream. After all she'd been through, the nightmare, the horror . . . This really was a dream.

But it might be a trap, she mused. If Goodhugh and the others had got together and lured her to the cottage to imprison and use her for crude sex . . . But they wouldn't have left the telephone connected. The priest or Goodhugh would have been there, ready to nab her the minute she entered the place. Listening to the singing birds, the breeze rustling the leaves in the trees, she grew increasingly sure that this was some sort of trap. At least Marianne now knew where she was, she thought. If Goodhugh did materialize and . . . Unless they were hoping to ensnare Marianne, too. Her head spinning, she had to stop thinking about all the possibilities.

Finishing her coffee, Charlotte left the cottage and

walked back down the lane. She couldn't just move into the place. She didn't know who it belonged to or whether she was expected to pay rent or . . . Perhaps her mother might throw some light on the situation, she mused as she again passed Goodhugh's shop. Fortunately, there was no sign of the evil man. The village seemed different now, she thought as she neared her mother's cottage. It was alien to her, almost as if she'd never lived there. She couldn't stay, she knew as she gazed at the church. Too much water had passed under the bridge. Too much sperm had passed between her lips.

Letting herself into the cottage, she was surprised to find that her mother had gone out. Something was going on, she was sure as she took her money from her bedroom. The cottage was a godsend, but she still wasn't sure whether to move in. If Goodhugh and the priest had keys and turned up in the middle of the night . . . Wishing she'd not told Marianne to meet her there, she again wondered what to do. Finally deciding to go to the boys' school and talk to the chaplain, Charlotte stuffed the money into her shoe and left the cottage. She had to find out more about Father James, discover exactly what had happened between him and Jenny Harrington. Perhaps the Harringtons had owned the cottage.

'Oh, Emily,' she breathed, finding Emily sitting by the stream. 'What are you doing here?'

'Feeling guilty,' the girl replied morosely.

'Why? What have you done?'

'I'm in a terrible mess,' she confessed. 'I . . . I'm sorry about your mum and the pictures.'

'Pictures?' Charlotte echoed, her dark eyes frowning.

'I sent the photographs to her. I was jealous, Charlotte. I was jealous of you and Marianne so I—'

'You sent them to my mother?' Charlotte gasped. 'When was this?'

'Yesterday. I'm sorry, Charlotte. What did she say? I'll bet she went mad, didn't she?'

'Yes, yes, she did,' Charlotte murmured, wondering why her mother hadn't said anything.

Sitting next to Emily, Charlotte now knew that her mother was deliberately turning her back on her daughter's decadent ways. But why? The strait-laced woman with her Victorian attitudes would normally have gone mad with rage and thrown her out onto the street. She obviously knew far more about the scam than she was letting on. She'd already told Charlotte that she'd known about the scandal of two decades ago, but why was she ignoring her daughter's wicked ways?

'You said that you were in a mess,' Charlotte said, gazing at Emily's naked thighs.

'You won't believe what's happened,' the girl sighed. 'I can't believe it myself.'

'Try me.'

'Goodhugh is . . . I don't know where to start. Goodhugh and Father James are blackmailing me.'

'*What?*' Charlotte gasped, feigning shock.

'It's a long story. Goodhugh said that I'd stolen a radio. He also said that he hadn't given you a radio. According to him, you paid for it.'

'He's lying. He gave me a radio. I was looking at them and he said that I could have one. I didn't pay for it. I had no money and—'

'Anyway, he wanted to take some photographs of me and I ended up naked.'

'Naked?'

'One thing led to another. It started with photographs of

me sitting on his desk and then he wanted me to open my legs and . . . He now has photographs of me posing naked with . . . As I said, one thing led to another. He's threatened to tell my parents if I don't have sex with him. And with that perverted priest.'

'God, that's terrible,' Charlotte breathed, again wishing she'd never sent the girl to Goodhugh's shop. 'You've had sex with Goodhugh and . . . God, I don't know what to say.'

'And I don't know what to do. I have to be at the church this evening for . . . for sex.'

'Don't go,' Charlotte said, deciding to pay the priest a visit before leaving the village.

'If I don't, then . . .'

'I'll see you later,' Charlotte smiled, rising to her feet. 'Don't go to the church, OK?'

'OK. Did you hear about the fire?' Emily asked.

'What fire?'

'There was an old shed at the back of the church. Someone set fire to it and burned it down.'

'Really?' Charlotte grinned. 'OK, I'll see you later. And don't worry. I think your problems might be over.'

Making her way to the church, Charlotte was sure that her plan had worked. Believing that Jenny Harrington had returned to the village, Father James had burned the shed to the ground and destroyed the photographs. No doubt Goodhugh would have cleared his shop and flat of evidence, she reflected as she wandered through the graveyard. Making her way around the side of the church, she gazed at the charred remains of the shed. It was impossible to tell whether the trunk containing the evidence had been in the shed. The priest might have stashed the photographs elsewhere, she knew as she went into the church.

SCHOOLGIRL LUST

'Father James,' Charlotte called, walking down the aisle. Entering the office, she wasn't really surprised to find the desk drawers and the filing cabinet empty. 'He's gone,' she breathed, wondering whether Goodhugh too had fled the village. Leaving the office she stood in the aisle, recalling the wooden partition, the penises she'd been forced to suck to orgasm when her naked body had been tied over the altar. 'The end of an era,' she murmured, leaving the church.

Sitting on the wall of the graveyard, she thought about the many unanswered questions. There was one thing she had to do, she reflected. And that was to discover who owned the cottage. She was about to walk back to Hampton Vale when she noticed Goodhugh and the gym mistress wandering across the road. This was all she needed, she thought fearfully as they approached. The woman was dressed as usual in a knee-length skirt and high-collared blouse. Far removed from the role of dominatrix, Charlotte reflected, wondering whether she'd be forced into the church and sexually abused over the altar.

'Good evening, Charlotte,' Goodhugh smiled. 'We're taking a stroll down to the pub.'

'Oh,' Charlotte sighed, wondering why they were holding hands.

'How is your mother?' the gym mistress asked.

'She's . . . she's fine.'

'I expect you've heard that Father James has left the village,' Goodhugh said, looking at the church. 'Apparently, he's had to go and look after his mother in Birmingham. She's been ill of late and he's gone to live with her.'

'Really?' Charlotte murmured, wondering what the pair were playing at. Why were they behaving as if nothing had happened?

'I'll see you at school on Monday,' the woman said. 'I'm thinking of making you captain of the netball team.'

'Oh,' Charlotte smiled as they walked off.

Perplexed, Charlotte slid off the wall and made her way to the woods. Something had happened to frighten the gym mistress, and Goodhugh. Had it really been mention of Jenny Harrington that had put the fear of God up everyone? The chaplain might know something, she mused, crossing the bridge and wondering where Emily had got to. It was a long shot, but the man might have heard from the priest and . . . Wondering why she was really going to the school, she thought she might be deluding herself. Was it the chaplain she wanted to see? Or did she want to meet the boys again? If she was going to live in the cottage, she'd need an income. She'd leave school, she decided. Leave school and . . . and become a prostitute? Wherever Father James had gone, he'd certainly left his mark, she mused. Crude sex, bondage whipping . . . Within a week, Charlotte had become a prostitute.

Had she not discovered her sticky inner thighs, had she not examined between the fleshy folds of her vagina, had she not talked about her concern to Emily . . . Hindsight was useless, she knew as she walked across the grass towards the old Victorian building. Slipping through the side door, she followed the maze of corridors to the chaplain's office. Tapping on the door, she peered inside at the man as he looked up from his desk.

'Sandy,' he smiled. 'I didn't think I'd be seeing you again.'

'I was passing,' Charlotte replied.

'Passing? Where were you going?'

'Just for a walk. I thought I'd come and say hallo.'

'It's funny that you should call in to see me. I've been thinking about you.'

SCHOOLGIRL LUST

'Oh?'

'I rang Father James and mentioned that one of his flock had been here.'

'What did he say?'

'He seemed to think that your name was Charlotte. He'd never heard of a Sandy Evans. Anyway, he rang back later and told me that he was leaving the village.'

'Did he say why?'

'No. That's the strange thing about it. When I first spoke to him, he said that he'd come up to the school to see me next week. He rang back a couple of hours later and said that he was moving away.'

'That *is* strange,' Charlotte smiled. 'Still, a lot of strange things happen in my village.'

'So, how are you? Did you write to Gibson-Brown?'

'No, I didn't. I'm moving to another village, actually.'

'Oh? Everyone's on the move.'

'Yes, they are. I'm going to live in Hampton Vale.'

'I know it well,' he chuckled. 'I lived there as a boy.'

'Do you know Thornycroft Cottage?' Charlotte asked hopefully.

'Indeed, I do.'

'Who lives there?'

'No one now. It's been empty for several years.'

'Who owns it?'

'It's strange that you should mention Thornycroft Cottage after our conversation the other day. It belonged to the Harrington family.'

'Jenny Harrington?'

'Yes. I don't know who owns it now.'

'Thank you,' Charlotte smiled. 'Well, I'd better be going.'

'Call in again when you're out for a walk,' the chaplain said, rising from his desk.

'Yes, I will. I'll probably call in regularly for a . . . a chat.'
'I'd like that, Sandy. You take care, now.'
'I will. Goodbye.'

Leaving the office, Charlotte realized that she was more confused than ever. Walking along the corridor, she reckoned that someone living in Hampton Vale must know who owned the cottage. Someone must have seen painters and decorators working on the place and asked questions. In a small village like that, everyone would know everything. The Harringtons must have sold the place, she mused. They wouldn't move to Australia and leave the cottage to go to rack and ruin. As she was about to leave the building, she heard footsteps behind her. Wondering whether it was the chaplain, she turned and waited.

'You'd better come to my study, young lady,' the headmaster scowled. 'What are you doing skulking around here again?'

'I came to—'

'I can imagine what you were after. Right, come with me.'

The sad pervert wanted sex, Charlotte knew as she followed him. She wasn't really in the mood for a caning or a mouth-fuck. But, if she was going to service the boys regularly and earn a good living, she'd best keep in with the old man, she thought. He locked the study door once they were inside, as she knew he would. Wasting no time, he grabbed a cane from a stand in the corner of the room and flexed it threateningly.

'You'd better pull your skirt up and bend over my desk,' he said, his trousers already bulging as he slapped his palm with the cane. 'I will not tolerate young girls roaming this school. As headmaster, it's my duty to punish you.'

This was a game to him, Charlotte knew as she walked

towards the desk. He was loving every minute of it, delighting in the prospect of ogling her rounded buttocks, thrashing her pert anal orbs with the thin bamboo cane. But, she had to admit, she too was enjoying the game. Playing the role of a naughty little schoolgirl sent delightful tremors through her young womb, inflated her clitoris and induced her juices of lust to ooze between her pinken love lips. She noticed the stain on the carpet as she stood before the desk and lifted her skirt up. A stark reminder of her last visit to the pervert's office, she mused. Would he like to watch her drain her bladder again? Undoubtedly.

'You're not wearing any knickers again,' the headmaster growled accusingly as she tugged her skirt higher over her back and leaned over the desk. 'I will not tolerate teenage girls wandering around my school without knickers.' He really was delighting in the game, she knew as she projected her buttocks further, the crease of her bottom opening to reveal the brown inlet to her duct of illicit lust. He'd no doubt be only too pleased to pay for her visits to his study, she reflected. The next time she was caught roaming around the school knickerless, she'd demand money in return for the caning.

Wondering what he was doing as she clung to the far edge of the desk, Charlotte turned her head. He was kneeling behind her, eyeing the firm mounds of her young bottom, the brown eye of her tightly closed anus, the alluring swell of her hairless vaginal lips bulging between her firm thighs. Was he going to push his fingers into the creamy duct of her cunt? she wondered, parting her feet further to afford him a better view of her gaping sex crack, the dripping entrance to her tight pussy. The dirty old man couldn't resist it, could he? She knew only too well that his cock would be solid by now, straining against the cloth of his trousers, desperate for the welcoming heat of her wet mouth, the hugging sheath of her teenage pussy.

Trembling as she felt his moustache tickling her naked buttocks, Charlotte closed her eyes. Kissing her anal orbs, he licked the full length of her bottom crease, his wet tongue repeatedly sweeping over the sensitive brown tissue of her anus. She wanted his cock-head there, his purple plum forcing its way past her tightly closed portal and driving deep into the tight sheath of her hot arse. Would he fuck her arse? she wondered as her arousal soared and her juices of desire poured from the sheath of her teenage cunt. His tongue trying to gain entry to her rectal rube, he parted the pert orbs of her buttocks. The gully of her bottom opening wide, her small hole fully exposed, he pushed his tongue deep into her anal canal.

'Yes,' Charlotte breathed as he parted her anal orbs further and licked the dank walls of her tight rectal tube. Heavenly sensations coursing through her trembling body, she breathed deeply in her illicit pleasure. Her clitoris brought her immense pleasure, but massaging the sensitive tissue of her tight bottom-hole took her to frightening heights of sexual arousal. A wet tongue licking her anal hole, delving into her dank channel . . . Had she known of the pleasure to be had from her anus, she'd have massaged and fingered herself there whenever she was in the privacy of her bed. If she moved into the cottage, she'd have candles by her bed, a huge cucumber, carrots . . . Anything she could push deep into her tight holes of lust. And if Marianne moved in, she'd have the girl's fingers to attend her intimate needs, her wet tongue to appease her yearning cunt.

The headmaster's finger gliding deep into her anal duct, Charlotte clung to the desk and gasped. His tongue lapping

SCHOOLGIRL LUST

the brown flesh hugging his finger, wetting her there, he groped between her thighs with his free hand and parted the fleshy cushions of her young cunt. A second finger thrusting into her bloated anal duct, she quivered uncontrollably in her decadence. This was sheer heaven, she mused as he massaged the hot inner flesh of her tight arse. And to be paid for receiving such pleasure . . .

'You're a naughty little schoolgirl,' the man said, driving three fingers deep into the wet sheath of her vagina as he pistoned her anal canal. 'Tell me that you're a naughty little schoolgirl.'

'I'm a naughty little schoolgirl, sir,' she gasped, the sound of her squelching love juices resounding around the room.

'You deserve the cane, don't you?'

'Yes, sir. I deserve to have my bottom caned.'

Charlotte was learning fast. She knew exactly what turned the old pervert on, and was determined to charge him for her services in the future. Marianne would never know of her secret life, her clandestine work. Sneaking off to the boys' school a couple of times every week and servicing the old man and a few pupils would bring in plenty of cash. She might suck twenty knobs to orgasm each week, allow twenty cocks to fuck her young cunt and spunk up her. Perhaps the boys would like to drink her creamy juices of desire from her cunt and lick her clitoris to orgasm. Grinning as the headmaster thrust his fingers in and out of her tightening lust holes, she was looking forward to her new way of life.

'I'm going to have to cane you for your insolence,' the headmaster said, sliding his fingers out of her inflamed ducts as he stood up. Listening to movements behind her, Charlotte waited in anticipation. She'd have to bring out the old man's spunk soon. Marianne would be arriving at the cottage and Charlotte was desperate to christen the new bed. Wondering whether to suck the man's spunk out or allow him the pleasure of fucking her tight cunt, she yelped as the cane swished through the air and struck the tensed globes of her young bottom.

Her vaginal juice spewing from the gaping mouth of her pussy, she clung to the desk as the cane landed squarely across her naked buttocks again. The old man would be desperate to pump out his sperm, she knew as the crack of the cane repeatedly resounded around the room. He'd probably been wanking, she thought as her clitoris swelled. He'd have pictured the swollen lips of her cunt as his sperm shot from his throbbing knob. Perhaps he'd fucked his wife, imagining he was driving his knob deep into Charlotte's tight pussy as he'd spermed the older woman's cervix.

'Six,' the headmaster gasped, bringing the cane down again. Her buttocks turning crimson as the gruelling thrashing continued, her juices of lust coursing down her thighs, she knew she wouldn't have time to attend the boys' knobs and suck out their fresh sperm. 'Seven,' the man breathed, the cane cracking loudly across Charlotte's bottom. After ten lashes, he dropped the cane to the floor and unzipped his trousers. As she heard him unbuckle his belt, she knew that he was going to push his solid shaft deep into her tight cunt and pump her full of sperm. The bulbous knob of his penis slipping between the swollen lips of her vaginal mouth, he suddenly thrust his huge shaft deep into her drenched sex duct.

'God, you're tight,' he gasped, gripping her hips and ramming his knob fully home. Her body rocking as he fucked her wet cunt, Charlotte listened to the slapping of his lower belly repeatedly meeting her weal-lined buttocks. His swinging balls battering her hairless mons, he grunted as he quickened his rhythm, pummelling her ripe cervix with his ballooning knob. He was going to come quickly, she knew as his gasps grew louder. Fucking a teenage girl's cunt . . . There was no way he'd last more than a few minutes. To add to his illicit pleasure, she let out long low moans of pleasure.

'You're so big,' she breathed. 'I've never known anyone so big.' His sperm jetting from his knob, bathing her cervix, he grunted with every penile thrust. She could feel his male liquid filling her spasming sex sheath, running down her inner thighs as he despunked his heavy balls. Again and again he rammed his bulbous knob-head against her spermed cervix, gasping and groaning as if he'd not fucked a pussy for years. Perhaps he hadn't, she mused as he finally stilled his massive cock, his knob absorbing the inner heat of her cunt. He'd be a regular client, that was for sure. Finally withdrawing his deflating shaft, he staggered back and flopped into a chair.

'I'll expect to see you here tomorrow,' he breathed, taking forty pounds from his wallet.

'I'll be here, sir,' Charlotte grinned, snatching the money and adjusting her skirt as she walked to the door. 'About the same time.'

'And if you're not wearing kinckers, it'll be the cane for you.'

'Yes, sir,' she smiled, leaving the study.

The poor old pervert was going to part with hundreds of pounds, Charlotte mused happily as she followed the corridor. Leaving the building, she headed across the grass towards the woods. There was no time to suck the boys off, she thought sadly as she trotted along the path. But there was always tomorrow, and the next day and . . . Deciding, as she crossed the stream, to call in on her mother she wondered again whether the woman knew about the cottage. Wondering whether she'd ever discover the truth, she opened her front door and called out for her mother.

The nightmare was over, Charlotte reflected, wandering into the kitchen. With Father James gone and Goodhugh acting as if nothing had happened, she knew that she didn't have to worry about blackmail and threats any more. Besides, the priest had shown her mother the photograph so he had nothing on her now. There wasn't anything to blackmail her with. Again calling for her mother, she frowned and shook her head. 'Where is she?' she murmured, scribbling a note saying that she was staying at Marianne's house for the night. Placing the note on the table, she left the cottage and walked up the hill. She'd finally made a decision. She was sure now that the cottage wasn't a trap set by Goodhugh. The man probably knew nothing about the place. She'd collect her clothes the following day and move in.

'Where have you been?' Marianne asked as Charlotte approached her new home. 'I've been waiting here for ages.'

'Sorry, I was held up,' Charlotte smiled, aware of sperm and girl juice running down her naked inner thighs. 'Come in and I'll make some tea.'

Marianne was wearing a short skirt, her naked thighs tanned from the summer sun. Her blouse partially open, revealing the alluring ravine of her cleavage, her erect nipples pressing through the material, she was sensual in the extreme. The girl asked a hundred questions as Charlotte showed her into the kitchen and made the tea. Her clitoris swelling at the prospect of lesbian sex, Charlotte suggested that they take their tea into the garden and sit on the patio.

'I wish you'd tell me who lives here,' Marianne repeated for the umpteenth time.

'I do,' Charlotte finally confessed, passing the girl her tea.
'*You* do? But . . .'
'I'm renting the place. It's my home now.'
'God, you're so lucky,' the girl gasped. 'Why didn't you say anything before?'
'I've only just moved in.'
'I expect your mother was sad when you told her that . . .'
'She doesn't know yet. I've only just got the keys.'
'She doesn't know? I would have thought that—'
'I don't want to go into the details,' Charlotte sighed as they walked out to the patio. 'Marianne, I don't want anyone to know about this place.'
'If you say so. But how can you afford it? It must cost a fortune.'
'I came into a little money,' she lied. 'A relative left me some money. Marianne, will you stay here with me tonight?'
'Yes, OK. I'll have to ring my mother and tell her.'
'Would you like to move in with me?'
'Yes, that would be great. I was talking to my parents about moving out. They weren't happy, of course. But they were OK about it. Once they see this place, see that I'm going to have a decent home . . .'
'I'd rather no one knew about the cottage.'
'They wouldn't tell anyone. If I explain that . . . Don't worry, no one will know.'
'The phone's in the lounge. Ring your mother now.'

Hoping that the owner of the cottage would make contact at some stage, Charlotte relaxed in one of the garden chairs and sipped her tea as Marianne went to ring her mother. The garden was lovely, she observed. Leaving school and visiting the headmaster and his boys twice a week, she'd have more than enough time to tend the garden. Life was going to be idyllic, she knew as she imagined inviting her mother round for afternoon tea. 'Fuck the English project,' she chuckled, again aware of sperm oozing from the tight sheath of her hot cunt. That would be Marianne's first job, she thought happily. Sucking the sperm out of her yearning cunt and cleansing her vaginal folds, the other girl would believe that Charlotte was wet with desire. Twice a week, she'd return from the boys' school with her cunt brimming with fresh sperm. And Marianne would suck out the male liquid and drink it.

'That's OK,' the girl said, stepping onto the patio. 'I told her that I'd be staying with you tonight. I also mentioned that I might be moving in permanently.'

'What did she say to that?'

'I said that you were renting a cottage and she seemed fine about it. But she doesn't want me to leave school.'

'And neither do I, Marianne. I'll be leaving but . . .'

'What about money?' the girl asked. 'I mean . . .'

'I have more than enough for both of us, so you needn't worry about that.'

'I'll stay tonight and collect my things tomorrow.'

'Good,' Charlotte smiled, lifting her skirt and parting her thighs wide. 'Just thinking about you has wet my cunt,' she said huskily. 'You'd better kneel between my legs and clean me with your tongue.'

Wasting no time, the other girl settled on the ground and gazed longingly at Charlotte's cream-oozing sex crack. Parting her legs wider and pulling her skirt high over her stomach, Charlotte watched her lesbian lover eagerly lap up the heady blend of sperm and girl-cum. The mother-of-pearl liquid smeared over her pretty face, Marianne parted Charlotte's swollen sex lips and sucked out the orgasmic cocktail. This was heaven, Charlotte mused, closing her eyes as the girl attended the most private part of her young body. To have a live-in lover, a sex slave, would be like a dream. Every day when the girl came home from school, Charlotte would lick the crack of her young vagina, breathe in the heady scent of her valley of desire and tongue her clitoris to orgasm. They'd spend evenings together, licking, sucking, fingering . . .

'You're so wet,' Marianne said, lapping up the intoxicating blend of spunk and girl-cream.

'*You* make me wet,' Charlotte smiled. 'Just thinking about you makes me *very* wet. Keep licking me. I want you to suck out all my juice and then finger me and lick my clitoris until I come.'

Obeying her new mistress, Marianne pressed her mouth against Charlotte's gaping vaginal entrance and sucked hard. Swallowing the creamy fluid, she parted the girl's sex cushions wider, her tongue delving deep into her hot lust sheath. Remembering the boys fucking her in the shed, Charlotte knew that she was going to have the best of both worlds. Solid cocks with huge purple knobs pumping spunk into her mouth, and the lubricious juices of Marianne's cunt to drink.

As Marianne thrust three fingers into Charlotte's tight cuntal sheath and sucked her pulsating clitoris into her hot mouth, Charlotte let out a rush of breath. As the evening sun dropped below the trees, its warm rays bathing the completely secluded garden, Charlotte was looking forward to many summer nights of lesbian lust. Marianne's long blonde hair tickled her inner thighs as she drank the juices of desire from her mistress and Charlotte held her head, forcing her open cunt hard against Marianne's mouth.

'I'm going to come,' she breathed, her young body trembling as her clitoris swelled and pulsated. 'Suck it hard,' she wailed as her pleasure built. 'God, my clitoris. Suck it and lick it.' Her orgasm exploding within the solid bud of her clitoris, her vaginal muscles tightening around Marianne's pistoning fingers, Charlotte tossed her head back and cried out in the grip of her massive climax. On and on the waves of lesbian lust coursed through her shaking body, her cunt milk squelching, spraying her inner thighs as she clutched her lover's head and ground her bared cunt into her sucking mouth.

'My bum,' Charlotte cried, her body shaking violently. 'Finger my bum.' Complying, Marianne pushed a finger into the wailing girl's anal duct and pistoned both her pleasure holes. Her orgasm peaking with the double finger-fucking, Charlotte brought her knees up to her firm breasts, giving the girl better access to her shafts of lust. Her juices pouring from her bloated cunt, her clitoris pulsating wildly, she cried out again as her mind spun in her sexual euphoria.

Her orgasm finally receding, Charlotte lay quivering in the chair as Marianne slid her fingers out of her spasming sex sheaths. As the mist of her sexual haze cleared, she focused on the girl's spermed mouth, the white liquid dribbling down her chin. The phone ringing, Charlotte wondered whether it was her mysterious benefactor. Trying to climb to her feet, her trembling legs like jelly after her multiple orgasm, she fell back into the chair and asked Marianne to answer the phone. Perhaps it was the priest or Goodhugh, she ruminated. No one knew the number, so . . .

'It was your mother,' Marianne announced as she stepped onto the patio.

'My mother?' Charlotte frowned. 'What did she say?'

'She'll be round in the morning with your things. She said that she hopes you'll be happy in your new home.'

'But . . .' Charlotte breathed, shaking her head. 'She doesn't know about this place.'

'Obviously, she does. And she has the phone number.'

'I just don't understand it.'

'I don't know what it is that's bothering you, but I think we should have an early night.' Marianne smiled, licking the sperm from her glistening lips.

'I'm dripping with confusion,' Charlotte murmured, following her lesbian lover into the cottage. 'And dripping with pussy juice.'

'Now I *can* help you with that problem. Come on, let's go to bed.'

'This is the beginning of our new life,' Charlotte grinned as they climbed the stairs.

'It is. Charlotte, you will be faithful to me, won't you? I mean, if I'm going to give you my body and soul, you won't betray me?'

'Never,' Charlotte replied, her vaginal muscles tightening as she thought about the boys in the shed, the headmaster's study. 'I'll never betray you.'